'Mirren, you did your duty – and more than your duty – towards Helen while she was still alive. You've given up enough of yourself for other people, including Donald, and perhaps now's the time to make up to yourself for all those years, while there's still so much living ahead of you.'

'I don't know . . .' Mirren said, but deep inside her, Aunt Catherine's words kindled a spark that had been lying dormant, waiting. As she went about her usual daily duties that spark became a flame; she hummed dance tunes to herself at her frames in the mill and practised steps in the confines of the kitchen at home, and even in the mill privies, where the girls often tried out new dances. She wanted to start dancing again, longed for it, but couldn't as yet quite bring herself to break with tradition and do it.

By the same author

The Silken Thread
A Matter of Mischief
The Damask Days
A Stranger to the Town
McAdam's Women
Pebbles on the Beach
Another Day
The Dancing Stone
Time and Again

A PROCESSION OF ONE

Evelyn Hood

WARNER BOOKS

A *Warner* Book

First published in Great Britain in 1999
by Little, Brown and Company
This edition published by Warner Books in 2000

A CIP catalogue record for this book
is available from the British Library.

ISBN 0 7515 1702 X

Typeset in Times by
Palimpsest Book Production Limited,
Polmont, Stirlingshire
Printed and bound in Great Britain by
Clays Ltd, St Ives plc

Warner Books
A Division of
Little, Brown and Company (UK)
Brettenham House
Lancaster Place
London WC2E 7EN

This book is dedicated to the Paisley mill-workers.

Acknowledgements

The story of Paisley's vast threadmills is complex, but I hope that I have managed to avoid making too many errors while using one of them, Coats' Ferguslie Mill, as the background to this novel. My thanks (and, if applicable, my apologies in advance) go to the following people, most of them former mill-workers, for their assistance in researching the book: Rena Shaw, June Quail, Jenny Leitch, Alex Rowand, Bill McDerment, Margaret Haldane, Archie Haldane, Margaret Blackie, Barbara Grant, Ellen Farmer, Helen Mitchell, Helen McGovern Haughey, Honor and Rick Raphael, Helen Dunbar, Rena Maxwell and Greta Ferguson.

I would also like to thank Lena Moore; Eleanor Clark, who gave me access to her own work on the history of the mills; Rena Murphy, for information on the Proctor family history and Patricia Burke and the staff of Paisley Reference Library for their assistance and patience.

A lane was made; and Mrs Hominy . . . came slowly up it, in a procession of one.

Charles Dickens, *Martin Chuzzlewit*

1

Blue and yellow gas jets flickered beneath the great vats of spitting fat as the door burst open. The April evening had turned wet and squally and the draught that caused the flames to dip and dance cooled Mirren's swollen, aching ankles pleasantly. The crowd of noisy youths who had caused the sudden cool gust surged in, each dangling a girl from one arm as though she was a trophy.

'Someone shut that door,' Vanni Perrini protested from the vats as the gas flames flickered again and threatened to go out entirely. He was answered with a chorus of insults, some friendly and others not, as the lads crowded the few customers already waiting at the counter.

'You heard the man!' Vanni's wife Maria had been working beside the vats, scooping the finished chips and pieces of battered fish out of the sizzling liquid fat. Now, as a handful of rain was tossed in through the doorway to spatter over the floor, she swung round. 'Born in a back-court midden, were ye? Shut that door afore my floor gets soaked,' she barked, impaling the newcomers on the honed points of her cold blue eyes. 'And mind yer manners if ye want tae be served in this shop.'

The youths cowered, their bravado suddenly gone. The door was closed and their girlfriends hastily tugged them into an orderly queue while the dancing gas flames settled down again.

'Aw, c'mon, Maria,' someone tried to protest, but in

a half-hearted way, while Vanni, turning from his work, said placatingly to his wife, 'No harm done.'

'Riffraff,' Maria snapped, 'can find another chip shop, for they'll no' be served in this one!' She gave the new-comers another icy look and most of them let their eyes flicker uneasily about the shop, while a few, the boldest, made a feeble, and futile, attempt to return her stare. Maria waited for a moment to see if anyone dared to pick up the gauntlet she had just thrown down, then, deciding that her customers had been suitably brought to heel, she ordered her staff, 'Get them served and get them out before they give the place a bad name!'

Ella Caldwell muttered something uncomplimentary beneath her breath as she swiftly folded and tucked a sheet of newspaper over a fish supper. She handed the neat bundle over to the waiting customer before turning her tireless, wide-mouthed smile to the young people and saying cheerfully, 'Yes, lads, what'll it be?'

Warmed by her friendliness and emboldened now that Maria had gone back to her work, they lined the counter, spreading their elbows out to mark their territories and giving their orders in a great clutter of words piled one on top of another. Mirren, working as fast as she could, shovelling chips onto sheets of waxed paper, adding crisp brown fish, shaking salt and vinegar over them, dipping into the pickle jar when required, then wrapping the food in neatly torn sheets of newspaper before handing it over, envied the way Ella could cope with these sudden invasions. They occurred every night as Paisley's public houses and dance halls emptied, but she herself had never managed to get used to them and always panicked when a crowd burst in through the door to fill the small waiting area with their chatter and their demands.

''Lo, Mirren.' Ruby Liddell, the desk girl in Ferguslie Mills' twisting department, where Mirren and Ella both worked during the day, grinned at her from within the circle of her boyfriend's arm. 'We've been tae the Palace. Have ye been in it yet?'

'No.' Mirren feverishly shovelled chips onto a square of waxed paper and shook the big heavy salt cellar over them. There had been considerable interest and excitement in the town when the Picture Palace had opened in the High Street two weeks earlier, but as she never had the money to spend on luxuries and had nobody to 'pay her in', now that Donald, her fiancé, was preparing a new life for them both in America, she had had little interest in the occasion.

'Oh, it's lovely!' Ruby's eyes glowed. 'When ye step in from the street the floor's all marble, laid out in black and white squares. Then further in there's this great big place with carpets. They're going tae have chairs there for folk tae sit on while they wait tae go in tae see the films. It really is like a palace! Ye walk through there and up the stairs tae get tae where they show the films . . .'

'. . . and the walls at the entrance are all panelled and there's a place where ye can buy chocolates and cigarettes,' one of the other girls chimed in. By now even Maria was interested.

'And there's going tae be a tea-room upstairs too, looking over the High Street,' Ruby glared at her friend and snatched the story back. 'And while ye're watching the films ye sit in soft chairs with seats that fold up when ye stand, tae let folk get past.'

'Only Jean's so skinny that her chair tipped up with her still in it,' Ruby's escort claimed and the entire group, with the exception of Jean, howled with mirth. The noise was enough to snap Maria back to the present.

'That's enough! This isnae a howff, it's a respectable shop. Get your orders and get out,' she snapped, and Ella and Vanni, who had slowed down to listen, hurtled back to work.

'We saw *Tarzan of the Apes*, with Elmo Lincoln.' Ruby

enunciated each syllable of the outlandish name proudly.
'He was lovely! All muscles.'

'If it's muscles ye want, hen, I'm the man,' her companion told her, squeezing her waist tightly. Ruby's
excited squeal was hastily bitten back as Maria whirled.

'If it's mussels ye want,' she said coldly, 'Go down
tae the sea-shore and look underneath a rock. We don't
stock shellfish.'

As Mirren handed over the packets of chips, Ruby
snatched hers and tore it open. 'I'm starvin'!' Jean, about
to follow suit, hesitated, glancing slyly up from beneath
pencilled eyebrows.

'There's no oose got ontae these chips, is there?'

'Cheeky bitch!' Ella flared back at her. Jean worked
in the mill's offices and the office staff considered themselves superior to other workers, because at the end of the
working day they left the mill with their clothes as neat
as when they arrived, whereas the machine workers were
covered in 'oose' or 'caddis' – the fine clumps of cotton
that clung to anyone who went near the machinery in the
manufacturing flats.

Jean smirked, but unfortunately for her, Maria had
overheard. 'What did ye say?' She rounded on the girl,
who took a step back, clutching at her greasy packet
of chips.

'It was just a j-joke,' she stuttered, while the rest of
her party, cowed again, fell silent.

'Joke, is it? I'll have no jokes about the cleanliness of
my shop or my staff, ye cheeky wee madam!' Maria's
hand shot out. 'Ye can just give back these chips!'

Jean's fingers flew into the packet's steaming depths
and reappeared with a chip. As she hurriedly bit it in half
her lipstick, probably only just applied, came off on the
uneaten half of the chip. Mirren had already been finding
the smell of the fat and the fried chips and fish difficult
to handle, and the obscene crimson smear against the pale
interior of the cooked potato was almost too much.

'I've started it now, so ye can't get it back,' Jean said indistinctly. 'Andy, pay the money, for I'm keepin' these.' The chip was roasting hot and she had to eat it open-mouthed, sucking in air to cool it. Mirren closed her eyes against the sight as Maria stormed round the edge of the counter.

'Out ye get, all of ye,' she ordered, throwing the door open. 'Out and don't bother comin' back!'

'Maria . . .' her husband remonstrated as the party fled, some squealing with nervous laughter, others cowed and embarrassed. Maria slammed the door shut behind them.

'We don't need their custom!' she snapped at Vanni. 'And if ye were half a man ye'd not have left it tae me tae deal with them!'

Mirren snatched up a cloth and made a pretence of wiping down the counter, breathing in deeply in an attempt to calm her queasy stomach, while Ella offered to make tea for the four of them.

Vanni brightened at the suggestion but before giving permission, Maria, who hated to see her staff enjoying a break, studied the empty area on the other side of the counter carefully, as though making quite sure that no hungry customers lurked unnoticed.

'I suppose ye . . .' she began just as the door opened to admit a harassed woman towed by three children clamouring for 'a poke o' chips!'

The newcomer looked as exhausted as Mirren felt. 'Mary hen . . .' she hooked herself on to the counter by two bent elbows, 'For any favour give these weans some chips and give me some peace!'

Maria, who had started life in Wellmeadow Street as Mary McGurk and altered her name on marriage to a man born in Scotland but of Italian descent, gave the woman a sour smile. 'Ella, serve Mrs Ogilvie. And ye might as well get some more potatoes peeled, Mirren.' Clearly, there was to be no tea.

By the time the children and their mother were served more people had come in, and customers continued to arrive in ones and twos until closing time was signalled by the arrival of Gibby, a head-scarfed woman as broad as she was high and the best cleaner in Paisley. Tonight she wore the Army greatcoat she had acquired from a relative on his return from the Great War.

'Christ, it's raw the night,' she boomed as she swept round the counter and into the back shop to take off her outdoor wrappings and collect her mop and bucket. 'Ye'd never think the winter was bye.'

Maria, impatient to close the shop and get home, hurried Mirren and Ella out as soon as they had bundled their coats on. As they left, Vanni, defying a glare from his wife, managed to slip two parcels of freshly cooked fish and chips into their hands. Then the door slammed shut almost on their heels as Gibby began swishing her mop over the floor.

Both girls had a walk ahead of them, for the shop was at the centre of the town, near the junction of Canal Street and Causeyside Street, while they lived at the west end, Mirren in Maxwellton Street and Ella in Well Street. As the door clanged shut at their backs they paused to pull their scarves up over their heads and turn up their coat collars against the persistent rain, which threatened to creep behind collars and down necks.

'Our Mary gets worse every week.' Ella opened up her package as she walked. 'Her temper seems tae rise hour by hour.'

'At least we usually get something home with us.'

'That's thanks tae Vanni, not tae her!' Ella said scornfully. 'If she could find a way of estimating just how many chips and how many pieces of fish would be bought every day, she'd not let that poor man fry one sliver of potato more. Then we'd not get anything. Are you not eating yours?'

'I'm not hungry.' The queasiness had eased but after spending an entire evening working with fish and chips and breathing in the smell of them, Mirren had no appetite.

'Keeping it all for Robbie again?'

'Lads are always hungry at his age. And mebbe Mam'll fancy a bit of fish tonight.'

'How is she?'

'Just the same. I wish the weather would get better. She might feel cheerier then.'

Ella finished her food, rolled the paper into a ball, shied it at a passing cat, then slipped a hand through Mirren's arm. 'Ye could do with some yersell. Ye looked awful tired tonight.'

'I'm fine,' Mirren said automatically.

'Why don't ye come with me tae this new Picture Palace on Saturday? It sounds grand and it'd cheer ye up tae have a peek at Tarzan's muscles,' Ella coaxed, and sighed when Mirren shook her head.

'You know that I can't afford it.'

'That older brother of yours should be putting something into the house. After all, your mam's his as well,' Ella said as they cut through Wardrop Street and along George Street.

'He says he can't spare it. Anyway, I'd as soon not be beholden to him.'

When they reached the foot of Lady Lane, where they usually parted company, Ella said, 'I'll just go on tae Castle Street with ye, it's as easy tae walk home from there as from here. If your Donald sends for ye tae go tae America,' she went on as they resumed their walk, 'your brother and his wife'll have tae see tae your mother, whether they want to or not.'

'You know fine that I couldn't leave Mam. And Donald knows it too.'

'It's a great pity that you and your brother Logan couldn't be melted down and stirred round, then remade,

like soap. Then he might get some of your kindness and
you might get some of his selfishness.'

'He's not being selfish, he's just being – like a man.'

'If you ask me,' Ella said darkly, 'it was men that started
that story just tae give them the right tae be selfish.' She
stopped at the junction with Castle Street, 'Well here we
are. It's me for Spinster Castle.' Since being orphaned as
a child she had been raised by three maiden aunts in their
small flat in Well Street. 'Are ye sure ye're all right on
yer own?'

Mirren freed her arm. 'On you go home and don't be
so daft. I'm old enough to walk home by myself.'

'I'll see ye tomorrow, then.' Ella waved, and went
swinging off up Castle Street while Mirren continued
along George Street, which stretched from east to west
through Paisley, keenly aware, now that she was alone,
of her muscles and bones feeling weak and rubbery.

There wasn't far to go now but she hadn't realised until
then just how much she had been relying on Ella's strong
arm linked through hers and on Ella's chatter to take her
mind off her own exhaustion. On the day Mirren had first
started work in Ferguslie Mills' twisting department Ella
had taken her under her wing and had even, when she
discovered that Mirren was the sole support of a schoolboy
brother and an invalid mother, persuaded Maria and Vanni
Perrini to employ her for four nights every week. Ella
herself worked there on two nights and on the other two
evenings Mirren's colleague was a morose older woman.
Mirren dreaded those nights, because as often as not it
was Ella's cheerfulness that kept her going.

The junction with Queen Street was terrifying; she
stumbled down the kerb and set off across a cobbled
desert, foot before foot before foot for an eternity, before
finally tripping and almost falling up the opposite kerb.
It was hard to believe that anyone could feel so tired
and yet still be alive. She wondered muzzily if it would
help to eat a chip or two. It had been a while since she

had last eaten; her mother had taken longer than usual to settle earlier, and Mirren hadn't had much time for her evening meal. She contemplated stopping to rest against a building while she opened the parcel she carried, then decided against it. Once halted she might not be able to get started again. So she plodded on, counting the mouths of the closes, since the space between lamp-posts was too vast to be contemplated, concentrating on placing one scuffed boot before the other with dogged determination. Passers-by were strangely blurred, their voices echoing from far away.

The next junction was Maxwellton Street, where she lived. Unfortunately it sloped down from Broomlands, an extension of the High Street, to George Street, which meant that a gentle rise had to be mastered before she reached the tenement building where she lived. Glancing longingly at the building on the opposite corner of the junction, she saw warm, welcoming light in the windows of the flat where her aunt Catherine Proctor lived, and half-thought of crossing over to take refuge there for five minutes before facing the final few yards home. Then, realising that once she sat down she would not be able to get up again, she turned her back on the lit windows and began to struggle up Maxwellton Street.

The lamplighter had been round and the single mantle near the street opening gave the interior of the narrow close a warm golden glow. At the far end stone steps soared up into darkness. These, she knew, she could never negotiate on her own, so there seemed little sense in trying to reach them. Instead she let her aching knees fold, lowering her body down to sit on the cold outer step, then leaned back against the wall and waited for Robbie. Sooner or later he would realise that she was late and come looking for her. The best nights were when he walked right to the corner to help her the rest of the way.

Waiting, she slipped into a pleasant dream world where she was dancing, whirling round and round in strong

supportive arms, laughing, dressed in something soft and
gauzy that lifted and moved with her. A dancing girl in
dancing clothes. It was a wonderful dream, and when the
chill of the step beneath her and a spattering of rain on
her face roused her, she was so disappointed that hot tears
began of their own volition to gather beneath her eyelids
and spill down her cheeks. Crying was a luxury that had
never been allowed in the Jarvis household, and for a
moment Mirren, alone and unseen, revelled in the pure
joy of letting her emotions go for once. Then she scrubbed
the back of one hand over her face as she heard a door
opening upstairs and feet clattering down the stairs.

'Mirren?' Robbie jumped the last few steps and ran the
short length of the close to gather her up. 'Ye shouldnae
be sittin' there, ye'll get chilled tae the bone,' he scolded
gently as he half-carried her up the stairs. The relief of
having him there, his strong young arm supporting her,
made light work of the flight that had been an impassable
barrier only moments before.

'I was only there for a minute, just taking a wee rest
before coming up.'

'Aye, that'll be right,' Robbie said in grim disbelief,
guiding her into the flat and nudging the door shut with
one foot. 'I've got a good fire going and some soup waiting
for ye.'

She could smell it. Suddenly she was ravenously hungry. She eyed the chair drawn close to the bright fire, and
the waiting slippers propped on the fender so that the torn
linings caught the heat from the flames. 'I should go and
see how Mam is first.'

Robbie was at the gas stove, ladling soup into a bowl.
'Mam's fine,' he said over his shoulder. 'I looked in on
her before I went downstairs. She can wait till you eat
some of this soup.'

The slippers were soft and warm and wonderful. 'I
brought you a fish supper.'

'We'll share it.'

'I'd rather just have soup and a chunk of bread, but you could leave some of the fish in case Mam fancies it.'

He brought the soup and bread to her, spreading a newspaper over her knee to protect her skirt from spills, then setting a kitchen chair by her side to hold the bread plate. Opening the packet she had brought, he carefully divided the fish, putting half of it on a plate in the oven for their mother before sitting down opposite Mirren to devour the rest.

'Robbie, don't eat it with your fingers! Put it on a plate and stop behaving like a heathen!'

He grinned at her, 'Fish suppers taste best eaten with fingers straight out of the paper,' he said, as always, and she gave up.

'You got some studying done then?' She knew that he had, because with Robbie, the tumble of fair hair falling over his forehead indicated that he had been concentrating hard on something. From his first day at school he had had the habit of playing with his hair while thinking.

'Aye.' He nodded, then frowned. 'But I don't feel right about you working in the evenings as well as by day, Mirren, while I'm studying. I should be the one tae do extra work.'

'You know fine that it's more important for you to finish your apprenticeship. Once you're a proper engineer bringing in a good wage I can start being a lady of leisure.'

'Ye will be, I promise ye that!' he said earnestly, and she smiled at him. She knew that he meant it, but Robbie was a good-looking lad in his final year as an engineering apprentice, working for one of the smaller local firms. Mirren had a suspicion that by the time he qualified and started earning more money he would have found someone special, and be thinking of setting up a home of his own. It had happened with Logan, the oldest of the family, and with poor Crawford, who had been killed at the Somme in the early days of the Great War.

Robbie popped the last small crunchy chip into his mouth, then crumpled up the empty packaging before yawning and stretching. 'I'm for my bed. And you should be, too.'

'As soon as I've seen to Mam. Sleep well.' Although she was the older of the pair by little more than two years, Mirren often thought that the love she felt for Robbie was more like that of a mother for her child than a sister for her brother. Like almost every other woman in Paisley she had been ravaged by fears throughout the Great War; in her case they had been for Donald, and for Robbie, who might become old enough to serve as a soldier before the fighting ended. Her prayers had been answered, but by that time her brother Crawford had been killed and relief had given way to guilt. Somehow it had never occurred to her that either of her confident, brawny older brothers could be in any danger, but each time she looked at her sister-in-law Agnes and her nephew Thomas, Crawford's now fatherless son, she wished with all her heart that she had devoted more of her prayers to Crawford. Sometimes she wondered if it would have made any difference, since she hadn't prayed for Logan either, and he had come home unscathed.

Guilt, she thought as she tidied the kitchen, seemed to be as much a part of her as her blue eyes or the soft fair hair pulled back each morning into a bundle at the nape of her neck. It had been fully fledged at the moment of her birth. It was because of her guilt over Crawford that she was determined to do all she possibly could to make their invalid mother comfortable, and to stay with her until the end, no matter how much she and Donald wanted to be together.

Tidying the books Robbie had left sprawled over the table, she found a copy of *Forward* tucked beneath them. That was something else to fret over – his growing interest in politics and his friendship with Joe Hepburn, an older man and an active member of the Independent Labour

Party. To Mirren's mind politics only brought trouble, especially to working-class folk. She was tempted to put the broadsheet with the rubbish waiting to be taken down to the midden in the morning, but instead she folded it and put it neatly on top of the pile of books before going into her mother's room.

The upper flat that Helen and Peter Jarvis moved into on the day of their marriage had consisted of a kitchen, a front parlour, both with bed alcoves, and a small bedroom which Peter, a plumber, had converted into a mere sliver of a room, where Robbie slept, and a lavatory, a triangular-shaped wedge that only just managed to contain a bath and water closet. Here, Helen and Peter had raised their four children; now, with only three adults in residence, it seemed quite spacious.

The parlour, the most elegant room of all, had been turned into Helen's bedroom when she became an invalid following the shock of her husband's sudden death.

'Is that you, Mirren?' Helen asked from the darkness.

'Yes, Mam. How are you feeling tonight?'

'Ye might as well put the light on for I cannae sleep. My back's that sore and I'm needin' tae go but the pot's full. I thought you were never comin' through.'

The bedclothes were tossed and tumbled, a clear indication that Helen had had a restless evening. Mirren removed the chamber pot from the commode and emptied and cleaned it, thankful that her father had had the wisdom to provide his family with indoor sanitation in an age when families thought nothing of sharing privies on the stair landings or out in the back courts. While her mother used the commode she plumped and turned pillows and smoothed out wrinkled sheets. After helping Helen back into bed she re-emptied the pot and cleaned it again.

'I've brought some fried fish for you. Could you manage it?'

'I'll have a try. Robbie gave me some soup earlier. He's

a good laddie, but it's not the same as having you here, Mirren,' Helen said with an invalid's fretfulness. 'There's things that a woman cannae ask a man to do for her.'

'I know.' When Helen had eaten the fish Mirren washed her then rubbed her back, before helping her into a fresh night-gown and combing her wispy grey hair. Once settled, Helen gave a sigh of relief.

'That's grand. I could mebbe sleep now.'

Back in the kitchen Mirren stripped and washed, then put on her night-gown and brushed out her long fair hair, before drawing back the chenille curtains that hid her inset bed by day. It was close on midnight now and she had to be up at six in the morning in order to get the breakfast ready and see to her mother before going off to work at Ferguslie Mills. As she turned down the top sheet the relief of knowing that another day had been got through and that she was free to slide between the sheets and lay her head on the pillow, was indescribable.

But it was not to be. When she went as usual to have one final look at her mother, praying as she opened the door a crack that she would hear the sound of steady breathing, Helen said, 'Mirren? I cannae settle, hen.'

'I'll sit with you for a wee while,' Mirren said with a sinking heart, knowing that it would be at least an hour before she could hope to crawl into her own bed and get the sleep her body and mind yearned for.

2

Paisley's Ferguslie and Anchor threadmills each employed some 5,000 workers, mostly women and mostly living within walking distance, which meant that on six mornings of every week any birds perched on vantage points such as the elegant spire of the Coats Memorial Church or the roof of the Clark Town Hall were able to view a mass of townsfolk streaming towards one or the other of the mill complexes.

When Mirren stepped out of the close every morning she could see a seemingly endless stream of men and women flocking westward along Broomlands Street on her right towards Ferguslie Mills' West Gate, while on her left a similar river of humanity poured along George Street towards the North Gate.

She could have chosen the West Gate herself, but instead she always walked down to George Street to meet Grace Proctor. On this particular morning she had spent most of the previous night in a chair by her mother's bed, lulled into sleep by the soft voice in the dark stillness, then startled awake when the tone changed or when Helen, amused by a memory, uttered one of her infrequent rusty laughs. The sick woman had finally dropped into a sleep as dawn began to filter through the thin curtains, and Mirren had slipped out of the room and into her own bed for a blessed hour of deep sleep before it was time to get up and make breakfast, then settle her mother for the day. Now she walked in a daze, head down, scarcely aware of her surroundings until her name was called out just as she approached the George Street junction.

'Agnes, what're you doing here? Is it wee Thomas?' Her mouth suddenly felt dry; Thomas was her mother's only grandchild and the apple of her eye. If anything should happen to him . . .

'He's fine,' her sister-in-law said breathlessly. 'I'm glad I caught you on your lone.'

'I'm on my way to work.'

'So am I. Mirren, I'm . . .' Agnes hesitated, the fingers of one hand plucking nervously at the shawl loosely wrapped about her head and shoulders, then said in a rush, 'I'm gettin' wed.'

'Oh, Agnes, I'm pleased for you!'

'Are ye? Are ye really?'

'Of course. Why shouldn't I be?'

'You don't feel that I'm turning my back on your Crawford?'

'You're doing no such thing. Our Crawford's dead and nothing'll bring him back to us. You've got a right to a life of your own, Agnes, and wee Thomas needs a father.'

Sudden tears filled Agnes's hazel eyes and her voice shook when she said, 'Ye've no idea how much I've been frettin' over havin' tae tell ye. I thought ye'd miscry me for forgettin' your brother. And I'd never ever do that,' she added fervently. 'Nor will Thomas . . . me and Bob'll always keep the memory of him there for the laddie.'

'Is that Bob McCulloch? He's awful nice,' Mirren said when Agnes nodded shyly. 'He'll be good to you both.'

'I know that,' Agnes said, and for a moment the small pale face, which looked older than her twenty-four years, was lit by an inward happiness. Then the light went out and the worry returned. 'But how's yer mam goin' tae take the news, Mirren, and what'll yer brothers say?'

'Whatever they say it's your business. You must do what you think best for yourself and the wee one.'

'Aye, that's what my mam says. I'd best run,' Agnes added as the Ferguslie bell rang for the second and final time. The other factories and mills in Paisley summoned their workforce by means of sirens and hooters, but Ferguslie had a great bell in the bell tower atop the original mill building. It rang every morning at seven o'clock precisely, and again at a quarter past the hour. Its voice could clearly be heard throughout most of the town, to ensure that every worker was in his or her proper place by the half-hour, when the machines involved in the detailed processes of turning baled cotton into thread roared into life.

'I'll bring Thomas on Sunday as usual,' Agnes called over her shoulder as she turned to run back down the length of George Street to the other end of the town. 'I'll mebbe tell yer mother then. Or mebbe it would be best tae leave it for a wee while . . .'

As Mirren crossed the road junction where George Street bisected Maxwellton Street, Grace Proctor emerged from the red-stone tenement on the opposite corner.

'Was that Agnes you were talking to?' Grace always watched for Mirren from the parlour window of the Proctors' first-floor flat. 'What's she doing at this end of the town just before the mills go in?'

As they joined the crocodile of people hurrying up Maxwellton Street towards the mill's North Gate, Mirren told her Agnes's news.

'How will your mother feel about it?'

'I doubt if she'll take it kindly,' Mirren admitted. 'Crawford was always her favourite and I don't think she'll like the idea of Agnes taking another husband.' It was just another worry to add to all the rest on her shoulders.

'Bob McCulloch's a good man. It's nice that he and Agnes have found each other, to make them happy again.'

Bob McCulloch, a quiet, civil-spoken man in his early

thirties, was one of the tenters, a team of mill-trained men adept at setting and adjusting the machines and dealing with minor problems that didn't require the skills of a trained engineer. A friend of Crawford's, he had fought in the Great War and survived, only to come home to find that his wife had been taken by the terrible flu epidemic that ravaged the world in the final months of the war.

'You look tired.' Grace changed the subject.

'It's cheery of you to say so!'

'Well you do. You know that Mother worries about you.'

'There's no need,' Mirren protested, though there was a certain comfort in knowing that someone was concerned on her behalf. She had been the one to worry about other people for as long as she could remember.

'She says to be sure to come on Sunday afternoon.'

'I don't know if . . .'

'You know she likes to see you. We all do.' Grace squeezed Mirren's arm as they turned left into a narrower street, known simply as Maxwellton. 'I saw George last night.'

'How is he?'

'He was much more like himself.' Grace's fiancé had only recently come home, having spent over a year in English hospitals and a convalescent home recovering from wounds that had almost cost him a leg.

'Is he settling in at his work?' Since George's injuries meant that he could no longer work at his former job as a van driver with Robertson's Marmalade Factory at the east end of Paisley, one of his uncles, an oiler in the mechanical department of the Anchor threadmills, had managed to obtain work for him as a desk man in the mill's stores.

'He didn't say much about it. It'll take a wee while for him to settle in.'

Glancing sideways at Grace, Mirren saw that despite

the other girl's happiness at having George home again, the little worry-line that had developed between her clear grey eyes since he had gone into the Army had deepened since his return. George Armitage had always been a chatterbox and the very fact that he didn't seem to have much to say nowadays indicated that something was wrong, apart from his injuries.

They were passing the Half-Time School, a handsome little building with intricate stone carving and polished granite columns set above the main entrance. Erected in the 1880s by the Coats family to enable their eleven- and twelve-year-old workers to continue their education for part of each working day, the school had closed in 1904, when under a new Education Act children below the age of fourteen were required to have full-time schooling.

Mirren knew from her mother, who herself had been a 'Half-Timer', that because of the new Act some 200 children had to be dismissed from the mill. 'And their parents were deprived of their wages. It was a good school, too, I liked it fine . . . and I enjoyed my work. Mind you,' Helen had often enthused while Mirren peeled potatoes or changed her bed or sat with her in the small hours of the morning, 'I'd a good gaffer, and if your gaffer was kind you were all right.'

Now the school had become the mill's book-keeping department and, as always, Mirren shot a wistful glance at it as she went by. If things had turned out differently, she might have been leaving Grace at this point to go in and take her place at a high desk, with an inkstand and a pen and a blotter as neat and snowy white as the blouse she would have been wearing. She had always been secretly glad that, born in 1900, she had been too young to start her working life as a Half-Timer, for she had loved school, and had been happy to stay in it for as long as possible. She had done well enough at school to be chosen for the mill offices when the time came, and had enjoyed every minute of the work, but a year later,

following her father's death, she had had no option but to
move to the twisting department, where she earned more
than in the offices.

Inside the mill gates they separated, Grace hurrying off
to the nearby Number 2 Spinning Mill while Mirren set
out for Number 9 Twisting Mill, adjacent to the West Gate
entrance. She had quite a walk before her; the sheer size
of the complex, with its offices and counting house and
stores and dyeworks, as well as the huge mill buildings
themselves, each between four and six floors high, often
astonished visitors to the town. Once Paisley had been
a weaving centre, home of the famous Paisley Pattern
shawls, but by the twentieth century thread production
had become the major textile industry, with the town
boasting the Anchor Mills, built by the Clark family on
the banks of the river running through the town centre,
and Ferguslie Mills to the west, built by the Coats family.
The mills had merged by the end of the nineteenth century
to become United Thread Manufacturers, but in the eyes
of the townsfolk they were still two separate businesses,
united in the common purpose of making the best thread
in the world but divided by friendly rivalry among their
workers. The Anchor employees were immensely proud
of the anchor motif on the bobbins that left their mills,
while the Ferguslie workers stayed true to their own
chain motif.

Ella caught up with Mirren as she reached the mill
entrance. 'Quick, we can catch that hoist, it's better
than having tae climb the stairs.' Together they ran to
the large wooden platform normally used to convey large
bobbins and 'cheeses' of yarn between the five floors of
the big building. The hoist was already full of women but
they made room willingly.

'It's a good thing the two of youse is thin,' one of
them said as the girls squeezed aboard and the metal
grille began to come down. 'God, I mind bein' a wee

skelf of a thing when I was your age. Wait till ye've got four or five bairns . . . ye'll no' be so skinny then.'

'I'd as soon keep my waistline as have all these bairns,' Ella told her, and the hoist, rising up slowly, almost vibrated to the derisive laughter of the married women on board.

'Ye'll no' have any choice, lassie,' said one. 'Just wait and see.'

The hoist shuddered to a stop and as the guard slid up the women poured out. In the twisting department the chatter flowed as they got ready for work, wrapping themselves in large calico aprons and taking off their shoes and stockings. The twiners all worked in their bare feet, partly because the floor was greasy from the trays of tallow used to lubricate the machines, and partly because they had to use their big toes to operate the switch that brought the spindles to a stop.

Someone had discovered that it was Ethel Gemmell's birthday and the poor girl, squealing and struggling, was seized and whirled round fifteen times, rebounding from one woman to the next. 'Think yersel' lucky ye're no' my age, hen,' Libby McDaid, grandmother to three, said as Ethel, released, staggered about, 'or ye'd have been birled intae candle grease. Happy birthday!' She gave the girl a hug and a smacking kiss on the cheek. 'God love ye, fifteen years old and never been kissed, kicked or manhandled.'

'Away ye go . . . that's enough tae make a horse laugh,' one of the other women scoffed. 'Ethel could teach ye a thing or two, couldn't ye, pet? I bet ye've passed most of us by on that path!'

Ethel, plain as a pikestaff, giggled and blushed with pleasure, then glared as Ruby Liddell said tactlessly, 'I don't know so much about that, with her looks.'

'Pay no attention, pet,' someone broke in quickly. 'Ruby is just jealous because ye're younger than her. Anyway, ye know what they say – ye might never get

a man, but ye can always be sure of a good pension if
ye work in the mills!'

The others nodded sagely. The pension rights established in 1918 were a matter of great pride to the female
mill-workers, not to mention a blessing to those women
who had lost sweethearts and husbands in the Great War
and found themselves facing a future without menfolk to
care for them.

'Aye, well, there'll be no pension if there's no job,
so mebbe ye should stop yer gabbin' and get to yer
machines.' The Mistress, the title given to female overseers in the mill, had arrived in time to hear the last
remark. Under her gimlet eyes the women scattered
throughout the huge, high-ceilinged room.

Once all the machines were in operation the noise was
deafening and the only way of communication was a
system of nods, winks, apron-flapping and lip-reading
developed over the years by the workers. Not that there
was much time to communicate, for each experienced
twiner had three machines to tend and the work was
continuous, with the machines stopping only if they were
being set up for the next job, or the thread had broken
and needed splicing, or if a tenter was making a necessary
adjustment.

Mirren, with four years' experience behind her, was
a 'six-sider', which meant that she was able to manage
three two-sided machines, each twisting the yarns from
a row of large bobbins together to form four- or six-ply
thread. Her main problem lay in trying to keep awake,
for the department was always kept warm – for the sake
of the yarn, rather than the workers – and the steady thrum
of the machines as the thread ran from bobbin to spindle
could be soporific.

Discipline within the mill was strong and rules had to be
strictly adhered to. Cleanliness was deemed to be essential
and any operators caught dozing at their machines were
instantly dismissed, a rule created on the basis of safety as

much as discipline. If a huge thundering machine caught hold of a wisp of hair or the tip of a finger, an arm or a head could be pulled into the intricate mass of cogs and wheels, and if one of the big overhead belts should break, all workers in the vicinity had to be sufficiently alert to run for their lives because, once released from tension, the broken ends could lash back and cause terrible injuries. Every department in the mill had its stories of employees who had been scalped, crippled or killed following an unguarded moment near a working machine.

Today Mirren kept sleepiness at bay by fretting over Agnes's news. There was little doubt that her mother would be bitterly opposed to the thought of another man becoming father to six-year-old Thomas. On a recent Sunday afternoon visit to Maxwellton Street with his mother, the little boy, a toddler when his father died at Gallipoli at the end of 1915, had innocently mentioned that 'Uncle Bob' had taken him up the braes to the west of the town to fly a new kite. Helen Jarvis had pointedly changed the subject while glaring at the woman she had never considered to be a suitable wife for her son. Not that anyone would have been thought suitable . . . Logan's wife Belle also fell far short of her mother-in-law's expectations as, no doubt, would the lass Robbie eventually chose.

To Mirren's mind, Agnes was doing the right thing in marrying again. She was only twenty-four, with a long life ahead of her and a child to support. When she and Crawford first met, Agnes had worked in a grocer's shop but, after being widowed, she had found better-paid work in the Anchor Mills Gassing Flat where cotton to be used as embroidery or crochet thread was passed through gas flames to burn off any loose fibres. The work was hard and dirty but Agnes, with a child to support, needed all the money she could earn. She had given up the nice little flat she had shared with Crawford and taken Thomas to live with her widowed mother, who also worked at the mills. As both women were on shift work they had been able, like many other women with children to care for, to work out a system that meant that when Agnes came off her shift, her mother was waiting at the mill gate to hand Thomas over before she herself started work.

Once the little boy started school, life had become a little easier, but the financial burden of caring for a lad with a healthy appetite and feet that were always growing and scuffing along walls or splashing in puddles was not easy. Mirren would have liked to help, but every penny she and Robbie brought in was needed at home, and Logan, working in his father-in-law's ironmongery, claimed that he too needed every penny of his wage.

'Belle's father's a right old skinflint,' he grumbled when Mirren tentatively suggested that he might pay something towards Thomas's keep. 'If I was a free man instead of his daughter's husband, he'd have tae pay me more and well he knows it.'

'You could go back to your own trade.' Logan had been a joiner before his marriage.

'And leave the way open for that sister and brother-in-law of Belle's tae creep in and inherit the shop when the old man's gone? We'll stay put, her and me. We're entitled tae that shop and we'll get it!'

Agnes's life would be much easier with a man's wage coming into the house again and it would be good for wee Thomas to have a father, Mirren thought. The only time she had peace to think things over was at work, where habit and repetition had trained her to control the frames under her supervision with hands and eyes only, leaving her mind free to range from one problem to another.

At midday, when she hurried home to feed her mother and see to her comfort, a letter addressed to her in Donald's sprawling writing waited on the doormat. All at once the day took on a special glow. She wrote to him every week without fail but, since Donald had never been much of a letter-writer, every letter from him was something to be treasured. She would have no time to read it during her afternoon shift, but even so she stuffed it into the pocket of her calico apron. Just knowing that it was there, the envelope stiff against her fingertips when she slipped one hand into the pocket, sent happiness coursing through her entire body.

When she first met Donald he had been just another boy in her class, one of a noisy group that delighted in pulling pigtails, flipping bits of blotting paper soaked in ink across the classroom when the teacher's back was turned, and generally irritating all the girls. When they happened to meet in Nardini's ice-cream parlour in Moss Street a month after leaving school, Mirren with Grace, and Donald – an apprentice electrician at the mills – with his pal, he had blushingly asked her if she would like to go for a walk one day. Her parents were at first reluctant to give their permission, but after Donald called for her and willingly answered a series of embarrassing questions probing his background, parentage and character – not to mention his intentions towards their only daughter – they agreed to allow Mirren to walk out with him 'since he worked in the mills'. Because the Coats and Clarks always insisted on high standards among their employees, it was a known fact among the Paisley girls that parents would approve of a young man employed by the mills. From then on Mirren and Donald had been inseparable until he was called up in 1917.

He survived the fighting to return home unscathed, but no sooner was he back in Paisley than his parents decided to move to America, where his father's brother was doing well for himself. Now Donald was working in Detroit and saving for the day when he could send for Mirren. As Grace had once said, it was like the stories of Cinderella, or the Sleeping Beauty, that they had read as children.

There was a special atmosphere in the mills on Friday

afternoons. The weekend was just around the corner, promising freedom from midday on Saturday, and the wages were distributed on Fridays. Once the clerks from the counting house had doled out the small brown envelopes from their big wooden trays there was a flurry of activity. Even as the twiners checked their money, a woman who sold home-made tablet on credit during the week to every department in Number 9 Mill arrived to collect what was owed to her, while the desk girl, who kept a check on the number of bobbins each machine used and the number of spindles woven, was in charge of collecting money for both the Holiday Bank and for Sma' Shot Day, Paisley's traditional works holiday. Grumbling but resigned, the women handed over the money they had just received.

'The rate I'm goin' I'll soon be payin' money out just tae work here!' one complained as she counted coins into a waiting palm.

'Ye shouldnae buy so much tablet.'

'I know that, but I can never resist it.' She sighed and shook her head over her depleted packet. 'When my man sees what I'm bringin' home he'll think I'm keepin' someone else in drink and no' just him.'

Mirren was the only twiner free of debt for the simple reason that she never spent her hard-earned wage on fripperies. When the tablet was brought round – smooth, golden sugary slabs neatly wrapped in waxed paper – she pretended that she disliked it, no matter how much her mouth might water. And she claimed that she had no wish to go on any trips to the coast when she secretly ached to be among the crowd piling onto the trains or into the buses for a happy, noisy day away from Paisley.

The money she earned in the mill and in the chip-shop was badly needed at home and any savings she managed to make went into a special bank account opened on the day Donald had broken the news that he was leaving for America. The account was never touched, no matter how much she might need money, for she was determined that when she finally went to Donald she would take with her a nest-egg, no matter how small, to prove to him and his parents that she knew the value of money and the art of saving.

She allowed herself one luxury, and that only because she would not have been able to cope with the hardships of her life without it. Mirren had grown up with a deep love of dancing, and when she first started earning a wage she had won permission from her parents to spend a little of it on classes at William Primrose's Dancing Academy in Forbes Place. She loved the small studio overlooking the River Cart and the sound of the yellow-keyed piano thumping out dance tunes, and she loved Mr Primrose himself, sawing busily at his violin as he walked among the dancers, roaring out instructions as he went and breaking off his playing now and again to rap some miscreant on the shoulder with his bow.

For a whole year she had attended the academy religiously once a week, and then her world had fallen apart. A year after Crawford and Logan went off to war, a burst stomach ulcer had killed her father. Helen Jarvis, never strong, had become an invalid, and overnight Mirren became the sole support of her mother and young brother.

The regular visits to the dance classes and to the occasional dance hall had now become sporadic, but she had not let them lapse altogether, even though her mother disapproved. Helen Jarvis recognised, reluctantly, that with no man to bring a full wage into the house, her daughter needed to earn extra money at the fried-fish shop, but she found it hard to understand why Mirren had to give up time to dancing.

'Oh, that's right,' she tended to say peevishly on these occasions, 'go if ye must . . . and I'll probably be dead when ye get home.'

She never was dead, but she did manage to create

enough guilt in Mirren to take a fair amount of the
pleasure out of her evening off. Ella and Ruby, her
companions when she visited a dance hall, were both
keen dancers and if it hadn't been for them Mirren
might have simply given up and stayed at home as her
mother wished. But the other two bullied her into going
with them as often as possible, arguing that having lost
Donald, although only temporarily, she should not lose
anything else.

She agreed, and tired and disheartened as she so often
was these days, she found that those occasional, treasured
visits to a local hall or to the little studio and the old
piano, and William Primrose with his violin, made her
life bearable.

3

Grace opened the door to Mirren as soon as she knocked. 'Is your Agnes visiting today?'

'She and Thomas arrived ten minutes ago.' The only time Mirren had to herself was on a Sunday afternoon when either Agnes or Logan and his wife visited her mother.

'Let the lassie get her coat off before you start questioning her, Grace,' Catherine Proctor admonished her daughter.

'I was only wondering if Agnes was going to tell Aunt Helen about Bob today?' Grace almost dragged Mirren's coat off.

'I don't think so. She came in looking like a ghost, and she wouldn't let Robbie take Thomas out for a wee walk.' Mirren sat down at the kitchen table. 'Good afternoon, Uncle James.'

'It's yourself, Mirren lass,' James Proctor said in his soft Highland voice, then having done his duty as host returned to his newspaper, leaving Mirren to get on with the subject in hand. 'She said it was because Thomas had a cough, but it's my belief that she wanted to keep him with her, because she knew she couldn't tell Mother in front of him. Then Logan and Belle arrived just before I left and I doubt if she'd tell them all together.'

'I'm sure she was a good wife to Crawford, God rest the poor lad's soul.' Catherine poured tea and placed a plate of home-made buttered pancakes on the table. 'But now she's free to marry anyone she chooses, whether Helen likes it or not.'

'It's not as easy as that, Aunt Catherine.'

'I know, I know. Nothing's ever as easy as it should be. Here, I'll put some raspberry jam on that for you, they go well together. How is your mother?' Catherine asked, ladling thick red jam onto a pancake.

'Much the same. She finds time lying heavy on her hands.'

'It must,' Catherine agreed with feeling. She herself was an active woman and had passed her energy and her interest in life on to the seven children she had borne and raised. Mirren was not at all surprised to find only Grace and her parents at home on this Sunday afternoon, for the Proctors were always out and about.

'Have you heard from Donald?'

'A letter came on Friday.' The ball of Mirren's left thumb automatically moved to touch the ring he had slipped onto her finger at the quayside before boarding the liner that waited to take him from her. At work she wore it round her neck on a length of string for fear that it might catch on the machinery. 'Everything's fine and he'll soon be able to start looking for a place of his own.'

'Your own,' Grace corrected her excitedly, and Mirren put her hands up to her face to cool the sudden heat that surged upwards from her throat at the thought.

'It won't be long now, I'm sure,' Catherine beamed at her cousin's daughter.

'There's no hurry, for I can't leave Mother.'

'Of course you can and you must, when Donald sends for you. You've got your own life to think of,' Grace protested. 'Surely Logan and Belle can look after Aunt Helen?'

'I doubt that.' Every moment of pleasure seemed to be outweighed by the problems it brought with it. Now joy at the thought of Donald was swamped by the worry of how they were to achieve their dream of being together.

'You'd not refuse to go to him?'

It was something that tormented Mirren occasionally in the dead of night, when she was too tired even to sleep. So far Donald had been busy settling in to his new life, but what if he was to claim her while her mother was still in need of her? Belle had made it plain that as far as she and Logan were concerned it was Mirren's duty, as the only daughter in the family, to care for her mother. All she could do was hope that the problem would resolve itself . . . though there could only be one resolution. Much as she loved Donald and longed to be with him, she could not bring herself to look forward to her mother's death.

'You wouldn't, would you?' Grace's voice rose in her anxiety and her father rustled his newspaper restlessly. Catherine put a hand on her daughter's shoulder.

'Don't go troubling trouble, Grace. Everything will work out as it was intended to before we were even born. Let's go through to the parlour and we'll put on some music and leave poor James in peace to read his paper.' She got to her feet, still as agile as in the days when she had been a dance teacher, despite a thickening of the waist and hips.

While her aunt sifted through the pile of records by the gramophone player and Grace settled herself in a comfortable chair, Mirren crossed to the big bay window. She loved the view from the Proctors' parlour, which, situated on the corner of the building, looked into Maxwellton Street from one side and George Street from the other. Standing at the large central window she looked down onto the cobbled road junction, her favourite view. There were, of course other similar road junctions in Paisley, but this one was special because right in the middle of it, set in stone, a horse-shoe marked the spot where a number of miserable wretches – men and women accused of witchcraft by the young daughter of the Laird of Bargarran, in nearby Erskine – had been burned in 1699. According to legend, the witches had first been strangled on the Gallows Green, now the large back court where Mirren hung her family washing. At Hallowe'en parties, when the games were over and the food eaten and everyone in a mood to be chilled to the marrow of their bones, Catherine Proctor was often called on to end the evening by telling the story of the Bargarran witches.

Lifting her eyes from the horse-shoe and the vans, cars and carts that passed by or over it, probably without their occupants giving a thought to its existence and meaning, Mirren had a panoramic view up the length of Maxwellton Street one side and almost down the length of George Street on the other.

'Are you still managing to attend Billy Primrose's?' Catherine asked.

'I haven't been there for a week or two,' Mirren admitted.

'Then a wee dance around the parlour'll keep you in trim. This one, I think.' Catherine selected a record from her precious collection and put it carefully onto the gramophone player. Although, to her unspoken disappointment, her children were not as interested as Mirren in dancing, they had all inherited her love of music. Bill, the eldest, married and the father of a small son, played the clarinet in the Paisley Theatre orchestra and also taught the instrument. A machinist by trade, he was also skilled in the saxophone, and had been a bandsman in the Army during the Great War. His brother John, also a machinist, leaned to politics rather than music, but Grace and her four sisters, Kate and Anne, Maggie and May, sang in their church choir and were all, especially auburn-haired Maggie, proficient on the highly polished rosewood piano that stood against one parlour wall.

Unlike most parlours, this room was uncluttered and the few pieces of carefully chosen furniture were set back against the walls, for Catherine and her children

often held small soirées on Sunday evenings for their
friends and liked to have room to dance. Now, as Grace
wound the gramophone, Catherine held out her arms to
Mirren in a graceful sweeping gesture. Her mother, too,
had been a dance teacher, and poise and carriage had
been instilled into Catherine from infancy. Her back was
always straight, her head with its neatly dressed grey hair
held erect and her straight, squared shoulders could have
been drawn in place with the use of a wooden ruler. As
she stood in the middle of the floor, poised for the dance
with arms outstretched, she almost looked as though
she was clad in satin and lace of the highest quality,
instead of her good Sunday dress of sprigged dark-blue
cotton with a pleated white-silk modesty-vest beneath the
cross-over bodice.

'May I have this waltz?'

Mirren curtsied deeply and moved into her aunt's
embrace. It didn't embarrass her a bit to be dancing
with a woman, for men were in the minority in Mr
William Primrose's small dance studio in Forbes Place
and the young women were often required to partner
each other.

Usually in the class Mirren was too busy trying to cope
with her partner's interpretation of the dance, but with
a good partner such as Catherine Proctor she was free
to let herself be lulled by the music into a daydream,
in which she dipped and swayed to the strains of 'The
Blue Danube' in a vast ballroom with pillars down both
sides and silken curtains at the tall arched windows, with
mosaic flooring beneath her slippered feet and chandeliers
sparkling high above her head. The music came, not from
the gramophone in the corner, but from a full orchestra
looking down from the musicians' gallery on a jewelled
kaleidoscope of dancers swirling around the floor.

So real was the fantasy that she could hear the murmur
of conversation, the occasional soft laugh, the swish of
the women's skirts as they dipped and swayed, the tinkle

of crystal glasses carried on silver trays by footmen wearing sumptuous livery and powdered wigs. Instead of the smell of the lilac soap that Aunt Catherine always used, Mirren's nose twitched slightly to the aroma of exotic perfumes and the flowers banked in alcoves along the walls.

And instead of her aunt's arm about her waist, her aunt's hand holding hers, her aunt's generous white-silk-covered bosom brushing her own rounded breasts as they moved together, she was with Donald, his beloved face only inches above hers, his brown eyes smiling down at her, his fair hair catching the light from the chandeliers. Together they circled the room before dancing out through open glass doors onto a balcony built over a rose garden and lit by stars from the night sky . . .

The music stopped and Grace, who had been curled up in a chair watching them, applauded vigorously. 'Very good!'

'You have a gift for movement and timing, Mirren,' Catherine said approvingly. 'It's a pity you can't use it more often, but you will, one day.'

'I wonder if they dance the waltz in America?'

'I'm quite sure they do, and other dances that you'll learn quickly. You must write and tell me all about them.' Catherine began to sift through the records again. 'Now you and Mirren, Grace.'

'Must I? You're much better at it than I am, Mother.'

'All the more reason for you to practise. Come on . . .' Catherine, who could be a martinet when it came to dancing, clapped her hands and Grace rose reluctantly.

'You'll have to be the gentleman, Mirren, for my daughter finds it hard enough to be the lady, let alone changing her steps. Now . . .' Catherine finished winding the gramophone, put the record on, and stood watching the dancers critically. 'Move from the hip, a nice smooth step . . . keep the ball of your foot on the floor, Grace.

Good, Mirren. Onto your heel now, Grace, as you move
to the back foot . . . No, the other foot is your back foot
now, Grace . . . stop!'

There was no possibility now of dreaming about ballrooms and chandeliers and Donald. Grace possessed none
of her mother's natural fluidity, and Mirren, who had felt
like a cloud during the waltz, found herself becoming
more and more awkward as she and her cousin lumbered
about the room. Fortunately for Catherine's temper, the
lesson was cut short by the arrival of her youngest child
Mary, who put her head round the door then let out a wail
of 'Dolores!' and sped into the room to snatch a large rag
doll from a chair.

'Someone's been sitting on Dolores!' She held the doll
close, glaring at Grace over its yellow wool head. 'It was
you, wasn't it?'

'So that's why I felt uncomfortable,' Grace said flippantly. Catherine had made the doll years before for
her youngest child, the delicate member of the family,
and Mary and Dolores were still inseparable. By chance
the Proctors' children were neatly graded by height with
James, the oldest, also being the tallest. Although she
was now seventeen years old and working as a clerkess
in an architect's office, Mary was less than five feet in
height; fussing over the gangling yellow-haired rag doll,
she could easily have been mistaken for a child.

Small though she was, Mary had made her mark as a
Proctor years earlier when her sweet soprano had won
her the honour of singing a solo at a school concert in
Paisley Town Hall. Standing alone at the front centre of
the large, high stage she had been right in the middle
of a superb rendering of 'Cherry Ripe' when both her
long black woollen stockings had parted company with
her suspenders and begun to slide down her thin little
legs. Ignoring the situation, Mary continued to sing right
to the end of the song, then she gave the audience a
dignified little bow and marched off the stage, folds of

black wool corrugated round her ankles and her head held
high. The applause had made the rafters ring, but she had
not returned for an encore.

Catherine had seen the incident as proof of her small
daughter's complete professionalism, while Mary's explanation had been simple but direct. 'I can pull my stockings
up any time but I only had that one chance to sing on the
Town Hall stage and I wasn't going to spoil it.'

As Mary fussed over Dolores, Mirren reluctantly prepared to return home.

'You know that I'm only just down the road if you need
me,' Catherine said quietly as she went to the door with
her niece. 'It would help you so much if I could just go
and sit with Helen now and again. Someone of her own
age, to talk to about the past, and the things that interest
us, can make all the difference . . . But we don't want her
to get upset, do we?' She kissed Mirren's cheek. 'Come
back soon, dear . . . and take care of yourself, for it will
do your mother no good if you fall ill.'

'I'm as strong as a horse!'

'In spirit, there's no doubt of that. But you've no colour
in your cheeks, lassie.'

'My skin's just naturally pale.' As a child Mirren had
longed for black curly hair, green eyes and pink cheeks,
but she had long since had to accept her fair hair and skin
and the light blue eyes that, to her mind, were simply
colourless.

'It's more than that. You're worn out and there's scarce
a pick of flesh on your bones. You need looking after and
the sooner your Donald takes that task over, the better.'

Mirren hugged the words to her as she walked the short
distance home. Catherine Proctor was an exceptionally
kind woman and Mirren always felt wanted and loved in
her presence, as though she was one of the family. The
Proctor house was also the only place where she remembered that she was only twenty years of age. At home she
carried the full responsibility of looking after her mother

and Robbie, as well as shopping, cleaning, cooking and attending to the household bills, while at Grace's house she could giggle and chatter and be cosseted by her aunt. It had been years since Helen Jarvis had cherished her children and even then, if the truth be told, her sons had mattered more to her than her only daughter.

At the mouth of the close she met Agnes and her son. 'You didn't tell her, did you?' she accused as Thomas, after a hurried greeting, scampered down the road to where a neighbour's pet cat ambled along the gutter.

'Logan and Belle arrived before I managed to find the right words. It's hard to know just how to put it.'

'You only need to tell her that you and Bob are to be wed. You'd not want her to hear of it through some gossiping neighbour, would you?'

'That would be even worse. Ye'll not let that happen, will ye?'

'What I'm saying to you is that the only way to prevent it is for you to tell her yourself.'

'I will, I will but . . .' Agnes stopped, then said wretchedly, 'she thought the world of Crawford. She'll wonder how I can bring myself to take another man in his place.'

'You're not replacing him. Crawford isn't like a bedsheet that's been worn out. You're just moving forward in your life. Marriage to Bob won't be the same as marriage to Crawford because they're different people.'

'Ye're right, I'm not really betrayin' Crawford, am I?' Agnes brightened. 'You put it so well, Mirren. Mebbe you should be the one to . . .'

'I know I offered before, but now I think it's best coming from you. If I tell her she'll only be offended that you didn't do it yourself, then it'll be even more difficult for you to face her again.'

Agnes chewed her lower lip. 'I'll ask Bob if we can keep it a secret for a wee while longer, just until she knows.'

'My mother's not a tyrant, Agnes, I don't know why you're so frightened of her.'

'It's one thing being a daughter and quite another being a daughter-in-law. Ye'll find that out for yerself one day,' Agnes said darkly as Thomas, who had had a hard time catching the cat, came puffing back to them with the animal dangling from his two small hands like an untidy and heavy tortoiseshell-coloured fur boa.

'It wants to be taken home,' he announced.

'He knows the way. If you just put him down he'll manage fine,' Mirren suggested, but he shook his head, clutching the cat to his chest.

'It'll run away if I put it down then I'll have to catch it again.' His small face, so like Crawford's, brightened. 'Uncle Bob says that when we're living in his house I can get a wee kitten all of my—'

'I'll take the cat back to Mrs Murray,' Mirren said hastily as footsteps on the stairs behind them indicated the possible arrival of Logan and Belle on their way home. She scooped the animal up and Agnes grabbed the little boy's hand and almost ran towards Broomlands Street, with Thomas protesting loudly at the end of her arm.

'I'm . . . I'm just returning Mrs Murray's cat,' Mirren said awkwardly as her brother and his wife, encountering her in the close, eyed the animal in her arms.

'You'll get cat hairs all over your good jacket, not to mention fleas,' Belle said with a shudder, pressing herself against the opposite wall, as far as possible from Mirren and her burden.

'Mind and brush your clothes and wash your hands before you go near Mother,' Logan instructed. 'The last thing she needs is fleas. She seems a wee bit down today. We've a tonic wine in the shop that might help. I'll bring a bottle when I visit next week.'

'You don't have to wait for a week before visiting her again. You could bring it any evening. She always enjoys seeing you.'

'We're both too wearied in the evenings,' Belle said firmly. 'That shop's harder work than anyone realises.' The cat, testing the possibility of escape, gave a tentative wriggle, and she eyed it nervously. 'Come along, Logan, we can't stand here talking all night.'

Mrs Murray was surprised to find her pet being delivered to her door. 'Ye shouldnae have bothered, hen,' she said, taking the cat. 'Did ye get a nice wee carry through the close, Jockie son? Did ye like it?'

Jockie wriggled free, landed on all fours with a soft thump, shook himself and eyed both women with contempt before flowing back out to the street.

'He'll come home when he wants tae,' his owner said easily as the tip of his tail vanished from sight. She folded her arms and settled one shoulder on the door frame, ready for a chat. 'How's yer ma, hen?'

'You're not usually away this long on a Sunday afternoon,' Helen Jarvis fretted when her daughter arrived home.

'I met Mrs Murray and she kept me talking. She says she'll come in and see you soon.'

'If I'd a pound note for everyone who says that I'd be a rich woman. They promise but they never visit.'

'What would you like to eat? I've got a bit of spiced meat and some sausages. D'you fancy beef olives?'

'I might manage that with some boiled potatoes, mashed. Or mebbe,' Helen said as her daughter was going out of the room, 'you should fry the potatoes.'

'I'll need to boil them first then fry them. That'll take longer.'

'I've got all the time in the world.' Helen threw out her thin hands to indicate the bed where she lay.

Starting work on the potatoes, Mirren glanced nervously at the clock. Robbie would be home at any moment, hungry and ready to eat immediately. If his meal wasn't ready he would 'make do' with all the

bread in the house and forget to leave anything for
the toast their mother often liked before settling down
for the night. He had better have his potatoes boiled so
that he could start eating as soon as possible, while she
fried a few potatoes for their mother. She counted what
she had peeled then began work on two more. Having
eaten his own meal, Robbie would be sure to want
fried potatoes as well when he smelled them cooking.
As for herself, she had lost her appetite, as so often
happened.

If her mother and Aunt Catherine could be friends
again it would ease her own burden a little. She knew
from the little that Catherine had said that they had been
inseparable as children, more like sisters than cousins. But
when they were young women there had been a falling
out and they had had nothing to do with each other
since. Catherine refused to tell Mirren more, insisting
that the rest of the story belonged to Helen Jarvis and
was not hers to tell.

Mirren hadn't even known of the Proctors' existence,
let alone her kinship to them, until the day when Grace,
in her class at infant school, had stumped up to her in
the playground and told her, 'You and me should be best
friends together because you're my cousin.'

Astounded, Mirren had confronted her parents with
the matter. Her father, a plumber at Ferguslie Mills,
had looked up from the shoe he was mending for small
Robbie on his cobbler's last and said mildly, 'Aye, that's
right, pet,' before being interrupted by his wife, swinging
round from the sink, wash-cloth in hand.

'But we have nothing to do with them, so you can
just forget about being friends,' she had said fiercely
and refused to discuss the matter further. Nor would
Mirren's father when she managed to get him on his
own. He adored his wife and would do nothing to upset
or annoy her.

'It's between your mammy and her cousin, pet,' he had

said uncomfortably. 'Best just leave things be, and say no more, for it frets Mammy.'

Always obedient, Mirren had held her tongue, but even so she had become best friends with Grace. And when Grace took her home one day after school to visit her Aunt Catherine and Uncle James and the rest of her cousins, Mirren had decided that trouble between the grown-ups need not affect her own friendships. And so before her tenth birthday she had learned the art of secrecy, an art that had stood her in good stead since.

Robbie arrived just as the potatoes were ready to dish out, full of enthusiasm for the political meeting he had attended. 'Joe got up and said a few words too, and ye should have seen the folks' faces,' he said proudly as he washed his hands and face before sitting down at the table.

Mirren winced. For months now Robbie had talked of little else but Joe Hepburn and politics. A decision one evening to attend a small meeting just to see what was being said had blossomed into an enthusiasm for politics that made Mirren uneasy. In company with her parents and her older brothers she thought of politics as all right, perhaps, for some, but dangerous for ordinary working folk like the Jarvises. She didn't like the way this Joe Hepburn – a welder at Fleming and Ferguson's shipyard by the River Cart and therefore an ordinary working man who should have known better – was leading her young brother into uncharted territory.

'Mirren, could you come and sort my pillows? They keep crumpling.'

'Coming.'

'I'll go. You sit down and have your meal in peace . . . what there is of it.' Robbie eyed the small helping his sister had set out for herself.

'I know the way she likes her pillows done.' As she hurried into the next room it occurred to Mirren that, although she had told Agnes that her mother was not a tyrant, Helen did possess the knack of getting the entire household to revolve around her. Her husband had always given in to her for the sake of peace and now Mirren was doing exactly the same.

Clearly there were many different ways of controlling others.

4

'She's still not said a word to my mother.' Mirren rested her basket on the counter and kept her voice low, mindful of the two assistants bustling about the shop, preparing for closing time. Mirren usually tried to shop in the Co-operative grocery shortly before closing, because it was quieter then and she had the opportunity to chat to her cousin Anne Proctor, the manageress.

'Bob'll be getting tired of waiting to name the day.' Although she was giving Mirren her close attention, while at the same time weighing the bacon she had just sliced, Anne's striking brown eyes regularly swept the shop to make sure that all was in order and that her staff were getting on with their work.

'She keeps telling me that she's going to do it, then she finds some excuse not to. I don't know why she's so frightened.'

Anne wrapped the bacon deftly. 'Has your Donald set a date for the wedding yet?'

'Oh, that's a while away. He's still to find somewhere for us to stay and then there's my—' Mirren stopped suddenly and the older girl, who, with her straight bearing and competent air, strongly resembled her mother, gave her a brisk nod.

'Exactly. You don't relish telling your mother that you're going off to America, do you?'

'But . . . I mean . . . that's different!'

'Not to Agnes. And remember that once Agnes marries Bob, she could turn her back on your mother and take the bairn with her.'

'She'd not do that.'

'Probably not, but she could, any time she had a mind to. That's what your mother'll fret over when she hears the news. Losing the wee one could mean to her that she's losing what's left to her of Crawford. Agnes might well guess how Aunt Helen's mind could work, and that would put her off the idea of breaking the news.'

'How d'you come up with these ideas?'

'You'd be surprised what a shopkeeper hears,' Anne said, while at the same time counting the packages on the counter and adding up the neatly written list. 'It's like a confessional in here sometimes, so it is.' She took Mirren's money then said as she gave her change, 'Tell Agnes from me that she should put Bob first for once. She's fortunate in having a good man wanting to marry her. For the second time in her life, too. Some of us poor lassies are still waiting for the first.'

'You're not in a hurry to wed, surely?' Anne had a lot of friends, but had never to Mirren's knowledge courted anyone. In the past eight years she had steadily worked her way up the Co-operative hierarchy from counter assistant to manageress and it was generally accepted by all who knew her that her work, which she loved, came before anything else.

Now she folded her arms across her neat waist. 'Not really, but times I think it would be nice to have someone special and to know what the future held. There's our Bill wed, and Kate. And Grace, soon.'

'D'you have a young man in mind?'

'Not a one.' The twinkle that was never far from Anne's eyes appeared. 'I tell you, Mirren, if I don't hurry myself on it's an old man I'll be needing, for I'm twenty-two now and not getting any younger.' Then the twinkle disappeared as the bell above the shop door jangled and she glanced over.

'Grace?'

'Oh, Anne!' Grace's pretty little face was distorted with barely contained grief. Anne ran round the edge of the counter, the colour gone from her own face.

'Is it Mother?' Her voice was sharp with apprehension. 'Or Father?'

'No, they're fine, everyone's fine.' About her neck Grace wore a pretty gauze scarf that her sister Kate had given her; one end hung loose, and her fingers were worrying at it.

'You're not fine. Mirren, bring that chair forward from the corner, will you? Beth, Annie, off you go home now,' Anne told her wide-eyed assistants as she guided her sister to the chair. When the girls had gone she locked the door then hurried back to Grace. 'Now . . . what's amiss?'

'It's George.' Tears began to spill down the girl's ashen cheeks.

'He's never ill again, is he?' Mirren saw that her friend's twisting, pulling fingers had torn holes in the fragile scarf, one of her favourite possessions.

'I wish it was only that! He's . . . oh, Anne, he's jilted me!'

'He's what?' Mirren asked in disbelief while Anne, grim-faced, stormed, 'He has, has he? Well, he neednae think he can just brush my sister off as if she was nothing more than a bit of thread on his jacket!'

'Look . . .' Grace held out a crumpled letter that had been clutched in one hand. 'I was just getting ready to meet him in the Fountain Gardens as we'd arranged when this c-came!' As she burst into noisy, frenzied weeping Anne gathered her into her arms, rocking her like a child.

'You read the letter, Mirren,' she said over her sister's head. The single-page letter held only a few lines, baldly stating that their engagement must be at an end, since

George no longer considered himself to be a fit husband
for any woman. It ended with his sincere hope that Grace
could forgive him, and his good wishes for her future. It
was signed with his full name.

'H-he's been saying such d-daft things,' Grace wept as
Mirren held the letter before Anne's eyes, 'about him not
earning enough in the mill storeroom to support himself
and his mother, let alone me and mebbe b-bair . . .'
The mere thought of the family that she and George
had once planned to raise brought on another bout of
heartbroken sobs.

It took some time for the two of them to calm her,
even with the smelling salts that Anne, ever practical,
kept in the back shop. When she did resort to gulping
and hiccuping, Grace's face was swollen almost beyond
recognition from the storm of tears. The scarf she had put
on for her meeting with George was shredded and tugged
until it was beyond redemption.

'I'll have a thing or two to say to Mister George
Armitage before this day's out,' Anne announced, making
for the back shop. 'Mirren, you take Grace home. I'm
going to see the man.'

'No!' Grace jumped up and ran after her sister. 'You
can't, you mustn't!'

'He needs to have some sense talked into him!' Anne
had already pushed her arms into her jacket sleeves and
was winding her own scarf about her neck.

'I'll not go begging and I'll not have anyone begging
for me!' Grace said with a sudden touching dignity, then
it all collapsed in another rush of tears as she wailed, 'I
just want to go home. I want my mother!'

Anne shrugged, defeated. 'We'd best take her home,
Mirren.'

'I'll have to get back to my own house,' Mirren told
her apologetically. 'There's the tea to get ready and I'm
due in the shop in an hour.'

'Oh Mirren, I was so taken up with our Grace that I

quite forgot. Off you go and I'll see to her. You'll come
to the house tomorrow afternoon?'

'I'll try,' Mirren promised. As she ran all the way home,
the heavy basket thudding against her leg at every step,
she felt as though she was deserting Grace in her hour
of need.

As ill-fortune would have it, she found herself plunged
into a domestic crisis of her own the following day,
when Agnes finally plucked up the courage to tell her
mother-in-law of her impending marriage. She arrived a
good hour before she was expected, marching into the
house and past Mirren as though she didn't exist, her
face pale and determined.

'Where's wee Thomas?'

'At home with my mother.' Agnes tossed the words
over her shoulder. 'I've got things tae say that don't
concern him.'

Mirren's heart sank. Not this Sunday of all Sundays.
Not when all she wanted was to go down the road
as soon as possible to see how Grace was. 'Agnes,
come into the kitchen and we'll talk about . . .' she
began, but her sister-in-law was already walking into the
front room.

Every Saturday night Mirren carefully wound locks
of her mother's salt-and-pepper hair round paper strips.
Despite the discomfort, the paper screws remained in
place until early on Sunday afternoons, when they
were removed and Helen's hair carefully brushed and
arranged before her visitors arrived. Nobody but Mirren
was allowed to see her on a Sunday until she was
ready to be seen; today she had undone the paper
curlers on one side of her head, and with the help
of a mirror propped against a cushion on her lap she
was brushing her corkscrew hair before unwinding the
other half.

By barging in unannounced and uninvited, Agnes was

breaking one of the household's unbreakable rules. She wasted no time. 'I'm here to tell ye that I'm gettin' wed to Bob McCulloch as soon as we can have the banns called,' she was saying flatly when Mirren got to the room door.

'What?' Helen, the hairbrush clutched in one hand and half of her head still dotted, hedgehog-like, with little screws of paper, gaped up at her unexpected visitor.

Equally demoralised by the sight of her normally neat mother-in-law in a state of chaos, Agnes gulped audibly then fisted her hands by her sides. 'I said I've come tae tell you that I'm gettin' wed. Me and Bob McCulloch've been promised tae each other for three weeks now and it's time you knew about it.'

Helen's thin body jerked in the bed and the cushion spilled off, leaving the mirror poised on the bump of her knees. 'You can't!'

'I can, and I'm goin' tae whether you like it or not. It's decided,' Agnes said in a high thin voice.

'But Crawford . . . what about our Crawford?'

'Crawford's dead, Mrs Jarvis, and I'm still alive and I want tae be happy again.' Agnes's voice began to tremble. For a moment she was on the point of bursting into tears but when Helen, gathering her scattered wits about her, said sharply, 'Don't be ridiculous, girl, you're not going tae marry anyone!', the younger woman stiffened and gained control of herself again.

'I'm a free woman!'

'You're my son's wife.'

'I'm his widow and I've been his widow for near on five years now! Is that not long enough?'

'I'm a widow too and even if I was able, you'd not see me grinding my husband's memory into the dirt and whoring after other men!'

Mirren felt the blood drain from her face while she watched the same thing happen to Agnes.

'That's a terrible thing tae say!' The younger woman's voice was little more than a whisper. 'If Crawford had ever heard you say that tae me . . .' She put a shaking hand to her mouth.

'Someone has tae remind ye where your duty lies!' Helen emphasised the point by banging the hairbrush down on the bed. Unfortunately the tortoiseshell backing hit the mirror sharply, shattering it. She gave a sharp cry and Agnes, horrified, lunged forward to pick up the mirror before the glass fragments fell out onto the bedclothing.

'Leave it! Don't you dare touch it!' Helen snatched up her precious mirror, a gift from her late husband. 'Look what ye've done, you wicked girl! That's seven years' bad luck!'

'Not for me. I've had five years of misery and it's over now that I've found Bob. Give it here, ye'll cut yourself,' Agnes said as Helen, distracted and confused, began to pat at the broken glass as though trying to mend it with her fingertips.

'Don't touch it!' Helen pulled the broken mirror to her breast protectively, then, as Agnes bent over her, 'Ye've been drinking. Ye're intoxicated!'

'I'm not.'

'I can smell it on yer breath.'

Bright colour flooded Agnes's ashen face. 'I've had one wee glass of port tae steady my nerves, just. It was the only way I could get up the courage tae face you, and Bob said that if I didnae do it this afternoon he'd do it for me.' In despair, she rounded on Mirren. 'Did I not tell ye what she'd be like? Wasn't I right?'

'You knew?' Helen's eyes narrowed as she twisted in the bed to look up into her daughter's guilty face. 'You knew about this . . . this hussy's plans and you didn't tell me?'

'Don't you call me names! I was a good wife tae your Crawford and it's not my fault he's dead.'

'I knew when he first married ye that he was making a mistake. I told him . . .'

'Aye, and he told me what ye said.' Whether it was the glass of port that loosened Agnes's tongue or relief that her marriage plans were no longer a secret Mirren didn't know, but the words began to spill out, tumbling over each other. 'We laughed about it, him and me. Why d'ye think he was so eager tae get wed in the first place? It was because he wanted out of this house, and away from you and the way you tried tae rule every minute of his life.'

'You . . .' Helen dropped the mirror and gripped the bedclothes in both hands. For a moment Mirren thought that the sick woman was going to scramble from the bed and throw herself at Agnes, but she settled for clutching the blankets so tightly that her knuckles went white. 'Ye besom!' she hissed, for all the world like the sort of 'common woman' she had always despised. Her eyes blazed. 'Ye'll not take my grandson intae another man's house, d'ye hear me?'

'The boy needs a father and Bob'll be good tae him and tae me.'

'I'll not have it!'

'Ye can do nothin' about it!'

'Get out of my house!'

'Ye didnae think I was goin' tae stay for my tea, did ye?' Agnes sneered defiantly and stalked from the room. A moment later the door leading to the landing slammed shut.

'Mother?' Helen had collapsed onto her pillows and was dragging in deep shuddering breaths. Alarmed, Mirren took the smelling salts from a nearby drawer – the second time within two days that she had seen smelling salts used, she thought as she opened the bottle and wafted it beneath Helen's nose. Her mother's eyes shot open and with a surprisingly strong grip on Mirren's wrist she pushed the bottle away.

'Put that back and go and fetch Logan. Why's he never here when I need him?'

Her hand flailed perilously close to the broken mirror. Mirren snatched it up out of harm's way and saw that although the glass had been cracked across, no shards had fallen out to lurk among the folds of the bedclothing. She put it aside carefully. 'He's probably on his way . . .'

'Fetch him, now!'

'Will you be all right on your own?'

'Just do as ye're told!'

Mirren snatched up her coat and ran out, only to find Agnes leaning against the wall by the landing window, shaking like a leaf. 'I havnae got the strength tae get down the stairs on my own,' she said pitifully, and Mirren put an arm about her.

'Come into the kitchen and sit down for a wee while,' she urged, but Agnes shook her head vehemently. 'I'll no' go back intae that house ever again! Just help me down the stairs, Mirren. Bob's waiting for me at the close-mouth. I'll be all right with him.' The tears began to flow and her trembling increased. 'I want Bob!'

As soon as Agnes saw the tenter pacing up and down outside the close she flew into his arms. He held her clumsily, blushing with embarrassment as passers-by stared. 'What happened?'

'It was terrible,' she wept into his chest. 'I said it would be and it was. Ye should never have made me face her. Sh-she broke a mirror, Bob!'

'She threw it at ye?' His mouth tightened. 'If she's hurt ye . . .'

'It was an accident,' Mirren tried to explain.

'Seven years' bad luck,' Agnes sniffled as Robbie rounded the corner of Broomlands Street and came swinging down towards them, his face clouding with concern when he saw his sister-in-law.

'What's amiss with our Agnes?'

Bob McCulloch's arms tightened about his intended. 'We're gettin' wed, her and me,' he announced, almost belligerently.

'That's grand news, man!' Robbie thumped the ten-ter on the shoulder, then added doubtfully as Agnes gave another wail, 'but Agnes doesnae seem too happy about it.'

'She's upset because Mother didn't take the news well.'

'Why not? It'll be good for wee Thomas to have a father again.'

'Go and fetch Logan, will you? Mother wants him. I'd best get back to her, and you should take Agnes home, Bob. I'll come and see you soon,' Mirren promised her weeping sister-in-law as she was led away.

Robbie was soon back with Logan and Belle, who had been on their way to Maxwellton Street when he met them. Leaving her mother, who had had time to take out the rest of her paper curlers and make herself presentable before their arrival, to break the news, Mirren escaped to the kitchen to make some tea. Robbie joined her after a few minutes.

'They're all carrying on in there as if Agnes had murdered poor Crawford with her own hands in order tae marry Bob.' He helped himself to a biscuit. 'What's wrong with them?'

'Mother's afraid that she'll lose Thomas.'

'She will if she makes an enemy of Agnes. What's wrong with her marryin' again? They should be pleased for her. I know I am.'

'And me.'

When she carried the tea-tray into her mother's room Logan was administering the smelling salts, but to Belle, not his mother.

'I'll be all right now,' she said feebly, waving the bottle aside. 'It was the shock.'

'She's not very strong at the moment,' Logan explained, putting the bottle down by his mother's bed.

'Are ye expectin' at last?' Helen demanded of her daughter-in-law, who shot upright in her chair with shock, squeaking 'Logan . . . !'

'For goodness' sake, Mother!' he was brick-red. 'It's nothing like that. Belle's just overworked and in need of a rest.'

Helen shot the younger woman a venomous look. 'Overworked, is it? And here's me a helpless old woman about tae lose my only grandchild, if none of ye can think of any way of puttin' a stop tae that besom's wickedness.'

'You're not goin' to lose Thomas, Mother.' Mirren began to pour the tea. 'I'm sure that Agnes's marriage won't make any difference.'

'It'll make one difference right away. I'll not have her under my roof again!'

'If you bar Agnes from the house, how are you to see Thomas?'

'She's not fit tae look after him.' Helen's fist thumped at the bedclothes. 'Logan, can ye not do something!'

'I don't see what. The woman's free to marry, I suppose.'

'She's thankless, that's what she is, thankless! After all we've done for her!'

Mirren was unable to hold her tongue any longer. 'And what have we done for Agnes, Mother?'

The other three looked at her in astonishment. For a moment Helen gobbled, then she rallied. 'We accepted her intae this family when our Crawford made up his mind tae marry her, for one thing.'

'And we supported her when he was killed.'

'In what way did we support her, Logan? Agnes has worked hard in the mills ever since Crawford died to feed and clothe and house herself and wee Thomas. She's not had a penny from any of us.'

'She gets her war-widow's pension,' Logan pointed out. Then, with a brightening of the eyes, 'And she'll stand tae lose that if she marries again. Has she thought about that, d'ye think?'

'If the pension was enough to live on she'd not have had to work. I'm sure that a living husband's worth more to her than a wee pension.'

'If ye can't be helpful, Mirren, ye might find yerself something else tae do,' Logan said coldly. 'Why don't ye go out for yer usual walk?'

'I will if you and Belle are going to stay with Mother for a while.'

He blinked then said, 'Robbie's here.'

'He's just gone out again.'

'In that case,' Logan said uncomfortably, avoiding his wife's eyes, 'we'll stop on with Mother for half an hour . . . but no more than that, mind.'

When she left the building Mirren automatically turned left towards the George Street junction and Proctor flat, then hesitated. Much as she cared for Grace and felt for the girl in her present misery, she herself had had more drama in her life that afternoon than she could cope with. Feeling like a traitor to her cousin, she pushed her hands into her coat pockets and walked in the opposite direction to Broomlands Street, where she turned left and made her way at a brisk, angry pace past the mills and out into the countryside.

If a letter had arrived at that moment from Donald asking her to leave at once for America and a new life as his wife she would happily have set her concerns for her mother's well-being aside and started packing.

5

To Mirren's surprise Grace looked cheerful when they met to walk to the mill in the morning. 'We were looking for you yesterday.'

'I couldn't get away. Agnes told my mother about marrying Bob and they had a terrible row. We'd to send for Logan and I was up half the night listening to Mother going on about it all.' She hesitated, then said tentatively, 'What did your parents say about . . .'

'About George's letter?' Grace asked lightly. 'Mother pretended that she wasn't surprised. Of all the things to say! She said that if he had been serious about wanting to marry me, he'd have seen to it as soon as he came home instead of keeping me dangling. She even said that she'd been wondering if he was the right man for me!' Her chin tilted. 'She was just trying to make me feel better and it was kind of her but George just needs time to settle back home after what he's been through.'

All the way to work she prattled on with scarcely a pause to draw breath, moulding the situation into something acceptable and believable. 'Father was so sorry for me that he made tea and went out and bought a box of cakes. He meant well, but I couldn't eat anything. I crumbled my cake all over the carpet without noticing till Anne fetched the dustpan and the brush and started sweeping round my feet. What a state to get into!'

'Anyone would get into a state if they received a letter

like that,' Mirren ventured as they walked through the mill gates.

'Oh,' Grace dismissed the letter with a wave of the hand, 'I was bothered about it at first, but when I woke up the next morning I realised that George just needs time to settle things in his own mind. Nob'dy but me understands what he's suffered, Mirren. The guns and the mud, and seeing lads he knew getting wounded and killed. He said a little about it when he was home on furlough but he wouldn't tell me everything. He said . . .' her voice wavered then steadied again, 'he said that he loved me too much to upset me. He just needs time to himself, that's all. I know him,' she insisted as Mirren said nothing. 'He's my fiancé. The best thing is to let him be just now, so that's what I'm going to do. I'll see you after work then.'

She waved and went off towards the spinning mill with the usual quick, brisk swing to her walk. Mirren stared after her, feeling that there was some flaw in her cousin's reasoning. But she was too tired to find it. After a very difficult night her mother had fallen into an exhausted sleep only two hours before the new day began, and Mirren's mind was fuddled with fatigue.

When there was no sign of Agnes at the usual hour on the following Sunday, Helen Jarvis tossed her head and declared that she was glad the lassie had had the sense to know she wasn't wanted. But by the following week she was fretting for Thomas.

'He's all I've got left of Crawford,' she wailed to the rest of her family. 'It's cruel of her tae keep him from me.'

'He's only half Crawford's,' Logan pointed out irritably. 'The other half's inherited from Agnes. Are you sure you want tae see him again, Mother?'

'He's the only grandson I've got! Here's Mirren with nothing in her head but the thought of running off tae

America tae birth her bairns as soon as that man of hers snaps his fingers, and by the time Robbie becomes a father I'll be cold and forgotten in my grave. And since that wife of yours hasnae seen fit tae give me grandchildren,' she added nastily, 'then wee Thomas is all I've got.'

Logan had always been self-centred and even un-likeable, but looking at the colour surge into his face now Mirren felt sorry for the man and glad that Belle had stayed home that day instead of accompanying him. He muttered some excuse about re-filling the teapot and hurried from the room, forgetting to take the pot with him. When Mirren carried it into the kitchen he was standing at the window, staring out over the huge back yard encircled by tenement buildings and known as the Gallows Green.

He cast a swift glance at her then turned back to the window. After a moment he said stiffly, 'With me and Belle kept so busy in her father's shop, it's a blessing we've got no bairns tae see tae as well.'

'Mother sometimes says things without stopping to think about how hurtful they might be.' She busied herself at the gas cooker. 'And now that she's not got any life of her own she's become bitter.'

'She always was sharp-tongued. Agnes was right when she said that Crawford left home for a bit of peace,' Logan said abruptly. 'He was always her favourite. Trust him tae be the one tae give her her precious grandson. Crawford always had all the luck.'

'Logan, the man's dead!'

'Aye, that's what I mean,' he snarled at her, and walked out of the room.

At first Mirren thought that Agnes's mother was going to refuse her entry to the flat in Gauze Street, then Mrs McNair, her face tight with resentment, stepped back to let her in. In the small kitchen Agnes was baking at the table, while Bob McCulloch and Thomas squatted on the floor in the midst of a flotilla of paper boats.

The big man scrambled awkwardly to his feet while Thomas ran to greet his aunt, brandishing one of the boats. 'Look what me and Uncle Bob made. He's goin' tae buy me a real boat with sails and we're goin' tae sail it on the pond in Barshaw Park. Have you come tae take me for a walk?'

'I thought you might like to visit your grandma. She's not seen you for two weeks and she's missing you.'

Agnes's hand immediately reached out and clamped itself onto her son's shoulder. 'He's stayin' with me. Go and pick up the boats, Thomas, there's a good laddie.'

'I've not come to cause trouble,' Mirren said low-voiced as the child obeyed. 'If you don't want me to take him to Maxwellton Street I'll not press you.'

'If yer mother's sent ye, ye might as well go back home now, for her mind's made up,' Mrs McNair said from the doorway. 'She's marryin' wi' Bob here and that's an end of it.'

'I know it is and I'm happy for her . . . for both of you,' Mirren said to the big, silent man who stood protectively by Agnes. 'Nobody sent me, I came on my own account because my mother's fretting for Thomas.'

'She should've thought of that when she miscried me.' The hurt was still in the young woman's eyes. 'She cannae expect me tae go on takin' him tae see her after what she said.'

'I could call for him, mebbe every second Sunday, and take him along for a wee while just so that they can see each other.'

Agnes was shaking her head when Bob said, 'It might be an idea, hen. After all, they're his blood kin.'

'He'll never forget his real father, we're agreed on that. Is that not enough?'

'He's got the right tae see Crawford's people and they've the right tae see him,' Bob argued gently. 'I'd not want tae be known as the man who came between Thomas and his own folk.'

'It'd be no great loss tae the laddie.' Agnes's mother spat the words out.

'Mebbe and mebbe not. Best let him decide that for himself when he's old enough. In the meantime he's got his rights and so dae his father's folk.'

'What if she tries tae poison his mind against ye . . . and against me?'

'She'd not do that,' Mirren said quickly, and Agnes gave a short mirthless bark of laughter.

'Ye think not?'

'If you let me take him to Maxwellton Street for one hour every other Sunday I'll promise to stay by him and make sure that nothing out of place is said in his hearing.'

'Have nothin' tae dae with it, or with her!' Mrs McNair told her daughter. Agnes hesitated, looking from one to another of the adults then down at Thomas, playing happily at her feet. 'Bob?'

His fingers squeezed her thin shoulder gently. 'Give it a try, lass.'

'Ye can call for him next Sunday,' Agnes told her sister-in-law.

Acting as Thomas's chaperone meant that Mirren's visits to the Proctor household were cut to every second Sunday, but there was nothing else for it.

'I hope your mother knows what you've given up for her,' Ella said during a lull in business at the fried-fish shop.

'She doesn't even know about Grace and Aunt Catherine, or about me having to beg Agnes to let Thomas visit. She thinks it was Agnes's idea.' Helen also saw it as an indication that Agnes recognised her own guilt and was trying to atone for it, but Mirren had decided that it was best to leave that be, since it made her mother happy and Agnes herself had no idea of it.

'You're too good tae be true, Mirren Jarvis. One of these days you'll be turned intae a saint when you're not lookin'. That family of yours takes advantage. God, it's hot in here!' Ella hooked a finger into the neck of her blouse, pulled the material away from her moist skin, and blew into the hollow between her full breasts. 'A fried-fish shop's no place tae work when the weather's gettin' warmer.'

'If ye don't like workin' here ye can leave any time ye want,' Maria snapped from behind her. 'I can find someone else easy enough.' Her own face glistened with heat, and poor Vanni, toiling over the big fryers, paused constantly to mop at his face and neck with a towel and drink deeply from a bottle of lemonade. Even though he was suffering more than anyone else he managed to flash a sympathetic smile at both girls as his wife hectored them.

Watching him tip the bottle back to drain it, Mirren noticed for the first time that he looked much younger than Maria, although she knew that he was the older by a year. They were both in their early thirties, but strands of grey were clearly visible in Maria's scraped-back brown hair and her tight mouth was dragged down at the corners and seemingly fastened to her chin by grooves cut into her sallow skin. There were deep frown lines, too, between her sharp eyes. Vanni, who had inherited the happy-go-lucky nature of his Mediterranean forebears, was round-faced and bright-eyed with not a hint of silver in his thick, curly black hair. As he gulped the lemonade the muscles of his throat moved smoothly beneath sleek skin the shade of milky coffee.

Mirren hurried to fetch another full bottle, and he thanked her with a sparkling, white-toothed smile as she opened it and placed it on the shelf by the fryers.

'I thought it was publicans that drank their profits away.' Maria's voice sawed through the warm air. 'Not fish-fryers!'

Vanni, who had frequently been punished with a tongue-lashing in front of employees and customers when he tried to remonstrate with his wife, prudently held his tongue, but Ella said, 'I'm sure I'd want tae drink the Paisley reservoir if I had tae work over the vats the way Vanni does. He could dry up intae a husk if he didn't keep on drinking.'

Maria whipped round like a snake ready to strike, but fortunately for Ella a group of customers came in just then and the older woman had to satisfy herself with casting evil glances at the girl and giving her all the hard, dirty tasks she could think of for the rest of the evening.

'Old bitch!' Ella said as soon as the two of them left the shop that night.

'I don't know how poor Vanni stands it.' Mirren was grateful for the night's coolness.

'He's got no choice, poor man. I'd hate tae have tae go home tae Maria with an opened pay packet. My Aunt Bea says that havin' a bad temper can make folk ill.'

'It doesn't seem to be doing Maria any harm.'

'Mebbe she meant it made the folk ill that had tae live with the ones with the temper. It's going tae kill Vanni if something isn't done about it,' Ella said sombrely, then, reverting back to their earlier, interrupted conversation, 'So you're lettin' your mother think that poor Agnes sends the bairn tae visit because she's in the wrong?'

'A few wee lies won't hurt anyone and if Mother's happy it makes my life easier.'

'If your Donald leaves ye here much longer he'll end up getting what your mother's chewed up and spat out.'

'Ella!'

'It's true. See ye tomorrow.' Ella tossed the words over her shoulder as she turned towards Well Street.

'It doesn't matter what our Grace says – that George Armitage has broken her heart.' Anne Proctor made certain that both her assistants were busy re-arranging shelves at the other end of the shop, then leaned over the counter so that her head was close to Mirren's. 'She might put a brave face on it during the day but she cries herself to sleep every night, and I can do nothing but lie there and pretend I don't hear her.' Tears came into her dark eyes. 'If she'd just talk to me about it I might be able to help, but she's too set on holding onto her pride. It's as if she's wearing a suit of armour. Has she said nothing to you?'

Mirren shook her head. As Anne had said, it was hard to watch Grace struggling to hide her hurt from the world. The girl's determined cheerfulness was so brittle that it seemed to be in constant danger of shattering.

The doorbell clanged as a customer came in and Anne immediately began to talk about the weather as she counted change into Mirren's palm.

Walking home, the weight of the shopping bags dragging her down, Mirren wished that she could spend more time with her cousin. If they had been able to go for walks as before, then Grace might begin to confide in her. But now that Agnes was allowing Thomas to visit his grandmother, the little boy needed Mirren's company and support. He was too young to be able to make conversation, and after asking him if he had been a good boy and quizzing him on what he had done at the school since his last visit, Helen tended to devote the rest of their hour together talking about his father. Mirren knew that her mother felt threatened by Agnes's marriage plans and was trying desperately to keep her son alive in the mind of the little boy, who knew him now only as a photograph. She had tried on several occasions to assure her mother that Agnes and Bob had no intention of allowing the child to forget Crawford, but Helen refused to believe her.

'Out of sight, out of mind, that's Agnes for ye. I knew the first time Crawford brought her home that she wasnae worthy of him, but try gettin' a laddie tae think straight when the fire's runnin' through his blood. And wasn't I proved right? There she is, chasin' after the first man tae take notice of her, with never a thought for poor Crawford, let alone his mother!'

'Agnes has been widowed for five years now and she never looked at another man until Bob came along.'

'When you're a wife and mother yourself, Mirren, you'll understand more about these things. And when that happens you'll wish you could come tae me tae tell me that I was right. But by then,' Helen added pitifully, 'I'll be at rest in my grave. It's the way of the world.'

The visits were an effort for Thomas. The child never complained but each time she saw him waiting for her, dressed in his good Sunday clothes, his hair brushed and oiled flat against his small skull, his mouth set firmly and his eyes heavy, Mirren knew. All the way to Maxwellton Street he tramped by her side, his hand clutching hers tightly, and as they entered the close she could feel his shoulders slumping. The words 'Abandon Hope, All Ye Who Enter Here' always came to mind as she led Thomas along the close and up the stairs.

In Helen's bedroom he perched on the edge of his chair, legs swinging in space, hands clasped tightly between his knees, following Mirren anxiously with his eyes when she left the room to make tea and pour the milk that Helen deemed suitable for him. Her suggestion that he might prefer lemonade had been dismissed by her mother, although Thomas himself had perked up slightly at the thought.

At the end of each visit he accompanied his aunt into the kitchen to have his hands washed and the milky moustache wiped from his upper lip, before returning to plant a dutiful kiss on his grandmother's thin cheek. And every time, as soon as he and Mirren stepped onto the pavement on the way home, he slid his hand free and skipped ahead of her, running back frequently to say something, freed from a heavy burden and as happy – as Agnes said when he burst into the house and embraced her knees – as a wee lintie. To her, his cheeriness was a sign that the visits to his grandmother did him no harm, and neither Thomas nor Mirren said a word to disillusion her.

'I can't bear it any longer,' Grace said suddenly one day as they walked home from the mill. 'I was so certain that George would . . . but he hasn't written again or come near me.' She clutched at her cousin. 'I don't know what I'm going to do, Mirren!'

'You're going to get on with your life and you're going to find someone else, someone much better for you than George.' Mirren took her cold hand and held it tightly. 'And one day you'll be glad of your freedom.'

'I don't see it.' Grace's eyes were filled with her pain. 'I still love him, Mirren, with all my heart.'

'But if he doesn't love you . . .'

'He does, I know he does! Nob'dy could say what he said or write what he wrote while he was away and not mean it!' Grace withdrew her hand slowly and carefully, as though the fingers were hurting and must be treated gently.

'Folk change, and George was away from Paisley for a long time.'

'Lots of lassies have married the men that came back to them after the fighting. Why should it change my George more than anyone else? If I could just see him, talk to him . . .'

'Best not,' Mirren advised hurriedly. The letter had been difficult enough for Grace. If she met George face to face and heard her rejection from his own lips, there was no knowing what it might do to her.

'I was thinking, mebbe if you were to speak to him for me . . .'

'Me? What could I say to make him change his mind?'

'Something . . . anything. You were always so good with words in school. You could tell him how much I love him and how him getting hurt won't make any difference at all. Tell him that it doesn't matter if we don't have much money,' Grace said eagerly. 'I'll go on working. I make good money in the mill and I could mebbe get evening work in the fried-fish shop, along with you and Ella. We could wait for a year or two before we have bairns . . . and tell him I'd not mind us living in his mother's house, so's I can take care of the both of them. Tell him anything that'll make him change his mind, Mirren!'

By the time they reached Grace's close-mouth Mirren had been coerced into making a promise, but as she completed the last short stretch of the walk home on her own, she felt for all the world as she did on those late nights when she trudged home from the fried-fish shop lacking the energy to climb the stairs.

How, she wondered in despair, could she possibly force George Armitage, a man she scarcely knew, to change his mind and marry Grace? And if she failed, what would Grace do next?

6

George Armitage lived with his mother in a tenement building in Love Street, at the east end of the town. Mirren walked past the close several times, rehearsing her speech, before finally plucking up the courage to go in. When the door opened in response to her timid knock, the sight of a stranger – when she had expected either George or his mother – wiped her mind clean of everything she had intended to say.

'Yes?' the man asked shortly, then as she opened her mouth and nothing came out, 'Well? I've got more tae d-do than st-stand here all day.'

Her mouth shut so abruptly that she heard and felt her teeth click together, then she opened it again and this time the words came out. 'I've mebbe come to the wrong place. I'm looking for George Armitage.'

His eyes narrowed and his thick black eyebrows tucked together in a sudden frown. 'He's not . . .' he began, then his head whipped round as a voice called from within the flat, 'Who is it?'

'Someone for ye . . . a lassie.'

'It's not . . . ?'

'Ye're all right, George,' the man shouted back, then, to Mirren, 'I s-suppose ye'd best c-come in.'

Mirren, who hadn't seen Grace's sweetheart since his return home, scarcely recognised the man who sat at the table, a half-empty glass and a beer bottle before him. As she recalled him, George Armitage had been a sturdy, red-haired lad of average height, easy-going and rarely without a grin on his open features. The man before her now was thinner and much older than the George she had known. The colour had even leached from his hair, which had become lank and listless and his naturally pale skin had an unhealthy tinge to it, as though he had been hiding from the daylight for years.

'Hello George. How are you?'

'Oh, I'm fine, just fine. Is that not what folk are always expected tae say when ye ask after their health?' he asked sarcastically, then, 'What d'ye want?'

'Grace asked me to talk to you.'

Two spots of colour suddenly glowed against George's pale cheekbones and his eyes, dulled from their former sea-green to grey, widened before he stared down at the glass between his fidgeting hands. 'There's nothin' tae say.'

'She's heartbroken, George.'

'I'd b-better be off,' the other man said, and George's head snapped up again, sharply.

'No, Joe, ye're fine where ye are,' he said swiftly, and Mirren stiffened at the name, then told herself that there were plenty of men in Paisley called Joe. She had no reason to believe that this was the man that Robbie was always talking about.

'If ye're sure . . .' He hesitated then gave a slight shrug and moved to lean against the wall. Since nobody had invited Mirren to take a chair, she drew one out for herself and sat down at the table, facing George.

'Grace is in a terrible state.'

'She'd be in a worse state if she married me. She'll get over it . . . eventually.'

'But why are you doing this to her? We've all known for years that one day you and Grace would get married. You were so happy together.'

'That was before. Things are different now,' George said to the beer bottle.

'Lots of men have been wounded in the war then come home and got married.' She used Grace's own argument. 'Being injured doesn't have to make a difference.'

'It does if I cannae earn money the way I used tae.' He leaned forward, a spark of life bringing the green lights back into his eyes. 'I was a van driver for Robertson's before I went away. I earned decent wages, enough tae set me and Grace up in a wee house. But look at me now!' He pushed his chair back so roughly that it fell to the floor and got up to stamp clumsily about the small room. 'Look!'

The injury was worse than Mirren had realised. His right leg was rigid at the knee and shorter than the left, causing George to lurch as he walked. He looked as though he was trying to move about on board a ship that rolled and tossed in a storm. Back and forth he went until his friend, who had set the chair upright again, stopped him with a hand on his shoulder and eased him gently back down.

'Y'see?' George grated at her. 'Ye think a man that cannae even walk properly can load a van, let alone drive it?'

'But Grace says that you've got another job.'

George gave a jeering laugh. 'If that's what ye want tae call it . . . nothin' but charity work my uncle got me by grovellin' tae the gaffers at the Anchor Mills.'

'The mills wouldn't take folk on out of charity. If you're there you're doing work that's needed.'

'I'm doin' somethin' that could be done as easy by a laddie fresh out of school or an old man past the age of being useful enough tae do anythin' better. And the wages are as poor as the job. How can I support a wife now, let alone bairns?'

'Grace says she'll go on working. She earns good money at Ferguslie.'

'I'll not be kept by any woman!'

'But it's what she wants. Will you just talk to her?'

'I said what I had tae say in my letter, and that's an end of it.'

'Y-you've had your answer,' the other man said suddenly. 'He's not going tae ch-change his mind. Ye'd b-better go.'

Mirren ignored him. 'Grace has been in a terrible taking since she got that letter. If you could see her, George . . . she's making herself ill over it.'

He crashed a fist down on the table and the liquid in the glass jumped. 'For any favour, what does it take tae get things through yer head, woman? What me and Grace had . . . that belongs tae another world that disappeared on the day the war was declared. It took me away from her and from Paisley and it made a cripple of me.' Spittle gleamed on the table and dribbled down his chin unchecked. 'And when it finally allowed me tae come back home because I was of no more use tae it, I found my mother turned intae an old woman because of the worry over what was happenin' tae me. I'm all she's got and what little I earn now's needed tae keep her. Grace is young enough and able enough tae make her own way in the world. Go and tell her that . . . and ye can tell her she'll thank me for this one day.'

Mirren put her two hands flat on the table and levered herself to her feet, then all at once her continuous exhaustion and all the misery that she and Grace were suffering between them became too much to bear. Suddenly she knew that if she didn't speak out, if she didn't do something, she would burst into tiny fragments and perhaps never become whole again.

'You know your trouble, George Armitage?' she heard herself say. 'You don't know how much you have to be grateful for. At least you're still alive and you've got a job and a lovely girl like Grace just desperate to marry you and look after you. Only you don't see that, because you're too busy feeling sorry for yourself to understand. You're right about one thing though . . . she's better off without you, and I hope she finds someone more worthy of her than you'll ever be!'

She stormed out of the room and out of the door onto the landing. At the bottom of the stairs she stopped and leaned against the wall to stop herself from falling on the stone flags. Her own voice still rang in her ears and her body shook with the loud, fast thumping of her heart against her ribcage. Vaguely she recollected seeing George's face uplifted to hers, eyes wide with shock and mouth agape.

A door banged above and someone began to come down the stairs at a run. Not wanting to be found slumped like a drunk woman against the wall, she drew herself upright and had taken a few shaky steps towards the pavement when her arm was grabbed from behind and she was whirled round.

'How dare ye speak tae the man like that!' George's friend Joe hissed down at her.

'Let me go!' She tried to pull free, but couldn't.

'Not until ye hear what I've tae say tae ye. Come here!' She was dragged back to the stairs, past them, and through the back close into the yard, a small square area of weed-infested flagstones and patchy grass. Once outside, he pushed her hard against the wall.

'If you don't let me go I'll . . .'

'Ye'll go when I'm ready and not before,' he said through gritted teeth. She tried to struggle free but he caught her upper arms, holding them so that she was pinned between the wall and his lean body. Her mind scurried frantically around the prison of her skull, seeking a solution to her predicament. The little yard was overlooked all round by the back windows of other tenements, but the man holding her prisoner was much taller than she was and no doubt anyone casually glancing down into the yard would assume, by the way she was pinned against the wall, that they were lovers stealing a moment alone together.

She thought of screaming for help but two things stopped her. One was that her face was almost against his chest, which would muffle the sound, and the other was to do with her upbringing. Helen Jarvis lived in constant fear of being an object of attention and she had taught her children throughout their formative years that crying, misbehaving or screaming in public was tantamount to committing murder.

'George Armitage never was a coward and never will be,' Mirren's captor said into her ear, 'and if you ever again accuse him of such a thing I'll . . .' He stopped, and she heard him swallowing hard. 'I was there when he got wounded. I helped tae carry his stretcher tae the field hospital. There'd been so many wounded brought in that there was no room for George. He was given somethin' that was supposed tae dull the pain, then dumped ontae duckboards they'd tae lay over the mud outside the hospital tents because it was so bad. I stayed with him because we'd all heard about the way the mud sometimes came up over the boards and drowned men too badly hurt tae get themselves clear of it.' He stepped back slightly so that he could look down at her, a tall gangly scarecrow of a man, with fierce blue eyes beneath brows as thick and black as the hair on his head. 'Can ye imagine what it must've been like for those poor bastards?' he demanded savagely. 'Helpless as bairns, drownin' slowly in thick mud with the folk all around them too busy or too hurt themselves tae notice or care? That's why I stayed with George and that's why I know the hell that man went through.' Although his eyes still held hers, she could tell by their blank look that he no longer saw her face just inches below his. Instead he was looking at something beyond her ken, something that still, two or three years later, had the power to sicken and frighten him.

'It was hours before they came for him and if he hadnae

been left unattended for so long, he might not be crabbin'
about the way he is today. He went away a man and he
came back a wreck. D'ye think he wanted it tae be like
that? D'ye think he enjoys seein' bairns pointin' at him in
the streets and folk feelin' sorry for him? Even sympathy
can be hard tae swallow at times. Specially sympathy from
the lassie he was goin' tae wed.'

He released his grip, and stepped back. 'Do as the
man says, will ye? Tell yer friend tae make a new life
for hersel' and leave him alone. It's what he wants, far
more than he wants her.'

He wheeled round and walked into the close. Mirren
heard him go back up to the flat where George sat,
not running this time, but moving slowly. The steps
faded, a door closed in the distance, then there was
silence.

Walking home, she felt as though her mind had been
hauled from her skull, turned inside out, scrubbed and
replaced. She desperately wanted to be angry with George's
friend for the terrible things he had said to her but at the
same time she had an overpowering feeling that he had
been in the right and she had been in the wrong when she
accused Grace's sweetheart of selfishness.

It wasn't until she was in bed that night that she realised that during his tirade in the back court Joe hadn't
stammered over a single word.

'But surely he understood how I feel!' Grace railed at her
on the way to work the next morning.

'Yes he does, but his mind's made up.'

'Are you certain you explained how miserable I am?'

'Grace, I said everything I could think of but he
wouldn't change his mind.'

'I'll have to go and see him myself.'

'No!' Mirren couldn't bear the thought of her cousin
being exposed to George's bitterness, or, even worse, to
his friend Joe's rage, if he should happen to be there. 'The

man's changed out of all recognition. It's as if the George you got engaged to died in France.'

'I wish he had . . . and I wish I had as well.'

'Grace!'

'There's nothing left for me here, Mirren.' Tears shone in Grace's eyes. 'I've been jilted. How am I to face the women at work?'

'They'll all be on your side.' The mill-workers had always supported and helped each other, a tradition that had become more noticeable since the Great War. Girls who had lost sweethearts in the conflict found their workmates closing ranks about them, helping them through their suffering. True, there were jealousies and rivalries and a certain amount of bitchiness, as was to be expected among groups of women anywhere in all walks of life, but when someone was in need, the solidarity among the mill lassies was matched nowhere else.

'It's their pity I can't take!' Without knowing it, Grace was echoing George's feelings. 'I hate working in that mill. George was going to make all the difference to my life. We were going to get a wee house, and bairns, and I'd have stayed at home and looked after him . . . and he'd have looked after me.' The tears flowed again. 'Everyone's getting married but me! Jessie Kennedy and her sister have just gone off to Canada, and you'll be in America with your Donald soon enough, and I'll be stuck here with n-nothing to look forward to for the rest of my life!'

As May progressed Mirren began to find every day a struggle. It became harder and harder to stay awake at her machine.

'God love ye, hen, ye look like a wee neglected flower that someone's jammed intae a vase and forgotten tae water. Here,' Libby McDaid reached into her shopping bag during the morning break and produced a bottle and a small wine-glass. 'Have some of my tonic.' She rubbed at the used glass with a corner of her apron and filled it almost to the brim.

'I'm fine, I don't need it.'

'Then take it tae please me. Every drop of it, mind,' Libby ordered, and Mirren had no option but to accept the drink. In the weeks before their summer holidays many of the mill women treated themselves to a bottle of cheap sherry. A glassful was removed and the bottle topped up again with phosphorine. Every day at the morning break the bottle was vigorously shaken and a small glassful taken. The mill-workers swore by the 'tonic' which, they claimed, gave them the energy to enjoy their holidays.

It was cloyingly sweet to the taste and strong enough to tickle the back of Mirren's throat, but she swallowed it down under Libby's watchful eye and handed back the empty glass.

'Ye should get yersel' a bottle of sherry, pet, and some phosphorine from the chemist,' Libby advised as she corked the bottle and stowed it back in her bag. 'There's nothin' like it tae set ye up.'

'Can I have some?' Ethel Gemmell asked eagerly.

''Deed no, milady, you're far too young tae be takin' spirits! Anyway, wee lassies aye have plenty of energy.'

'Mirren's not much older than me. How is it that she needs sherry and I don't?'

'Mirren works hard at home as well as here. Her mammy's ill, not like yours, waitin' tae put yer dinner on the table every night . . . and tuck ye up in yer bed and read ye a story an' all,' Libby added, and the girl flushed and stuck out her lower lip.

'Nob'dy takes me seriously in this place.'

'That's because ye're the youngest and the newest, hen,' Libby told her, putting her bag out of the way and moving to her machines as the Mistress's approach signalled the end of the work break. 'Another wee lassie'll come in sooner or later, then it'll be your turn tae torment her the way we torment you.'

*   *   *

'We were wonderin', me and Bob, if ye'd stand with me at my wedding,' Agnes said tentatively when Mirren brought Thomas back from his Sunday visit to his grandmother.

'Me?'

'Aye. Bob's first wife's brother's standin' with him and I'd like you tae be my witness.'

Mirren looked from one to the other. 'But what'd my mother say?'

'Does she have tae know?' Agnes's fingers were twisting round each other nervously.

'She'd be sure to find out. Is there not someone you work beside that you'd like to ask?'

Bob's hand closed about Agnes's shoulder. 'Aye, but Agnes wants you,' he told Mirren in his usual quiet, firm way. 'We talked about it and we both feel that we should have family from our first marriages at our weddin' tae show that we're keepin' faith with those who've been taken from us.'

Mirren looked at the two of them, so perfect for each other and so determined to do everything properly. 'I'd be honoured to stand with you, Agnes,' she said, and the young woman's face lit up.

'Yer mother needn't ever know.'

'She will, for I'm going to tell her.'

'D'ye think that's wise?'

'I'm not going to let your marriage be turned into something that has to be kept secret. I'm going to tell them all,' Mirren said firmly.

Logan, Belle and her mother all stared for a long moment, open-mouthed, when Mirren told them that she was to be one of the witnesses at Agnes's marriage to Bob. Then Helen said flatly, 'Ye'll have nothin' tae do with it.'

'I've given my word.'

'Then ye can just take it back again. Logan, tell her!'

'Mother's right, Mirren. Ye can't have any part in this . . . this business.' He made it sound like a public hanging.

'Why not?'

'Because it's not decent,' Belle said.

'What's not decent about it?'

'Ye know well enough,' Helen snapped. 'Agnes promised herself before God tae our Crawford for the rest of her life.'

'And for the rest of his life too. She's Crawford's widow now.'

'It's not his fault he's dead,' Logan said through lips so pursed that the words had to squeeze themselves out.

'It's not her fault either.'

'Don't be cheeky!' Helen ordered, and all at once Mirren understood why young Ethel felt so frustrated and humiliated when the other women in the twining department treated her like a child. But having gone this far she wasn't going to give in.

'I'm not being cheeky, Mother, I'm just telling you that I've given my word to Agnes and I'm standing by it.'

'If our Crawford was here . . .' Helen began ominously.

'If our Crawford was here, Agnes wouldn't be thinking of marrying Bob McCulloch. I'll make some tea,' Mirren said, and escaped to the kitchen.

Robbie followed her a few minutes later. 'I doubt if there's been such a stir in Maxwellton Street since they burned the Bargarron witches. They're all huddled together in there, fretting over yer insubordination.'

'I don't see that I'm doing anything wrong.'

'Neither do I, and I'm pleased for Agnes and wee Thomas.'

'I wish you'd said that earlier.'

'Ach, I cannae be bothered with those family consultations. I don't even listen tae half of what's said. But I did speak up for you after ye'd left. That's why I've been banished in here. I'd like tae attend the wedding too, if ye think it'd be all right with Agnes and Bob.'

'Oh, would you, Robbie? It would mean a lot to Agnes!'

'Why not? We'll have a good time for once.' He eyed the trembling pile of saucers and cups in her hand, 'Mebbe I should take them.'

She relinquished her burden to him with relief, and held her hands out before her. 'Look at the way I'm shaking!'

'Ye shouldn't let them upset ye.'

'I know. It's just . . .' She shrugged and let the words trail away. It was just everything – missing Donald, worrying about Grace, who seemed to be locked for ever into a downward spiral of misery now that she had lost George completely; and over and around everything there was the tiredness that never left her and made all the little everyday problems in her life take on gigantic proportions.

7

'Ye still look awful peelly-wally, hen. Come dancin'
with me and Ella on Saturday,' Ruby Liddell suggested
as Mirren parcelled up her order in the fried-fish shop.
'It'll do ye good.'

'Aye, we could go tae one of the Glasgow dance halls.
What d'ye say, Mirren?' Ella coaxed.

'I don't know. I have to think of Donald . . .' To
Mirren's mind the Glasgow ballrooms, more sophisticated than anything Paisley had to offer, were not suitable
venues for engaged women.

'Och, we're only goin' out tae enjoy ourselves, not
huntin' for husbands,' Ella protested.

'You speak for yersel',' Ruby told her, leaning comfortably against the counter and opening one end of the packet
Mirren had just wrapped for her.

'Mebbe you are, Ruby, but I'm not.' For some reason
known to nobody but herself, Ella always insisted on
going home unescorted, no matter how much she had
enjoyed her evening. 'We can just have a nice evenin''
out then take ourselves home. Come on, Mirren, ye need
tae do somethin' just for yerself now and again.'

'Ella's talking sense tae ye,' Vanni chimed in. The shop
was empty apart from Ruby, and Maria was in the back
shop peeling potatoes. Vanni checked his bubbling vats
with a quick glance, then came to lean on the counter.
'You're too pale. What is it they say about all work and

no play making Jack a dull boy? You work hard and if ye don't enjoy yerself sometimes, there's no reason for living.'

Ella raised an eyebrow at him. 'You work hard too, Vanni. When d'you get the chance tae enjoy yerself?'

He gave a wry shrug. 'I'm married. For me it's different.'

'The best perfume in the world, that. Fresh chips with plenty of vinegar on them.' Ruby sniffed deeply at the steam rising from the paper packet in her hand, then pulled a chip out and blew on it before popping it into her mouth. 'By God that's hot!' she mumbled through the mouthful.

'Vanni'll fry them in cold fat for ye next time,' Ella offered.

Ruby settled herself comfortably against the counter as she chewed. 'You should enjoy yerself while ye can, Mirren, because we never know what's ahead of us. I mind when my Auntie went, God rest her, her oldest lassie insisted on keepin' tae a year of mourning for her. She wouldnae go anywhere or wear anythin' but black. She even kept the curtains drawn all the time. And what happened?' Ruby paused for dramatic effect and took the chance to eat another chip.

'We don't know, since it's you that's supposed tae be tellin' the story,' Ella pointed out.

'She went down with the tuberculosis six months intae her mournin' time and she was lyin' alongside her ma before the year was up. Just seventeen she was. They buried her in her black clothes so's she'd not break her pledge.' Ruby licked her fingers delicately.

'A sad story,' Vanni commented, while Ella jeered, 'So ye're telling poor Mirren here that she should enjoy herself because she might come down with tuberculosis any day now?'

'I'm sayin',' Ruby corrected her with dignity, 'that we have tae take our pleasures when we can, for we never know what might lie ahead. And that goes for all of us, even you with yer smart-alecky tongue, Ella Caldwell.'

Ella ignored her. 'So ye'll come tae the dancin' with us, Mirren?'

Tired though she was, Mirren felt her spirits lift and her feet itch at the prospect of dancing to a proper orchestra in a real ballroom. 'Mebbe just this once . . .'

Ella beamed, just as Maria arrived unexpectedly in their midst.

'This isn't a restaurant,' she snapped at Ruby. 'Once ye've bought the goods ye're supposed tae eat them somewhere else, instead of holding my staff back with yer natterin'!'

Ruby swept a glance round the empty shop as Vanni hurriedly returned to his vats and Ella and Mirren did their best to look busy. 'I cannae see a single person waitin' this side of the counter.'

'There's more tae their work than servin' the likes of you. There's floors tae be swept and counters tae be wiped, and potatoes tae be cut up and fish tae be battered ready for the rush after the picture houses empty. Though I grant ye,' Maria said, her glare piercing her husband and her two assistants in turn, 'that most of the folk on this side of the counter seem tae think it's all done by the elves when they're not lookin'. And don't encourage customers tae stand around like that,' she ordered her staff when Ruby flounced out, muttering. 'Ella, get another bag of potatoes peeled and cut. Mirren, you can do the fish.'

Fortunately Robbie was at home on Saturday evening, so Mirren was able to go out with a clear conscience after seeing to her mother. It had been a silent week; Helen's fury at her daughter's defiance still thickened the air and Mirren was glad, as she plumped up the pillows and tucked in the bedclothes, to be getting away from it for a few hours.

'I'll not be late back.'

'Don't spoil your evening on my account,' Helen said huffily. 'I'm only your mother . . . my wishes don't matter a bit.'

Mirren refused to be drawn. 'Robbie'll be in the kitchen if you need anything,' she said briskly, and escaped. 'You'll mind and make her a cup of tea at nine o'clock, Robbie? And mebbe a biscuit if she's in the mood to take one.'

'I know, I know.' He had settled himself at the table with his engineering books. 'Go and enjoy yerself . . . and try tae forget all about this place for a wee while.'

Ruby was waiting for her at the top of Well Street. As they hurried down the street she complained vigorously that the one thing she didn't like about going dancing with Ella was the way everything had to be kept a secret.

'I've tae go through this palaver two and three times a week just because she likes these old aunties of hers tae think she's workin' in the fried-fish shop every night. Ye'd think that at her age she could just tell them straight out about the dancin' and be damned tae what they think.'

Like Mirren, Ella loved dancing, but her aunts had refused to allow her to enrol in Mr Primrose's academy. When she found evening work in the fried-fish shop, however, they approved since she was earning extra money, while at the same time keeping herself busy and out of harm's way. The trusting souls were under the impression that she worked in the shop six evenings a week, when in actual fact she only worked two evenings, leaving four available for pleasure.

'I think she enjoys the mystery of it,' Mirren said as they went through the close.

'Well I could do without the mysteries.' Ruby stuck her head out of the close to survey the back court. 'Good, there's nob'dy here.' She bounced into the open space and Mirren, following her, was almost struck by a cloth bag that suddenly descended from above.

'That happened tae me the first few times. Ye have tae
be ready for it.' Ruby deftly caught the bag and after a
few minutes Ella came skimming down the stairs to strip
off the clothing she usually wore for the fried-fish shop
in the shelter of the close.

'I'm sayin' tae Mirren, why don't ye just tell yer aunties
the truth?' Ruby grumbled. 'What can they dae tae you at
your age?'

'They'd find some way tae make my life a misery. Hold that.' Ella dumped her blouse and skirt, still
warm from her body, into Mirren's arms and hauled
her dance dress from the bag. Slipping it over her head
with the dexterity of one in the habit of dressing swiftly,
she emerged from the folds to say, 'The last time I
did something tae annoy Aunt Lilian they didnae feed
me for a week. If it hadnae been for Vanni and his
fish suppers, I'd've died of starvation. Button me up,
Mirren.'

'That's terrible!' Mirren had never met Ella's aunts,
and the more she heard of them, the less she wanted to
make their acquaintance. Her fingers slipped and stumbled over the buttons in her haste to get away from the
close before one of them appeared.

'That's the way they've punished me since I got to be
too big for the strap. Ask Ruby . . . sometimes she'd share
her playtime piece with me at school because I'd not had
any food at home.'

'Then the two of us went hungry,' Ruby grunted,
stuffing the discarded clothes into the bag while Ella
combed out her hair.

'What would happen if your aunts discovered that you
don't work at the shop every night?' Mirren wanted
to know.

'They won't because they'd never dream of buying
food they'd not cooked themselves. Where's my handbag?'

'Here, but leave the lipstick till we get tae the hall,'

Ruby ordered. 'We'll miss half the evenin' if we don't go now!'

The bag, now holding Ella's working clothes, was wedged into a small space behind the bins, and the three of them ran through the close and up the street, arriving at the tram stop in Wellmeadow just as a Glasgow tram came along.

The ballroom was huge, and crowded. Chandeliers sparkling above poured bright light over the throng and a full-piece orchestra played on the stage at one end of the great hall.

'There's empty seats.' Ruby scurried ahead to claim the chairs while Ella, her face now glowing prettily with colour from the little tubes and bottles in her bag, took Mirren's arm and pulled her along. 'Stop gawpin', we don't want folk thinkin' we've never been tae a Glasgow ballroom before.'

'I haven't been to anywhere as fancy as this.' When Mirren first left school her parents would never have allowed her to go to any of the Glasgow halls, and since Donald was an indifferent dancer with no interest in learning, the Paisley halls had suited both of them. 'Do you and Ella come here a lot?'

'Oh yes.'

Mirren wished that she hadn't agreed to come with the other two. Most of the girls there were dressed in what seemed to her eyes to be the height of fashion. Even Ella and Ruby were smart and sophisticated and, beside them, Mirren felt shabby in her best navy-blue frock with white dots. It had been her best for years and it was sadly out of date, but she couldn't afford to spend money on luxuries like new clothes for herself. Ella bought clothes with the money she earned at the fried-fish shop; strict though her aunts were, they allowed her to keep it, under the impression that it was all being put away in a bank account. Although Ruby didn't earn any more than Mirren in her job as a desk girl, checking the yarn into then back out of the twisting department and keeping a record of each machine's output, she considered herself to be a little above the barefoot women who worked the machines. Because of that, and because she came from a large family, all as yet at home and all earning, she made a point of dressing well when out for the evening.

In an effort to take her mind off her own appearance Mirren concentrated hard on the dance floor. 'What dance is that they're doing? I've not seen it before.'

'It's the fox-trot,' Ruby told her airily. 'It's from America.'

'Can you do it?'

'Of course.'

'She cannot, she's just bragging,' Ella said, then before Ruby could retaliate, 'See those two sitting at the table by the stage? The man in evening dress and the girl in the blue satin?'

Mirren craned her neck and could just make out the man's Brylcreemed head as he leaned towards his companion. Then he sat back in his seat and the girl came into view, fair-haired and smoking a cigarette in a long elegant holder. 'Yes, I can see them.'

'They're demonstrators. They'll perform the fox-trot in a wee while, then ye'll see what it should really look like.'

'Demonstrators?'

Ella sighed as though finding the continual explanations tedious. 'Trained professional dancers. They travel all over the place showin' folk like us how the new dances are done. They're the ones tae watch.'

As the orchestra struck up a waltz three young men swaggered across the floor towards them. 'We're goin' tae be lifted,' Ella said low-voiced, and Mirren panicked.

'What? I don't know about this, Ella. I could just wait here . . .' But the youths had arrived, their eyes drifting over the three girls then flickering away without making contact.

'Y'dancin'?' one of them asked Ella's right shoulder.

'Don't mind.' She got up and followed him onto the dance floor while the second youth gave a little jerk of his head. Ruby immediately rose, grabbed his arm and whisked him away. The third man stood silent, then as Mirren looked at him, confused, he said impatiently, 'Well, come on then, I'm not goin' tae carry ye.'

'Oh.' Understanding dawned, and she stumbled to her feet and hurried after him onto the floor.

His jacket stank of cigarette smoke and the scent from his hair-oil was almost overpowering, but once she had shut out these irritations and begun to concentrate on the music everything changed. Regardless of the tuneless humming above her head and the jerky way he moved, she gave herself up to the pleasure of dancing on a real floor instead of Aunt Catherine's parlour or the scuffed, scarred boards in Mr Primrose's studio, and to real music from a band instead of a wind-up gramophone or an elderly piano and a violin.

'Not bad,' her escort said when the music finished. 'Been here afore?'

'No.'

'Where're ye from?'

'Paisley.'

He shrugged then turned away, leaving her to make her own way back to her friends.

'Now mind,' Ella lectured. 'You're comin' home with me so don't let anyone else say they'll take ye. Ye've got tae be careful in places like this, ye never know what men'll be like when they get ye on yer own in a dark street.'

'Ach, you're too fussy,' Ruby said comfortably. 'Most of them's all right.'

'Ye'd not say that if ye got one of the wrong sort,' Ella warned darkly.

'Have you?' Ruby challenged, irritated.

'No, of course not!' Then Ella's head whipped back towards the dance floor as the music started up again. 'Look, they're goin' tae demonstrate the fox-trot now.'

Most of the others were standing up to get a better view and Mirren joined them, eager to learn the new dance. The professional dancers were in sole possession of the floor, poised and still as statues as they waited to move into the music. She had never seen such beautiful people. The man and the woman were both tall and slim and dressed in the height of fashion, he in a beautifully fitting evening suit with a snowy-white shirt, she in electric blue satin cut so that it clasped her slender hips snugly and shimmered with every movement. Her blonde hair was short and permed into tight waves, and as she came closer during the dance Mirren saw that her mouth was full and red, her skin creamy and her eyebrows arched.

'Make-up,' Ella whispered at one side of Mirren. 'She probably looks terrible in the morning.'

'She's just jealous,' Ruby said into Mirren's other ear.

'Shhh!' She wanted to be left in peace to drink in the way the couple moved together as though they were one; their feet – his shod in gleaming black patent leather, hers in Louis-heeled blue satin strapped shoes with elegantly pointed toes – skimming over the floor, scarcely lifting from it, yet not quite seeming to touch it either. The dancers' control, making them look completely relaxed even when they were executing intricate turns, was quite amazing.

When the music came to an end she joined enthusiastically in the burst of applause, clapping until her hands were sore. The demonstrators bowed elegantly to each side of the hall, then to the band-leader, before strolling nonchalantly back to their table, while Mirren clapped on, only stopping when Ella tugged at her arm and said, 'Will ye stop givin' me a red face? Everyone else has finished!'

The music began again, this time for a one-step, and again all three girls were taken onto the dance floor. This time Mirren's partner was a little more talkative, but she was glad to escape back to the others afterwards. Then came a slow fox-trot, not as fast and complicated as that danced by the demonstrators. To Mirren's relief the other two were claimed and she was left on her own, happy to watch the people on the floor and startled when someone thumped down onto the empty chair by her side.

'Mirren? I thought it was you,' said Gregor Lewis, one of the tenters in the Ferguslie twisting mill. 'I didn't know ye came here.'

'I don't,' she said at once, dismayed at being discovered by someone who knew her. 'I never come here. I mean, I've never been before.'

'Would ye like tae dance?'

She had not known that Gregor was a dancer, but as soon as she moved into his embrace they seemed to slide into the rhythm of the music, moving and dipping and almost floating in a way she had never experienced before.

As usually happened she closed her eyes and imagined that she and Donald were dancing in an American ballroom while others watched enviously. 'Who is that?' she heard someone whisper in an accent alien to Paisley. 'Why, it's Mr Donald Nesbitt and his young bride from Scotland,' came the reply. 'Isn't she the best dancer you ever saw?'

'I didnae know ye could dance.' Gregor's voice broke into her dream. 'Where did ye learn?'

'At Mr Primrose's class in Forbes Place.'

Gregor laughed. 'Me too. My mother made me and my sister go when I was still at school. I hated it at first, but then I started enjoying myself once I got the hang of it and he stopped hitting my knuckles with his violin bow. Does he still do that?'

'Oh yes.'

'But not tae you. Ye're good.'

They danced together for the rest of the evening and he would have escorted her home if she hadn't insisted on going with Ella, as arranged. Ruby was with them, disconsolate because nobody had offered to take her home.

'That's what comes of livin' in Paisley . . . Ye'll not often get a lad willin' tae go all that way on the tram then all the way back home.'

'You could have gone with Gregor.' Ella winked at Mirren.

'No thanks. I didn't come tae Glasgow just tae go home with someone I see every day.'

'He asked Mirren.'

'Did he? Ye should have said yes.'

'I'm promised to Donald!'

'Och, he's in America and Gregor's here. And it makes sense tae keep in with a tenter,' Ruby pointed out. The relationship between machinists and tenters was always fragile and some mill-women were known to make regular gifts of sweets or home-baked cakes to one or other of the tenters in their department. By doing so they hoped to ensure that their machines were never left waiting too long for the tenter's attentions and that he would tend the machine efficiently. Those who fell foul of the tenters could be made to pay by having to wait while other machines were set up or altered. The system worked both ways, for difficult and demanding machinists could make a tenter's life a misery.

'Gregor Lewis might be a good dancer but that doesn't mean I'm interested in going out with him . . . especially just so's you can have your machine seen to before anyone else,' Mirren said firmly, adding as they got up to leave the tram at Paisley's west-end, 'Anyway I'm not interested in him. Donald'll be sending for me any day now.'

'At least we all got danced,' Ruby consoled herself. 'Some nights the lads are too busy talkin' in the bar

tae bother with us. When that happens we've tae sit
out half the dances, haven't we, Ella, lookin' at the
band and them lookin' back at us and feelin' sorry for
us.'

'You could always dance with each other,' Mirren
suggested, and Ruby gave her a cold look.

'I don't pay tae get intae a dance hall just so's I can
dance with a lassie!'

Robbie was writing at the kitchen table when she arrived
home. 'Did ye have a good night?'

'It was grand. You should have seen that dance hall,
Robbie – it was so big! And there were these two
professional dancers . . .' She launched into her story
then stopped as she saw him glance back down at the
page before him. 'Were you wanting to get on with your
studying?'

'I finished all that an hour ago.' He held the paper out
to her. 'This is a report on a meeting for the *Gazette*.'

'A political meeting?' Her heart sank.

'Yes.' His level gaze challenged her as he held out the
paper. 'D'ye want to have a look at it?'

She didn't, but she couldn't say so. Instead she took the
sheet of paper and began to read, skimming the words at
first, then settling down to read them properly.

'This is good,' she said when she had finished, and
he flushed with pleasure. 'For the *Gazette*, did you say?
I didn't know you were a writer.'

'I quite like it . . . factual things like meetings, I mean,
not stories. That part's the speech Joe gave – he's a grand
speaker, though some are too thick-headed tae realise the
truth when they hear it.'

For a moment Mirren thought that he had noticed the
way she had winced at the name she had come to detest,
then she saw that he was examining the skinned knuckles
of his right hand.

'Robbie, have you been fighting?'

'Not really.' He twisted away when she tried to examine his hand. 'It was just a few hot-heads tryin' tae break up this afternoon's meetin'.'

'Does this happen often?'

'Now and again. Nothin' we can't handle. We can land punches just as hard as they can.'

'Oh, Robbie!'

His face darkened and he twitched the article from her fingers. 'If ye're going tae start preachin' I'm off tae my bed!'

Alone, she looked in on her mother, who was sound asleep for once, then got ready for bed. In an attempt to avoid worrying all night about Robbie she summoned up the memory of the chandeliers, the moving, shifting figures, and the music. A few bars drifted into her mind, and she hummed them aloud into the darkness of the bed recess.

The demonstrators danced across the screen of her closed lids, the man's hair gleaming as richly as his shoes, the woman's blue dress shimmering, her fair head thrown back and her pretty face lifted to her partner's. They dipped and skimmed and turned and swirled, and Mirren spun with them, drifting into sleep as light and as free as the air.

8

'Canada?'

'Why not?' Anne Proctor asked jauntily.

'But it's so far away!'

'Aye . . . far from George Armitage. That's the whole idea.' Anne finished slicing bacon, popped it into Mirren's basket, and noted the cost on the list before her. 'Anything else?'

'I'll have a small brown loaf. Whose idea was it to emigrate to Canada?'

'Mine.' Anne raised an eyebrow, then as Mirren shook her head she started to add up the list.

'And Grace is happy about it?'

'She near jumped at me with excitement when I suggested it. That's one and sixpence ha'penny. I got the idea from a bit I saw in the newspaper,' Anne went on as Mirren scraped about in her purse for the money. 'The Canadians are looking for Scottish lassies to work in their hospitals. They'll pay our fares and we'll have positions to go to.'

Mirren, catching the faint strains of a brass band in the distance, scooped coins hurriedly from her purse and handed them over. If she was quick she could get home before the Sma' Shot procession went past on its way from Ferguslie Mills to Gilmour Street railway station at the other end of the town. Anne cocked her head to one side, listening. 'Is that not the mill band?'

'I don't think so.' But the music was growing louder, and Anne's assistants, followed by the one other customer in the shop, were already hurrying to the door.

'It is.' Anne rounded the counter. 'Come on . . . you can leave your basket here until they've passed.'

Reluctantly Mirren followed the others out onto the sun-splashed pavement. She had had to wait in a queue in the grocery shop and then Anne's news had kept her back. Now she had no option but to watch the parade; she would have had trouble getting across the road in any case, for the pavements were already crowded with people gathering to see the mill-workers on their way to their annual day's outing.

'They've got a bonny day for it,' Anne said as the mill-band arrived, the musicians already looking uncomfortably hot in their uniforms but playing for all they were worth. After them came the workers dressed in their best, laughing and excited, waving to the folk on the pavements and calling out to their friends.

Sma' Shot Day owed its origins to the previous century when the Paisley weavers had won a long battle for payment for the plain binding thread on their looms, known as the sma' shot because it was not part of the pattern. They had promptly bestowed the name of their victory on the local one-day holiday, a custom that had been upheld in the town ever since.

As most of the 5,000 workers from the Ferguslie Mills were involved, the procession took some time to pass. To the east of the town an equally long parade would be wending its way from the Anchor Mills; both groups would meet up at the station and split into smaller groups before departing in specially hired trains for destinations up to a hundred miles away.

Mirren had only managed to get to one Sma' Shot outing, before the war. They had gone to Ayr, and it had been the best day of her life. In the evening, with the races run and the prizes distributed and the food eaten, she had danced every dance with Donald. They had travelled together in the train back to Paisley and walked home hand-in-hand through the summer darkness, dazed with the sheer joy of being together.

Now that she couldn't afford such pleasures Mirren pretended to her colleagues at work that she didn't care for outings, and preferred not to see or hear the Sma' Shot celebrations. It was at times like this that she missed Donald so much that she could scarcely bear the pain of it.

'Don't they look grand?' Anne waved vigorously by her side. 'I'm going to miss this sight when me and Grace are away from here.'

'What do Aunt Catherine and Uncle James think of your plans?'

A shadow passed over Anne's handsome features. 'They don't know yet. We're telling them tonight.'

Mirren had always admired her Aunt Catherine's serenity, no matter what the members of her large and active family might be up to, but on the day after the Sma' Shot outing the woman was distraught.

'Can you believe it, Mirren? My two innocent lassies wanting to live three thousand miles away with nobody to look after them!'

'We can look after ourselves, Mother,' Grace protested.

'How d'ye know that? You've never had to before!'

'Everyone has to learn. And I'm not a bairn,' Anne pointed out. 'I've been manageress of a branch of the Co-op for the past two years, nearly.'

'What difference d'ye think that'll make in a country like Canada? I doubt if they even have a Co-op there.'

'They have at least one hospital and that's where we'd both be working.' Anne brandished the newspaper cutting. 'They're looking for Scottish lassies to work there and we'll even get free passage over.'

'I don't know, pet.' Even James Proctor, who usually left all the family decisions to his wife, was concerned. 'It's an awful long way tae go. What if ye don't like it?'

'Then we'll come back.' For the first time in weeks Grace had some colour in her face and a light in her eyes. 'The only way to find out whether we'll like it or not is to go. Canada's part of the British Empire, Mother, we'll still be under the same flag.'

'Ye'll be taken advantage of, two young lassies on your own,' Catherine predicted. 'And your father and me too far away to do anything about it!'

Despite their parents' opposition, the sisters travelled to Glasgow a few days later to an office where, Grace told Mirren the next day as they walked to work, they had to wait in a long line of hopeful applicants then answer a lot of questions and fill in forms.

'It took half the day, but it's done. Now we just have to wait.'

'What about Aunt Catherine and Uncle James?'

Grace wrinkled her nose. 'They're still behaving as if we'd decided to kill ourselves, but if we're accepted we're going. I need to get away from here, Mirren. I'd have liked to try America, what with you going there yourself soon. But,' she squeezed Mirren's arm tightly, 'Canada's not far from America and once we've worked out our contracted time in the hospital they send us to, we could mebbe move across the border. You and Donald could help us to find work near you.' She spoke, Mirren noticed, as though the distance between the two countries was as easy to cover as the distance between Paisley and Glasgow, some twenty miles away. Geography had never been Grace's strong point at school. 'Have you heard from Donald at all?'

It was the first time for weeks that she had asked about him.

'I got a letter last week. He doesn't have much to say –

you know Donald, he was never a great letter-writer. But he's fine, still working away and saving for our house.'

'Imagine,' Grace said. 'One day you and me might be sitting in America talking about the old days in Paisley. And I'm sure that we'll both be very happy with our new lives.'

Bob and Agnes had decided to marry at the beginning of August so that they could take advantage of the annual Paisley Fair Fortnight, when the mills closed for the summer holidays. Mirren, with no money to buy clothes for the event, was rescued by Anne Proctor, who loaned her a particularly stylish cream-coloured georgette dress with a matching hem-length jacket. A single button fastened the jacket at the waist, and the cuffs and collar were dark blue, as was the brimmed straw hat. Both dress and jacket, a little too large for her, had to be pulled in with safety pins, each placed where it wouldn't be seen.

'Just don't take the jacket off,' Anne had said as Mirren revolved before her for final inspection. 'If you do you'll get us both red faces, for the pins at your waist'll easily be seen.' Then, with a frown, 'You know, Mirren, you should eat more. You're too thin.'

Agnes wore a jersey-silk jacket and matching skirt striped in light and dark green. The tailored style and shawl collar suited her slight figure but beneath her small black velvet hat, decorated with a pale-green silk bow pinned at one side, her face was knotted with worry.

'Am I doin' the right thing?' she burst out as soon as her mother ushered Mirren into the small flat.

'For any favour lassie, will ye tell her? I'm tired of sayin' it, but she'll no' believe me,' Mrs McNair said wearily.

'Of course you're doing the right thing. You and Bob are perfect for each other.'

'I couldnae sleep last night for wonderin' if yer mother was mebbe right and I was turnin' my back on Crawford.'

Mirren rescued the pale-green glove from her sister-in-law, who seemed bent on twisting it into a rope. 'I knew Crawford for longer than you did and I can promise you that he'd want this marriage for your sake . . . and for Thomas's. The wee lad needs a father. Where is he?'

'Ben the hoose.' Mrs McNair indicated the other room in the small flat with a jerk of the head. 'I set him down in a chair tae look at a picture book and he's been well told not tae move till he's fetched.'

Mirren glanced at the sunlight streaming in the single kitchen window. It was a perfect August day. 'You'll not have a fire on . . . ?'

'No, but the armchair's up against the grate.' They had guarded against leaving Thomas alone in a room with an empty hearth ever since the day when, aged fifteen months and too small to reach up to the handle of the closed door, he had tried to escape boredom via the chimney. Showering soot all the way, he had been carried by his mother at arms' length to the landing, where he had been forcibly detained on several sheets of newspaper while a tub was filled with warm water. It had taken a good hour to rid him of the soft clinging soot and a day or two to clean the stuff from the front room, the rest of the flat, and the clothes Thomas and Agnes had been wearing at the time.

'Do I look all right? D'ye think Bob'll like it?' Agnes's mind, which had been conditioned to worry from the day her young husband had gone off to war, settled on a fresh problem.

'You're beautiful and he'll be fair delighted with himself for having had the sense to choose you,' Mirren assured her, and the young woman glowed.

'You look lovely too, doesn't she, Ma?'

'Aye, ye'll make a bonny bride when yer own turn comes, lass.'

Mirren flushed with pleasure and thanked her lucky stars for the Proctor family's generosity and dress sense.

'Look . . .' Agnes lifted back a tea-cloth that had been laid on the draining board by the sink to reveal two perfect roses, one pink and one red, lying on a nest of tissue paper. Each flower, just opening into full beauty, nestled against a spray of fern. 'Bob sent them, the pink one for me and the red one for you.' She lifted them reverently, her eyes star-bright. 'Wasn't that kind of him?'

'And there she is, wonderin' if she should marry the man,' Mrs McNair put in, raising her eyes to the shabby ceiling. 'If I was you, our Agnes, I'd run tae that church as fast as my legs'd take me just in case some other woman gets a hold of him first.'

By the time the roses were pinned on and Mrs McNair had arranged her favourite bunch of artificial violets on her own lapel, they were due to leave for the North Church, where Agnes and Bob were to be married in the vestry. While Mrs McNair, in black as always, skewered her practical hat to her head with large hatpins, Mirren opened the front-room door and Thomas bounced free, spotless in a little sailor suit Bob had bought for him. The sight of his mother, grandmother and aunt in unfamiliar finery brought on an attack of shyness and it took some coaxing and bribery in the form of a penny before he agreed to leave the flat.

When they turned the corner into Love Street, Bob and Robbie and a third man were waiting at the door of the church. 'He came!' Agnes said joyfully.

'Of course he came. Did you think he'd jilt you?'

'Of course not.' Agnes beamed at her sister-in-law. 'Not my Bob!' As she almost ran along the pavement, Bob, a pink rose identical to hers on his jacket, hurried forward to take both her hands. Mirren, following at a more sedate pace with Mrs McNair, smiled at the couple, then felt the smile chill on her lips as she looked beyond them to the man by the church door. Today his black hair, longer than was usual for 1920, was sleeked back and he wore a pinstriped suit with a red rose on the lapel instead of a shirt and braces, but there was no mistaking his height and the gangly way he held himself, or the long thin face, dominated by direct blue eyes under shaggy brows.

'Isn't this a stroke of luck!' Robbie chortled as Mirren reached the church door. 'I'd not realised that Bob and Joe were related. Joe, this is Mirren, the sister I'm always talking about.'

Joe Hepburn's dismay at this second meeting was as great as Mirren's. His hand barely clasped hers and their greetings were muttered, but nobody noticed in the scurry to get into the vestry where the black-robed minister awaited them.

In order to involve Thomas in their wedding day, Bob and Agnes had allowed him to choose the venue for their wedding breakfast, which meant that once the brief ceremony was over the small group walked from the church to Nardini's ice-cream parlour in Moss Street, where Bob ordered large dishes of ice-cream with raspberry sauce for all.

Mrs McNair found the whole thing embarrassing, especially as the sight of the little party dressed in their best and with flowers in their lapels aroused the interest of everyone else in the parlour. 'I could have made sandwiches, and wee sponge-cakes as well,' she explained earnestly to Mirren and Joe Hepburn. 'We could have gone back tae my house and had somethin' proper tae eat.'

'I know, Ma, but we needed tae let Thomas be part of the day,' Agnes explained, her attention divided between mopping red-and-white smears from her son's face and admiring the narrow gold band circling the third finger of her left hand. Crawford's wedding and engagement rings had been put away carefully in a small satin-lined box.

'I l-like ice-cream.' It was almost the first time Joe Hepburn had spoken, and it was the first civil thing Mirren had ever heard from him. He smiled at Thomas and dug his spoon into the crimson-splashed mound of ice-cream on his own plate.

'Me too. I think I'll have exactly this sort of feast at my wedding if I ever have one,' Robbie agreed enthusiastically, while Mrs McNair poked her own spoon at the melting heap before her.

'I cannae take tae it myself. It's awful cold.'

'That's why it's called ice-cream, Ma, because it's cold.'

'I know that! Ye're gettin' awful cheeky, our Agnes, now that ye're callin' yerself Mrs McCulloch,' her mother told her, and Agnes flushed and giggled and rolled her eyes at Bob, who was also pink with pleasure. 'Just wait till yer teeth have reached my age. They cannae be doin' with hot and cold when they get older. It jabs right through the gums. We'll all go back tae my place for a wee cup of tea after, will we?'

'I'll take your ice-cream, Granny,' Thomas offered.

'Ye will not,' his mother said swiftly. 'Ye'll make yerself sick, and we don't want that tae happen when your granny's left tae look after ye. Lean over here a minute, ye've got cream all over yer face.' She took a handkerchief from her bag, folded it and spat neatly to moisten it. When she tried to wipe her son's face he shied away from her, and Bob, who had scraped up the last of his ice-cream, took out his own snowy handkerchief.

'Over here, son. It takes a man's 'kerchief tae dae a man's work, eh?'

'Aye.' Thomas agreed gruffly, slipping from his chair and going to stand by his new step-father, who used one corner of the handkerchief to wipe cream and raspberry sauce from the small pursed mouth before tying it round the child's neck to protect his sailor suit.

'There, that's the sailor all ship-shape again.' Bob lifted the little boy up onto his chair while Agnes beamed proudly at her new family. Watching the three of them,

Mirren wished that her mother could have been there to see their happiness.

Joe Hepburn left them when they emerged from the ice-cream parlour, after shaking hands all round.

'We'll need tae have ye over once we've settled in,' Agnes told him, and he ducked his head briefly and said, 'Aye, m-mebbe.'

'Hold on, Joe, I'll come with ye.' Robbie planted a kiss on his sister-in-law's cheek and shook Bob by the hand. 'It was a grand wedding and I hope you'll both be very happy . . . the three of you,' he added, bending down to shake Thomas by the hand.

'Joe might not come visiting,' Bob warned his bride as the rest of the wedding party set off for Mrs McNair's flat. 'He's always been a solitary kind of man, not like Molly at all. It was tae do with his upbringin'.'

'What about his upbringing?' Agnes wanted to know.

'It was all a bit of a mixter-maxter from what I heard. The old man – that'd be Joe and Molly's grandfather – was a right rascal, fond of the drink and of . . . well, too fond of the sort of company a decent man shouldnae seek,' Bob improvised, a red wave rising from his high white collar. 'And a bully too, in his younger days. Joe's father was the opposite, a decent, God-fearing soul who'd never say boo tae a goose.'

'Weak,' Mrs McNair diagnosed crisply.

'I'd not say that. Just . . . not good at making decisions since his father had never allowed him tae have a crack at it. It was Molly's mother that ran their house and seemingly she was bent on makin' sure that her son was neither a drinker nor a womaniser . . . nor a man who couldnae make up his own mind. Molly said her mother was harder on Joe than on her lassies. It sounded tae me like a strange kind of household,' Bob finished.

'Me too.' Agnes shivered and tightened her grip on his arm. 'We'll not have that sort of life at all, will we?'

Thomas was staying with his grandmother for a few

days so that the newly married couple could enjoy some privacy in Bob's flat, then the four of them, Agnes's mother included, were going off for a week to the seaside. There was no such pleasure on the horizon for Mirren; after taking a cup of tea with what was left of the wedding party, she hurried home to change out of her wedding finery and see to her mother before going off to work in the fried-fish shop. Maria and Vanni never took time off, nor did they ever consider that their assistants might like to have a holiday. Usually Ella went with her aunts for a week in Troon, ignoring Maria's mutterings, but this year, as her Aunt Margaret was in indifferent health and the holiday had been cancelled, Ella had decided to go to work as usual.

'And yer mother never said a word about it, even when you and Robbie went off all dressed up?' She shovelled just the right amount of chips onto a waxed paper square.

'Nothing at all, but she had me running after her from the moment I got back. I scarcely had time to change out of my good clothes.' Mirren passed the big salt container and the vinegar bottle along the counter and watched, her stomach rumbling, as Ella distributed just the right amount of each, then tucked and folded the paper. She hadn't had time to eat anything before hurrying out, and tonight the smell of chips and fried fish, which she normally couldn't stomach, was tempting. But wherever she was, whatever she was doing, Maria had eyes as sharp as an eagle's and nobody, even Vanni, dared to eat even one crispy little chip that wasn't paid for.

'A fish supper, is it?' Ella tossed a glance over her shoulder at the empty tray and told the next customer, 'Ye'll have tae wait for the fish, but it'll not be long.' Then, flashing the warm smile that captivated everyone, 'And it's worth the waiting. Vanni's the best fryer in the town. Is that not right, Vanni?'

'That's me.' He tossed a grin over his shoulder then

went back to his work, shoulders hunching as Maria's voice cut like a cold knife through the hot air, 'He'd be the fastest too, if he didnae waste time chatterin'.'

'I hope I never turn out like your mother,' Ella said on the way home. 'I know she's not well and that must be terrible for her, but it's surely not a reason to be so nasty about Agnes. Will the wee one keep visiting her?'

'Agnes says yes. It gives her and Bob a chance to have some time on their own every other Sunday.'

The last part of the walk home, once Ella had gone, seemed even harder than usual for Mirren tonight. Her feet dragged along one after the other like whining children having to be pulled along a road, and every muscle in her legs and back ached. It would have been quite easy just to give up and lie down on the hard stone pavement and drift into a deep sleep. When she finally managed to trudge up the slope from the bottom of Maxwellton Street she found Robbie already sitting at the close-mouth.

'I thought I'd get a breath of fresh air.' He reached up a hand and drew her down beside him; then, easing the packet of fish and chips out from under her arm, 'And I was hungry.'

'What would you have done if I hadn't brought anything home with me?'

'Sent ye back for it.' He started to unwrap the paper, sniffing appreciatively.

'Wait till we get upstairs,' Mirren protested, but he was already breaking the battered fish in two.

'I'm too hungry tae wait. Anyway, it's nice eating out in the fresh air . . . like a picnic. Have some.' He held the packet out to her.

'What about Mother?'

'Asleep. I looked in on her five minutes ago, and she's well away. Go on.'

Mirren took a piece of fish. It melted in her mouth, and so did the next piece. Between them they devoured the food, eating with their fingers, sitting shoulder-to-shoulder on the hard step while tramcars rocketed noisily along nearby Broomlands Road. When they had finished they wiped their greasy fingers carefully on a clean area of the newspaper in which the fish supper had been wrapped, and sat on, enjoying the soft warm twilight.

'It was a nice wedding, wasn't it?' Robbie said suddenly. 'I think Agnes has done the right thing.'

'There's no doubt about it. I just wish Mother and Logan could understand that.'

'Ach, there's no changing some folk.' There was a pause before he said soberly, 'One of the lads that just finished his apprenticeship was turned off today in the factory.'

'Why?'

'Because there's not enough work for everyone.'

The serious note in his voice awakened an anxious tremor in Mirren's stomach. 'Was he in the same department as you?'

'No.'

'Well then . . . you'll be all right when your time comes.'

'There's rumours going round, Mirren. The factories are letting men go, just here and there, one or two at a time. But it's happenin'. I'm wonderin' if it's worth finishin' my time at all.'

'Of course it is! You've only got a few more months to go.'

'And then what?'

'Then they take you on as a tradesman. And if they don't,' she rushed on, as he opened his mouth to speak, 'There are other places . . . plenty of them!'

'I don't know. Joe says there's unemployment coming and the first tae go'll be the younger men like me, because once apprentices become time-served men the employers have tae pay them full wages.'

'What does Joe Hepburn know about employment!'

'He goes tae a lot of meetings and he's attended classes too, so he's got a good idea of what's going on in this country.'

'He's got no right to worry you over something that might not happen.'

'Joe's a fair man,' Robbie protested. 'He'd not say anythin' unless he believed it.'

'We'd best get in.' Mirren began to scramble to her feet. 'Mother might have wakened up.'

She was stiff from standing all evening, and Robbie offered her his arm. 'May I have the pleasure of your company, my lady?'

She laughed, but as they started up the stairs she was glad of his support.

9

'Robbie's out,' Mirren said hurriedly.

'I know that.' Joe Hepburn, hat in hand and wearing the same dark suit he had worn at Agnes's wedding the day before, looked as embarrassed as she felt. 'That's why I'm here. It's you I came tae see.'

'I can't think why.' It was an inane thing to say, but she was so taken aback at the sight of him on her own doorstep that her brain wouldn't function properly.

Colour flooded his face. 'I c-came tae say that I'm s-sorry for the way I behaved at G-George's house.'

'Oh. You'd best come in,' Mirren said reluctantly, stepping back. Somehow his apology was even more difficult to cope with than his rage on that first occasion. In the kitchen she remembered to offer him some tea.

'No thank you. I j-just came tae s—'

Helen called from the front room and Mirren had to excuse herself. When she returned he was standing awkwardly by the table, hat in hand.

'Will you not sit down, Mr Hepburn?'

'First I w-want tae say that I'd no r-right tae treat ye as I did, that day. I didnae realise ye were Robbie's sister.'

'Are you saying that you'd have treated me different just because you know my brother?'

His flush deepened. 'I've p-put things very b-badly.' The stammer was even worse now. 'I c-can only ask ye t-tae forgive m-me.'

'If I do, will you sit down? Then I do,' she said briskly when he nodded. 'Now will you take a seat, and tell me how George is?'

'Still very l-low in spirits.' He drew back one of the upright chairs by the table and folded himself down into it. 'I believe he's p-pining for your friend.'

'She's not pining for him . . . not any longer. She's planning to make a new life for herself in Canada.'

'I'm glad tae hear it. If she was tae m-marry poor George the way he is now they'd b-both be miserable, through no fault of hers – or of his,' he added hurriedly. 'The man's sufferin' so much that he c-cannae spare any k-kind thoughts for others.'

'He used to laugh all the time,' Mirren remembered. 'He was never serious. I even wondered sometimes if he was ready for marriage. I never thought to see such a change in him.'

'War can do more than damage men physically, and it did its w-worst with George. He cannae come tae terms with what's happened, and tae t-tell the truth his mother doesnae help. She's well-meaning, but she treats him like a helpless bairn, when it might aid him better tae be treated as the man he s-still is.'

'Grace would have done that if he'd let her.' Mirren still felt more sympathy for her cousin than she did for George.

'It wouldn't have w-worked for them. When George courted her he was whole and strong, and able tae care for her as a man should in a marriage. After he . . . came back, he couldn't b-bear the thought of having tae be dependent on her for everythin'. Every time he looked at her he saw the man he had been reflected in her eyes.'

'He said that to you?'

'No, but I could see it in his face and hear it in his v-voice.'

'So you're the one with the elegant turn of phrase?' she asked, surprised.

'If I am, it comes from bein' a prolific reader. Which reminds me . . .' He reached into his coat pocket and handed her a well-worn book. 'I thought ye m-might like the loan of this.'

Surprised, she glanced down at the lettering on the spine. '*Oliver Twist*.'

'D'ye know the works of Charles D-dickens?'

'I've heard of him but I don't think I've read his books.'

He relaxed visibly. 'He's a grand writer, a man who made a close study of what he saw about him. There's no hurry tae return it,' he added swiftly, 'I know from what Robbie says that ye're kept busy, what with w-working and looking after yer mother.'

On cue, Helen called again, and he stood up. 'I've taken up enough of yer time. I'd best g-go.'

'Just a minute, Mr Hepburn. I'll be in in a minute, Mother,' Mirren called from the kitchen doorway, then turned back to her visitor. 'While you're here I might as well tell you that I'd appreciate it if you'd stop filling my brother's head with all this political nonsense of yours.'

He stiffened. 'Ye think it's nonsense tae care about what happens tae yer fellow w-workers and their families?'

'Not entirely. I mean, I can see that there are times when someone needs to speak out, but . . .'

'But not yer b-brother.'

'He's young and impressionable and . . .'

'And he has a good head on his shoulders, and the wit tae use it. But perhaps not,' he added drily, 'the freedom.'

This time the colour that surged into her face came from anger, not embarrassment. 'We're ordinary folk, Mr Hepburn, and we've enough to do just getting by, without becoming involved in things we don't understand.'

'Then take the t-trouble tae understand them. Come with me tae a political meeting some evening. Listen tae what the speakers have tae s-say. They might help you tae understand what folk like me and Robbie are f-fighting for.'

'I've got more to do with my time.'

'That's a pity.' He picked up his hat, then said, 'Robbie tells me that ye like dancin'.'

'I suppose you disapprove of such frivolity?'

'Oh no. I'm not a dancer myself, but I believe that folk should be free tae follow their own inclinations. And that includes yer b-brother,' he added deliberately. 'Why don't ye try g-goin' tae a meetin' instead of tae the dancin' some evenin'?'

'Mr Hepburn,' Mirren said coolly, going ahead of him to open the door, 'I'll attend one of your precious meetings when you take up dancing. Good afternoon to you.'

When she returned to the kitchen she picked up the book. It was well thumbed, with a shabby jacket. Clearly, it had been well read. She herself had very little time to spend on books though she had once enjoyed them. Goodness knew when she would find the time to sit down with this one.

She said nothing to Robbie about his friend's visit, or their quarrel about him. And since he never mentioned either, she guessed that Joe Hepburn had, like her, decided to keep his visit secret.

There were two envelopes, one addressed in splendid flowing writing to Miss Anne Proctor and the other to Miss Grace Proctor. They arrived in the early afternoon, not an hour after Anne, who always came home in the middle of the day, had returned to work.

Catherine Proctor laid the envelopes carefully on the kitchen dresser, then, finding that she couldn't work with them in the same room, took them through to the front room, placing them on the big carved sideboard that had been a wedding present from her parents. All afternoon she kept going in to look at them . . . for all the world, she told herself shamefacedly, as though she expected them to get up and leave the house on their own if they were left unattended for too long.

Once she even put her hat and coat on, preparing to take Anne's letter to the shop, then on the point of picking it up she changed her mind. Bad news, she thought as she put her outdoor clothes away again, came soon enough. No sense in going to meet it.

Now that the family was grown-up, the weekday evening meal was a rambling affair. A sociable clan, the five younger Proctors still living at home were usually out in the evenings on some ploy or other, which meant that their meals had to be fitted in between arriving home from work and going out again. Tonight Maggie and May were off to a concert while John, as usual, had a meeting to attend at the Liberal Club. As the three of them left the house, Catherine followed them onto the landing and leaned over the banisters.

'Mind now, John, I want you home by half past ten at the latest!'

All she could see of him was the top of the bowler hat that he had carefully painted black because he thought that it looked more dignified, but a hand flapped up at her. 'Aye, Mother, aye!'

Catherine tutted as the clatter of feet died away. There was every danger that after the meeting John would get involved in some political discussion and forget the time. And then she would have to sit up to wait for him, for she would not allow anyone but herself to lock the house up for the night. Once she had locked him out to teach him a lesson, and unbeknown to her the weather had suddenly turned colder in the early hours of the morning. The poor lad had caught pleurisy and although the incident hadn't taught him anything about punctuality, Catherine had never quite forgiven herself for making him so ill.

It didn't help to know that he had probably inherited his ambition and his grand ideas from her. As a young woman

Catherine had found that her dancing skills brought her into social contact with people she would otherwise never have met. She had become used to visiting some of the fine big houses in the area and mixing with girls who, unlike herself, would never need to earn their way in the world, but would move instead from the comfort of their father's houses to the comfort of marital homes.

Clearing the used dishes from the table and setting places for her husband, Grace, Anne and herself, Catherine recalled only too clearly her own mother's disapproval. 'You're tryin' tae climb too far up the stairs, lassie, and the higher ye go, the more chance of fallin' and gettin' hurt. Keep tae your own folk!' It was almost exactly what she herself said often enough to John, with his dreams of one day becoming a politician. It was true that everything moved in a circle and the seeds sown in one generation flourished in the next.

To her relief her husband James arrived home before the girls. Catherine flew to meet him when she heard his key in the door and almost dragged him into the front room. 'Look!'

James, as was his wont, took his time over examining both envelopes back and front, studying the names and addresses closely. 'You think it's to do with Canada?'

'What else could it be? They've been accepted!'

'You cannot know that,' he said in his precise Highland voice.

Catherine snatched up one of the envelopes. 'Feel it – it's got quite a few pages in it. If they've been turned down there'd surely just be the one sheet of paper.'

'Aye, mebbe.' He carried both envelopes into the kitchen and laid them on the table, one by Anne's plate, the other by Grace's. Then he sat down and started taking off his outdoor shoes.

'What are we to do?'

'There's nothing we can do, lass. The letters are not addressed to us.'

'We're their parents, and they're too young to think of going so far away on their own!'

'They'll have each other and they'll be going to work that's been arranged. The folk that are paying their way there will surely look after them.'

Catherine automatically fetched his slippers and laid them down by his stockinged feet. Then on an impulse she went down on her knees beside them, her hands clasped on her husband's knee. 'James, is there no way we can stop them?'

'Even if there was I'd be loath to do it, Catriona.' Only he called her by the Highland version of her name, the version that he had been used to as a child. 'I'll miss them as much as you will and I'll fret about their safety alongside you, but I'll not stop them if their hearts are set on it. They must do as they think best.' He touched her face gently. 'You've brought them up to be straight and true and honest, Catriona, and now the rest is up to them.'

'Oh, James, you're the best father, and the best husband!'

'Nonsense, woman,' he said, but a pleased smirk flickered beneath his moustache and when she moved from the floor onto his lap to give him a hug and a kiss he didn't try to stop her. For all the wealthy, well-set-up young men she had met through friendship with their sisters, she had had the good sense to marry within her own class. Even then her parents had taken some persuading, for James Proctor was not a Paisley man but a Highlander, brought as a youngster to the town by his parents from the village of Clachan in Argyllshire.

A Gaelic speaker, James had suffered greatly at his Lowland school, jeered at by the other children because of his way of speaking English clearly and carefully with a soft lilt to the words. Once he told Catherine that at times he had been forcibly held down in the school playground by the other children and made to speak 'that

silly Highland jabber' for their entertainment. As a result
he had often arrived home bruised and with torn clothes,
earning himself a thrashing from his poverty-stricken,
homesick parents. And so James had learned to fight
and to stand up for himself, although he had managed
to retain his gentleness and much preferred to reason his
way through conflict rather than use his fists.

'I suppose,' Catherine said now against his greying
hair, 'that they'll all go eventually, whether it's to the
other side of Paisley or across the water.' She heaved
a deep sigh, then said resolutely, 'But as long as we've
each other I'll be able to face that.'

'That's my lassie.' James patted her cheek, then eased
her to her feet and went into the hall. Following, she found
him rooting about in the big 'press' where everything not
immediately needed was stored.

'What are you doing in there?'

'Looking for this.' He backed out of the press, dragging
the large trunk they had always used for family holidays
to Gourock when the children were small.

'Oh, James!' Catherine pressed the fingers of one hand
to her mouth.

'We should show willing, lass.' He opened the lid and
looked at the winter clothing she always stored in the
trunk, 'Help me to clear this thing.'

'What about your dinner?'

'I can wait till the girls come in.'

As she often did these days, Grace had gone from the
mill to the Co-op so that she could walk home with Anne.
When they finally arrived it was to find the kitchen table
moved against one wall and the large family trunk standing on an old sheet spread out before the fireplace. Their
parents knelt on either side of it, busily pasting strips of
wallpaper and lining the inside of the trunk with them.

'What on earth are you doing?' Grace asked, bewildered. The family holidays had lapsed after Bill and

Kate married and the others had become involved in their own lives.

Her mother sat back on her heels and smiled up at them. 'If you're going off across the ocean you'll need a good trunk. We're just making it nice and fresh for you.'

'You mean you don't mind us going?' Anne asked cautiously.

'Mebbe we've little choice.' Their father nodded at the table and Grace, following his gaze, gave a squeal of delight and pounced on the waiting letters. With shaking hands she tore hers open.

'Well? Don't just stand there reading it, Grace . . . tell me!' Anne demanded.

'Read your own if you want to know.'

'Tell me!'

Grace looked up from the paper, her face one big grin. 'I don't know what they've said to you, but I'm off to Canada!'

As Anne gave a yelp of excitement and pounced on her own letter, James Proctor reached for his wife's fingers and gave them a squeeze. 'We did the right thing in getting that trunk out . . . eh, lass?'

She smiled mistily, clinging to his hand as though it was a lifeline. 'Aye, James, the right thing,' she said.

'Our steamer tickets and everything,' Grace told Mirren on the way to the mill the next morning. 'We're to sail from Glasgow in September and when we arrive in Quebec – does that not sound romantic: Quebec! – someone'll meet us and see that we get to the hospital where we're working.' She giggled. 'It eased Mother's mind a lot, knowing that we're to be looked after by the Canadian Government. There'll be other folk from Scotland and England travelling with us, of course.' She hadn't looked so happy since the day she had heard that George was alive and in a convalescent hospital.

'I'm going to miss you!'

'I'll miss you too, but it won't be for long. You'll be off yourself one of those days, and once you're in America we can visit each other.'

'Have you looked at a map, Grace? America and Canada aren't like Scotland and England, you know. They're a lot bigger for a start.'

But nothing could dampen Grace's spirits. 'Even so, we'll find some way of seeing each other. It'll be wonderful, Mirren – you and me and Anne, all with our new lives!'

There were a number of dance halls in Paisley, but the one above Burton's the tailors at the Cross was Mirren's favourite, mainly because of the great glass panels set into the end wall, giving the impression that the hall stretched on and on into the distance and was filled with dancers.

As usual, weariness fell away from her shoulders like a discarded coat as soon as she, Ella and Ruby walked into the hall. It was as if she had stepped into a picture frame, leaving her everyday life behind.

It was the custom for all the girls to sit along one long wall while the young men gathered opposite. Almost as soon as the three of them had found seats Ruby indicated the other side of the room with a nod of the head. 'Ye're all right, Mirren, Gregor's here.'

'What's that to me?'

'He told me that you're the best dancer he's been with. See?' Ruby said triumphantly as the three-man orchestra struck up and Gregor immediately set off across the no-man's-land of the dance floor, heading in their direction.

Mirren had to admit that she found the young tenter to be the perfect partner. They had both learned from Mr Primrose the importance of control and balance, of holding their heads up and level, and of moving easily and lightly with the music, controlled yet relaxed. She was able to trust Gregor implicitly and follow as he dictated the pattern of the dance.

'There's a good film showin' at the Picture Palace next week,' he said as they swept across the floor. 'Would ye go with me?'

'I can't.'

'Why not? Ye don't work in that shop every night, do ye?'

'No, but I've got my mother to see to, and you know fine that I'm promised.'

'I'm not askin' ye tae walk out with me; it's just the films.'

She well knew that going to the cinema together would be followed by a meeting by appointment at the dance hall, then another film . . . 'Best not,' she said, and his irritated sigh ruffled her hair.

'You two make a grand couple,' Ruby said enviously as Mirren returned to their table.

'Ye could go in for competitions together, with a bit of practice,' Ella added.

'Don't say that to Gregor, he's trouble enough as it—' Mirren began, then swung round as a voice behind her said, 'M-may I have this dance?'

'What are you doing here?' The words were out before she could stop them.

'T-taking up your invitation.' In his one and only good suit, which was old-fashioned, Joe Hepburn looked uncomfortable and out of place.

'Invitation?' She was keenly aware of the other two girls gawking.

'You s-said that if I came tae the dancing ye'd attend a m-meetin' with me.'

'I didn't mean . . .'

'Would ye c-care tae dance?' he insisted, and with a helpless glance at Ruby and Ella, she got to her feet and followed him onto the floor.

'I'm not very g-good at this,' he said as the band struck up. It was obvious, even before they took the first step, that he spoke the truth. While the other couples danced

past them, Mirren had to guide his arms into the correct
hold then insert herself into them like a folded sheet of
paper going into an envelope.

'Keep your left elbow up and look straight ahead. Now
move forward with your right foot . . . no, forward . . .
and move to the music. One – two – three, one – two
– three. Just keep counting,' she said in despair as he
narrowly missed stepping on her toes. How could anyone
avoid following the natural, flowing rhythm of a waltz?
'One – two – and close. One – two – and close. It's the
easiest dance there is.'

'I don't think it's easy at all.'

'That's because you keep looking at your feet. Look up
– over my head,' she added as he fixed panic-stricken eyes
on hers, 'and just let the music tell you what to do.'

She almost wept with delight when the dance finally
ended and they were free to return to where the other
two waited, eyes bright with curiosity. 'Where did ye
meet him?' Ruby hissed as Joe went to fetch lemonade
for the four of them.

'He's Robbie's friend, not mine.'

'So why's he dancing with you and not with Robbie?'

'I told him he should try an evening at the dancing, but
I was only joshing.'

'Did ye see Gregor's face?' Ruby asked, smirking. 'He
was givin' that lad of yours a right squint. He thinks ye
shouldnae dance with anyone but him.'

'Joe Hepburn is no lad of mine, and I don't belong
to Gregor Lewis either,' Mirren snapped, exasperated.
It was seldom enough that she got the chance to enjoy
a night out. Did it have to be spoiled for her like
this?

Gregor claimed her for the next dance, which happened
to be a fox-trot.

'Who's that ye were up with the last time?'

'A friend of my brother's.'

'What does he do?'

'He's a welder in Fleming and Ferguson's.' She wished that he would keep quiet and let her enjoy the dance.

'A tradesman? Ye're goin' up in the world, aren't ye? It'll soon cost tuppence tae talk tae ye.' There was resentment in his voice. Tenters weren't skilled tradesmen as such, since they learned their craft on the shop floor. Most of them had started as messenger or store boys.

'Gregor,' she said as they completed a deft reverse turn, 'You're good at your job. You're just as important as any tradesman – more important as far as I'm concerned.'

'Am I?' His hold on her eased and he held her back slightly so that he could look down into her face.

'When one of my twisting machines needs re-setting, a welder's not much use to me, is he? I need someone with your talents.'

Gregor beamed on her. 'Right enough,' he said, and swung her into a series of intricate turns and dips. He was more skilled than she was, possibly because he was free to go dancing more frequently. Tonight he was on top form and it took all Mirren's concentration to keep in step with him.

'That was grand,' he said enthusiastically when the dance ended. 'We'll have the next dance too, eh?'

'All right.'

This time she felt more relaxed and able to give herself up to the sheer pleasure of following and even anticipating him. As one, they moved across the floor and by the time the dance came to an end most of the other couples had stepped back to the edges of the floor to watch them.

As their audience applauded Gregor grinned down at her. 'See? Ye can have a better time wi' me than wi' that three-legged friend of yours.'

'He's not a dancer.'

'Ye're right there,' Gregor said contemptuously. 'He'd be best tae stick tae his weldin'.'

Looking into his flushed, self-satisfied face Mirren realised that the dance she had just enjoyed so much

had been deliberately staged to show Joe Hepburn up.
'As a matter of fact,' she said coldly, 'he only came here
because I challenged him. At least he'd the courage to try
it even if it did make him look foolish.' And she turned
on her heel and marched back to the others to announce
that she had a headache and was going home.

'I'll walk p-part of the way with ye.' Joe unfolded his
lanky length from his chair.

Outside in the dark street she turned on him, furious
with him for ruining her evening and for putting her in a
position where she had to defend him to Gregor Lewis.
'You don't have to walk me home. I know the way well
enough.'

'In that case I'll say goodnight. I don't believe ye're
workin' next Wednesday evening?' he added as she
began to turn away from him. 'There's a meetin' in
Glasgow . . . John McLean's speakin' and he's always
worth the listening. I'll call at the house for ye at half
past six.'

'Call for me?'

'Tae take ye tae the meetin'. It was your suggestion,'
he went on calmly as she began to splutter. 'Ye said ye'd
attend a political meeting if I went dancin'.'

'I didn't mean it as a promise! It was like saying . . .'
she floundered and could only come up with, 'like saying I'd go to one of your meetings when the moon
turned blue.'

'Ye should never say things ye d-don't mean. Half past
six, then, next W-Wednesday,' he reminded her before
walking into the darkness.

10

Right up until the last moment Mirren told herself she would go dancing with Ella and Ruby, or go out for a walk or visit Agnes and Bob – anything to ensure that she was not at home when Joe Hepburn called to take her to Glasgow. But Robbie was determined to make her see it through.

'You agreed tae go. Ye gave him yer word.'

'I did not agree! I was just joshing when I said that I'd go to one of his meetings if he went to the dancing. I never for a minute thought he'd do it.'

'I've never known Joe tae turn aside from a challenge.'

'Robbie, I don't even know the man!'

'Ye don't need tae know him. Just do as ye promised and attend the meetin' with him. He went tae the dancin', didn't he?'

'And a right fool he made of himself . . . and of me. I'd to leave early because of him. He must be desperate for folk to attend those meetings if he'll hold me to a promise I didn't even make!'

'Ye're not lettin' Joe down,' Robbie said in a new, firm voice she had never heard before. 'He's my friend and I'll not have my own sister standing him up and making him feel foolish all over again.'

Thanks to his insistence and her own guilty conscience, she was ready and waiting when, at exactly half past six as specified, the doorbell rang.

'Ye'll enjoy yerself,' Robbie said soothingly as he got up to open the door.

'How can anyone enjoy going to a meeting?' Mirren snapped, pinning her hat on before the mirror.

'Miss Jarvis.' Joe Hepburn, wearing his one and only good suit, greeted her formally when he followed Robbie into the kitchen.

'Mr Hepburn.'

'Ye're awful formal, the two of ye,' Robbie objected. 'Can it not be Mirren and Joe? So ye're goin' tae hear John McLean, eh?'

'Aye. A grand speaker. I thought Miss . . . your s-sister would find him interesting.'

'Sure to. I'll mebbe come along myself.'

'Did ye finish that article ye said ye'd write for the paper?'

'There's still a bit of work needin' done on it,' Robbie confessed.

'That's more important than the meeting. We'd best be g-going,' Joe said, and opened the door for Mirren.

She insisted on paying her own tram fare and they scarcely spoke to each other during the journey. The audience in the hall Joe took her to was mainly made up of men, but there was a good smattering of women too. They were all plainly dressed, some shabbily, and Mirren, who had agonised over what to wear for the occasion, was glad that she had opted for a grey skirt with a three-quarter-length belted matching jacket. The seating consisted of rows of benches and when they arrived, a good twenty minutes before the meeting was due to start, the place was so full that they only just managed to squeeze into two empty spaces on a bench near the back.

From the moment the speeches started her companion forgot that she was there at all. He leaned forward, listening intently to every word, nodding or shaking his head, drumming on the floor with his feet now and again and applauding vigorously. Once he jumped to his feet to ask a question, almost knocking Mirren from the bench as he did so.

John McLean was the final speaker and the man with the most to say. When he had finished the place erupted in cheers and rapturous applause. The entire audience jumped to its feet, Joe catching Mirren by the arm and pulling her up with him. His face glowed as he watched McLean and as he banged his hands vigorously together he looked as though he had just witnessed a miracle.

He was still glowing when they finally left the hall and made for the tram stop. 'He's a wonderful man. A wonderful speaker! What did you think?'

'The man's not well, you can see it in his face.' McLean looked as though he had once been burly, but now the flesh seemed to Mirren to hang on his big frame.

Joe stopped short. 'Is that all ye can say after listenin' tae him?'

'I didn't understand the half of what he said.'

'That's only because it's all new tae ye . . . Socialism, and the rights of workers. Ye'll learn, the way the rest of us have.'

'No I won't, for I've no wish to learn,' she said, but it was as though she hadn't spoken.

'It's as if we're strugglin' up through the ground like plants.' His pace quickened as his voice gained enthusiasm and Mirren found herself walking faster to keep up with him. 'Then suddenly one day we break through the crust and come intae the light and discover a whole new world spread out before us. And it's ours, only nob'dy ever told us that before. They liked keepin' us in the dark, crawlin' on our bellies in the mud and grateful for any crumbs they threw tae us. The pity of it is that it took a terrible thing like a war tae open our eyes tae truths we should have known all along.'

'How could war teach folk anything apart from how daft it is to kill each other?'

'It taught us that they need us, mebbe even more than we need them. Look at women,' Joe rattled on as they reached the tram stop, the stammer completely gone. 'With the menfolk all away at the war, women came forward and took on all sorts of work that they'd never done before. And they managed it.'

'Then the men came home and took the jobs back.'

'What else could they do, those poor souls that did manage tae get back? But the important thing is that women found out truths about themselves too. Were ye never involved in the Suffragette movement?'

'No.'

'Ye don't believe in rights for women?'

She bridled at the sharp note that had come into his voice. 'Of course I believe. I'd be daft not to, but I never had time to march or protest. I was too busy going to school, then caring for my mother and working in the mills during the day and in the fried-fish shop at night to earn the money to keep us.'

'There ye are, then! Ye know that most women have tae work just as hard as men, and that means they're entitled tae have a say in the way their country's run. These politicians don't know anythin' about real life, so how can they decide things for us?'

He talked on and on in the same vein all the way home, while Mirren stared out of the window and longed for the journey to be over.

When they alighted in Paisley he said, 'Ye didn't enjoy yerself, did ye?'

'No more than you enjoyed going to the dancing last week.'

He shrugged. 'There's no point in pretendin' that I did.'

'Why go, then?'

'Because you thought I wouldnae do it. I don't like givin' in.'

'Just like John McLean. He should be home in his bed, not making speeches in draughty halls.'

'Robbie told me that I'd never open yer eyes tae politics.'

'Robbie was right.'

'But how can we change things if we don't know what we're up against?'

'I've got enough to do managing my own life without meddling in other folk's,' Mirren said, irritated. He walked in silence by her side for a few moments before asking, 'Have ye managed tae look at that book I loaned you?'

'I've started on it.' There was no denying that Charles Dickens was a skilled writer and whenever Mirren found time to open the book, she immediately became absorbed in the story about poor little Oliver Twist, born in a workhouse, orphaned within hours, growing up hungry and intimidated and forced to sleep in one of the coffins his employer made, escaping only to fall into the hands of the terrible Fagin. Her problem lay in finding the time to read, for when she was at home there was always something else to be done and when she did manage to make a fifteen-minute oasis for herself, her mother almost always commandeered it.

Recalling the story now, she shivered. 'It's awful sad. That poor wee laddie, growing up in poverty, with nobody to care about him.'

'There are still whole families living in poverty and misery. Dickens was an unusual man – even though he never had to live that way himself, he knew that there were others who did, and he wanted to make everyone aware, so that somethin' would be done about it.'

'He didn't succeed, if it's still happening.'

'He managed tae make a small difference. That's what it's all about,' Joe Hepburn said patiently. 'If people can each make just a wee bit of difference then it adds up. And the more folk try, the faster it adds up.' He dipped into his pocket. 'I brought you another of his books.'

'But I've still got that one to finish . . .'

He brushed her protest aside. 'This is easier tae read. *A Christmas Carol* . . . it's one of my favourites.'

She took it from him, then asked reluctantly as they reached the close-mouth, 'D'you want to come in for a cup of tea?'

'I'd best be gettin' home.' He held out his hand. 'Goodnight, Mirren.'

'How was John McLean?' Robbie wanted to know as soon as she went in.

'He doesn't look well.'

'Is that all ye've got tae say?'

'Yes,' said Mirren, and went through to her mother. Robbie was still writing when she came back, but a cup of tea waited for her on the table.

'That stammer of your friend's seems to come and go,' she commented as she drank it.

'Stammer?' he asked blankly, then, 'Oh yes, I've heard it sometimes. It's because of something that happened when he was away at the fighting. He never seems tae have it when he's teachin' a class or talkin' tae folk he feels comfortable with.'

That would explain why the man's speech had been clear and easy when he got onto the subject of his beloved socialism. Mirren rinsed her empty cup, and Robbie's, at the sink, then yawned and looked pointedly at the clock. 'Are you not ready for your bed? I know I am.'

As she undressed she felt the weight of the book Joe had loaned her in her pocket. She took it out and put it in a drawer, knowing that it would send out reproachful signals until she managed to find time to finish *Oliver Twist* and start on it. Reading in bed was useless; apart from the shadows in the alcove that held her bed, she tended to fall asleep as soon as she swung her bare feet from the linoleum and onto the bed.

Her best opportunities came at work where, if her six frames were working smoothly, she could stand behind one of the machines, safely out of sight of the Mistress's sharp eyes, and read the book she had smuggled into her apron pocket. But that luxury had its own dangers, for as soon as she opened the book at the place marked by a torn scrap of brown paper everything vanished . . . the thunder of the machines, the flooring under her bare feet, sticky with oil and lumpy with the fragments of yarn, the reek of the oil from the racing machinery. And she became so absorbed in Oliver's travails that she forgot to keep an eye out for Mrs Drysdale. On more than one occasion Libby McDaid, who worked beside her, had alerted her just in time.

In early September Robbie completed his apprenticeship and a few days later he came home from work, white-faced, to announce that he had been laid off.

Mirren had snatched a few minutes' respite to concentrate on the bed-jacket she was crocheting for her mother's Ne'erday gift. With little money to spend on luxuries, she usually started knitting and crocheting round about Easter in preparation for the New Year celebrations. Now the soft blue wool, bought ball by ball from her weekly wages, fell from her fingers and her mouth went dry. 'But why?'

He threw his cap towards the back of a fireside chair. It missed and fell to the floor, where it lay neglected and ignored. 'Because they don't want tae pay me a time-served man's wages,' he said savagely. 'It's cheaper tae use apprentices.'

'They can't do that, surely?'

'They can do whatever they like, Mirren. They're the bosses, we're just dross under their feet.'

'Is that what Joe Hepburn says?'

'He speaks more sense than most.'

'Mebbe it's believing in the likes of him that's lost you your job.'

'I've got my own opinions and a right tae them. I suppose you'd prefer it if I was one of those mealy-mouthed boot-licking creatures that fawn round the bosses?'

'Robbie, the likes of us can't afford to speak out against those who pay our wages!'

'It had nothin' tae do with that!' He had started to take his jacket off; now he shrugged it back over his shoulders and looked for his cap. Finding it on the floor behind the chair, he clapped it on his head.

'Where are you going?'

'Out.'

'But your dinner's nearly—'

'I'm not hungry,' he snapped, and stormed from the flat.

Mirren, in a quandary, had to ask Mrs White, who occupied the flat across the landing, to sit with her mother so that she could go to work at the fried-fish shop.

She served, salted, wrapped fish and chips, took the money and counted out the change in a dream, moving automatically and scarcely speaking to anyone. It was one of Ella's nights off and the other assistant could scarcely bring herself to speak to the customers, let alone her fellow workers. This suited Mirren, for all she could think of was Robbie and how they would manage if he had trouble finding another job. He had brought in a very small wage as an apprentice and for years Mirren had been living for the day when he would be able to contribute more to the running of the house. Now the time had come – and had been taken from them even before his first decent pay packet had been brought into the house.

Like the children of all working-class people she had been taught at an early age to fear unemployment. Without wages, people could lose their homes and perhaps starve to death. No work, no pay. The Jarvis family had always managed to support themselves, but now the spectre of poverty was hovering over her head and she didn't know what to do about it or where to turn. She felt helpless and frightened.

When she went to the counter by the vats to get some

more fish Vanni put a hand on her arm. 'Is anything wrong?'

'No, nothing.'

'You look ill tonight. Tell me,' he insisted when she shook her head.

'It's just . . . my brother was turned off today.'

'That's bad.' His brown eyes were filled with sympathy. 'But he'll get other work, eh?'

'I'm sure he will.' Mirren summoned up a smile, then as Maria called her name she hurriedly scooped up the fish and turned back to the counter.

As she was leaving that night Vanni pushed a larger parcel than usual into her hands. 'For you and your brother.'

'Vanni . . .'

'Sshhh. Fish is good for the brain. This'll help him tae think about where tae find more work. And if I hear of anything, I'll be sure tae tell you,' he said, then shooed her outside and closed the door behind her as Maria, who had been in the back shop, suddenly appeared at the other side of the counter.

When she arrived home, wearied to the bone as always, she had to struggle up the stairs on her own, for there was no Robbie to help her. Mrs White smilingly assured her that Helen had settled down early and had slept all evening.

'Any time ye need me, hen, just chap my door. Yer mammy's never any bother at all and Scrap doesnae mind me leavin' him as long as I pop across the landin' tae speak tae him now and again.' Mrs White's dearly loved little terrier dog meant more to her than anyone in the world.

'Thank you. Here,' Mirren handed over one of the fish suppers Vanni had given her. 'There was quite a lot left over at the fried-fish shop tonight. Mebbe Scrap could manage some of this.'

'Are ye sure?' Mrs White's eyes lit up at the sight of the food. 'Oh, that's kind of ye, pet. I'll be sure tae tell him it came from you.' Pride would not allow her to accept the food for herself, but Mirren knew, as she watched her neighbour scud across the small landing clutching the parcel, that both Mrs White and her dog would go to bed that night with full stomachs.

As soon as she opened the front room door Helen said, 'I thought ye'd never come home! I need tae use the commode and the sheets are all wrinkled. I cannae get comfortable at all.'

'You should have asked Mrs White. She doesn't mind helping you.'

'I don't like tae be beholden to folk,' snapped her mother, who had never considered Mirren to be 'folk'. 'And her bletherin' bothers me.'

'I thought you'd enjoy listening to her news.' Mirren, her bones screaming for rest, took Helen's full weight as the older woman shuffled from the bed to the commode.

'Mebbe, at times, but not tonight. She was boastin' about that grandchild of hers that lives in England, with no thought for me that's just lost mine.'

'You've not lost Thomas at all, Mother. He still comes to visit you every other Sunday.'

'It's not the same.'

'I'm sure Mrs White would be more tactful if she knew about Agnes marrying again.' Helen had forbidden the family to mention her errant daughter-in-law's remarriage.

'I could do with another pillow, too,' she said from the commode, watching her daughter re-make the bed. 'My back's been awful sore all evening. I couldn't sleep for it.'

'Would you like a nice bit of fish?'

Helen shook her head fretfully. 'My stomach wouldnae take it. Mebbe a mouthful of soup, if you have any.'

'I'll heat it up after I've got you back in your bed.'

By the time Robbie came in, smelling of drink and looking shamefaced, his mother was asleep and Mirren sat by the kitchen fire with a pile of darning in her lap.

'Vanni sent a fish supper for you.'

'I'm not hungry.'

'You need to eat something. Please, Robbie.'

He pulled the plate from the oven and studied its contents. 'You'll need tae have some of it too, then.'

She wasn't a bit hungry but she forced some food down in order to encourage him. At first he picked at his meal, then his normally good appetite took over and he emptied his plate, then hers. She was pleased to see him eating, knowing that it would help to dilute the drink he had taken. When he had finished he washed the dishes.

'How did ye manage with Ma tonight?' he asked from the sink.

'Mrs White sat with her.'

'I just needed tae get out for a while.'

'I know. It was all right, Mrs White didn't mind.'

Robbie dried his hands and sat down opposite her, elbows on his knees, staring at the floor between his feet. 'I suppose bein' out of work means that I'll be able tae look after her more,' he said bleakly.

'You'll get another job in no time at all.'

'Ye think so?'

'Of course. You're a good engineer.'

'With very little experience.'

'And you'll find something soon. I'll ask around the women at the mill. Mebbe someone's husband or son or father knows of a position you could apply for. You'll find something soon,' she repeated firmly, clinging to an old childish belief that if something was said often and strongly enough, it would come to pass.

'Aye,' he said without much conviction, and went to his bed.

11

Grace took one look at the tender rocking gently at the bottom of the steps, then looked further out on the river at the even more frightening sight of the huge TSS *Carpathia* moored in deep water at the Tail of the Bank, off Greenock, and said flatly, 'I'm not going. I can't go!'

'Of course you're going . . . you promised the Government folk.' Anne was as white and tremulous as her younger sister, but her mind was made up. 'You'll get into terrible trouble with them if you turn back now.'

'Mammy . . . Daddy . . . ?' It had been years since Grace had called her parents by these baby names.

'Ye'll be fine, my darlin',' her father assured her. 'Anne'll be with ye.'

'What if I don't like it?'

'Then we'll find a way tae fetch ye back home, no matter what their Government has to say about it.'

Maggie had been unable to get off work and Kate was busy with her small baby, but Catherine and James were there, together with Bill, John, May and Mirren. Stepping aside slightly to let the Proctors say their final farewells as a family, she found herself confronted wherever she turned by identical tearful groups of people all over Greenock's Princes Pier. Mothers and daughters, fathers and sons, brothers and sisters and sweethearts clung to each other while officials with lists to check and men transporting luggage to a second tender worked around and among them, indifferent to the personal grief they saw day in and day out.

It had been like that for centuries, Mirren knew, for the Scots had a history of emigration and resettlement in far lands, often with little choice in the matter. She had never forgotten a picture in one of her school books called *The Emigrants*, and today she was keenly reminded of it, although the women in the picture had been dressed in shawls and bonnets. But the grief was just the same. She had first experienced it for herself on this very pier when, shortly after welcoming Donald back from the fighting, she had had to bid him goodbye again when he set sail with his parents for America.

One day she herself would be here to board a tender on the first lap of her journey to America and her married life. She wondered how she would feel when the time came, but it was difficult to forecast. She knew only that if she had the chance on that lovely September day she would have taken Grace and Anne's places without a backward glance.

There was a sudden flurry on the pier as a man with a handful of papers took his place at the top of the steps, ready to mark people off as they boarded the tender. As Mirren hurried back to rejoin the Proctors, Grace threw her arms about her.

'You'll not forget to write to me?'

'Every week. And you mind and write back.'

'I will. Oh, Mirren, I wish I'd never said I'd go!'

'You'll be happy there once you settle down. And we'll see each other when I go to America.'

'Let it be soon!' Grace prayed, completely forgetting that only Helen Jarvis's death could unlock the door to her friend's future.

'Mirren.' Anne's hug was brief, her face composed. She stepped back, picked up her bag, smiled at her family, then said, 'Come along, Grace,' for all the world as though they were only taking the train to Glasgow for the evening. Mutely Grace followed her to the edge of the pier, where they joined the queue of people waiting to go down to the tender. They had almost reached the steps when Mary darted towards them.

'Mary! Mercy me, she's not going to try to go as well, is she?' Catherine asked in a panic. She would have run after her daughter if her husband hadn't caught hold of her arm.

'She can't go, Mother,' John said reasonably, 'Her name's not on the list.'

Grace stepped out of the line to meet her young sister, who rummaged in the large bag she carried and pulled out a shawl-wrapped cocoon with a splash of yellow wool surging from one end. Grace tried to argue but Mary pushed the bundle into her sister's arms, then gave her a fierce hug before running back to her parents.

'Dolores?' Bill asked in amazement as she rejoined them. 'You gave Dolores away?'

'They need to have a bit of home with them. Anyway, she's just loaned and that means they'll have to bring her back to Paisley some time,' Mary said stoutly, then burst into tears as first Anne, then Grace, hugging the rag doll's smiling face to hers, descended the steps and disappeared from sight.

They waited until the tender had gone out to the *Carpathia* before making their way back to the station to catch the next train back to Paisley. On the outward journey they had chattered like budgerigars, partly because nobody wanted a silence to fall and partly because there was so little time left to say all the things they wanted to say before Grace and Anne left Scotland. On the return journey, however, they were all busy with their own thoughts. Bill and John stared straight ahead and Catherine only lifted her eyes occasionally from contemplation of the floor to look down at Mary, huddled against her shoulder, her face blotchy with tears.

James too kept his eyes on the floor apart from occasional worried glances across the carriage at his wife and youngest daughter. Mirren, keenly aware of the relentless approach of Ne'erday – New Year's Day – had brought her knitting with her; now she took Robbie's jersey from its bag, the clack of her needles echoed by the rattle of the train over the points. As fields and trees, roads and houses whipped by she kept wondering what Grace and Anne were doing at that moment.

Grace had begun to have her doubts as soon as they had their tickets in their hands and a firm date for the sailing, and on several occasions she would have pulled back from the whole notion of emigrating if Anne had allowed it. Only Mirren knew how close Anne herself had come to changing her mind.

'I can scarce sleep at nights for thinking of it,' she had suddenly confessed one evening when the shop was quiet. 'And I'm so frightened!'

It was one of Mirren's few nights off from working in the fried-fish shop and she had a lot to do at home, but clearly Anne needed to talk to someone. She rested her basket of groceries on the counter, folding her arms across the handle. 'If you don't want to go, you don't have to.'

'I do. I must. You saw the state our Grace got herself into over George, and that'd all just start up again if we stayed. She needs to get away and to tell the truth, so do I. My life's not going anywhere. There's our Kate happy with her bairn and Maggie'll not be long in marrying, for she's the beauty of the family and she's never lost for admirers. The same goes for Mary, too . . . and Grace herself, come to that.'

'You're not exactly ugly yourself, Anne!'

'Mebbe not, but I'm the practical one. I've got my mother's capable nature and they're all beginning to rely on me, Mirren. In the mornings I stay behind when the others leave so that I can help Mother by cleaning out the fireplace and taking the ashes down to the backyard midden. Then I polish up the fender and the fire-irons before I come to the shop. And at midday I always go home to have something with Mother, because I know fine and well that if I didn't she might not bother eating at all and that's not good for her.' She looked down at the counter, tracing a scar on the wood with the tip of a finger, then said in a rush, 'It's a terrible thing to say, but I can see myself turning into the one that stays at home and nurses her old parents, and becomes good old Auntie Anne with no real life of her own.'

'That's nonsense! There's nothing to stop you getting married and having a husband and a home and bairns.'

'There's one person can stop me, and that's myself. My trouble,' Anne confessed, 'is that I'm too pernickety. I've never met a man yet that didnae end up irritating me in some way or another. And I couldnae stand to spend the rest of my life with someone who irritated me, Mirren.'

'You think the Canadian men are going to be better than what we've got here in Paisley?'

Anne laughed. 'I'm not that daft. I know full well that folk are folk no matter where they live or how they speak. I just know that I need to make a change in my life. And I have to be strong for Grace. If she gets half a chance she'll change her mind, and it seems to me that as long as she lives in the same town as George Armitage she'll pine for him, though I can't see why myself. So,' she straightened and became her everyday practical self, 'we're going . . . even if the fear of it does keep me from sleeping at nights.'

By the time the train drew into Gilmour Street station one sleeve of Robbie's jersey had almost been completed. There was still a jersey to be knitted for wee Thomas and a waistcoat for Logan and a cardigan for Belle. And, Mirren had hoped, a warm jersey for Donald, who had written that the winters could be fierce. But it was now the middle of September and she was beginning to run out of time.

The small group walked silently from the station along Paisley High Street, past the Central Library and the Museum and the magnificent Baptist church, all built by members of the Coats family. High Street gave way to Wellmeadow then to Broomlands, and not a word was said. Even talkative Mary was silent. As they turned down Maxwellton Street and reached Mirren's close-mouth, Catherine, who had been leaning heavily on her husband's arm, hugged and kissed her.

'Don't be a stranger, pet, just because our Grace is gone,' she said, the tears welling in her striking dark eyes. 'We'll need you more than ever now.'

Day after day Robbie trudged round the engineering firms in Paisley and the neighbouring engineering town of Johnstone, but without finding work. His apprentice's wage, small though it had been, was sorely missed and Mirren found it harder with each week that passed to make ends meet. Although the weather was mild, Helen tended to feel the cold and Mirren had to keep a fire going, usually day and night, in the front room.

Her mother had some money, she knew, but Mirren couldn't bring herself to ask for any of it. Once a month one of the clerks from the mills called to deliver the small pension due to the widow of a former employee. His visit was always turned into a special occasion, with Helen insisting on looking her best, which meant that her hair had to be done and she required a clean night-gown and bedjacket. The bed had to be changed and every speck of dust removed from the room as though, Robbie used to say, she expected the clerk to carry out a minute inspection instead of just handing over a small envelope. The man was always invited to take a cup of tea and a biscuit with Helen and, while Mirren was permitted to serve the refreshments on a tray, with the best tray-cloth the house possessed, she was always banished before the transaction itself took place.

The money was carefully stored in a handbag kept by the side of the bed and every week Helen doled out a small set amount to cover the housekeeping costs. The trouble was that she was quite oblivious to the way prices had risen since she herself had run the house, but she guarded so jealously her small income and the power it brought her, and made such a ceremony of counting out and handing over the weekly allowance, that when the money ran out, as it almost always did before the week's end, Mirren found it easier to make up the difference from her own wages rather than ask her mother for more and have to undergo a lecture on thrift and common sense.

As the weeks dragged by she took to going to the shops just before they closed because in those final minutes the merchants, anxious to get meat, vegetables and bakery produce off their hands while they were still fresh enough to sell, cut their prices. She bought stale bread and toasted it at the fire, or crumbled it and added it to stews and mince to make them go further, or soaked it in a mixture of milk and water, sprinkled a little sugar over it, and served it up as bread pudding. She bought bones for soup, scraping what meat she could from them and serving it with potatoes as a main dish, and she stayed up late making pancakes and scones because it was cheaper than buying them.

Handing over precious pennies in return for small but essential bundles of firewood, she envied those mill-workers with access to the small wooden bobbins used for sewing thread. Nothing was supposed to be removed from the mills, but even so the faulty bobbins were smuggled out – in the case of women, often tied round their waists beneath their skirts – to use as firewood.

Things had become so difficult that she was not only unable to add to the little savings account she had started for herself and Donald when he left for America, but was forced once or twice to break her firm pledge to herself never to dip into it.

Robbie grumbled about the poor food, but then Robbie grumbled about almost everything these days. Mirren, knowing that he was sick with humiliation and worry, had to bite her tongue at times against the temptation to snap back at him, but she wasn't a saint and there were days when she was so tired and so worried herself that she couldn't remain silent in the face of his complaints.

'But you like stovies,' she tried to reason with him one evening when he complained about his dinner. Helen had often relied on stovies – potatoes and chopped onions simmered slowly in a little water, then mixed with oatmeal – to fill her children's bellies when times were hard. It made for a tasty and nourishing meal and, if the family was fortunate enough, there might be a few spoonfuls of mince to give added flavour.

'I know I like them, but not every day.' Robbie pushed his plate away and added peevishly, 'I cannae stomach this!'

Her patience suddenly ran out. 'Then you look after the house for a change,' she raged at him. 'You do the shopping and make the meals, for I'm tired of it all!' Then, as he snatched up his jacket and made for the door, 'Robbie, where are you going?'

'Out tae a meetin'.'

'With Joe Hepburn?'

'What business is that of yours?'

'At least he's bringing some money into his house,' Mirren said bitterly, then at the sight of her young brother's stricken face, 'I didn't mean . . . I wasn't accusing you, Robbie.'

'I'm off.'

'But I've to go to the fried-fish shop to . . .' Her voice trailed away as the door closed behind his back. She stared down at his rejected dinner then sank into the chair he had shoved back so angrily, pushed his plate aside, rested her head on her arms and burst into tears.

*　　*　　*

'Are ye sickenin' for somethin'?' Ella whispered as the two of them stood shoulder to shoulder at the counter, ladling chips onto sheets of paper.

'No.'

'Is it yer monthlies, then?'

'It's nothing.'

'Ye're looking right peely-wally – there's somethin' wrong with ye. That'll be ninepence,' Ella told her customer, then as Maria took the money and doled out change, she moved swiftly on to the next person in the line snaking from the counter to the door. She was serving three or four people to each one Mirren dealt with tonight, working fast and keeping up a constant flow of chat and banter with the customers. When a lull came she almost bullied Maria into allowing them to have a cup of tea.

Mirren was sent into the cramped back shop to make it. 'And be sure to add plenty of sugar to yours,' Ella whispered as Mirren passed. 'Ye need the energy.'

The tea helped to revive Mirren's drooping spirits a little and keep her on her feet until closing time. Ella was a good listener and as they walked home arm-in-arm, Mirren, driven by despair beyond the family rule that squabbles should be kept secret, told her friend about her row with Robbie.

'I can understand how he feels – a young married lad in our close is in the same boat and he's just fading away with the worry of tryin' tae find work,' Ella said. 'But your Robbie should think about how it is for you as well as him.'

'He does, usually. He's a good lad, but . . .'

'But he's a man, and men arenae good at dealin' with disappointment and worry. They tend tae leave that tae the womenfolk,' Ella said sagely. 'I've heard all that time and again from my aunties. Why d'ye think they never married? They saw my gran havin' a terrible time of it with my grandfather, and when they were younger than you and me they made up their minds never tae marry.'

'Will you get married, Ella?'

'Oh yes.'

'Who to? You won't even let a lad take you home from the dancing.'

'I'm looking for the right man,' Ella said positively. 'And I'll know him when I see him. So far I've only met the wrong ones.'

When Mirren arrived back in Maxwellton Street she found Mrs White, who had again agreed to look after her mother, approaching the close from the opposite direction, her old dog toddling along by her side.

'We've just been out for our bedtime walk, haven't we, Scrap?' Mrs White asked the dog, who peered up at Mirren from beneath a fringe of brown hair, eyes bright and nose alert to the aroma from the parcel she carried.

'My mother . . .'

'Don't fret, hen, I'd never leave her alone. Your Robbie's home. Oh my,' Mrs White said as they reached the end of the close, 'These stairs'll be the death of me. Can I take yer arm, hen?'

With Scrap huffing and shuffling ahead of them they climbed the stairs slowly, and if Mrs White noticed that Mirren leaned on her rather than supporting her she said nothing about it. When they reached the landing the woman lowered her voice, turning her back to the Jarvis's door as though fearing that Helen might be crouched on the other side, listening.

'I'm a wee thing concerned about yer mammy, Mirren.'

'What d'you mean?'

'She's no' lookin' as able as she was. Sometimes a difference can be so slight that those closest never notice it,' Mrs White hurried to explain. 'It's just a . . .' she fumbled for the right words, 'a sense of somethin'. Ye might want tae ask the doctor tae look in on her sometime.' She peered up into Mirren's face. 'Ach, don't worry, lass, it's probably nothin'. I'll let ye get in tae yer

bed, ye'll be ready for it.' She opened her own door for
Scrap, then turned back to say, 'Ye're a good daughter,
Mirren. Helen's fortunate tae have the likes of you.'

Robbie, surprisingly, was down on his hands and knees,
polishing the fender and the tiles round the fireplace.
'Just tae save ye in the mornin',' he explained awkwardly, scrambling to his feet as his sister came into
the kitchen.

'You didn't need . . .' she started, then amended it to,
'thank you, Robbie, that'll be a good help to me.'

In the front room Helen was sound asleep. Mirren,
with Mrs White's words ringing in her head, longed to
put the light on so that she could study her mother more
closely, but instead she had to tiptoe out again, leaving
Helen to the deep sleep so badly needed and so rarely
granted.

Back in the kitchen she fetched two plates from the
cupboard and was unwrapping the fish supper when
Robbie said abruptly, 'I don't want any.'

'Of course you do.'

'I'm not hungry. You eat it . . . you earned it,' he said
gruffly.

'Robbie, you're having your share, same as always.'

'I don't deserve it!'

'Neither of us deserves what's happening to us just
now. So we've got the right to enjoy what comes to us.
And thanks to Vanni that includes the occasional fish
supper.'

A grin flickered round his mouth before it gave way to
the bitterness that was ageing him these days. 'Ne-erday's
comin' and I'd such plans for this year . . . I was plannin'
tae buy decent gifts for you and Mother because I thought
I'd be earning a man's wage at last. And now look at us!'

'There's a whole week before September ends; you'll
have found work long before Ne'erday. Even if you don't,
we've never made much of the season anyway.'

'Mirren, I'm sorry about . . . the way I was earlier.'

'It was my fault, I shouldn't have snapped at you.'

'You do the best ye can tae keep us all goin' – ye always have. I don't appreciate it enough.'

She pushed a plate of food at him and collapsed thankfully into a fireside chair with her own share. 'Just appreciate your chips for now, then we can both get to our beds,' she told him, and knew by his laugh that all was well between them again.

'D'you think Mother's looking worse?' she asked as they were finishing the food.

'She looks the same tae me. Why?'

'Just something Mrs White said when I met her on my way in.'

Robbie reached for her empty plate. 'I'll wash them. If Mother was ill I'm sure Logan and Belle would have said something. You know how Logan always behaves as if you were a housekeeper he'd hired tae look after Mother.'

'You'd noticed that as well?'

'It's hard not tae notice,' Robbie said.

Mrs White's concern for Helen haunted Mirren. She knew well enough that women who had raised families and cared for ageing parents and, in some cases, had been looking after small brothers and sisters when they were little more than babies themselves tended to have a sixth sense about other folk. Her own mother was among those who could glance at a slender, carefree young girl and know that she was 'expecting' long before the girl herself was aware of it. Such women could accurately foretell the sex of an unborn child or even, again with uncanny accuracy, determine whether a complete stranger was Catholic or Protestant. And they could see death approaching from a distance – how, she didn't know and nor did they. But they could.

For that reason she took Mrs White's words seriously enough to confer with Logan and Belle on their next visit.

They looked blankly at each other then Logan said, 'Has she been complainin' of ill-health?'

'No, but Mother never complains.' That wasn't true. Helen complained all the time, about everything, but Mirren had a suspicion that if her mother felt really ill she would never admit to it.

'Well then.'

'It's just, mebbe I should fetch the doctor, just in case.'

'If ye want.'

'The thing is,' Mirren said awkwardly, 'the doctor costs money.'

'I hope ye're not goin' tae ask me for it,' her brother said at once. 'You know I'm scarcely paid any wages tae speak of.'

'Robbie's not found work yet.'

'What about Mother's pension?'

'I can't ask her for money to pay for a doctor's visit. She'd only say that she didn't need one and anyway, I don't want to alarm her.'

'Then use yer own money,' Logan suggested. 'Mother told me when Donald Nesbitt went off tae America that ye were puttin' somethin' aside from yer wages every week towards yer own journey. Is that not why ye took the job in the fried-fish shop?'

'Yes, but it's meant for a new life for me and Donald when the time comes. I've already had to use some of it, and I do everything else for Mother,' she made herself point out.

'That's a daughter's duty,' Belle told her, while Logan added self-righteously, 'Surely ye'd not deny a doctor for yer own mother when ye've got money sittin' in the bank doing nothing?'

12

'What d'ye think, Mirren!' Catherine planted herself in the middle of the pavement, halting Mirren when she would have trudged past without looking up. 'A letter's arrived from our Anne! D'ye have a minute to come to the house and hear what she says?'

Mirren hesitated, glancing up Maxwellton Street. She dearly wanted to know how Grace and Anne were faring and at the moment Robbie was at home with his mother. The two of them could surely do without her for another five minutes or so.

'Just for a minute or two,' she agreed, then as she and her aunt walked the few steps to the Proctors' close-mouth she hesitated again. 'Mebbe I should go home first and tidy myself . . .'

'Nonsense, lassie, it's not that long since our Grace used to come home every day lookin' as though she'd walked through a snowstorm.' Catherine urged her into the close. Spotlessly clean, with the walls tiled to halfway between floor and ceiling, it was more modern and much more attractive than the close leading into the building where Mirren lived. 'I've still got her old sheet, you can use that.'

The Proctors' lobby was large and square, with room for a cupboard as well as a coat-rack. Calling out, 'Mirren's here, Maggie. Put the kettle on and fetch Anne's letter,' Catherine whisked the sheet from a cupboard shelf and spread it on the floor. 'Step on that and I'll give your coat a good brushing,' she ordered. 'And no arguments. I used to do this every day for our Grace, and to tell you the truth it's a pleasure to be doing it again.' Then as the cotton, dislodged by her vigorous brushing, drifted from Mirren's shoulders, 'It makes me feel closer to her when I'm doing this.' Sudden tears sparkled in her fine dark eyes and she brushed them away impatiently with her free hand. 'A bit of oose must have got intae my eye. Turn round, lassie, and I'll brush your back.'

Catherine wasn't the only one to be moved by the little ritual. As she stood submissively beneath her aunt's deft hands, Mirren was reminded sharply of her early days in the mill, when her mother had been strong enough to perform the same service for her every day. Now she always had to see to herself.

When all the caddis had been brushed away Mirren stepped off the sheet and helped her aunt to gather the corners together neatly without allowing one speck of cotton to escape. 'We'll just put it in this corner and I'll take it down to the midden later. Now come on . . .' Catherine swept her into the kitchen, where James and Mary were finishing off their evening meal and Maggie waited to pour fresh tea for their visitor.

'They've reached the hospital safely,' she said as soon as Mirren appeared, 'and a lot of the folk speak French . . .'

'Now don't go putting the cart in front of the horse, Maggie,' her mother admonished. 'Mary, hand round the cake while I read the letter out.'

Anne had a good way with words, and Catherine had a flair for drama. She read the letter so well that Mirren could easily sense the claustrophobia of the tiny cabin that Anne and Grace had shared with two other Scottish girls. She saw in her mind's eye the four bunks, two bolted to each wall, and the tiny hand basin opposite the door, and she felt the lift, tilt and plunge of the steamship as it fought its way through the North Atlantic.

'It was a relief,' Anne wrote, 'when we entered the shelter of the St Lawrence River and went on deck for our first proper sight of our new home. The day was sunny and the air invigorating, though cold. After docking at Quebec on the following day we had to disembark and find our luggage in the great mass of items brought from the ship's hold. That was a worrying time, for we couldn't think how we would ever find our own pieces among such a lot. But we did, finally, then we had to spend hours and hours with the customs inspectors, who required us to open every bag and suitcase. Grace and I were very glad that we had packed so neatly and made certain that everything was in good order.'

That ordeal over, the Proctor sisters, together with the fifteen or so other girls who had sailed with them in search of a new life, were directed to a huge arrival hall, where there was great relief when one of them spotted a tall man holding aloft a placard with 'Board of Trade' written on it.

'It took us quite a few minutes to fight our way through the crowds towards him,' Catherine turned a page and read on, 'but when we got there we found that there were three nurses with him, wearing their uniforms under warm coats. We were welcomed in a very strange accent, which took some getting used to, but has turned out to be the Canadian form of English with a strong French accent. Many of the people in this part of Canada are of French extraction and speak the language whenever possible.

'Once we were all safely gathered in, like the sheaves in the hymn, we were taken to omnibuses waiting outside and driven to the nurses' home, where Miss Gentles, the lady in charge of our group, saw to it that Grace and I were given a double room so that we would not be separated. She told us that they had a great need in the hospital for more workers, and that was made evident by the haste in which they got us started to work the next morning.'

The Scottish girls had been wakened at six o'clock on the following morning and by eight o'clock were equipped in their new grey uniforms – 'Not stylish by any manner of means, but practical and easy to care for' – had had breakfast and been given a lecture by the head nurse as to the sort of work they would be required to do. 'We were then taken to the various wards and put into the charge of the ward sisters. Our days are filled with work and learning how things are done here, and at night we are too tired to do anything but sleep. Being busy keeps us from moping too much with homesickness, and the people are pleasant. We are both in good spirits and, although we miss you all very much, we are both firmly agreed that we did the right thing in coming to Canada.'

The letter finished with a promise that they would both write often and that nobody needed to worry about them. And there was love to everyone from Grace, Anne and Dolores, who, Mary was assured, was enjoying her new life and spent her days on the windowsill of the room the sisters shared and her nights tucked into Grace's bed.

'There!' Catherine's face glowed as she folded the pages and tucked them carefully into their envelope. 'So now we know that they're safe and doing well.'

'Did I not tell ye that time and again, woman, when ye were fretting about them?' her husband asked mildly. 'They've got good Scots heads on their shoulders and good Scots tongues in their mouths. Of course they'd be all right.'

'I know, I know, but even so . . . There's times when being a mother's a right heartache,' Catherine said, and then, as Mirren got up to go, 'I'll walk down to the close with you and empty that sheet in the back court.'

'What's amiss?' Catherine asked her niece as soon as they were out of the house.

'Nothing.'

'You're not very good at telling lies. Honest folk never are.' Catherine paused on the landing. 'Out with it, now.'

Mirren bit her lip. She had been brought up to keep her own counsel and never discuss family matters with others.

It was as though Catherine could read her thoughts. 'When all's said and done, lassie,' the woman urged gently, 'I'm your own blood kin.'

'It's just . . . it's my mother . . .'

Once started, she couldn't stop. Catherine listened intently while Mirren poured out her worries, then she announced, 'I'll come and see Helen tomorrow afternoon.'

'But you and Mother don't get on.' Mirren followed as her aunt began to descend the final flight of stairs.

'I need to see her for myself, and if there's one of us not getting on, it's Helen. I've no quarrel with her and it's high time we spoke to each other again.'

'But she doesn't know that I visit you. She mustn't know!'

'Don't fret yourself, lassie, I'll tell her that I heard about her health from a neighbour. It's surely my Christian duty to call on my own cousin in her hour of need, and it's all right to lie a little bit, as long as the lie does no harm to anyone.'

'I don't know, Aunt Catherine . . .'

'I'll not stand by and watch you fretting yourself to death like this. Let me see Helen for myself, then we can decide together what should be done for her – since your brother and his wife don't seem to be bothered,' Catherine added with a steely edge to her normally placid voice.

'Aunt Catherine, what happened to make you and my mother fall out?'

'As I said, the quarrel was all on her side, not mine, so that's for her to tell you, if ever she has a mind to. Off you go home now, and don't fret yourself any more.'

Daylight had begun to ebb and Mirren stepped out of the close into the softness of late afternoon on a mild mid-October day. It was a time of the year that she normally enjoyed, when the leaves on the trees fringeing the town were turning soft shades of brown and red and yellow, and the night air had a hushed feel to it, as though gently mourning the passing of summer while at the same time waiting, with bated breath, for winter to stride confidently over the horizon. But today Mirren had more on her mind than the weather. She didn't know whether to feel relieved or worried. It was grand to know that someone was finally listening to her, and willing to help her with advice. On the other hand, she felt apprehensive about being in the vicinity when her mother met the cousin she had not spoken to since they were girls.

True to her word, Catherine Proctor called the next day. 'You must be Mirren, dear.' Her clear voice echoed round the small landing. 'How d'ye do? I'm your mother's cousin, Catherine Proctor. I've come to call on her.'

Now that the moment had arrived Mirren's courage all but deserted her. 'I don't know . . . She's not so well this evening . . .'

'All the more reason for me to see her.' Catherine swept the objections aside and marched into the small hall, a basket filled with packages on one arm. 'Where is she?'

Instinctively Mirren glanced at the front-room door. 'I'll just ask if . . .' she began, but her aunt was already pushing the door open and advancing into the room, where Helen struggled to sit upright, her face tight with anger.

'What are you doing in my house?'

'I'm doing what I should have done years ago – visiting my cousin.'

'I don't want you here!'

'Don't be daft, Helen,' Catherine Proctor said calmly. 'I've brought you some calves' foot jelly.'

'We don't need your charity!'

'Mother!'

'It's not charity, woman. I'm sure that if I was unwell you'd do the same for me.'

'I would not. You tried to steal my man away from me!'

'Tut, Helen, I did nothing of the sort. I'm sure we could both do with a nice cup of tea, if you've the time to make one, Mirren.'

'I don't want any tea.' Helen was behaving like a sulky child. She threw herself back against her pillows, fingers plucking at the tumbled, twisted blankets over her thin body.

'As I mind it, you were always a right tea jenny, Helen,' her cousin chided her with a smile. 'Remember when you used to drain my mother's big teapot dry all on your lone?' She dipped into her basket and took out a paper bag, which she handed to Mirren. 'I brought us some nice tea biscuits from the Co-op in Broomlands Street. My daughter Anne used to be the manageress there, but she's gone off to Canada. I'll tell you all about that while Mirren makes the tea.'

When Mirren returned with a tray her mother, bright spots of angry colour on each cheekbone, was lying back against pillows that had been punched into shape and skilfully arranged to make a comfortable backrest. The bedclothes had been tidied and Catherine Proctor had shed her fur-collared coat and was sitting by the bed, talking. She got up and took the tray, settling it on the table by the window and pouring tea as calmly as if she was in her own home, while Helen watched, her eyes bright with dislike.

'Why don't you take your tea into the kitchen, Mirren? I don't want to interrupt your work, and your mother and I have a lot of memories to catch up on.'

The tea cooled unnoticed in Mirren's cup as she tried in vain to concentrate on the business of polishing the big kitchen dresser that had always been her mother's pride and joy. She collected the hand-painted plates from the top shelf first and carefully washed them, before fetching the cloth and tin of beeswax, her ears straining all the time to make sense of the soft murmur of voices from the front room.

Twenty minutes dragged by before Catherine brought the tray out, calling cheery goodbyes over her shoulder to her cousin. Once the kitchen door was firmly closed behind her, the smile disappeared.

'The woman's not well at all, Mirren.' She looked closely at her niece. 'Have you the money for the doctor? I'd be happy to help. If there's anything I can do for poor Helen . . .'

'No, we can manage.'

'If you're sure, but remember that you only have to ask,' Catherine said, then gave a little gasp of pleased surprise as her eyes fell on the dresser. She reached out and touched it, a fond smile temporarily smoothing out the worried frown between her eyes. 'I mind this piece well. Aunt Beatrice – your grandmother – kept it gleaming, and she had lovely plates set out on the top shelf.'

'We've still got some of them.' Mirren indicated the plates she had carefully washed and stacked to dry.

'Oh yes, there they are. She was a lovely woman, your gran. And Helen was such a bonny lassie.' Catherine's voice trembled and she scrubbed the back of one hand across her eyes. 'I cannae believe she's come to this. I wish I'd made up with her years ago when she was well.'

'There's still time.'

'Not for us, my dear. Your mother's turned against me completely, and the way she is, it would only upset her if I tried to call on her again.' Catherine shook her depression off with a determined effort and started to unload the basket she carried. 'But it's not too late for me to help in other ways. Here's the calves' foot jelly I mentioned, and I bought a nice bowl of potted hough in the Co-op. Helen might fancy some for her tea. Now I'd better go, she'll be wondering what we're talking about.'

At the door she kissed Mirren on the cheek. 'Remember that James and I think of you as one of our own, and we're just down the road if you ever need anything.'

'What took you so long?' Helen wanted to know when her daughter went into the front room. 'What were you and Mrs High-and-Mighty Proctor mutterin' about in the kitchen?'

'We weren't muttering, she was just asking me about the mills and about how Robbie was.'

'That's none of her business . . . and I'll not have her here again, Mirren, d'you hear me?'

'She was just trying to help, Mother.'

'We don't need her help!'

'She's your blood kin. I thought you'd be pleased to see her again.'

'If I'd wanted to see her again I'd have seen tae it long before this. Now mind me, Mirren, she's not welcome,' Helen stormed, then, all the fire suddenly draining out of her, 'I have to use the commode.'

Mrs White had been quite right when she said that it was difficult to notice changes in someone close. It was only now that Mirren had seen her mother and her aunt together that she could assess Helen's deterioration. Despite her advancing years and a lifetime of hard work, Catherine Proctor was still sturdy and erect and the lines about her wide strong mouth and around her eyes were those of a compassionate woman easily moved to laughter. She was still in her prime, while Helen Jarvis looked old. Her colouring was bad and the lines on her face were hard and deeply grooved, her mouth pulled down by bitterness and pain. Helping her from the commode and settling her back into her bed, Mirren was suddenly aware of her mother's frailty and the way her bones were barely covered by skin, let alone fat or muscle. Remembering how easily Helen had carried her up the stairs from the close-mouth when she was a small child, Mirren was frightened. Aunt Catherine was right, it was time to summon medical help.

She was making soup when Robbie came in, his shoulders hunched against the cold outside, his face bleak. She knew with one glance that he had not had any luck with his job-seeking.

'Aunt Catherine Proctor called to see Mother today.'

'Oh?'

'Mother was furious and she says she doesn't want to see her here again. She even said that Aunt Catherine had tried to take Father away from her.'

A spark of interest lit Robbie's eyes. 'D'ye think it's true?'

'I can't see it. Aunt Catherine and Uncle James seem so fond of each other.' Mirren chopped busily. 'Their first meeting was very romantic. Anne told me about it once. It seems that Aunt Catherine had a friend from a well-to-do family – someone she'd met through her dancing – and this lassie had a sweetheart in the Army. Because her parents didn't think him good enough for her they wouldn't agree to an engagement, then the young man was posted off to India and while he was away the girl engaged herself to a Glasgow businessman – someone her parents liked. The church wedding was all set and the wedding breakfast was to be held in the Town Hall, and Aunt Catherine was one of the bridesmaids. But on the day . . .' Mirren stopped chopping carrots and turned to face her brother. 'The bride was just about to walk down the aisle when her Army sweetheart burst into the church and shot her dead. Her beautiful white wedding gown was crimson with blood, Anne said.'

Her voice shook slightly, for the story never failed to

move her. 'Uncle James was in the congregation that day and when he saw poor Aunt Catherine almost fainting with all the commotion and the fuss over the bride, and folk trying to take hold of the man and subdue him, he took Aunt Catherine by the arm and led her outside and sat her down on a gravestone in her pretty dress. Then he talked to her and calmed her . . . and a year later they were wed.'

'What happened tae the soldier?'

'He was locked up in an asylum for mad people, poor man.'

Robbie looked sceptical. 'I cannae see a thing like that happenin' in Paisley.'

'Anne said it did, and she'd never lie to me. Anyway,' Mirren turned back to her work, 'folk are folk, no matter what town they live in. You should come with me to visit the Proctors some time, Robbie. They're nice people, they'd make you very welcome.'

'Aye, mebbe.' Robbie liked to choose his own friends and had never shown any interest in meeting his relations.

'Robbie, Aunt Catherine thinks we should get the doctor.'

'Ye mean Mother might be really ill this time?'

'I hope not, but it's best to get the doctor in.' Mirren scooped the last of the vegetables into the soup, gave it a good stir, checked the flame beneath the pot, then took her coat from its hook on the back of the kitchen door and fetched her Paisley Provident Co-operative Society share book from its drawer. 'I need to go out for a wee while. Will you remember to stir the soup now and again to stop it getting too thick?'

'What's for the dinner?'

'Potted hough,' she said, and for the first time in weeks his face lit up. He loved the dish, which had been a family favourite in the days when their father and Crawford had been alive. It consisted of a shinbone and some meat simmered with onions, carrots and a bayleaf to add a spicy flavour to the stock, then poured into bowls and covered with equal amounts of stock. The stock turned to jelly as it cooled and the dish was sliced and eaten cold.

'Potted hough? We must be doin' all right if you can afford tae buy that. Have ye been made up tae the post of Mistress at work?'

'No, I'm just good with money.'

'I'll peel the potatoes while ye're gone,' he offered.

Despite all her efforts to leave the Co-operative dividends alone to multiply into a reasonable amount, Mirren had been forced since Robbie lost his job to use some of the money. In the Paisley Provident Co-operative Society office, an impressive building in Causeyside Street, she withdrew all that was left; it came to one shilling and threepence, not enough to pay for a doctor's house call. Slowly she walked back up St Mirren Brae to the High Street, where she turned in at the door of the Paisley Savings Bank. It had been such an effort to build up the American account, almost penny by penny, and now it was dwindling. The last withdrawal had been for a nice necktie to send to Donald as his Ne'erday gift. Her mother's deteriorating health meant that she had had after all no time to knit a warm jersey to protect him against the American winters. It hurt to see her precious savings melting away, but she had no choice other than humiliating herself by begging from Logan, who would only refuse her in any case.

'There's little I can do for her,' the doctor followed Mirren into the kitchen, where Robbie paced the floor nervously. 'Your mother's heart – her entire body, come to that – has simply worn out.'

'Is there no medication we can try?' Robbie was stunned. He was used to his mother being an invalid, but clearly he had never considered her condition to be life-threatening.

'Only good nourishing food and mebbe a wee glass of tonic wine every day. And try to keep her spirits up,' the doctor said as he picked up his bag and held a hand out for his fee.

As Mirren followed him onto the landing he said, 'There's one blessing, my dear. At least you're saving money because your mother has no need of medication.'

Mirren flinched as though he had struck her in the face, then recovered herself and looked him straight in the eye. 'I'd have been very happy to find whatever price the medication might cost if I could only restore my mother to health,' she said clearly, and the man had the grace to flush with embarrassment before hurrying down the stairs.

13

Mirren didn't know what she would have done without Aunt Catherine to turn to. Ella was a sympathetic listener and Agnes still one of the family, but neither of them had Catherine Proctor's maturity and wisdom, nor her serenity. Just talking to her helped to ease Mirren's anxiety.

She listened without comment to the story of the doctor's visit, then asked a few questions about Helen's past health. 'She was never all that strong after Robbie's birth, but it was Father's death, then Crawford's, that brought her to her bed,' Mirren explained miserably, glad that she had found her aunt at home alone for once. 'And I suppose she's right when she says she has little to live for now.'

'There's always something to live for! There's her wee grandson, and mebbe others to follow when you and Robbie marry.'

'I'll be away in America, and now that Agnes has married again and given wee Thomas a stepfather . . . That's not going to take him away from Mother, but she keeps fretting herself that it will.'

'Oh, my poor Helen. I always mind her as being so brave. I was a tomboy in my youth and she wasn't, but whatever I did she'd follow no matter what. She'd face anything rather than be left behind. It near broke my heart to see her lying there last week, so frail and helpless and . . .' Catherine paused, then said huskily,

'. . . so old-looking. It made me realise that I'm not getting any younger myself. Look, Mirren.' She opened a drawer and brought out a small faded photograph. 'I found this just the other day. It's me and your mother when we were just going into our teens.'

The likeness showed two young girls, their arms about each other's waists, standing beside a pillar bearing a large leafy plant in an urn. Mirren recognised Catherine at once; she was the taller of the two, and her strong jawbone and erect posture were unmistakable. So, too, were the clear direct eyes and the wide, well-shaped mouth that looked as though it was trembling on the verge of a peal of laughter.

Helen, nestling against her cousin, was the smaller and slighter of the two. Her delicate little face was solemn and the smile that hovered about her lips was more nervous than amused, yet Mirren could see the determination Catherine had described in the way that Helen's pointed chin jutted out and in the set of her mouth. Catherine's dark hair hung down over her shoulders beneath a straw boater with a bow at the front, and a draped knee-length skirt could be seen below her fitted hip-length jacket, while her cousin's long fair curls were held back from her face with a velvet band and she wore a high-necked smocked dress of broad light and dark stripes, with sleeves puffed from shoulder to elbow and tight-fitting from elbow to wrist.

'I'd forgotten I had that, but I still mind the day it was taken as if it was just yesterday. It was my mother who came up with the idea of us going to a photographer's studio, and your gran was all for it herself. She was the one who took us and between us we near drove her wild with exasperation, for we were in one of those silly giggly moods that day. I mind that the photographer had a terrible time getting us to stay still.' Catherine's finger rested briefly on Helen's long fair locks. 'You've got your mother's hair, lassie, but I do believe . . .' she

turned Mirren round so that she could study her face
closely, 'that you've got my mouth and my eyes. And
you've certainly got my love of dancing. Helen gave it
a try when I became so fond of it, but she didn't have
the same sense of rhythm. Poor Helen, it vexed her that I
could dance better than her, though of course there were
other things she did better than me. Would you like me
to have a copy made of this?'

'Oh yes, please.' Mirren could scarcely take her eyes
off the portrait of her mother as a girl. This was a Helen
she had never known and never could know, for her
mother was not one to talk of her childhood, claiming
that what was gone was gone and of no interest to her.

'Then I'll see to it tomorrow. I just wish that Helen
and I could be close again.' The ball of Catherine's
thumb caressed the likeness of her cousin's small, pointed
face. 'We were so sure in those days that we'd always
be together, no matter what,' she said. Then, putting
the picture down and straightening her shoulders, 'At
least I can help by seeing that she gets any wee thing
she needs, and she needn't know that it came from
me.'

'We can manage fine,' Mirren said at once. Grateful
though she was for her aunt's strength and support, she
was not yet ready to accept financial charity. Not as long
as she could manage on her own.

'I've no doubt that you can, lass, but I want to do my
share and you'll surely not deny me that wee pleasure.
For a start,' Catherine said briskly, 'I've got in more
of that calves' foot jelly for her, and a bottle of tonic
wine. It did our John the world of good when he had the
pneumonia.'

At the beginning of November Robbie came home and
announced that he had found a job.

'In your own trade?'

He grinned broadly. 'Aye.'

'Oh, Robbie, that's wonderful!' She hugged him, laughing as he danced her about the kitchen. 'Where is it?' she asked when he finally let her go.

'Promise ye'll not put on that disapprovin' face.'

'Why should I disapprove of you getting another job? Goodness knows you deserve it, and you've looked hard enough for it.'

'It wasnae me that found it, though. It was Joe.' He eyed her narrowly. 'It's in Fleming and Ferguson's engineering shop.'

'Oh. He works for them, doesn't he?'

'In their shipyard. It was good of him tae get them tae take me on.' There was a faint warning note in his voice.

'You must have got the job on your own merit.'

'Of course I did. But Joe arranged for them tae give me the interview.'

Mirren bit her lip then said, 'In that case I'm grateful to him.'

'So am I. Now,' Robbie said to show that the matter was over and done with and he would not be interested in further discussion, 'what's for the dinner? Ye'll need tae feed me up now that I'm a workin' man again.'

'Feed you up? A horse couldn't eat more than you already do!'

Seeing him go off to work each morning, walking with his old jaunty swing, his self-respect regained, Mirren could do nothing other than accept the situation and be grateful to see him bring home a decent pay packet again at the end of each week.

In the fried-fish shop Maria Perrini had become even more waspish than usual; sometimes, as the evenings dragged by, Mirren was reminded of the tight-rope walkers in a circus she had once visited with Donald. Shovelling chips and taking money and counting out change, she recalled holding her breath, one hand clutching at her throat and the other gripping Donald's sleeve, as she watched three small figures – a man and two women, all dressed in tight-fitting spangled clothing – make their way slowly across a swaying rope high in the air, with injury or even death just one slip of the foot away.

At times when Maria's temper was at its worst she felt just like those circus people. One word, one mistake on her part, and Maria's sharp tongue would slice ruthlessly through the rope and send her spinning into space, out of control and out of the extra work she so badly needed, particularly now that her mother was so frail and required little extras to tempt her failing appetite.

'If Maria was older I'd say she'd reached that time when women get all dried up and past their prime,' Ella said one night as the two of them plodded home. Even she was finding it hard to stay cheerful in the shop these days.

'Mebbe she's expecting.'

'Not her. She makes sure that there won't be any bairns.'

'How d'you know a thing like that?'

'Vanni told me.'

'Ella!' Mirren was horrified. 'You talked to the man about things like that?'

'No, he talked tae me one Saturday afternoon when we happened tae meet in Barshaw Park. The poor soul gets right down at times, and he has tae talk tae someone,' Ella said defensively. 'Being Italian and a Roman Catholic, he's always wanted bairns. He says he loves bein' with his wee nephews and nieces. But Maria's determined not to have any, ever.'

'She might change her mind.'

'That's what Vanni's hoping but I think he's just foolin' himself. That selfish bitch'll not change her mind once it's made up.'

'If she doesn't want children and he does, why did he marry her in the first place?'

'If you ask me, she let him think that she was as fond of bairns as he was just tae get her hands on the shop. It belongs tae his family. He told me that they're all over Scotland, with at least one shop in nearly every town. As the young ones grow up, the older ones put the money together tae buy them a wee business. They know how tae look after their own, the Perrinis. But there's a bad apple in every barrel and as far as you and me are concerned, that's Maria,' Ella finished in disgust. 'Times I can't stand tae be near her, knowin' what she's doing tae poor Vanni, and him such a civil soul, too.'

'You could stop working there.'

'And leave you and Vanni on yer own? Ye both need someone sensible like me tae keep an eye on ye,' Ella said, squeezing Mirren's arm. 'Besides, who would I carp about if I didnae have Maria?'

Robbie was waiting at the close-mouth, pacing the pavement impatiently. 'There you are!' He took her arm and hurried her into the close and up the stairs. 'I've been waiting for you tae come home so's I could get out tae a meetin'.'

'At this time of night?'

'I'll have missed most of it now, but I can find out what went before.' They had reached the landing and, without waiting for her to lift the latch, he swung round and began heading off down the stairs again, taking them two at a time.

'Robbie!'

'Put some of that fish in the oven for me,' he called back over his shoulder as he went. 'And don't wait up. I'll come in quietly so's not tae disturb ye.'

'What's all the noise about?' Helen asked peevishly when Mirren went in to see her.

'Just Robbie going out to some meeting.'

'As late as this?' Helen shook her head then said indulgently, 'It's probably a lassie. I mind the way his brothers were at his age. Is there any more of that tonic wine left, Mirren?'

'Aye, there is. Could you take some fried fish with it?'

Going to fetch the wine and the small piece of fish that Helen thought she could manage, Mirren wished that it was a girl that held Robbie's interest rather than Joe Hepburn and politics. She had to admit that Joe had a right to be bitter about the grand vision of a new Britain presented by Parliament during the Great War – a vision of a land fit for the heroes who had left home, hearth and loved ones to fight and be injured like George Armitage, or die like Crawford, for their country. The land for heroes had never materialised, but even so she did not care for the idea of ordinary men such as Joe Hepburn and her Robbie taking what had been promised, if it wasn't given to them freely. Such attitudes could lead to trouble and if there was any trouble around she had a feeling that Joe was sure to be in the thick of it. Recalling the evening when Robbie had proudly shown her his bruised knuckles, she worried.

'That's good,' Helen said appreciatively after her first sip of wine. She had become quite fond of it and had no idea that it was Catherine Proctor who supplied it. She only picked at the fish before pushing the plate away.

'You need to eat more, Mother.'

'What for? Eating's for keeping your strength up, and I'm not using any lying here. I'm never out in the fresh air to get an appetite.'

'Mebbe when the weather's better we could get you down to the back court.'

'Aye, mebbe,' Helen said listlessly. For once she was not in the mood to talk, and when the wine was finished and she had been settled for the night she dropped into a doze, leaving Mirren free to return to the kitchen, where she got out her notepad, pen and ink, and started a letter to Donald. She loved those letters, for while she wrote them she stopped being a daughter and a sister and a friend, and became a woman in love, longing to be with her man again and frustrated by the circumstances that kept them apart.

'I know that Aunt Catherine would help, but Mother refuses to have anything to do with her, or with Agnes now that she has remarried. And Logan and Belle already have their hands full. But the day will come if we're just patient, though I know that that is not easy for either of us,' she wrote, wishing that she could put herself into the envelope and post herself across the water to him.

Robbie came in soon after she had gone to bed, slipping like a shadow into the kitchen to fetch the food she had kept warm for him. She pretended to be asleep, but when he gave a sudden exclamation, followed by a soft curse, she asked from the shadows of the bed recess, 'What's wrong?'

'I've burned my fingers on this damned plate!'

She could see his figure outlined against the small window. 'There's a towel on the back of the chair nearest you. Use that to hold the plate. And light the gas if you want.'

'No,' he said abruptly, then, 'go tae sleep, Mirren, I'll take the food intae my own room.'

She listened for a while to his soft movements on the other side of the wall before sleep took hold of her.

When Mirren saw the envelope with its unfamiliar stamps lying on the doormat she pounced on it, her tired heart soaring. Donald's letter must have crossed hers, she thought, then a second glance showed that the stamps weren't American and that Grace's name had been printed clearly in one corner.

Although she had very little time in which to see to her mother before running back to the mill for the afternoon shift, she managed to start on the close-packed pages as she heated the soup that was all Helen wanted.

'I'm sorry to have taken so long to sit down to this letter,' wrote Grace in the neat copperplate writing that had been dinned into them both at school, sometimes with the aid of the teacher's heavy wooden ruler across their knuckles, 'but there has been so much to do and so much to learn, and I know that Mother will have shared Anne's letters with you, so you will have heard of our excitements and adventures. Anne is so good at writing, no matter how tired and harassed she might be. I do not know how she finds the energy, since she works every bit as hard as I do. We all have to work hard, but at the same time we are treated kindly and fed well, so we cannot complain.'

Anne had written only of the pleasant aspects of their lives, but Grace clearly felt more free with Mirren, who learned for the first time about the dreadful sea-sickness both her friends had experienced during the crossing between Scotland and Canada, particularly early on as they sailed across the North Atlantic.

'It was very cold and so stormy that I was certain that we would sink at any moment. The cabin was extremely small with no windows, not even those little round port-holes. It put me most unpleasantly in mind of a coffin. We were all four of us dreadfully sick and I have to admit to crying bitterly for my mother, just like a little child. I wept so hard and for so long that I believe I was as much in danger of drowning in my own tears as in the terrible sea. But even though she was sick too, and longed to be home just as much as I did, Anne was so brave and so determined that we would arrive in Canada safe and sound that she kept the rest of us going, when we were more than ready to advance on the captain and demand that he turn about and take us back to Scotland.'

Once the sickness passed and the weather eased, life became much easier for Grace and Anne and their companions. There were walks on deck, the pleasure of meeting some of their fellow travellers, and as much food as anyone could want. 'Though what I still wished for more than anything was to be back home with Mother and Father and all the others, and watching from the parlour window to see you come down the street with your pretty, anxious face set in its usual worried frown.'

Mirren set the letter down and raced to the mirror, pushing her fair hair back from her forehead so that she could examine it closely. Grace was right – there were lines across it, and more tucked between her eyebrows. When she smoothed them with her fingers they re-appeared as soon as she let go. They deepened when she heard the Ferguslie bell ringing for the second time and realised that she would have to run like a hare in order to get back to work.

It was late at night before she was able to return to Grace's letter and read about the sisters' arrival on dry land. 'The uniformed customs men looked at us very sternly,' Grace wrote, 'and they seemed quite reluctant to let us into their country. Although I was still homesick I was also determined that, having come so far, we were going to remain there. Eventually, after searching through every corner of our bags and our big trunk, they allowed us to go through. Then followed an anxious time until we found the Board of Trade gentleman and the nurses who were to take us under their wing. Anne and I were fortunate because we were put in the charge of an English lady, who made sure that we shared a room in the hospital, being sisters, and also explained our duties clearly and told us to go to her if we were in doubt about anything.

'We are kept busy from morning to night changing beds and mopping floors and carrying trays and bedpans. I confess that I much prefer the trays! And we must always be ready to help the nurses with whatever they might require of us. As Anne says, it is fortunate that we two were raised to be obedient and hard-working, and therefore the daily routine is easier on us than on some of the girls who have been accustomed to an easier life. The Canadians, patients and nurses alike, are very nice people, and they take such a delight in our Scottish accents, so we all get on very well together and have a fairly cheerful time. I believe that Anne may well end up training as a nurse but, for myself, I am not certain that I would wish to do that.

'Although I am settling in happily I do miss Paisley and my family and you, my dear cousin. Promise that you will not forget me and that you will write often. And one day you too will be crossing the sea, and we will meet . . .'

Helen's voice was heard from the front room and Mirren, hauled back in an instant from Canada to Paisley, put the letter down, looked regretfully at her waiting bed, and went to her mother.

'You're looking awful drawn, pet.' Catherine Proctor peered at her niece. 'Are you sickening for something?'

'I'm fine. Just a bit tired.'

'Is Helen sleeping badly?'

'She's scarcely sleeping at all,' Mirren confessed. It was such a relief to have someone to confide in. 'She dozes during the day, just.'

'When you're having to work.'

'Mother can't help that.'

'I know.' Catherine opened a drawer and took out three wrapped parcels, 'Before you go. This is for your Ne'erday, and Helen's and Robbie's. I know Helen won't accept her present if she knows it's from me, so if it comes to it you can say it's from you. And we'll have no thought of you buying anything for us,' she said firmly as she tucked the parcels into Mirren's bag, along with a jar of calves' foot jelly and a bottle of wine, 'for there are too many of us and you've got more than enough to do with your silver.'

Robbie pounced on the parcels when Mirren unpacked them, shaking the one that bore his name, then hefting it in his hands to calculate its weight. 'Can I open it now?'

'You cannot . . . not until Ne'erday.' Like most Scots, the Jarvis family always celebrated New Year rather than Christmas, and any gifts exchanged were opened on Ne'erday morning. 'Give it to me,' Mirren ordered as Robbie rubbed a fingernail gently over the paper, clearly hoping that it might tear and give some indication of its contents. She took it from him and put it under her bed together with the other two, ignoring his grumbling. He might be a man now, but he still had the eagerness of a child.

Ella and Ruby did their best to persuade Mirren to go to the Hogmanay dance in the drill hall. 'It'll be wonderful . . . they have streamers, and a punch-bowl, and every kind of dance from the Dashing White Sergeant to the fox-trot. And at midnight when the bells start ringin' in the New Year, everyone goes round kissin' everyone.' Ella winked. 'If ye're lucky ye can manage tae get more than one kiss from the lad ye might fancy. Ye'd enjoy it. And it's time ye'd a treat.'

'How can I leave my mother?'

'She'd surely not begrudge ye a wee bit of pleasure on Hogmanay,' Ruby protested.

'No, of course not, but it would be no pleasure for me thinking of her on her own at a time like that.'

The other two looked at each other, then Ella suggested, 'Tell one of yer brothers that it's his turn this year.'

'Logan and Belle are always expected to see the New Year in with her father, and Robbie should be free to go out with his friends. One of us has to be with Mother when the bells ring.'

'I don't see why it always has tae be you,' Ella grumbled.

Secretly, Mirren was quite relieved to stay at home, for she was worn out. It was the custom for every corner of a Scottish house to be scrubbed clean on Hogmanay so that it was in pristine condition for the start of the New Year.

Mirren well remembered the resentment she had felt year after year because, even from the days when she was a tiny child scarcely able to toddle across the front room unaided, she was expected to help her mother with the Hogmanay cleaning while her brothers were sent outside, supposedly to get from under their mother's feet, but in actual fact to enjoy themselves while she, as a female, was expected to work.

Now she had it all to do on her own, and as the hands of the front-room clock inched towards midnight and she went into the kitchen to fetch the tray bearing shortbread and to add three filled glasses – sherry for herself and Mrs White, who always came in to listen for the bells ringing, and tonic wine for Helen – she briefly massaged her aching back and looked longingly at the curtains hiding her bed from view.

She herself envied the English their Christmas celebrations, for Hogmanay and Ne'erday could be sad occasions, with older folk tending to look back rather than forward, thinking of happier days and of friends and family long gone. Sure enough, as they waited for the town's church bells to ring in the welcome to 1921, both Helen and Mrs White fell silent, and there were tears in their eyes as they drank to the New Year.

Almost as soon as the bells had stopped ringing, folk would be out on the pavements to work their way round their friends' houses bearing with them the traditional gifts of coal, whisky and black bun. There would be partying until dawn all over the town, but nobody was expected at the Jarvises door. Watching the older women, their faces closed as they grappled with their own thoughts, Mirren remembered with a pang that the last person to come laughing into the house bearing the gifts that traditionally represented wishes for health, wealth and a warm hearth in the New Year had been her brother Crawford, a scant month before he was called into the Army. Agnes had been with him that night, rosy-cheeked and giggly from excitement and the pleasure of being with her man, not to mention the effects of the single unaccustomed drink she had had. They had brought Thomas with them, well wrapped in shawls against the cold night air, bright-eyed and intrigued by the sudden and unexplained change in his usual routine.

Helen, Mirren recalled, had ranted at them for taking the child out so late at night, and Crawford had told her cheerily that since he was soon away for to be a soldier he was determined to go first-footing once, at least, with his own son. The comment had triggered another burst of anger from his mother, who had accused him of spoiling her New Year by reminding her that he was going off to fight and might never come back to her. Agnes had burst into tears, and so had Thomas. Crawford, his good mood destroyed, had turned on his heel and taken his small family home.

The bells began to ring, a great clamour of sound from every church in Paisley, and Mirren, wishing passionately that she had recalled earlier, happier Hogmanay celebrations rather than that one, kissed her mother's cheek.

'Happy New Year to you, Mother.'

'No doubt it'll be the last for me,' Helen returned sourly, 'And mebbe that'll no' be a bad thing.'

14

By the time Mrs White returned to her own flat and Mirren washed her mother and helped her into a night-gown, a few more glasses of tonic wine had mellowed Helen's mood. And made her talkative, which meant that Mirren had to sit by the bed for a while listening to her ramble on about her time as a mill-worker.

'What about your childhood?' she asked when Helen paused to catch her breath. 'You never talk about the games you played, and your friends, and the things you did together.'

'We played just the same games as you did – skipping ropes and spinnin' our peeries, and hopscotch and Bee Baw Babbity. Och, what is there tae say about being a child?' Helen's voice was suddenly crotchety. 'These years are over and done with fast enough.' And she turned the talk back to the mill and the Half-Time School.

Eventually her blue-veined eyelids, fragile as tissue paper, began to flutter and her voice to drift. When the lids finally closed and the memories had been replaced by very faint snores Mirren sat on, listening to the voices of revellers passing by outside and watching her mother's face, grey against the white pillow. Once, Helen had been a slender girl with long fair hair, trying valiantly to keep up with the adventurous cousin who had been her constant companion. Mirren would have given much to know more about the shy child she had seen in the old photograph, but it seemed now that she never would.

As she pulled the quilt more securely over her mother's shoulder, Helen opened her eyes and said sleepily, 'Ye're a good girl, Mirren. I mebbe don't say it as often as I should, but I notice.'

'Yes, Mother. Have a good sleep now.'

'I notice . . .' The last word floated Helen off into sleep like a hand gently pushing a boat into a stream.

In the kitchen Mirren peeped beneath the recess bed where Catherine's Ne'erday gifts, a large parcel from Donald and the few things that she and Robbie had bought for each other and for their mother nestled in the shadows. Together they made quite a respectable showing, and she gave a satisfied little nod before poking the fire into a comfortable glow. Then she drew the best gift of all from beneath her pillow and settled down in a chair with it. Donald's latest letter had been clamouring to be read for the past two weeks but she had refused to allow herself to open it until after the bells, telling herself that reading it then would be like beginning the New Year with him.

It was longer than his usual letters, and more intense. Instead of writing about his daily routine and mentioning towards the end how much he looked forward to the time when they would finally be together, he had, in a most unScottish way, poured out his need for her over some three pages.

'The day when we first started walking out together seems to me now to be so long ago that it belonged to another life, and so does the day I kissed you and held you in my arms before leaving Scotland. Another year is about to begin and I don't want it to end with us still apart, Mirren. I am in a position at last to leave my parents' house and find somewhere for us to live together as man and wife. I have good friends here, all looking forward to meeting my wife-to-be. All I lack is you, and I must confess that I cannot bear to wait much longer. I know that your mother is unwell, but there are others in the family who could and must care for her. You have done more than your fair share and now it is my turn . . . our turn. Please, if you still care for me, write and tell me that you have booked your passage to America and will soon be here by my side where you belong.'

Mirren dried her wet cheeks then wept again as she re-read the letter several times more. The pain in it, and her own pain, wrenched at her heart. She felt more keenly than ever before that she was being torn in two. When she had cried herself dry, she kissed each page of the letter before folding it away and tucking it beneath her pillow again. Then she washed her face and put more coal on the fire so that the place would be warm for Robbie when he got home.

She started working on some mending, then jerked awake, startled, when her brother came in, flushed and happy and slightly unsteady on his feet.

'Still up?' He bent to kiss her, his breath rich with alcohol fumes. 'Happy Ne'erday, Mirren.'

'Happy Ne'erday. D'you want some tea?'

He shook his head, then winked and dragged a small bottle from his coat pocket. 'I saved a night-cap for myself. There's enough tae do us both.'

'You have it, I don't want any.'

'Yes ye do.' He fetched the wine glasses she had rinsed and left on the draining board, poured a minute quantity of whisky into each, and topped it up with water. 'Here's tae us, you and me.'

'I hope . . .' The whisky must have been cheap, raw stuff, for even though most of the drink consisted of water, it made her cough and choke and brought tears to her eyes. 'I hope this is the best year you've ever known, Robbie,' she said when she got the use of her voice back again.

'I doubt it, but there's no harm in wishing.' He was suddenly serious, staring down into his empty glass.

'That's all that folk like us have – the right tae wish for better things. They've not found a way of takin' that from us yet.' Then, with a sudden change of mood, he jumped to his feet and fumbled in the pocket of his coat. 'I near forgot . . . I've somethin' for ye.'

'For me?'

'Aye. This is from Joe.'

She looked in dismay at the book in her hands. '*Martin Chuzzlewit*. But when I gave the last one to you I said to tell him that I didn't have time to read any more.'

'He says there's no hurry. And he wishes ye a happy Ne'erday.' He was back in his chair and now he wriggled his backside more firmly into the seat and stretched his legs across the front of the fire to soak up extra heat, holding his glass up to the light and sighing contentedly. 'That's Joe for ye: generous tae a fault.'

When the three of them unwrapped their gifts in the morning Robbie was happy with the sweater Mirren had knitted for him, and Helen delighted with her warm bed-jacket. She herself, unable to go out to the shops, gave her son and daughter money from her 'pension handbag'.

Robbie presented his mother with a small bottle of lavender water and for Mirren he had a necklace of blue beads. 'I got them because they're the same colour as yer eyes,' he said bashfully when she enthused over them.

'Robbie, they're beautiful! But how did you . . . ?' She knew that he had very little spending money.

'Ye're not supposed tae ask where the money comes from for gifts,' he told her firmly, adding, 'And ye're not the only one good at managin' it.'

On the previous Sunday Agnes had handed Mirren a large tin of shortbread for the family and Thomas had brought a wrapped picture which, he informed his grandmother proudly, he had made all by himself. Now, unwrapping it, Helen looked perplexed.

'What d'you think it is?'

'A building?' Robbie guessed through a mouthful of shortbread, although it was only mid-morning. 'A big grey building in among some funny-looking trees. Only it doesnae have any windows in it.'

'A jail, mebbe?' Helen puzzled.

'Why would the bairn draw a picture of a jail, Mother?' Robbie asked.

'No, it's an elephant. See, there's its trunk.' Mirren pointed. 'And these are palm trees. D'you not mind a few Sundays ago when he brought his new schoolbook and read us a story about elephants in Africa? There were pictures in the book.'

Catherine Proctor's gifts, a hand-knitted scarf and gloves for Robbie, a lovely blouse for Mirren and a filmy scarf in pretty pastel shades for Helen, had to be passed off as extra gifts that Mirren had managed to buy.

'I hate having to lie,' she fretted afterwards to Robbie, who shrugged and said, 'It's a lot easier than tellin' the truth at times.'

Donald's parcel had arrived two weeks earlier and Mirren had been hard put not to open it early. Now she fetched it from below her bed and unwrapped it to reveal a colourful patchwork quilt for Helen, a handsome pair of mother-of-pearl cufflinks for Robbie and, for her, a box containing a pair of tortoiseshell combs studded with glittering stones.

'Put them on,' Robbie ordered as she ran her fingers over them, bedazzled by their beauty.

'They're too nice to wear just now. I'll keep them for when I go to America.'

'Away! They're meant for wearin' – and anyway, do Mother and me not deserve tae see them as much as Donald does?'

Mirren obediently unpinned her long fair hair from its usual bun on the back of her neck and caught it back with the jewelled combs. 'There. What d'you think?' she asked self-consciously.

Robbie's eyes widened, then he joked, 'If ye werenae my own sister I'd ask ye tae walk out with me. You should always wear yer hair like that, it makes ye look younger.'

'But it's not practical. Mother . . . ?' Mirren, admiring herself in Helen's hand mirror, turned her head this way and that to let the light flash on the paste stones in the combs.

'They're very pretty,' her mother said, then, dismissively, 'But you're right, they're not practical at all.'

Mrs White, who had no family save a married daughter who lived in England and never came North or invited her mother to visit, came across the landing later for her Ne-erday dinner, bringing with her a small chicken and a home-made clootie dumpling. In the evening Logan and Belle arrived bearing their gifts – a bottle of sherry and an enormous tin of biscuits.

As usually happened on Ne'erday they were bilious from over-eating and irritable after spending an entire day with Belle's father, a sharp-tempered and difficult old man. Belle eyed the new combs enviously and remarked that it must be nice to have a young man with so much money to throw around. Logan, taking her comment as criticism, flushed and declared that, speaking for himself, he considered glittery trinkets to be ostentatious and vulgar.

'Pay no heed tae these two,' Robbie comforted when he went through to the kitchen to find his sister gazing anxiously into the mirror and fingering the combs. 'And don't you take them out . . . I know fine that that's what you're thinkin' of doin'.'

'They're too bright for Paisley.'

'The town needs a bit of brightenin', and Belle and Logan are just jealous. You didnae tell me,' he went on with a touch of jealousy himself, 'that Mother had sent you out tae buy gifts for them.'

'I never thought to mention it,' Mirren said evasively. 'She gave us money, and I'd as soon have that as a gift just now.'

Her brother snorted. 'What she gave us wouldn't have covered the bottle of whisky and the bonny brooch they got. It seems tae me that in this family it's the ones that are close at hand and doin' all the work that get the least appreciation.'

Fortunately the kettle came to the boil just then and there was no time for any more talk.

'It's funny how the New Year never feels any different from the old one,' Ella said as the women shed their shoes and donned their calico aprons in the twisting department on the following morning.

'Ye'd know the difference, hen, if ye'd a man like mine.' Libby McDaid scratched her greying head and yawned widely. 'He sees Hogmanay and Ne'erday as an excuse tae fill the house with his pals . . . and who's expected tae find food for them tae mop up the drink? Then, when they finally went off down the stair, his snorin' kept me awake for the rest of the night. I'm glad tae be back at work for a rest!'

To young Ethel's delight another girl was starting work that morning, replacing her as the baby of the flat. As always, Mirren's heart went out to the poor child, bewildered by the strangers surrounding her, afraid of the huge machines and of making a fool of herself, and still pale and shaken from the obligatory visit to the first-aid room to undergo a head examination. Nobody liked that ritual.

'Checked ye for nits, then, have they?' Libby boomed at her, and the girl's pale face flushed crimson.

'We've never had head-lice in our family,' she said in a frightened peep of a voice. 'My mother would never have allowed it.' Humiliated tears glistened in her eyes. 'If she knew . . .'

'Ach, it's nothin' personal, pet,' Libby assured her cheerfully. 'They do that tae all the new starts. It's no' for our sakes, ye understand, it's for the machinery. The machines in here are treated like precious bairns, and the gaffers cannae afford tae let them catch nits off any of us.'

The girl's eyes widened. 'Can machines get lice?'

'Of course they can, and they suffer terrible when that happens, for they havenae got fingernails like us. The poor things go daft tryin' tae scratch themselves.' Libby roared with laughter at her own joke and went off to her machines, while Ethel led the newcomer officiously to where a large blackboard bearing the department's rules stood in one of the window recesses. The girl's first task would be to study the rules until she could repeat them, without pause or error, to the Mistress. After that she would be given her calico apron and one of the twiners would be appointed to train her.

'The Hogmanay dance was grand,' Ella murmured as she and Mirren made their way to their allotted machines. 'Ye'd have enjoyed yerself.'

'Did you click?'

Ella shrugged. 'I could've had my pick of the lads, but you know me, I don't believe in steady sweethearts. Mind you, there was one . . .' Then she caught the Mistress's eye, and hurried to her own machines.

As soon as she opened the door and heard the strange sounds, half-snoring, half-grunting, from the front room, Mirren knew that something was terribly wrong.

'Mother?' She dropped the basket of messages she had brought with her and raced into the room to find Helen sprawled across her bed, her head resting uncomfortably on the edge of the bedside table, breathing noisily through a slack, gaping mouth. When Mirren, after a struggle, managed to hoist her mother back onto her pillow she saw that her face was flushed darkly.

'Mother!'

Helen gave no indication that she had heard. Even though she was now lying back on her pillow, the noisy breathing continued. A line of spittle ran from one corner of her mouth to her chin and her eyes were half-open.

'Oh no . . . oh no . . .' Mirren kept whimpering as she ran from the house. Robbie was on his way up the final flight of stairs, whistling. 'Thank God you're home!' She caught at his jacket, almost lifting him bodily up the final tread. 'I think Mother's had a seizure. Run to the doctor's and tell him to come at once!'

Without waiting for a reaction she sped back into the kitchen to dampen a clean towel, knowing that whatever her condition, her mother would want to look as decent and respectable as possible for the doctor's visit. As she bathed Helen's face she noticed that one side seemed to have slumped downwards from her eyebrow to the corner of her mouth, as though her features had been melted then re-set.

'Your mother's had an apoplectic seizure, my dear,' the doctor said gently when he had completed his examination.

'Is it . . . Will she recover?'

'There's no way of knowing at the moment. We must just keep her warm and comfortable and hope for the best.' She could tell by his expression that he did not expect the outcome to be favourable.

Catherine Proctor was on the doorstep within the hour. 'Paisley's still a small community, for all that it's a big town,' she said, sweeping past Robbie and into the house. 'I've come to help with nursing Helen.'

'But she . . .'

'Don't bother telling me that she wouldn't like it, Mirren. She's in no fit state to know who's with her, and you two can't be expected to manage on your own at a time like this.' Catherine went into the front room and stood looking down at Helen for a long moment. When she glanced up again tears shone in her eyes and on her cheeks. 'We never thought when we were bairns together that it would come to this,' she said, with a catch in her throat. 'And the New Year not a week old.'

Helen lay for three days without regaining consciousness. Sometimes her eyes opened and even followed movement in the room, but she seemed to be unaware of what was being said when anyone spoke to her.

'She's not really awake,' Mirren said to Robbie. 'If she was, she'd be angry to see Aunt Catherine tending to her, but she doesn't recognise any of us. She's not the same person. It's as if her eyes are windows in an empty house.'

'She's not an empty house, she's our mother!' he told her fiercely. Clearly he had always assumed that even though his mother was an invalid there was never any danger of her dying. Now that the possibility was with them, filling the air around them and clouding their futures, he found it hard to cope with the situation. After his first visit to the front room he had refused to return and Catherine advised Mirren against trying to persuade him.

'Best leave him to remember his mother in his own way. She knows nothing about it, and if she gets better you'll find that he'll more than make up for not seeing her just now,' she said. And she supported Agnes, too, when she refused to give in to Logan's demands that little Thomas should be brought to his grandmother's bedside. 'It could scare the wee laddie into convulsions, seeing his grandma like that. And that'll not do Agnes much good in her condition.'

'Mother would want to see Thomas more than she'd want tae see Mrs Proctor,' Logan ranted at Mirren, who was past caring.

'Aunt Catherine's been a godsend to me the past few days, Logan. I'd as soon listen to her as to anyone else.'

'Then let it be on your own conscience, for I despair of you,' he snapped back at her and stormed from the house.

Even now he and Belle were of little use, claiming that they were both needed in the shop. It was Catherine who, with Mrs White's help, cared for Helen during the day so that Mirren and Robbie could continue to go to work. For the first time in years Mirren knew the luxury of coming home to find a cooked meal waiting on the table for her, and the house clean and neat.

'There's plenty at home to look after my house and see to James,' Catherine said placidly when Mirren tried to thank her. 'And it means a lot to me to be able to help Helen in her time of need. It helps me to feel that I'm making up for all those daft wasted years when we were strangers to each other.'

'Aunt Catherine, what happened between you?'

Catherine hesitated, then shrugged. 'I don't suppose there's any harm in telling you now, lassie. It was one of those daft wee misunderstandings. Your parents met each other at a dancing class I taught, but the pity of it was that Helen was never much of a dancer, while Peter was very good at it.'

'My father liked dancing?' Mirren found it hard to believe that the quiet, withdrawn man she had known could ever have given a good account of himself on a dance floor.

'Oh yes, he'd a grand sense of movement and he loved the dancing. When Helen stopped attending they went on walking out together, for Peter worshipped her . . . not that she seemed to realise it. He kept on with his dancing, though, because of his fondness for it. He'd always the hope that he'd be able to encourage Helen to take it up again, but instead she got it into her head that he only stayed at the class because he'd taken a fancy to me.'

'Had he?' Mirren, remembering the vivacious girl in

the old photograph, wouldn't have been surprised if he had.

Catherine, filling in a spare moment by cleaning cutlery, rubbed hard at a fork. 'No, of course not, it was always Helen he wanted and anyway, I was walking out with my James. But she never had much faith in herself – it was the way she was raised. Your grandparents never praised her for anything, though they were always fast enough when it came to criticism. So one day Helen told poor Peter that he had to choose between her and his dancing, and of course he gave it up there and then. He never danced again, but even when we were both wed, Helen would have no more to do with me.' She put the fork down. 'Sometimes when folk get an idea in their heads it can be impossible to get it out ag—'

She stopped, lifting her head to listen. Mirren did the same, but by the time she had registered the sudden silence in the flat, Catherine was out of her chair and on her way into the front room. When Mirren got there her aunt was by the bed, holding one of Helen's hands in her own.

'Mother?'

Gently, Catherine smoothed the hair back from Helen's forehead then laid her hand down.

'Sit here by her, lassie, and say your farewells while I make us a cup of tea.'

Mirren let her aunt push her gently into the bedside chair. When she took her mother's hand it lay in hers, inert but warm. It was hard to believe that Helen wasn't just sleeping. 'The doctor . . . ?' she heard herself say from far away.

'After we've had our tea,' Catherine told her. 'She's in no hurry for him now, God rest her.'

15

'How much money did Mother leave?' Logan asked bluntly when he and Belle came into the kitchen after paying their respects to the silent figure on the front-room bed.

'How should we know?' Robbie's voice was sharp but the hand he laid on Mirren's shoulder was gentle.

'There's a funeral tae be arranged and paid for. We have tae know how much money we can spend on it.'

Mirren felt her brother's fingers tightening. 'She always put her pension money in the black handbag down by the side of the bed,' she said swiftly, unable to face a row. 'The last payment was made just before she took ill.'

'How much is in it?'

'I don't know, I never looked in it myself.'

'I'll fetch it while you make some tea, Mirren. Belle's fair worn out by grief.'

'So's Mirren,' Robbie called after his brother. 'I'll make the tea.'

When Logan opened the bag his eyes bulged. 'Look at this!' He drew a handful of notes from the bag's roomy interior and went to the table to count them. Belle, her grief forgotten, leaned on his shoulder.

'Seventy-four pounds, four shillings and ninepence halfpenny! Tae think,' Logan said passionately, 'of the times when Belle and me were in sore need of help and there she was, sittin' on all that money and not sayin' a word about it.'

'It was for her old age,' Mirren sprang to her mother's defence, while Robbie chimed in, 'She didnae give us any of it either, if that's what you're thinkin'.'

'Why would you have needed it?' Logan wanted to know. 'You two were still livin' comfortably in the family home while I was havin' tae deal with all the responsibilities and expenses that marriage brings. I cannae believe that Mother withheld knowledge of that money from me!' He gathered it up and stowed it away in an inner pocket. 'At least we'll not be out of pocket over the funeral.'

'The nerve of him!' Robbie exploded when his brother and sister-in-law had gone home. 'Ye can be quite certain we'll not see a penny of whatever's left over once he's paid the funeral expenses.'

'It doesn't matter,' Mirren said wearily. 'It'll all be meant for him anyway, as Mother's oldest son, and at least he's going tae arrange the funeral. I don't think I could bear to have to do that.'

Helen Jarvis was buried in Broomlands Cemetery, not far from her home. Mirren had fully expected that only the immediate family would attend the funeral, but to her surprise a fair number of people were waiting to pay their last respects when she and her brothers and Belle arrived at the cemetery. Vanni and Mrs White were there, together with the entire Proctor family, and she was startled to see Joe Hepburn among the group waiting by the grave. Despite the bitter cold of the January day, Agnes and Bob had brought young Thomas, wide-eyed and subdued in his new black clothes.

'Bob thinks he's too young for funerals but tae my mind it's only right that he should represent his father,' Agnes whispered to Mirren as they gathered at the graveside. 'I'll not have him sayin' when he grows up that I kept him from payin' his respects tae his granny.'

'Mother and Crawford would both have appreciated that, Agnes.'

'I'm not so sure they'd appreciate . . . this.' Agnes bit her lip as she glanced down at her rounded belly. 'Ye'd think I was further on than five month, but I was like this with Thomas too. I cannae help it.'

'It's not as if these folk are family,' Logan said under his breath as they all left the cemetery and began the short walk to the Martyr's Memorial Church hall, hired for the funeral tea.

'Vanni's been kind to us and Aunt Catherine Proctor was Mother's full cousin. She helped us a lot during those last few days.'

'Aunt Catherine, is it?' He gave her a sidelong glance. 'You sound tae be well in with that lot already.'

'Grace Proctor's been my best friend since we were at school together. We didn't even know we were cousins then.'

'Hmphh. And there's Agnes, flaunting herself before everyone. Ye'd have thought she'd've had the decency tae stay at home. Funerals arenae the place for women, specially when they're in . . . her condition. And with her new man too!'

'Bob brought Agnes and Thomas to pay their last respects to Mother, and as for flaunting herself, the poor lassie's almost walking all doubled up, trying to hide her condition.' Mirren didn't want to quarrel with her brother today of all days, but it was hard to keep her temper. 'Not that there should be any need for her to be ashamed, for there's nothing wrong with a respectably married woman being in the family way,' she added tartly, and Logan grunted, then hurried ahead to join his wife and father-in-law.

In common with many West of Scotland men, the Jarvises were all under six feet in height, which meant that Logan was dwarfed by his wife's exceptionally tall father, still erect and burly in late middle age. Now that she had met him, Mirren could understand why her brother and sister-in-law were in such awe of Fergus Lamont. His shock of white hair surmounted a strong face with hooded eyes and a hard mouth that looked as though its owner always got in the final word. His handshake when Logan introduced them had almost crushed her fingers, and his lips had scarcely moved as he said, 'It comes tae us all' – the only words he was to speak to her all day.

'Are you all right?' Robbie arrived by her side.

'I'll be glad when it's all over and we can get back home.'

'I don't know why Logan and Belle had tae hire the church hall and turn the day intae a circus.'

'It's the done thing, Robbie.'

'Funeral teas are meant tae be for folk who've had tae travel long distances tae attend the burial,' he pointed out. 'Since everyone here lives in the town there's little sense in feedin' them before they set off for home.'

'Mother would have wanted everything done properly.' It was true what folk said, Mirren thought wearily. No matter how carefully any funeral was planned, someone was sure to find fault.

In the church hall Logan and Belle set themselves up as the host and hostess for the occasion and Mirren was more than happy to leave them to it. A row of trestle tables held plates of sandwiches, biscuits and cakes, with teacups waiting in a prim, somehow subdued cluster at one end. Most of the guests filled their plates with sandwiches, then scurried to the chairs set around the hall's perimeter, where they balanced plates and saucers with difficulty. A few wandered restlessly, as though in search of a way out.

'I was sorry to hear of your l-loss.' Joe Hepburn appeared before Mirren.

'Thank you.'

'Losing a m-mother is like bein' cast adrift in a boat without a c-compass.'

She stared at him for a moment, startled by his perception. He had put her own sense of bewildered helplessness into words that she would never have considered. But he was quite right.

'Bob told me that your own mother died of the influenza just before the end of the Great War.'

'That's what it s-said on her death certificate. But in truth it was a lifetime of hard work and not enough nourishment that k-killed her. If the doctors had any courage they'd write that fact on the death certificates of most working c-class folk.'

Mirren, suddenly sure that she was about to hear a political speech, shot an anguished glance past his right sleeve, which was swathed in the black armband he had donned for her mother. Fortunately she caught Catherine Proctor's eye, and her aunt detached herself from the group she had been talking to and came over.

'Can I have a wee word with you, Mirren?' she asked, then when Joe, with a nod to them both, moved away, 'Don't tell me he was pestering you?'

'Just starting one of his lectures on the rights of the working classes.'

'Well meant, but even so this isn't the time or the place.'

'I wish Robbie wasn't so friendly with him, Aunt Catherine. He's sure to get into trouble if he goes around with firebrands like Joe Hepburn.'

Catherine led her to a seat. 'Stop fretting over Robbie and start thinking of yourself for once. I hope you've written to your young man to tell him that you'll be joining him soon.'

'I can't do that yet,' Mirren protested, while thoughts of Donald's impassioned Christmas letter swam to the surface of her mind. 'It would be unseemly.'

'Oh, tut! I've never seen the sense in periods of mourning for those who've gone before us. Now that poor Helen has no more need of your kindness, you must think of yourself . . . and your sweetheart. You've kept him waiting long enough.'

'What would people say?'

'What does that matter to you, since they'll be here in Paisley and you'll be in America? Even the Paisley gossips can't clack loud enough to be heard that distance away. Write to him,' Catherine said firmly.

Logan and Belle arrived the following evening to see to Helen's few possessions. While his wife rifled through the few clothes in the cupboard, Logan reached under his mother's bed and dragged out the old suitcase that had always housed the family papers, spreading its contents across the stripped and empty bed where Helen Jarvis had been forced to spend her final years.

First came the family's marriage, birth and death certificates, then every letter that Logan and Crawford had sent to their mother during the Great War. Beneath them, at the bottom of the suitcase, lay an envelope with 'Last Will and Testament of Helen Louisa Jarvis' on it in Helen's best writing.

'Ye didnae tell me that she'd made a will, Mirren.'

'I didn't know. Did you, Robbie?'

He shook his head as Logan ripped the envelope open and dragged out the single sheet of paper it held. He turned white then red as he read it.

'This is a nonsense!' he exploded, then, to Mirren, 'It's all your doin'! You took advantage of my mother when she was too sick tae think straight!'

'Logan . . . ?'

'"Everythin' that I own tae my daughter Mirren Jarvis, in gratitude for all she has done for me,"' Logan read out, his voice thick with rage. 'Everythin'!'

'That means this flat and everythin' in it,' Robbie said. Most folk in Paisley lived in rented accommodation, but Peter Jarvis had taken the unusual step of buying his flat in order, he always said, to ensure that if anything happened to him, his widow and family would have a roof over their heads.

'Let me see.' Belle snatched the paper from him and scanned it. 'It's a trick. It'll not stand up in law!'

'It's signed and witnessed,' Robbie pointed out, reading over her shoulder. 'Mrs White's signed it, and an Albert R. Erskine. Who's that?'

'The clerk from the mill,' Mirren said through stiff lips. 'The man who brought her pension every month.'

'What did she mean, in gratitude for all you've done for her?' Belle wanted to know. 'What did you do for her that we didn't?'

'Cooked and washed for her. Changed her bed and emptied her chamber pot and sat up at nights with her,' Robbie said. 'When did ye last empty my mother's pot, Belle?'

'You mind yer tongue!' Logan snapped, while his wife gasped and put a hand to her throat. 'Mirren only did what any unmarried daughter would be expected tae do. We did just as much for Mother in our own way. And much good it did us!' he ended bitterly.

'I didn't know folk looked after their own just for gain,' Robbie said mildly. 'And here was me thinkin' you visited every Sunday out of affection.'

Logan ignored him. 'This . . .' he had stuffed the will back into its envelope; now he shook it in Mirren's face, 'is goin' tae the lawyer's first thing in the mornin'. He'll soon tell us if it's worth the paper it's written on!'

'I'll meet you outside his office just before it opens and we'll go in together,' Robbie said as his brother, followed by Belle, stormed through to the front bedroom to fetch his hat and coat.

'And you can just sort through the clothes yourself,' was Belle's parting shot to Mirren as she followed her husband out of the flat. 'Since it seems that you own them lock, stock and barrel!'

'It's at times like this that ye know what folk really

think,' Robbie said as the door slammed. 'They didnae even wait for a drink of tea.' He steered Mirren into the kitchen, where he filled two cups with tea that had been waiting so long by the fire that it was stewed, then added milk and plenty of sugar before handing one over. 'Sit down and drink that.'

'But Robbie . . .'

'Just drink yer tea and let's take a minute tae think things over.'

By the time she had downed half a cupful, Mirren's racing pulse had slowed and her mind was clearing. 'Why would Mother leave everything to me and not to Logan, or between the three of us?'

'Because you were the one who did most for her.'

'Mebbe the will's not legal. Mebbe everything'll go to Logan, or be divided three ways.'

'That's why I said I'd meet Logan at the lawyer's office tomorrow. I want tae hear for myself what the man's got tae say.'

'You can't take time off your work, Robbie, you've not long started there.'

'I'll go along early tae Mr Field's house and explain that it's a legal matter concernin' my mother. He'll surely let me go in an hour late for once.' Mirren had drained her cup and was rinsing it at the sink when Robbie's hand reached over her shoulder and took it from her. 'Leave it be for now, we're goin' tae ask Mrs White about that signature.'

'At this time of night?'

'We'll neither of us sleep until we know.'

When Mrs White finally came to her door she was wearing a heavy coat over her night-gown and her hair was in paper curlers. Her little dog yapped up at the visitors from beneath the uneven hem of the gown.

'We're sorry tae disturb ye so late at night,' Robbie apologised, 'but we need tae ask ye . . .'

'. . . about the bit of paper I signed for yer mam,' the old woman finished the sentence for him, turning to shuffle back into the gloom of her flat. 'Come in and shut the door. The night air's cruel, and me and Scrap don't want tae catch our deaths of cold.'

Her kitchen was crammed with a lifetime's collection of furniture and ornaments, and smelled of a mixture of things . . . stewed tea, camphor, damp clothes hanging on the ceiling pulley to dry, and old dog. Among the many items on the dresser Mirren recognised two large curved and fluted rose-pink shells and a huge ostrich egg on a stand, both brought back to Scotland years before by the long-dead Mr White, a seaman. As a child, visiting Mrs White with her mother, Mirren had been fascinated with these strange objects. She had never been allowed to touch the fragile egg, but her palms still recalled the cool hardness of the shells.

'It was a month or so back, not long before the poor soul's seizure.' Mrs White settled herself into her fireside chair while her visitors chose to stand. The dog collapsed on the rug, its head on the old woman's slippered foot. 'Helen got me tae call in at the lawyer's office when I was out gettin' my messages, tae ask him tae visit her at a particular time that afternoon. When he came, he called me across the landin' tae sign somethin'. The man from the mill was there as well. That's all I know, as I told your Logan.'

'Logan was here?'

'Not half an hour ago. That's how I knew what you were goin' tae ask me. They were just in and out of the place, him and that wife of his.' Mrs White's round wrinkled face, topped by the curlers, looked like an over-decorated pudding. 'They were in an awful hurry. And in a right tid as well, the both of them.'

'There ye are,' Robbie said as they returned to their own flat. 'I was right – everything's legal and there's nothin' Logan can do about it.'

'It doesn't seem fair.'

'Why not? It's true what I said tae Belle. Ye did everythin' for Mam . . . and for me. You even put more of yer wages intae payin' the rent and buyin' the food than ye should have . . .' The final words were blurred by a yawn. 'Now go tae yer bed and let me do the same. We've both got things tae see tae in the mornin'.'

'I trust,' Belle said aggressively, 'that Logan might at least be allowed to choose a keepsake to remember his mother by.' The lawyer had pointed out that Helen's will, which was legal, covered everything, including her clothing and the furniture.

'Of course, Logan, you must choose something,' Mirren hastened to assure her brother, who said promptly, 'In that case I'll have the chiffonier-sideboard in the front room.'

'The chiffonier-sideboard?' Astonishment brought Robbie right out of his chair. 'I'd scarce call a big piece of furniture like that a keepsake!'

'It has sentimental value tae me.' Logan's face, already filling out and beginning to show the first touch of middle age, though he was only in his late twenties, began to flush dangerously and Mirren hurriedly assured him that he was welcome to the chiffonier-sideboard if he wished it.

'I'll arrange tae have it picked up tomorrow evenin', then.'

'Fine.' Robbie smiled sweetly at his brother, though his grey eyes were angry. 'We'll empty it out tonight and have it all ready for you.'

'And I,' Belle put in, 'would like to have her blue enamel pendant with the pretty stones around it.'

'I'll fetch it,' Mirren said swiftly, before Robbie could object.

'Ye realise that this is probably worth a fair bit of money?' Robbie asked that evening as he helped Mirren to empty the chiffonier-sideboard. 'He'll probably have it sold within the month.'

'He can do what he wants with it. I can't take it to America with me, and I doubt if you'll want it.'

'No, but ye could have sold it yerself.'

'I've already done well . . . better than I should have,' Mirren fretted.

'Ach, be quiet, woman. Speakin' for myself, I don't believe in inheritance. That's what's wrong with this country – far too many of the bigwigs are daft gowks who'd be nobodies if it wasnae for the money they inherited. Folk should work for what they get instead of just collecting it from rich relatives. And they should be paid what they're worth, too.'

'Is that what Joe Hepburn thinks?'

'It's what I think . . . and so do you, surely.'

'I suppose I do,' she admitted, adding at once, 'That's why I don't feel right about Mother's inheritance.'

'I've told ye, Mirren, you earned every penny of that money. The people I'm talking about did nothin' but sit on their fat arses expectin' everyone else tae run after them.' Robbie ran a hand down a carved spindle which, with its partner on the other side of the sideboard, supported a small bookshelf. 'It's bonny, isn't it? It's strange how ye take somethin' for granted just because ye grew up with it. I've never taken a good look at this piece before.'

'I'll fetch the polish. It deserves to look its best when it leaves.' When Mirren came back she found Robbie glancing through the pile of items they had removed from the chiffonier-sideboard.

'Where are ye goin' tae put all this stuff?'

'It'll have to go. Mother scarcely used any of those tablecloths and traycloths.'

'And the papers from the drawer.' He lifted a handful. 'It looks as though most of them are recipes and household hints cut out of newspapers. Here's a picture – two right bonny wee lassies. I wonder who they were?'

'That's Mother,' Mirren said round a lump that had suddenly appeared in her throat, 'and that's Aunt Catherine Proctor.'

'Mother?' She had taken the photograph from Robbie and now he leaned on her shoulder to take another look. 'How d'ye know that?'

'Aunt Catherine gave me a copy of the same photograph not long ago. I wanted to show it to Mother, but I thought it might anger her. Wait till I tell Aunt Catherine,' Mirren said as she looked down at the two young faces, one cheerfully confident and the other with a tentative smile trembling on her lips, 'that Mother cared enough to keep her copy too.'

'Have ye written to Donald yet?' Robbie asked, losing interest in the photograph.

'Not yet.' Mirren polished vigorously. 'It seems too soon after the funeral.'

'Too soon? Ye've been apart for a long time and if ye've got any thought of stayin' here for my sake, ye can just forget it. I can manage fine.'

She rested for a moment, sitting back on her haunches. 'But I'd like to see you settled first. Where'll you live, Robbie?'

'Not here, anyway. I'd not want tae stay on in the family house once you go. I'll find somewhere easily enough.'

'Is there no lassie who might share this house with you one day?' Robbie had brought girls to the house once or twice, but not since his mother's illness had progressed. Now he shrugged the question off.

'I'm not interested in courting just now. I've got other interests.'

'When you meet the right one you'll not want to do anything but court her.'

'Mebbe. But we werenae talkin' about me,' he reminded her. 'We were talkin' about you. Think of yerself for once and write tae Donald tonight.'

It was her turn to say, 'Mebbe,' but he was having none of it.

'Tonight, Mirren. There's a new life waiting for ye, and a man who can look after you the way ye deserve.'

'Tonight, then.' While she longed to be with Donald, she knew that it would be hard to leave her young brother. He had been as steady as a rock during the past week, and she doubted if she would have managed to cope with everything if he had not been there.

'Robbie,' she said on a sudden whim. 'Why don't you come to America too?'

'Me? What would I do there?'

'I'll ask Donald if he could find work for you. You're a time-served engineer, trained in Scotland. Surely America can do with folk like you? We could both start a new life.' She wondered why she hadn't thought of it before. If he agreed, and if Donald could find work for him, she wouldn't have to leave Robbie behind after all. And, better still, he would be removed once and for all from Joe Hepburn's influence.

'I'd need tae have a good think about it. But there'd be no harm in askin' Donald when ye write,' Robbie said, interest beginning to glow in his eyes.

16

'By God and it's a bitter wind the day,' one of the women said as the hoist rose slowly towards the twisting department. 'There's snow on the way.'

'Call this cold weather?' Libby McDaid jeered. 'Ye should try a winter in Russia.' Libby had spent almost five years in Coats' St Petersburg mills, helping to train local workers. Once she had shown Mirren her certificate of agreement, in which the company had undertaken to pay her travel expenses and provide free lodgings in Russia as well as 'fire and light' and a wage of three pounds per fifty-seven-hour working week. The Paisley girls had been lodged in a flat with a chaperone and a young maid who, to Libby's great sorrow, had eaten their pet goldfish.

'Are they all heathens in Russia?' Mirren had asked, horrified by the story.

'No, hen, just hungry sometimes. The wage was good,' added Libby, who had started work in the mills at thirteen years of age, attending the Half-Time School and being paid two shillings a fortnight to sweep floors. 'My ma got fifteen shillin' of my pay every week while I was away, and I got thirty shillin' tae myself. And the mill here put the other fifteen shillin' intae the bank, so when I came home tae marry wi' my sweetheart I was quite a catch in more ways than the usual.' She winked and nudged Mirren in the ribs.

Although she had received only a basic education, Libby possessed a natural talent for words and her descriptions of life in St Petersburg, holidays in Finland and the wild Cossacks who sometimes rode their horses right into Mill property in search of young women were vivid. On more than one occasion the manager had been forced to lock Libby and the other Paisley workers in his office to keep them safe from the marauding horsemen.

What Libby casually referred to now as 'the Russian shift' came to a sudden end in 1917 when Russia was torn asunder by revolution. Summoned home, Libby and the others had endured a ten-day journey from Moscow to Archangel in an unheated train in the dead of winter, followed by a long, terrifying walk across an ice-bound harbour. After being hauled like bales of cargo up the side of the ship waiting to take them to freedom, they had had to endure weeks of anxiety as the ship made one detour after another to avoid packs of German U-boats. When they finally arrived in Paisley, Libby, her Scottish accent unaltered by the years abroad – she had worked for two years in the Italian mills in Pisa before going to Russia – had settled down again as though she had been no further away from them than her own home in King Street.

It began to snow in mid-afternoon and by the time Mirren got home her jacket and the scarf wound round her head were white with snow as well as with oose. The first thing she saw was a letter on the doormat. She pounced on it, and a ripple of excitement ran through her as she saw that it was from Donald.

She set it up on the narrow wooden ledge where she kept her clothes brush so that she could devour it with her eyes as she spread out the old sheeting on the floor. Her hands trembled with excitement as she brushed the worst of the cotton, wet with melting snow, from her jacket and skirt. Once or twice in her haste the brush slid from her grasp and had to be retrieved from a dark corner of the tiny lobby.

Since her mother's death she had systematically sorted out all her possessions and decided what she would take, and she was now ready to leave whenever Donald sent for her. All that was needed now, she thought as she hung her coat up, was a promise of work for Robbie.

Normally she would have taken the cloth down to the back court to be shaken out over the dustbins, but tonight she folded it carefully to keep the caddis inside, then hurried into the kitchen with the letter. Before opening it she put a match to the fire she had carefully laid that morning. It wasn't the chill in the air that made her shake so badly that she had difficulty in slitting the envelope open, but the knowledge that the letter within represented a doorway leading to her future. Although she had thought that it would be pleasant to have some time to herself at last, she felt lonely and unsettled on those evenings when she was at home and Robbie was out. She kept thinking that she heard her mother calling, and on more than one occasion she had caught herself opening the front-room door quietly to look in on the bed, which was being used to store towels and linen, now that the chiffonier-sideboard had gone to Logan and Belle. It was time, she knew, to say goodbye to one life and start out on the journey to another.

When she had finally released the single sheet of paper she smoothed it out and settled down to read it.

Donald was sorry, more sorry than he could ever say in a letter, but he was no longer certain of his feelings for Mirren. 'We have been apart for so long now and we have both changed,' he wrote. 'At times it is as though the life where we knew and loved each other was lived by someone else, not the person I have become since arriving in America.' Then came the worst part of the brief letter. 'The truth is that I have become very friendly with an American girl and as a result I am confused as to my true feelings. If you had only been able to leave Scotland a few months ago, when as you remember I

begged you to, then things might have been different
for us both. I needed you so much then, Mirren, and I
felt that your presence would have resolved the turmoil
I was experiencing. But you had other commitments and
I have now decided that it would be wrong of me to ask
you to leave your family and make the journey here, only
to discover that we had indeed grown too far apart from
each other for a marriage to be considered. I am therefore
asking you to be understanding and give me more time,
as I have given you time in the past.'

He ended by assuring her of his confidence in her
generosity and understanding, and his enduring affection
and admiration at all times, no matter what the future held
for them both.

There was no need to make an evening meal, for Robbie
was going directly to Glasgow after work to attend a large
meeting and Mirren couldn't have eaten a bite. Instead
she sat in the kitchen, Donald's letter in her lap, staring
at the wall.

It had happened to poor Grace, but even so it had never
once occurred to Mirren that it might happen to her. She
had been so sure of Donald and now he had finished with
her. Jilted her. The word clanged in her head like a tolling
bell. Jilted. Spurned, unwanted, cast aside.

For the first time she truly knew what pain poor Grace
had suffered. Losing Donald and the future they had
planned together was even worse than losing her mother.
Helen's death had been inevitable, whereas Donald had
held the key to the rest of Mirren's life. There was no
doubt in her mind that, although he had hinted at a
possible change of heart, it would not happen. He had
found someone else and that was that.

Glancing at the clock she realised with dull surprise
that it was almost time to start work in the fried-fish
shop. For a moment she considered staying at home,
but the thought of being alone in the house with nothing

to do but read Donald's letter over and over again was unbearable. Instead she got ready, moving stiffly about the house like an old woman.

Outside, the snow was thickening underfoot and great soft flakes tumbled down from the dark sky, blinding her and drifting between her parted lips. In little less than two hours the everyday appearance of the streets and houses had changed dramatically, just as Mirren's life had changed. But eventually the snow would melt and disappear down the drains, and the town would become its familiar self again, while nothing would ever be the same for her. She felt as though she had been wrenched out of her world, spun around like a child in a game of Blind Man's Buff, then discarded to reel about on her own, sick and giddy and without any sense of direction.

'The bairns'll have a grand time tomorrow mornin' if this goes on,' Ella said cheerfully as they met outside the shop door, pausing to stamp snow from their feet and brush it from their coats before going in. A blast of warm air met them, together with Maria's 'Make certain ye've got rid of all that nasty wet stuff before ye come in here! We'll be moppin' at the floors all night as it is, with other folk trampin' it in heedlessly!'

'Are you all right?' Ella asked as they took their coats off in the small back shop and put on their aprons.

Mirren nodded, too ashamed to tell the other girl what had happened. Every nerve-end in her body had been stripped of its protective covering and left exposed to the open air, and even the sympathy of a good friend would have hurt beyond bearing. At least she hadn't cried one single tear over the letter, so there was no problem with red or swollen eyelids. The tears would no doubt come later, when she was alone in bed at night, but at the moment she felt too numb to weep.

The evening ground on, second after second, minute after minute. Fish was battered, potatoes were peeled and sliced into strips. The food was cooked, laid out on waxed paper, ritually blessed with a shake of the big salt cellar and a generous sprinkle of vinegar, wrapped in sheets of newspaper, paid for and borne out of the shop. Outside, the snow continued to fall and Maria insisted on having the floor mopped every five minutes. They were kept busy with never a break, for there was nothing more comforting than a piping hot fish supper on a cold winter's night. Mirren was glad of the constant procession of hungry customers; they kept her from remembering, and she began to believe that she was going to get through the evening safely, but the Fates that had just dealt her such a cruel blow hadn't finished with her yet. With barely half an hour to go before closing time the tears arrived, quite without warning.

They began when Mirren was helping Maria to scoop chips from one of the vats and they arrived in a sudden rush that filled her eyes, brimmed over, and splashed into the bubbling liquid fat before she could put up a hand to wipe them away.

'For pity's sake,' Maria squawked as the fat hissed and spat its resentment. 'D'ye want tae burn yersel'?' She snatched at Mirren's arm and swung her round. 'Ye should know better than tae cry intae one of the vats!'

'I'm s-sorry . . .' The words came out as a rush of saliva and there was nothing Mirren could do about it but stand there, tears pouring down her face and even from her nose and mouth. It was as though she had turned into a fountain.

'Pull yersel' together!' Maria was outraged.

'Maria, there's somethin' wrong with the lassie . . .' Vanni began.

'And there's customers tae be seen tae! You stay where ye are,' Maria added swiftly as Ella turned from the counter. 'It's bad enough havin' one of ye makin' an exhibition of herself, without the other encouragin' her!

You . . .' she pushed Mirren towards the back shop. 'Get in there and wash yer face!'

'She needs more than that. Here.' Vanni pushed a dishcloth into Mirren's hands then put an arm about her. 'Come with me. Come and sit down.'

'Vanni!'

For once he ignored his wife, apart from saying over his shoulder as he led Mirren into the back shop, away from the gaping faces of the customers waiting to be served, 'See tae the vats for me, Maria.'

In the peace and quiet of the shop he sat Mirren down, then knelt before her, taking the cloth and mopping gently at the tears that kept flowing.

'Let them come,' he said when she tried to apologise. 'Ye need tae cry, so cry. There's nothin' wrong in that.'

As she had feared, sympathy only made things worse, but at last the tears began to ease. Vanni got up and began unhurriedly to make tea, leaving Mirren to calm herself. 'Now . . .' he came back to her and put a cup into her hands, tucking her fingers carefully round it. 'D'ye want tac tell me what's wrong?'

'I'd best get back to work.' She started to rise but Vanni pushed her gently back into the chair.

'Maria . . .'

'Maria and Ella can see tae things for a wee while. Drink yer tea. It might help the hurtin'.'

'You're very k-kind, Vanni.'

'I care about ye,' he said simply. 'Me and Maria employ you, and we want ye tae be happy. If we . . . if I can do anythin' tae help, ye must tell me.'

'Nob'dy can help.' The tears threatened to return, but this time she was able to blink them back as she fished in her pocket then held the letter out to him. He looked at it doubtfully.

'Ye're sure ye want me tae read this?' he asked, then when she nodded he took his time about it, his brown eyes moving slowly from word to word. When he looked up

at her again his mouth was tight and there was a frown
between his brows. 'This man has done ye a great wrong!'
His voice was cold and hard; she had never heard Vanni
speak like that before.

'He can't help falling in l-love with someone else.'

'The two of you are engaged tae be married, aren't
ye?'

'Y-yes, but . . .'

'There is no but,' Vanni declared, his expressive eyes
flashing. 'You've kept your side of the bargain, workin'
all day, then comin' here tae earn more money for yer
future with him. Ella's told me about it,' he added as
she blinked at him. 'She wasnae gossipin', just frettin'
about you havin' tae work such long hours and care for
yer mother as well. I was worried about ye myself,' he
added. 'Ye're too young tae have such responsibilities.'
He took the scarcely touched teacup from her and set it
down, then clasped her hands. 'Ye've good friends who
care about ye, Mirren,' he said, the anger gone and his
voice soft again. 'Always remember that.'

His hands on hers were so strong and reassuring, his
dark eyes so filled with compassion, that she longed to
put her head on his shoulder like a child and demand that
he look after her and make the hurt go away. Instead she
asked in despair, 'What am I going to do, Vanni?'

He set the sodden dishcloth aside and took a spotlessly
clean white handkerchief from his pocket. 'First ye're
goin' home tae rest. The shop's about tae close anyway,'
he added as she opened her mouth to protest. 'And tomorrow,' he mopped at her eyes, then put the handkerchief
into her fingers, 'ye'll feel stronger and more able tae
decide what ye want tae do about this man, who doesn't
have the sense tae appreciate ye. Come on now . . .' He
drew her to her feet then helped her on with her coat,
settling it around her shoulders. 'Are ye ready tae go
home?'

She nodded. 'My face must be all red and swollen.'

He studied her, then wiped a stray tear gently from below one eye with the ball of his thumb. 'It is gettin' dark. Nob'dy'll notice.' His palm cupped her cheek for a moment. 'Ye've the gift of courage, Mirren. Everything'll come right for ye. Ready?' he asked, and when she nodded he led her into the shop.

'Ella, fetch yer coat, and see Mirren home.'

'Vanni!' Maria protested, her eyes flashing dangerously.

'We can manage between us for another half-hour. Mirren's had some bad news. She needs tae go home and rest.'

While Ella fetched her coat he made up two packets of fish and chips, ignoring Maria, who looked on, her face white with anger and her mouth drawn into the shape of a small button. The shop was empty for once and Mirren huddled into her coat, praying that nobody would come in and see her in her misery.

When Ella came back Vanni walked with both girls to the pavement, his arm about Mirren's shoulders. 'Mind what I said, get a good night's rest.' The snow was still falling and under the light of a nearby gas street-lamp flakes glittered on his thick curly hair. 'Ella, take her right tae her door . . . and don't pester her for information on the way.'

Ella nodded, subdued. 'No, Vanni,' she said meekly. Then, as soon as the two of them started walking, 'What's happened?' she wanted to know.

There was no sense, now, in hiding anything. 'Donald's found someone else.'

Ella gasped. 'Your Donald? The rotten . . . how could he do this tae ye?'

'He just got tired of waiting. It's my fault for not going when he asked me.'

'Of course it isn't! He's promised tae ye, isn't he?'

'That's got nothing to do with it!' Mirren snapped. 'I don't want a man who l-loves someone else!'

Her voice wobbled dangerously over the final words and Ella put an arm about her, holding her close as they walked on under the falling snow. 'No, of course ye don't. He's not worth frettin' over, Mirren.'

'I know, but that doesn't make it any easier!' She began to weep again and Ella drew her into a shop doorway, rocking her soothingly until the tears slowed. 'I didn't know that a body could hold so many tears,' Mirren sniffled as they set off again. She dabbed at her eyes with Vanni's handkerchief. 'Vanni was awful kind, Ella.'

'He's a decent man and he likes ye.'

'He'll get into terrible trouble with Maria for being so nice to me.'

'Och, he's used tae that. Mebbe this time he'll give her as good as he gets. One of those days he's goin' tae have tae stand up tae her,' Ella said.

She insisted on going all the way home with Mirren. Within a few minutes of their arrival Robbie came in, calling from the tiny lobby, 'I brought Joe home for some supper, Mirren. What a night! It's beginning tae ease off, tho . . .' The words died away as he came into the kitchen and saw his sister's wan face. 'Mirren? What's happened?'

'That miserable creature that promised tae marry yer sister's changed his mind,' Ella told him crisply. 'Ye'll have a cup of tea?'

'Donald's jilted ye? But . . .'

'Mebbe I'd better just go,' Joe said uncomfortably.

'No, ye'll not. Take yer coat off and sit yourself down,' Ella ordered. 'I've just mashed the tea and there's two fish suppers tae share between us . . .'

'. . . and plenty of bread and some cake.' Mirren pulled herself together and began to think like a hostess. It was unforgivable, in the West of Scotland, to treat a visitor shabbily, even one who was not invited or expected. 'Sit down, Joe, we'll have it ready in a minute.'

It helped to be busy. While both girls worked Robbie

draped his own and his friend's caps and coats over the clothes-horse to dry near the fire, then sat down to read the letter Mirren handed to him. When he had done he tossed it down on the table. 'If I could get my hands on Donald Nesbitt!'

'Don't fret yourself, Robbie, what's done's done.'

'And the fish is getting cold,' Ella added, clattering cutlery onto the table. 'Sit down, everyone.'

'I couldn't eat anything, not tonight.'

'Now, Mirren, ye must eat somethin',' Ella fussed, as much in control of the kitchen as if she had lived there all her life. 'Ye'll feel better with somethin' in yer belly.'

It was easier said than done. While the others enjoyed their supper, talking animatedly about anything that came into their heads, Mirren listlessly turned a piece of fish over on her plate, just as she was turning the wreckage of her future over in her mind.

'I must go,' Ella said as soon as the meal was over. 'I'll wait for ye at the top of the street tomorrow, Mirren, so's we can go into the mill together.'

'Tomorrow! Ella, what am I going to tell them all at work?'

'Tell them the truth: that the man jilted ye because he hadnae the sense of a sparrow.'

'But what'll they think of me?'

'Why should they think any the less of ye?' Joe Hepburn wanted to know. 'Ye've done nothin' wrong.'

'Joe's quite right.' Robbie gathered up the plates and took them to the sink. 'Ye've nothin' tae be ashamed of.'

'Best tae just face everyone with the truth and be done with it,' Ella advised, fastening the buttons of her jacket. 'They'll all understand. I'd stay and wash the dishes but my aunts'll be getting worried by now.'

'I'll see tae the dishes,' Robbie told her. 'I usually do.'

'Oh, here – a man who knows his way around a sink?

You're a pearl beyond price,' she teased, and he grinned, flushing.

'First I'll walk ye home.'

'I'll do that.' Joe reached for his coat and cap.

'That's a nice cheery lassie,' Robbie approved when he returned from seeing them out. 'What're ye doin'?'

'Washing the dishes.'

'I said I'd see tae them.' His hip gently bumped her away from the sink. 'You sit down.'

'Robbie, what'll Logan say?'

'Who cares what he says . . . And what business is it of his anyway?' Robbie wanted to know as he splashed water into the sink. 'Speakin' for myself, I'm glad ye're staying on, because it means I'll not have tae look for lodgings now. We'll be all right together, you and me. You'll see.'

In a way it was Grace who helped Mirren to survive the crushing blow Donald had dealt. Remembering her cousin's distress over the shame of being jilted she decided, in the long dark misery of that first sleepless night, that the only answer was to meet the situation head-on and vanquish it.

It took all her courage to walk into the twisting mill in the morning and baldly announce to the other women that her sweetheart had found someone else and she would not now be going to America, but to her surprise they all – even those known for their gossiping and their sharp tongues – retaliated by surrounding her with sympathy. Even the Mistress, a chilly, aloof woman, showed a spark of understanding. It was as though a wall had been built round Mirren, holding her safe until she found a new sense of direction. Her mother had been right when she said that it was best to tell the truth and shame the devil.

Grateful though Mirren was for their rough kindness, they could do nothing to ease the bleeding wound deep within. Catherine Proctor, concerned for her, suggested that she should consider joining Grace and Annie in Canada. 'It might do you good to get right out of Paisley, the way our Grace did.'

Mirren shook her head. 'Grace wanted to get as far away from George Armitage as possible. If I go to Canada I'll be nearer Donald, not further from him.'

'A wee holiday then, somewhere down by the Clyde.'

'At this time of year? Anyway, I can't take time off from my work. The truth is,' Mirren said helplessly, 'I don't know what I want to do with myself.'

'There must be something special that you've always wanted to do,' Catherine said, then clapped her hands. 'Of course – you must dance! It's what you like best, isn't it? And it would do you the world of good.'

'I can't go dancing so soon after my mother's death. What would folk say?'

'Mirren, you did your duty – and more than your duty – towards Helen while she was still alive. You've given up enough of yourself for other people, including Donald, and perhaps now's the time to make up to yourself for all those years, while there's still so much living ahead of you.'

'I don't know . . .' Mirren said, but deep inside her, Aunt Catherine's words kindled a spark that had been lying dormant, waiting. As she went about her usual daily duties that spark became a flame; she hummed dance tunes to herself at her frames in the mill and practised steps in the confines of the kitchen at home, and even in the mill privies, where the girls often tried out new dances. She wanted to start dancing again, longed for it, but couldn't as yet quite bring herself to break with tradition and do it.

17

Now that there were no demands on her free time Mirren took to strolling along Paisley's High Street with Ella and Ruby on Saturday afternoons. Her favourite shops were the haberdashery and drapers' emporium. To most folk they were merely shops, but to Mirren they were a treasure trove. Here lay card upon card of buttons – small and large, plain and fancy, white and coloured, flat and rounded, made of jet, glass, cut-steel, brass, wood, mother-of-pearl – as well as bobbins of sewing thread and 'dollies' of embroidery thread in all the colours of the rainbow. There were thimbles, scissors, tape measures, seamstress's pins, darning needles, packets of sharp-pointed little sewing needles for making tiny delicate stitches, and reels of lace, ribbon and tape.

Mirren, who had had no use for years for anything other than darning wool and large darning needles, drank in the colour and beauty of it all and would have stayed longer, but the other two were ever impatient, always pulling her back to the pavement and into the next shop before she had a chance to look her fill.

On this particular Saturday Ella was impatient to take another look at a silk blouse she coveted.

'What d'ye think?'

'It's very nice,' Mirren agreed.

'I could mebbe afford it next week if it's still here.'

Ella stroked the sleeve and Ruby suggested, 'Try it on, just tae make sure it fits.'

The two of them disappeared into the curtained fitting cubicle with the blouse while Mirren wandered to the back of the shop. When they came looking for her she was standing before a dummy wearing a black short-sleeved georgette dress, cut straight across at the neck. There was scarlet piping across the neckline and at the wrists, and a silk scarlet flower caught the broad hip-level belt at one side.

'The blouse didnae look right on me after all,' Ella said sadly.

'That's nice.' Ruby's eyes found the dress. 'I think I'll try it on.'

'If ye ask me, it'd suit you better,' Ella whispered to Mirren as they waited. 'Why don't you try it too?'

'I couldn't afford it even if it did fit. Anyway, Ruby'll probably buy it.'

But when Ruby emerged from the cubicle she was wearing her own clothes. She thrust the dress at the waiting assistant, said tersely, 'It's not as nice on as it looked on the dummy,' and sailed from the shop.

'That means it didnae fit her but she doesnae want tae let on,' Ella whispered as the two of them followed in her wake. Outside the shop they parted, Ella and Ruby to go home to get ready for the evening's dancing, Mirren to return to the haberdashery store, where she bought a card of pretty glass buttons to replace the plain ones on her navy-blue frock. Then her feet drew her back to the clothes shop, to have another look at the black and red dress.

'Would you like to try it on, madam?' An assistant appeared at her elbow.

'I don't think . . .'

'No harm in just trying it,' the woman coaxed, and within seconds Mirren was curtained off from the other customers, unfastening her jacket with shaking fingers.

The georgette folds slid over her head and fell into place around her body as though it had been made especially for her. 'It's perfect for you, pet,' the shop assistant said when she stepped outside the curtained changing booth. Then, surveying Mirren critically, 'D'you mind if I try something?' She drew a chair forward. 'Sit here for a minute.' Deftly she drew the pins from the tight bun at the back of Mirren's head, combed out the long fair hair then pinned it up again. 'You've got bonny hair, it's a shame to pull it back so hard,' she reproved, then stepped back. 'There . . . have another look at yourself.'

The black material gave Mirren's fair skin a pearly sheen, and below the broad black-velvet belt sitting snugly on her hips, the subtly flared skirt lifted slightly with each movement she made, then settled into place again. Where she herself always dragged her hair back, the shop assistant had allowed it to lie in soft wings that framed her thin face and had pinned it in a soft coil, rather than a bun, on the nape of her neck. Mirren's cheeks glowed with the pleasure of wearing the dress and she looked like a different person entirely.

She stared at her reflection in the mirror, wanting the dress as she had never wanted anything – other than Donald – before. It was made for dancing, and it was made for her. 'How much is it?' she asked fearfully. It was, of course, far more than she could afford. It would take weeks to save up the money and by that time the dress would have gone to someone else. Unless . . .

'Could you keep it by for me, just for an hour?' she asked timidly.

'We don't usually do that, but you suit it so well, dear, that I'll make an exception . . . if you promise to let me know within the hour whether you're taking it or not.'

Once outside the shop Mirren took to her heels and ran all the way home to fetch the bank book that had once been so precious to her, because it symbolised her future in America with Donald.

There wasn't much money left in the account now, but there was just enough to pay for the dress. She took a deep breath, then without giving herself time for second thoughts drew it all out, left the bank without a backward glance and returned to the shop, where the dress was waiting for her, already parcelled. Back home she tried it on with trembling fingers, and was relieved to see that it was still perfect for her. She tried a few dance steps, loving the way the skirt lifted and swirled and fell back into place. Her heart lifted with it. At last she was free, free of both her mother and Donald. Free to be herself.

She knew when and where Ella and Ruby were meeting to go dancing. Tonight she would be there too, in her beautiful new dance dress, and be damned to what anyone said about mourning and duty. Aunt Catherine was right: she had done her share of both.

She recalled a phrase that had caught her attention in one of the books Joe had loaned her, about a woman who had walked alone through a crowd in a procession of one. She said the words aloud, and they fitted her as well as the dress did. From now on she was determined to walk alone, in her own very special procession of one.

Although March had come in like a lion it showed no intention of going out like a lamb. The wind held sway, rampaging across the skies, snatching up any clouds that might be considering rain and hurling them across to the horizon and out of sight; fragmenting smoke as soon as it ventured from the chimney stacks and melting it like ice-cream on a child's tongue.

Just as the sailors of old had harnessed the wind's power to drive their ships under great stretches of canvas, so the womenfolk of Paisley hurried to make use of it. For months, while the back courts had been washed by rain or hidden beneath snow, they had been forced to dry the family wash in their small kitchens, either on overhead pulleys or draped onto clothes-horses set before the fire, shutting out the heat and causing complaints from husbands and bairns anxious to huddle round the grate. Now that they had the chance to get their washing dried and freshened outside they were bustling to and fro like ants, re-filling the lines as soon as the first wash was dry enough to be taken in.

Seen from the Jarvises kitchen window, the big back court that served tenements on all four sides was a vast tossing sea of blankets, sheets and clothing, and even quilts, all bucking and straining against the wooden pegs that held them to the ropes, yearning to be up and away. Every line in the court was festooned and the wash-houses built onto the back of the tenement buildings had been busy all day.

Since she had come home from the mill at midday Mirren had taken advantage of her free Saturday afternoon and now, as the light began to go outside, she turned from the window and looked with satisfaction at the pile of dried laundry on her bed. The room smelled sweetly of the fresh air trapped in the folds of sheets and shirts, curtains and blouses. The hours of back-breaking ironing to come offset the pleasure of a big wind-dried wash, she thought as she fetched the shabby old laundry basket that her mother had used for as long as she could remember and set off downstairs to bring in the last of the clothes. But the bulk of the drudgery could be put off until the next day, for she and Ella were going to the dancing at the Denniston Palais in Glasgow.

The wind almost took the breath from her as she went out of the back close, and she had to hold her skirt down with one hand as she advanced on the washing lines, where sheets snapped and cracked like sails on the lines. Here and there women or children chased after some smaller item of clothing that had managed to break loose from its clothes pegs and make a bid for freedom.

As Mirren cleared her washing line, deftly folding the clothes before putting them into the basket, an elderly woman nearby said to her neighbour without bothering to lower her voice, 'Would ye look at that frilled petticoat, and her mother not cold in her grave yet. Some folks have no respect for the dead!'

'Nice day, Mrs Chalmers,' Mirren called cheerfully. 'I see you're taking the chance to get your kitchen cloths washed.'

Some of the women nearby tutted disapproval while others, the younger women, giggled behind their hands, pleased to see Peggy Chalmers treated with the disrespect she so often vented on others. Mrs Chalmers, who, Helen Jarvis had once commented in Mirren's hearing, had a tongue that could saw firewood and stir hot tar, glared as she hauled her best curtains off the line.

'Ye're a cheeky wee midden, so ye are, Mirren Jarvis. If yer poor mother could see ye now, flauntin' yersel' in the streets and goin' intae dance halls instead of wearin' decent black for her, she'd break her poor heart.'

'I don't see why. I did right by her when she needed me. I've got the right to live my own life. At least,' Mirren said pertly, 'I'm not interfering with anyone else's . . . unlike some folk.'

Mrs Chalmers snatched up her basket and slammed it onto one hip. 'You'll come tae a bad endin', mark my words!'

'If I do, it'll be an ending of my choosing and not one that other folk decide for me,' Mirren retorted, going to help Mrs White, who kept disappearing into the sheet she was trying to take down from her line.

'This kind of wind's worse than a mischievous laddie,' she panted as Mirren unwrapped her, before reaching up to unfasten the remaining pegs and bring the sheet down from the line. 'Thanks, lassie, I'll just bundle it up for now and fold it properly in the house, else it'll be up and away. Was that Peggy Chalmers havin' a go at ye?' she asked as the two of them reached the back close. 'Don't mind her, she's aye been an interferin' busybody.'

'I know,' Mirren shrugged. 'She doesn't bother me.'
Once she would have cringed and flushed scarlet and
almost died with shame when criticised by the likes of
Peggy Chalmers, but those days were gone.

'It's an old way of life, this business of goin' intae
mournin' for a whole year. Young folk don't want tae
be doin' with such customs, specially since the war,'
Mrs White panted as she led the way upstairs. 'That
changed an awful lot of things. Ye're quite right tae go
yer ain way.'

'I will.' The smile Mirren put on for her neighbour's
benefit died as she returned to her own flat. The metamor-
phosis from submissive daughter to independent woman
had not been easy, but she had come through it, and
had become strong enough to ignore people such as
Mrs Chalmers, who had offered no assistance when she
was struggling to care for her mother, yet gossiped and
whispered her disapproval now.

Logan and Belle had been foremost among her critics,
making no secret of their belief that Mirren had become
a fast woman.

'Going out tae the dancin' during a time of mournin'!'
Logan had raged at her. 'How could ye do this tae me?'

Facing up to him was the hardest part because he was
her elder brother and Helen had clung to the conviction
that men should always be looked up to. But Mirren
refused to give way to his blustering. 'It's got nothing
to do with you. I don't ask you for the entrance money
to the halls, do I?'

'Don't try tae pretend ye don't know what I mean,
Mirren. Ye're bringin' down the family name. I'm a
local businessman – one day Belle and me'll own her
father's shop. How can I hold up my head among the
other shopkeepers when they know that I have a sister
who frequents dance halls?'

'I doubt if they care what I do.'

'Ye know nothin' about business,' Logan snapped,

while Belle chimed in with 'And have ye even realised that with every step ye take ye're dancing on yer own mother's grave?'

'I thought she was buried in the cemetery along the road, not under the floorboards at the Co-operative Halls,' Robbie said innocently, and his brother and sister-in-law both sucked air in so loudly that, as he said later, he almost expected the pictures to be pulled off the walls.

'I've never heard the like!' Logan said when he could speak again.

'That's blasphemy!' Belle's hand fluttered at her throat.

Robbie was unruffled. 'I'm just pointin' out that our Mirren can't possibly be dancin' on Mother's grave. And even if she did such a thing, I'd consider it her right tae do as she pleased.' He got up from where he sat by the table, raising his voice above the babble set up by his brother and sister-in-law. 'Nob'dy worked harder tae make Mother's life easier than Mirren, and I know what I'm talkin' about for I saw it all. I was the one that had tae help her late at night when she came back from the fried-fish shop too tired tae crawl up the stairs on her own . . .'

'Robbie . . .'

'You keep out of this, Mirren. I've held my tongue for months and it's time I had my say. When other lassies were enjoyin' themselves, Mirren was workin' tae earn the money tae buy special invalid food. When you and me were sleepin' in our beds she was sittin' up as often as not because Mother couldnae sleep. If ye ask me she's got more right tae lead her own life any way she chooses than any of us, and if ye don't approve of her then mebbe ye'd be better tae just stay away.'

Logan's face had been reddening steadily throughout his younger brother's lecture. Now he turned on Mirren, a vein throbbing in his right temple. 'This is your doing. You've been allowin' the laddie tae run loose and mix with the wrong sort.'

'For pity's sake, Logan,' Robbie said wearily. 'I'm not

a schoolboy tae be told what tae do by Mirren or by you. Just go, will ye, before ye start blamin' her for startin' the Great War.'

'If I go now I'll not come back, and neither will Belle.'

'We'll not argue with ye on that one,' Robbie told him, and with a final outraged snort Logan swept out, his wife hot on his heels.

'Oh, Robbie!'

'Don't fret yerself, they're no loss. Logan's just itchin' tae get both of us under his thumb. It'd make up for the way he has tae fawn round that old father-in-law of his and act the lackey.'

'He might not come back.'

'That,' Robbie said grimly, 'wouldnae upset me.'

'But he's our blood kin.'

'That doesnae mean that we have tae like him or do as he says. We'll manage fine without him, you and me.'

Neither Logan nor Belle came to the house after that, and although at first Mirren suffered pangs of guilt over her older brother's absence, she had to admit that Robbie was quite right when he said that Agnes, Bob and wee Thomas were better company and more like family than Logan and Belle had ever been. Thomas and his step-father doted on each other, and Agnes, four months from the birth of her baby, had never looked healthier or happier.

As Mirren washed and then carefully slipped the black georgette dress over her head she hummed a snatch of dance music to herself. She tidied her hair, then smiled at her mirrored reflection as she dabbed some rose-scented cologne behind her ears. In a surprisingly short time she was recovering from the blow Donald had dealt her. She had come to enjoy walking in a procession of one.

The wind was still blowing strongly as she waited for Ella that evening outside the Denniston Palais. Despite the fact that she had pinned her hat on firmly, Mirren had to keep a hand on it as well, but was forced to let it go when a sudden gust of wind came swirling along the pavement, whipping about her legs and whisking her skirt up to display her petticoat to all and sundry. Prettily edged and beribboned as it was, she had no desire to let it make an exhibition of itself. But the petticoat and her hat were apparently in league. As she pulled her skirt down with both hands, her hat, released to follow its own inclinations, immediately flew from her head to be deftly fielded by a young man coming along the pavement.

'Yours, I believe . . .' he said, then as Mirren reached for it and her skirt flew up again, he took her arm and hurried her into the shelter of the doorway. 'In here. You stand there, Martin,' he ordered his companion, 'and I'll stand here, and between us we'll keep the worst of the wind off the young lady while she pins her hat back on.'

'Thank you.' Mirren jammed the pins in willy-nilly in her haste, so that they pricked her scalp more than once. 'Thank you,' she repeated, and made to return to the pavement.

'Are you not going in to the dancing?'

'When my friend arrives.'

'We'll mebbe see you inside?'

'Mebbe.'

He tipped his hat and she watched the two of them going in through the doors. They looked and sounded like respectable young men, and the one who had helped her had lively eyes and a cheerful smile. She might indeed watch out for them once Ella arrived.

Mebbe.

'Sorry,' Ella panted when she finally arrived, 'It was Aunt Bea's fault.'

She always seemed to be busy with one or other of her aunts these Saturday afternoons, shopping or house-cleaning or helping with a difficult knitting pattern. Mirren and Ruby, who usually accompanied them, had become accustomed to arriving first when the three of them went out together on a Saturday night. When she was meeting the other two at the dance-hall, Ella smuggled her dance dress and shoes and make-up out, and changed in the close before scurrying up Well Street towards the tram stop, head down, hoping that none of her aunts happened to glance out of the window and recognise her.

'Come on . . .'

'Is Ruby not here yet?' Ella hung back as Mirren hurried through the doorway.

'She's to go to her granny's birthday tea tonight, d'you not remember? Come on,' Mirren repeated, impatient to be on the dance floor.

Ella chattered on as they took off their coats and changed into their dance shoes in the ladies' cloakroom. 'I thought Aunt Bea would never make up her mind. We spent the whole afternoon going up and down the High Street and along Gilmour Street, then down New Street and Causeyside. No wonder nobody else'll go shopping with her! Finally I got her down tae a decision between two blouses.'

'Which shop?' Mirren glanced enviously at a girl just leaving the cloakroom as they entered, her hair in a loose, casual bob that was both stylish and easy to tend.

'That was the problem. One of them was in Naismith & Scott's in the High Street and the other was in the Co-operative Stores in Causeyside Street. We were back and forward so much between the two that I doubt if I'll be able tae dance a step tonight. Ye'd never have guessed today that she's over sixty and she's supposed tae have a weak heart. Finally she settled for the Co-operative one and I got her home. Then there was the tea tae make . . .'

Mirren smoothed the skirt of her black and red dress and studied her reflection critically. Now that she was free to sleep at nights and to take her meals properly, instead of eating when she could find the time, her face had rounded out. There was more colour in her cheeks, and the eyes that had once looked as though all the colour had been washed from them had now taken on a healthier shade of blue. Her hair, worn now in the softer style demonstrated by the woman in the dress shop, had a shine to it. 'D'you think I'd suit a bob?'

'I don't see why not.' Ella's dark hair was long, but she kept it that way because it was sleek and smooth and attracted compliments.

'What if I didn't like it once it was done?'

'It'd grow back in fast enough. Come on,' Ella urged impatiently, 'we've lost enough time already.'

18

As they went into the crowded hall Mirren, despite herself, searched the crowd for a glimpse of the young man who had rescued her hat. Clearly, he had been watching out for her as well, since he smiled and nodded at her as he danced past.

'Who's that?' Ella wanted to know.

'Just a lad who caught my hat for me when the wind blew it off.'

'He looks quite nice.' Ella gave her a nudge in the ribs. 'Mebbe he'll dance ye.'

'And mebbe not,' Mirren scoffed, just in case. But as soon as the dance was over the two men sought her out. 'I see your friend got here all right,' said the one called Martin.

'Always late but never absent, that's me.' Ella beamed up at him, and jumped to her feet when he asked her for the next dance.

The other man smiled at Mirren. 'It looks as if you're stuck with me. Would you care to dance? I've not seen you here before,' he said as they moved smoothly into the whirlpool of dancers.

'We've been a few times but we usually go to one of the Paisley halls.'

'So you enjoy dancing?'

'Oh yes.' He was a few inches taller than Mirren and when she glanced up at him she saw that he had amazingly blue eyes set in a square, cheerful face. He danced quite well and she was pleased when he fell silent, allowing her to relax and enjoy moving to the music.

When the dance was over he shook her hand formally. 'Thank you, I enjoyed that. I'm Albert Latto. My friends call me Bert.'

'Mirren Jarvis.' She wasn't used to such courteous treatment. Most men simply walked away at the end of a dance, leaving the girls to make their own way back to their friends. Occasionally Mirren had been escorted to her seat, but nobody had shaken her hand before or exchanged names.

'Would you and your friend care for a drink?'

She hesitated, then said, 'That would be very nice.'

Martin – taller, slimmer and fairer than Bert – had already had the same idea.

'They're right gents, aren't they?' Ella whispered as the men went to fetch glasses of lemonade. 'More refined than most of the lads we've met here. I wonder where they work?' Her brown eyes sparkled. 'Hasn't Martin got lovely hair? We could be in for a grand evenin', Mirren!'

They sat the next dance out, getting to know each other. It turned out that Martin and Bert were both draughtsmen at John Brown's shipyard in Clydebank.

'So, what do you do?' Bert wanted to know, producing a cigarette case and a lighter.

Mirren shook her head as he proffered the case. 'We work . . .'

'. . . in a lawyer's office in Paisley,' Ella completed the sentence as she accepted a cigarette. 'We're clerkesses. That's how we know each other.'

'And you both live in Paisley?' When he smiled he revealed an attractive dimple in one cheek. 'So it's true what they say about all the Paisley girls being good dancers.'

'Do they?'

'It's well known.' He stood up and held his hand out to Mirren as the band struck up a waltz. 'Come and prove it to me again.'

As she moved into his arms Mirren heard Ella cough as she drew on her cigarette.

When the evening ended Martin and Bert asked if they could take the girls home.

'To Paisley?' Ella asked in astonishment. Normally the young men from Glasgow had no notion to escort a girl all the way to Paisley, for it meant having to face a long journey back again late at night.

'I've got a motor-car,' Bert said casually. 'It's no bother.'

'Well . . .' Ella looked doubtfully at Mirren, who smiled sweetly back at her, then at Bert, and said, 'That would be very kind of you. Thank you.'

'Ye know fine that we always go home on our own,' Ella accused when they went into the cloakroom to change their shoes and claim their coats.

'It's not every day we get the chance of a ride in a motor-car. And as you said yourself, they're very respectable. They'll behave themselves.'

'Are ye sure of that?'

'They can take you home first if you like. Come on, Ella,' Mirren urged, aflame with a sudden sense of adventure. 'I've never been in a motor-car before. Wait till we tell the girls at work about this!'

'Ye're right.' Ella giggled. 'Can ye imagine Ruby's face when she hears about it? The one night she wasnae able tae come with us and we meet these two.'

'Mind you,' Mirren looked critically at the reflection of her newly lipsticked mouth, then ran the top of a little finger over it to smooth out the colour, 'it's just as well she's not here, then there'd have been three of us and only two of them.'

'You've changed, Mirren Jarvis,' Ella said in awe. 'A

few months ago ye'd have refused tae have anything tae do with them and their motor-car.'

Mirren smiled at her in the mirror. 'A few months ago I was a daughter and a fiancée. Now I've got nob'dy to please but myself. And a few months ago,' she added, suddenly remembering, 'I wasn't a clerkess in a lawyer's office. What made you say a thing like that?'

'They're draughtsmen – skilled tradesmen! They'd not be interested in us if they knew we were mill-girls.'

'I don't see why not.'

'They probably just go out with lassies that work in offices. I'll need tae . . . to . . . watch the way I talk,' Ella fretted.

'See? You do want them to see us home and ask us out again.'

'Mebbe, I don't know . . . D'ye think . . . ?' Ella began, but Mirren, with an impatient, 'Oh, come on!' grabbed her arm and pulled her out to the lobby, where Bert and Martin awaited them.

Both girls gasped when they saw the car. 'It's beautiful!' Mirren said in awe.

'It's not bad,' Bert cast a casual eye over the gleaming vehicle. 'Quite old, but reliable. That's why I've kept her on.'

'He's kept her on because he's passionately in love with her,' Martin scoffed and his friend scowled at him, then beamed when Mirren said, 'I'm not surprised, I could fall in love with it . . . her myself.'

Both girls, unused to cars, required help to scramble up onto the running board then step over the low sill into the car's interior. Ella, who was to sit in the back seat with Martin, had to negotiate a second, slightly higher step; even though she tugged her skirt down as she climbed onto the running board, Mirren noticed both men eyeing the swift display of shapely ankle and calf.

'The roof folds down, doesn't it?' Ella asked as they set off.

'Yes, but it's too cold and windy for that tonight,' Bert called back over his shoulder.

'Can't you do it anyway?'

'No, he can't,' Mirren said sharply, thinking of the havoc the wind could wreak with her flyaway hair.

'Best not . . . but I tell you what,' Bert suggested, 'we'll take you both for a spin next Saturday afternoon if you're free. You can try motoring with the top down then.'

It was a new and exhilarating experience to be bowling past the tram stops in a comfortable private motor-car. Despite her nervousness Mirren was quite sorry when they reached the top of Well Street and Martin helped Ella to alight.

'I'll walk to your door with you.'

'Er . . .' Ella cast a panic-stricken glance at Mirren, who managed to scramble down from her seat unaided.

'I'll come with you both, I could do with stretching my legs.'

At the close-mouth Martin shook Ella's hand and wished her goodnight. 'I look forward to seeing you on Saturday. She's shy, isn't she?' he continued as he and Mirren walked back to where Bert waited in the car.

It was not the word she would have used to describe Ella. 'She lives with her elderly aunts,' she explained, swallowing back a smile. 'They worry about her safety.'

'I'm sure they'll find that they've got no need to concern themselves over me and Bert,' he said with amusement.

'What did I tell you?' Mirren asked as she fell into step with Ella at the mill-gates the next morning. 'They were perfect gentlemen, the two of them.'

'They seemed all right. Ye just need tae be careful when ye first meet up with folk.'

'I said we'd see them at the Cross at two o'clock on Saturday.'

'Saturday?'

'Surely your aunts can manage without you for once. You never used to be so busy with them on a Saturday.'

'They're gettin' older,' Ella said by way of excuse. 'I'll make sure tae have the afternoon free. What are you goin' tae wear?'

'My navy blue dress, of course. It's the only good one I've got apart from the black georgette. And that fawn jacket Annie Proctor didn't take to Canada with her. Bert's got two sisters, so he's going to bring the duster coats they wear when they travel in motorcars.'

Ella caught her arm and drew her into the shelter of one of the high mill buildings as one of the horse-drawn carts used to transport the yarn between the various buildings came clattering past. The young carter whistled at them as he went by, and waved his whip. Ella waved back.

'Nice laddie,' she said, 'but a poor dancer.' Then she asked incredulously as they started walking again, 'Did you say coats made of dusters?'

Mirren had thought that herself when Bert first raised the subject, but as soon as she got home the night before she had riffled through some fashion magazines passed on to her by Maggie Proctor, so she was able to correct Ella in what she hoped was a slightly bored, sophisticated tone. 'They're long coats ladies wear when they travel in motor-cars. They're made of gabardine and they're loose, so that they can go over your other clothes. Bert says to bring long scarves to tie over our hats so's they won't blow off.'

'It's exciting, isn't it? Wait till we tell the rest of them!'

But when they arrived in the twisting department the other women were clustered round Greta Cochrane, a plain, dumpy girl who usually had little to say for herself.

'I am not!' she was insisting loudly, flushed and simpering as she fiddled with her apron.

'Ye've got a sleekit look about ye,' Ruby said. 'Ye're up tae somethin'. Go on, Greta, we'll have tae be at the machines in a minute . . . out with it.'

'If ye must know, I'm gettin' wed,' Greta announced, then went into a fit of giggles.

'Married? God bless ye, pet!' Libby McDaid gave her a hug and a kiss.

'Ye're expectin', aren't ye?' Isa Wallace's sharp eyes ran down the girl's thick body.

The giggles gurgled to a halt. 'What d'ye mean?'

'Expectin' a wean, what did ye think I meant?'

'It's none of your business, Isa,' Libby said sharply. Isa and her sister-in-law Beattie spent all day and every day sweeping the department floor, clearing away the thread ends and caddis that fell like snow from the machines. The best of friends, their frequent fallings-out were spectacular because they were given to setting about each other with wet cloths, floor brushes or anything else that came to hand. On more than one occasion the sub-manager had had to be called in to separate them. The air around them both always reeked of the peppermint snuff they took . . . to cover the smell of alcohol, it was rumoured.

'Ye are, aren't ye?' Isa pressed, and Greta bit her lip.

'Aye . . . but just a wee bit.'

'A wee bit's all it takes,' someone said drily, and Beattie chimed in with, 'Ye're right – my man's proved that five times over.'

'How did ye know?' Greta asked as the group dissolved into shrieks of laughter. She pressed her hands hard against her belly. 'It's not near far enough on for it to show.'

'Why else would the likes of—' Isa winced as Libby's sharp elbow jabbed into her back.

'I was thinkin' just that myself, Isa,' Libby said glibly.

'Why would a lassie as young as our Greta get married if she didnae have tae?'

'Marryin' young's better than workin' here all my life,' Greta said truculently.

'D'yer mammy and yer daddy know, hen?' Libby probed.

Greta flinched at the question. 'My mammy was the one that told me, and she's made sure that Pat'll stand by me.' Her fingers worried at the hem of her apron. 'But if any of youse see my da, ye'll no' say nothin', will ye? I darenae let him know about the bairn till we're safely wed. My da's awful particular. He'd murder Pat!'

'Not a word, pet, not from any of us here . . . if we value our lives,' Libby said with heavy meaning, her eyes on the cleaning women. Then as they shrugged and turned away, robbed of their pleasures, she took the girl's face, plain to the point of ugliness, between her hands and kissed it. 'Bless ye, I hope ye'll both be as happy as the day's long.'

'The day's gettin' longer by the minute, and not a one of you at her machine,' the Mistress's voice broke in and the group scattered.

'We were just congratulatin' young Greta here, Mrs Drysdale. She's tae be wed,' Libby took time to explain. As well as being a long-serving employee in the depart-ment and a reliable worker, Libby had worked beside Teenie Drysdale, spinster, before the woman automati-cally became Mrs Drysdale, spinster, on the day of her promotion to the post of overseer. Although Libby never presumed on their former working relationship or expected any favours because of it, she enjoyed a little more leeway than the rest of the twiners.

'Indeed? So ye'll be leavin' us, Greta?'

'Aye, Mrs Drysdale, in a few weeks.'

'Oh aye? It'll be in a few minutes if ye don't get yer machine started. And that goes for the rest of ye as well.'

'Lord love the wee soul,' Ruby murmured as she passed behind Mirren on her way to her desk, 'The laddie cannae be very particular.'

Ella said much the same thing when the two of them left at the end of the shift. 'Greta's got a good heart,' Mirren protested.

'I'll give ye that. It's just that the box it came in isnae much tae look at. But this means we can have a bottlin' when she leaves. We've not had one of them for a while. I was sure that the next would be . . .' she stopped suddenly.

'For me. You can say it without me bursting into tears,' Mirren told her, and Ella squeezed her arm.

'I'm glad ye're not goin' tae America. I'd probably go mad in the fried-fish shop and throw all the chips over Maria, if ye werenae there tae keep me respectable. Here,' she giggled, 'did ye see Ruby's face when I just happened tae let drop about us meetin' Martin and Bert, and them havin' a car? She gave us a right squint!'

'She did that.' In mill-language, giving someone a squint was much the same as giving them an evil look, and Ruby had certainly glowered when Ella finally found an opportunity to mention casually the previous night's experiences. Ruby had flounced back to her machine, tossing her head, and had scarcely had a word to say for herself for the rest of the day.

'I felt sorry for her,' Mirren admitted.

'That's more than she'd feel for you if the boot was on the other foot. Save yer pity for someone worth it!' Ella advised briskly.

Bert's glossy dark-blue car, looking even more impressive with the top down, drew up beside the two girls at exactly two o'clock on Saturday afternoon. Heads turned and small boys came scampering like iron filings drawn to a magnet as the two young men, elegantly casual in tweed jackets and grey flannel trousers, leaped out and helped the girls into long, loose coats.

'Button 'em up to your chins. It can be really windy because of the speed we'll hit,' Bert advised. 'And tie your scarves over your hats, for I don't fancy having to walk back to hunt for them.'

They set off with a flourish, Bert tooting the horn for the entertainment of the cheering youngsters lining the pavement. As they drove along Broomlands Street, with passers-by staring, Mirren suddenly noticed Mrs Chalmers, the neighbour who had criticised her for going dancing so soon after her mother's death, gaping disbelievingly at her from a shop doorway. She waved and gave the woman a sweet smile.

'Someone you know?' Bert asked as Mrs Chalmers tossed her head and flounced back into the shop.

'Just an acquaintance.' Mirren sank back into her padded seat, smiling to herself. That would give the malicious old biddy something to talk about to her cronies!

They drove through the engineering town of Johnstone then struck out into the country, bowling through villages and past farms. Bert was right, the wind was strong and without the all-enveloping duster coat Mirren would have been chilled. She was also grateful for the long scarf that held her hat on and kept her soft hair from breaking away from the hairpins that anchored it in place.

There was something wonderfully exhilarating about the speed and the wind's buffeting. When Ella tapped her on the shoulder and shouted into her ear, 'Isn't this grand?' Mirren nodded enthusiastically, then gasped and clutched at the door as the car's long elegant bonnet tipped forward and they started to descend the long, steep, winding Haley Brae into the seaside town of Largs. At first there were only brief glimpses between the trees of the Firth of Clyde glittering quite far below them, but coming closer and closer with each glimpse, until they finally entered the town and drove down the main road past the railway station. Then, suddenly, there was the water, dotted with vessels, from passenger steamers to rowing dinghies.

They parked the car close to the shore and went to a café, where they ate ice-cream topped with grated chocolate out of tall glasses. Spooning the cold, smooth stuff into her mouth, Mirren was reminded of the last time she had had ice-cream, at Agnes's wedding breakfast. Ella, sitting by the window, was as excited as a small child. She could scarcely take her eyes from the view. 'I love the seaside.'

Martin smiled indulgently on her. 'It's the river, actually.'

'But it's salty. I can smell it on the air. And there's seaweed.'

'Because it opens onto the Irish Sea,' he explained. 'So the river has sea-water in it.'

Ella stuck out a creamy tongue at him. 'And that's why we've always called it the sea, so there.'

Afterwards they took a long and leisurely stroll along the front, stopping now and again to lean on the railings and watch the boats. Martin suggested taking a rowing boat out, but Ella firmly vetoed the idea.

'Water's all right to look at but I'll not go onto it for love nor money.'

'Not even in a big steamer?' Martin coaxed, but she shook her head firmly.

'Here's one coming in.' Bert caught at Mirren's hand. 'Come on . . .'

Together they ran along the length of the pier, arriving at the end just as the great length of the boat slid smoothly and easily alongside. Bells clanged in its depths as crew members hurled mooring ropes, deftly caught by the men waiting on the pier, and looped them over great bollards.

'Have you ever been on one of those?' Mirren asked, entranced.

'Often. Haven't you?'

'Mebbe when I was small, but I don't remember it.'

'I'll take you on a trip one day,' he promised, tucking her hand into the crook of his elbow.

When the steamer had departed they left the pier and strolled along the shore to the Pencil, a tall, slim monument erected to commemorate the Battle of Largs, when in 1263 the Scots had successfully beaten back an invasion threat from a great host of Viking warriors. Looking out over the water Mirren tried without success to replace the rowing boats and cabin cruisers, and yachts and puffers and passenger steamers, with Viking long-boats, each with its high prow, carved dragon's head and its fearsome crew. But the present kept drawing her back.

When they finally walked back into the town they had tea at one of its many restaurants before clambering back into the car and returning to Paisley Cross, where they parted company after arranging to meet a few nights later.

Now that she had spent more time with the men, Ella was much more relaxed in their company. 'I can't believe it,' she marvelled as they watched the car drive away. 'You and me, Mirren, with two perfect gentlemen and a motor-car. D'ye think we might end up marryin' them?'

'Don't be daft, we've only just met them!'

'It would be nice, friends like us gettin' wed tae men who are friends. We might even be able tae live near each other . . .' Ella prattled on as they walked home arm-in-arm, her speech lapsing into its usual comfortable ways now that they were alone. Mirren left her to her dreams, thinking that she never knew which way Ella was going to jump, but perhaps that was one of the reasons she liked the girl so much.

'If they havenae even tried tae kiss ye they can't be very interested in ye,' Ruby sniffed on Monday when Ella recounted the story of their afternoon in Largs, detail by detail.

'They're interested all right, aren't they, Mirren? They want tae see us again. See's those scissors over.' A small group of the girls were huddled in the privy, making bows and rosettes from coloured paper for Greta's forthcoming bottlin'. The girl's indomitable mother had found a single-roomed flat to rent, moving quickly in order to get a ring on her daughter's finger before the proposed bridegroom took to his heels, opined Isa, who knew the family Greta was marrying into. Whatever the reason, the banns had been posted and Greta would soon be leaving the mill to marry Pat.

'What sort of lad doesnae try tae kiss a lassie when he's spent money on her?' persisted Ruby, furious at having been absent when her friends met the two draughtsmen.

'A gentleman, Ruby, that's what sort. And don't you worry, they'll kiss us all right when we decide tae let them. They're just waitin' for permission.'

'Mebbe when ye give them yer precious permission ye'll find that they're not bothered.'

'You're in a right twitchy mood the day, Ruby. Has yer sister been makin' yer knickers again?' Ella retaliated, and the other girl flushed scarlet while everyone else giggled. Poor Ruby would never live down the evening she had gone to the dancing with Ella and Mirren, wearing a pair of drawers made for her by her sister, who was learning dressmaking at the time. Pretty though the underwear was, with lace round the legs, poor Ruby had had a miserable evening, most of it spent shifting restlessly in her seat in an attempt to get comfortable, complaining that the drawers were far too small and turning away any young men who asked her for a dance. The reason for her discomfort hadn't dawned on her until she returned home to be met by an apologetic sister, holding out the gusset she had forgotten to sew into the new undergarment.

'I'm sayin',' Ruby protested, glaring at the gigglers, 'that I've never known a lad who waited for permission tae kiss a lassie.'

'You don't know every lad, Ruby,' someone pointed out.

'She knows most . . . and they know her, an' all.'

'And what d'ye mean by that, Ella Caldwell?' Ruby asked dangerously.

'I mean there's no need tae tar me and Mirren with the same brush ye use on yerself,' Ella retorted, and a fight might have blown up, if the girl left out in the corridor to keep watch hadn't scratched on the door to warn of Mrs Drysdale's approach. The mill privies were a haven for the workers, being the only place where they could relax, gossip, practise the latest dance, hold a sing-along, experiment with each other's make-up, pierce each other's ears or do each other's hair. In every department the foremen and forewomen were obliged to visit the privies regularly to chase their staff back to work.

'Have you been smokin'?' Mrs Drysdale wanted to know as they scurried out into the corridor like field mice scattering before a harvester, pockets crammed with coloured paper. 'Or were the lot of you caught short again?' Then as they muttered and scudded on past, heads down, 'Ella?'

'Yes, Mrs Drysdale?'

'Tuck yer tail in,' the Mistress advised, the faintest glimmer of a twinkle in her eye as she pointed to the long strand of red crepe paper dangling from Ella's pocket. 'If Greta sees it she might begin tae suspect that ye're planning a bottlin' for her.'

19

It was hard to believe, Mirren thought, that a town as ordinary as Paisley could house a magical place like the Picture Palace. One minute she and Bert, arm in arm, were following Ella and Martin along the High Street and the next, just by making a left turn from the pavement, they were in a sultan's palace, crossing a marble floor set out in black and white squares. Through an inner set of glass doors they went, to find themselves in a huge carpeted foyer scattered with comfortable chairs.

'Will ye stop gawkin',' Ella hissed, leading Mirren to a chair while the men bought chocolates at the kiosk. 'Anyone'd think ye'd never been in the place before.'

'I haven't.'

'Don't let them know that!' Ella jerked her head towards their escorts. 'We're supposed tae be clerkesses, remember? Clerkesses probably visit places like this all the time.' She sneaked a swift glance around then said with longing, 'If we go on walkin' out with them we could visit here often.'

Mirren was too busy staring at the pictures and the soft wall lighting to pay her much heed. 'It's like being inside a palace!'

There was even more to see when they mounted the wide carpeted stairs leading to yet another big lobby, also carpeted. From there they went through another double set of doors to reach the auditorium itself, with its huge screen – hidden by curtains when it was not in use – and row upon row of soft comfortable tip-up chairs.

As a child Mirren had gone once or twice to the Glen Cinema at the Cross with her brothers, but the Glen had none of the comfort of the Picture Palace. The film on the screen before them was a dramatised account of the discovery of America by Christopher Columbus, and it was the most exciting thing she had ever seen. She quite forgot about the comfort of her surroundings as she watched the brave men battle their way in sailing ships across uncharted seas in search of new land.

During Columbus's first encounter with Red Indians she suddenly became aware that Bert's arm, which had been casually laid along the back of her seat, had moved so that his hand rested on her shoulder. It was a pleasant feeling and she was happy enough to snuggle in when his hold tightened and she was drawn against his body, though she was not so happy when he turned towards her and let his lips brush over her cheek while his free hand crept across to hold hers.

The four of them had been keeping company for a few weeks now and it wasn't the first time he had kissed her, but that had been in secluded corners. Even though the cinema was dark, the thought of sharing intimate caresses in public made her uncomfortable. In any case, she wanted to follow what was happening on the screen. She pulled back and was relieved to find that although he kept his arm about her and her hand in his, he didn't try to kiss her again until later, when they were saying goodnight in the privacy of the close in Maxwellton Street.

'See?' he teased when he lifted his mouth from hers. 'You're not such a little Miss Prim Paisley as you pretended to be in the picture house.'

'I don't like it when folk can see us.'

'The place was in darkness, and they were all looking at the screen in any case.'

'We don't know that.'

'I do.' He pulled her into his arms again and the next five minutes passed pleasantly for both of them. Then Mirren drew back as Bert's kisses began to become more intense. 'Martin'll be waiting for you.'

'You're so strict . . . you should have been a school ma'am instead of a clerkess. D'you want me to walk you to your door?'

'I know the way.'

'See you next Saturday then?' They had arranged to go down to Barassie, on the Clyde.

She nodded and hurried up to the first landing where she waited for several minutes, praying that none of the doors would open. When she finally tiptoed downstairs again Bert was gone, but even so she peeped cautiously from the close-mouth before venturing into the street, where she scurried along to her own building, which was smaller, older and shabbier than the one in which he thought she lived.

She hated this game of subterfuge that Ella had started with her pretence that they worked in an office. Up the stairs she sped, wondering if for some reason he might come back and find her, not feeling entirely safe until she was in the house with the landing door closed at her back.

Safely gaining the lobby, she walked into the kitchen then stopped short, one hand flying to her throat. 'Oh my God! What's happened?'

Robbie, trying to clean blood from Joe Hepburn's face, straightened up quickly. 'It's nothin',' he said, guilt written all over his open face. 'Just a wee disagreement that got out of hand.'

'A wee disagreement?' Mirren heard her voice soar into a subdued shriek. Joe, sitting in one of the upright chairs, had turned his head towards her when she came in, revealing a face covered in blood.

'I'd best go . . .' He began to get up but Robbie held him down with two hands on his shoulders.

'Don't be daft, man, you cannae go walkin' in the streets lookin' like that. Mirren . . . ?'

'Stand up. Robbie, move the chair over here where there's more light. No, I'll take the chair, you give him a hand,' Mirren added hastily as Joe rose to his feet and stood swaying. Assisted by Robbie, he limped over to the chair like an old man, clutching at his stomach and wincing. Robbie lowered him back onto the chair as gently as if he were a mother lowering her first-born into its crib. When he straightened his young face was tense with anger.

'They beat him down ontae the ground and then the bastards gave him a right kickin'. His face as well as his body.'

'Let me see.' She tipped Joe's face up towards the light from the gas mantle and drew in her breath sharply as she saw the wet red sheen from forehead to chin. It was probably not as bad as it looked, she told herself, gritting her teeth. Blood always made things look worse.

'Get me a cloth, Robbie – not that one,' she added as he proffered the wet, bloody ball he had been using to clean his friend's wounds. As he tossed it into the sink a corner flapped out and Mirren saw from the embroidered pattern that it had once been Helen's best tray-cloth. 'In the bottom drawer there, the clean dish towels. And fetch the wee dark-brown bottle from the shelf in the bathroom.'

Slowly, trying not to hurt Joe, she bathed the worst of the blood from his face and neck. Once that had been done she could see that the worst wound was a cut over one eyebrow. There were two more, one across the bridge of his nose and the other on his cheekbone. His nose had been bleeding profusely, and here and there the facial skin was scraped as though he had been dragged over rough ground. Once he was clean she set about with Robbie's help bathing the individual wounds with disinfectant. Joe sat in silence throughout, though several times as she dabbed at an open wound he drew his breath in sharply and his lips pulled back from his teeth. Beneath her fingers she felt him wince.

'I'm sorry to hurt you,' she said, 'but I must make sure that all the dirt's out, else you'll suffer even more.'

'I know,' the words came out as a grunt, 'and I'm grateful. Never mind me, just do what has tae be done.'

When she finally finished Robbie fetched what was left of Helen Jarvis's tonic wine, since there was nothing stronger in the house; while Joe drank it, Mirren emptied the basin, watching the bloody water swirl down the drain.

'Now, where else are you hurt?'

'Nowhere.'

'The way you're holding your arm across your chest I'd say you've mebbe broken a rib or two. You should really go along to the infirmary tonight.'

'There's no need. If I have, it'll not be the first time. They'll mend themselves in time.'

'Who did this to you?'

'It was . . .' Robbie began wrathfully, but Joe cut across the words.

'Nob'dy in particular.'

'It must have been somebody. You should report them to the police.' Both men exchanged glances before Robbie said, 'That wouldnae be a good idea.'

'Why not?' Then, as he shrugged and Joe stayed silent, 'It happened at one of your meetings, didn't it? Did I not tell you that you were playing with fire, Robbie?'

'If nob'dy ever lights a fire,' Robbie said, 'the whole world could freeze tae death.'

'That's not your concern. Look at you!' She caught him by the arm and pulled him over to the wall mirror. He fingered the bruise that was beginning to form on one of his cheekbones.

'It's nothin'. And if things arenae my concern, Mirren, then who the hell's concern are they? If it was left tae the likes of you, nothin' good would ever happen for our sort!'

'You call this good? It'll be you next. D'you think I want to have to mop up your blood and see your face cut to ribbons?'

They faced each other angrily across the kitchen, forgetting Joe until he began to struggle to his feet. 'Best if I w-went home,' he began.

'Best if you saw a doctor in the morning.'

'I'll be fine once I get a night's sleep.'

'And ye'll get it in this house,' Robbie told him firmly. 'Ye're not goin' out onto the streets tonight. Not after what happened.'

'Robbie . . .' Mirren protested, while Joe said, 'I cannae stay here. Ye've both done enough for me.'

'There's a bed in the front room and enough beddin' tae do ye. Come on now, I'll see ye settled down.'

'Why can't you let the police deal with it?' Mirren wanted to know when her brother came back into the kitchen to make tea. 'They'd take him to the infirmary for proper treatment and they'd catch the men who did that to him.'

Robbie gave her a pitying look. 'The police are the last people we want tae see here.'

She stared at him. There was something strange in the way he had spoken. 'You're not telling me that it was the police that did that to him?'

'I'm not tellin' ye anythin'.' He fetched the big wooden tray Mirren had used to transport her mother's meals, put two mugs on it, then filled them with tea. 'The less you know the better for all our sakes.'

'If it was the police then it means that Joe was breaking the law . . . and if you were helping him, you were breaking it as well!'

Robbie added sugar and milk to the mugs and stirred the contents. 'Some laws are like prison walls, made tae keep folk locked in.'

'Robbie, if the police are looking for that man then I'm committing a crime just having him in this house.'

He turned at the door. 'Mirren, tonight's meeting was very important. Mebbe Joe should just've run like the rest of us when the police arrived, but he'd a lot on his mind. Mebbe he was even spoilin' for a fight. If so, he'd good reason. His friend George Armitage went missin' yesterday. His mother's been mad with worry, and me and Joe've been lookin' everywhere for him. He was pulled out of the River Cart down by the Inchinnan Bridge a few hours ago.'

Mirren woke in the morning to find Robbie, fully dressed, moving about the kitchen. She blinked groggily at him, half-dazed by lack of sleep. She had lain awake most of the night, unable to forget the bloody mess that had been Joe Hepburn's face and plagued by the memory of the last time she had seen George Armitage, lurching about his mother's little kitchen, demonstrating what the war had done to him. Wondering, too, if Joe was also lying sleepless only the thickness of a wall away.

'What time is it?'

'Early yet. I wanted tae see tae Joe before I went out.'

She raised herself on one elbow. 'How is he?'

'Sore. He'll not manage tae get tae work today.'

'You go into the front room and let me get dressed then I'll make the breakfast.'

She made enough for three, and ate hers alone while Robbie took his in the front room with Joe. When he returned she was almost ready to leave for the mill. Ignoring his protests she pulled Robbie over to the window to examine his bruised face in the watery light from the window.

'It's not bad at all, going yellow already.'

'I got off lightly because it wasnae me they'd come tae the meetin' for.'

'What'll you tell them at work?'

'The truth. That Joe was set on and beaten. He says he'll be all right for tomorrow. I'll come back at midday tae see tae him.'

'You'll not manage to get here and back in the time.' Robbie and Joe worked down at the harbour, on the opposite side of the town. 'I'll come home. It's easier for me.'

'Ye're sure? Thanks, Mirren,' he said when she nodded.

'Ye'll have tae put a stop to that,' Ella said when she heard about Bert's overtures the night before. 'Never let a man take advantage of ye!'

'He wasn't taking advantage,' Mirren protested as they went into the mill building. 'He just . . .'

'Ye think not? Let him go too far and he'll stop respectin' ye. And a man won't marry a lassie if he doesnae respect her.'

'How many times do I have to tell you that I've no intention of marrying anyone?' The ground-floor hoist was full, which meant that they would have to walk up a half-dozen or so flights of stairs to get to the twisting department. 'I don't know what's wrong with you these days, Ella Caldwell,' Mirren fumed as they climbed. 'One minute you're worrying about us going out with them, and the next you're bragging about them all over the place and putting poor Ruby's nose out of joint. And one minute you're talking about Bert as if he's some sort of monster, then the next you're telling me I should want to marry the man. What's got into you?'

'Listen, Mirren, they've both got good jobs and they dress well and talk nice. Look at Greta, tyin' herself tae a lad who'll give her nothin' but bairns and hard work. She'll grow old before her time worryin' about money while he spends every night at the pub. That's no life for a lassie.'

'Greta's happy with her choice.'

'But she's not made any choice, d'ye not see that? She's marryin' because she's havin' a bairn and because if her father finds out the truth before she's got a weddin' ring on her finger, he'll give her the leatherin' of her life then half-kill her lad.'

'I've no intention of letting that happen to me.'

'Even if it doesn't, what's ahead of you and me? We'll probably marry lads like Gregor Lewis and spend the rest of our lives lookin' after poky wee houses and birthin' bairns, and frettin' about makin' the money stretch tae the end of the week. I don't want that sort of life, Mirren, and I don't want the other sort either – stayin' on with my aunts and lookin' after them, then findin' when the last one dies that I've become old myself, with nob'dy tae care for me the way I'll have cared for them.'

'You're havering! Your aunts are hale enough yet and there's a long way to go before you're an old woman.'

Ella's eyes were haunted. 'Time has a way of passin', Mirren. That's why I'm sayin' that Bert and Martin . . .'

'Are nice laddies, and it'll be a long time before I begin to think of them as anything else,' Mirren said, and sped up the rest of the stairs so quickly that there was no breath left for further conversation.

Joe was up and dressed and moving stiffly about the kitchen when she arrived home in the middle of the day. He had made tea, sliced a loaf, and set out a slab of cheese from the small larder.

'I didn't know what ye'd w-want,' he said awkwardly, not quite looking at her.

'This is fine.'

As he poured tea for them both she saw that the knuckles of his hands were bruised and skinned.

'I'm s-sorry.'

'That's the second time you've said that to me in this kitchen.' She felt just as awkward as he did. Now that he was sitting down and in her line of vision she found herself tending to speak to his ear, rather than look him in the eye. 'D'you have a book to lend me this time as well?' she asked flippantly.

'Not with me, but I've s-some in the house that I'm sure ye'd l-like.'

'No doubt you have,' she said drily.

'Look . . . I shouldnae have let Robbie b-bring me here last night and I shouldnae have stayed.'

'You weren't in a fit state to go home on your lone.' For the first time since coming in she ventured a look at his face. The bruises and cuts reminded her of the coloured map of the world on the classroom wall at school. 'It'll take a while for your looks to get back the way they were.'

'Aye.' They sat in an uncomfortable silence, both trying to eat. Finally Mirren said, 'Robbie told me about George Armitage. I'm sorry.'

'It's a terrible waste of a good m-man. His mother's in a r-right state. I saw her after they . . . after they found him. George was all she had in the w-world.'

'Was it . . . Did he . . . ?'

'He died of war wounds but unfortunately for him, the man that d-did the job bungled it so George had tae finish it himself. That takes more courage than I'll ever have.' Joe stood up abruptly and reached for the teapot, then stopped and clutched at his chest.

'You should see a doctor. You might have broken ribs.'

'I'll b-be fine.'

'Will you not go to the infirmary? I'm worried about you.'

He gave a short, surprised laugh, then explained sheepishly when she looked across the table at him, 'It's been long enough since someone said a thing like that tae me. I think myself that it's just b-bruisin' and mebbe a pulled muscle. I'll mend. I've survived worse and no doubt there'll be worse tae c-come.'

'For you, mebbe, but I don't want this sort of thing to happen to my brother.' Mirren got up and carried her cup and saucer and her plate to the sink. 'And it will happen, if he goes on keeping company with you. I've asked you before to leave him alone.'

'And I've told you before that Robbie's old enough and wise enough tae make his own decisions. Mebbe ye should bear in mind that he's a man now, not a wee bairn for ye tae mother.'

'I do not mother him!'

'No? Leave that,' he added as she turned the tap on. 'I'll see tae the dishes.'

'I can manage,' Mirren snapped, then looked round as she heard the ring of coins landing on the table. 'What's that?'

'That's the money for my keep last night, and my food.'

'Don't be daft!'

'I don't take charity,' he said levelly. 'If I cannae show my appreciation by clearin' up after myself then I must pay ye.'

'Put that money away!' She turned to confront him.

'Step aside from the sink,' he invited calmly, a gleam in his eye. That, and the fact that his stammer had disappeared, made her realise that he was enjoying the confrontation and would no doubt be prepared to stand there arguing with her for the rest of the afternoon. He had the time, but she didn't. A swift glance at the clock showed that it was almost time for the fifteen-minute mill-bell to ring.

He nodded, reading her mind. 'Ye'll be late if ye don't go now,' he said.

Mirren had just gained Broomlands Street when the bell began to toll. She took to her heels and got into the twisting department just in time. When she got home at the end of the afternoon the flat was empty, the dishes washed and dried, the table set for herself and Robbie, the fireplace cleaned out and black-leaded, and the bedding Joe Hepburn had used had been neatly folded and left on the mattress.

She was pleased to see that there was no money lying on the table.

Because she had always had to hurry home to see to her mother as soon as the sirens signalled the end of the day's work, Mirren had never been able to take part in a 'bottlin', the traditional send-off given to a female mill-worker when she left to get married. She looked forward to the occasion as much as Greta herself, and was happy to devote her free evenings to working on the necessary decorations, which couldn't all be made during brief, snatched visits to the privy.

When the day arrived she and Ella and some of the other girls spirited Greta's coat away during the short afternoon break in order to decorate it with streamers and bows. Between them they had gathered together the traditional accessories – a baby's feeding bottle, a cheap toy doll, a chamber pot and plenty of salt to fill it with. When the Mistress, in a lenient mood for once, allowed them to stop their machines half-an-hour earlier than usual they pounced on Greta, who blushed and squealed and put up a half-hearted show of protest.

'My, ye're bonny,' Ella said when they had pushed her into her coat and pinned a colourful paper bonnet on her wiry hair. 'Now, here's yer bairn . . .' the doll was pushed into Greta's arms, 'and don't forget yer chanty in case ye're caught short.'

The chamber-pot, filled with salt and with the feeding bottle sticking out of the top, was shoved into Greta's free hand before she was whisked to the stairs to be paraded in and out of the other departments.

'Lord love the lassie,' Libby muttered as they watched the men in the stores lining up for the privilege of kissing the bride. 'This is probably the best day of her life. It'll all be old clothes and porridge from now on.'

'Marriage isn't that bad, surely,' Mirren protested.

'It depends on who ye marry, and from what I've heard of that fellow wee Greta's fallen tae, she'll no' have her sorrows tae seek,' Libby said, then as the bride fled back towards them, shrieking with excitement and pleasure, her mood changed like magic. 'Come on, lass, we'll walk ye home and show the town the bonnie mill-bride,' she shouted, and they whisked Greta out of the mill gates and along the streets.

20

Joe Hepburn and Robbie were sitting at the big table with such tragedy in their faces that Mirren's heart chilled when she and Ella, who had fallen into the habit of going back to Broomlands Street for half an hour after an evening's work at the fried-fish shop, went into the house.

'What's amiss? It's not Agnes, is it, or wee Thomas?'

'It's John M-McLean.' Joe had become a regular visitor and even though he and Mirren had their differences, he had grown comfortable enough in her presence to lose his nervous stammer. On this occasion, however, sheer agitation tripped his tongue. 'He's b-been thrown in the jail ag-gain.'

'Is that all?'

'All?' both men said in unison.

'No, I didn't mean that. I know it's bad news, but I thought . . .'

'Who's John McLean?' Ella asked in a sympathetic whisper. 'Joe's uncle?'

Mirren put on the kettle. Normally Robbie had it simmering on the stove, but tonight he had seemingly been too downcast to think of it. 'An important man in the Independent Labour Party.'

'Oh.' Ella fetched four plates and began to divide two lots of fish and chips between them. 'What happened tae him?'

'He and Sandy Ross have been charged with sedition and inciting revolution.'

Ella's eyes widened while Mirren merely asked, 'And were they?'

'In this country any workin' man that doesnae keep his mouth shut, apart from thankin' the employers for lettin' him kiss their boots, is out tae cause trouble.' Joe's voice was bitter and his eyes blazed blue fire. 'It's a trumped-up charge, that's what it is – brought because he's less of a threat tae them inside the jail than outside it.'

'From what I saw of him he's not well enough to be in a prison cell.'

'That makes no difference tae them,' Robbie scoffed, while Joe, the glitter in his eyes intensifying, said, 'There'll be demonstrations about this.'

'You're not going to do anything daft, are you?' Mirren appealed to her brother when Ella and Joe Hepburn had gone.

'For any favour, Mirren. D'ye think John McLean worries about whether folk like you think the things he has tae do are daft?'

'I know he doesn't. That's why he's a sick man in jail at this minute. But I'm sure that if he's got a sister, she must be fretting about him getting into trouble just the way I fret about you!'

He flicked an impatient glance at her then remembered, 'There's a letter for ye, from Grace. I put it on the mantel.'

'You're trying to take my mind off what you and Joe Hepburn might be getting up to!'

'Mebbe I am,' Robbie said, and went to bed.

As Mirren took the close-written pages from the envelope and smoothed them flat she could tell by the way Grace's writing sprawled that her friend had special news to impart. A Boston lady, wife of a prominent surgeon, had been rushed into the hospital where Anne and Grace worked after going into premature labour while accompanying her husband to a medical conference in Quebec. As it happened, her room was one of several under Anne's care, and while the young Bostonian recovered from the birth of her daughter, she had developed such a liking for the cheerful, capable Scottish nursing assistant that when she was well enough to leave she and her husband offered Anne the post of nursemaid in their home, caring for the new baby and their older child.

'Imagine,' Grace wrote, 'America!' As Mirren read the word the pages seemed to jump in her fingers. Even though she knew that America was vast and held millions of people, she thought of Donald every time she came across the word.

'Anne was so alarmed at the thought of leaving me behind in Quebec that she refused the offer at once,' Grace wrote. 'And thank goodness she did, for friendly though everyone is here, I would be desolate without her. Mrs Fitz asked the reason for her refusal and when she heard that Anne had a sister working in the same hospital she asked to see me. I went with Anne on our afternoon off, and I was very taken with Mrs Fitz, a pretty and charming lady with the sweetest little baby.

'She must have liked me too, for since recovering and travelling home with her husband she has written to say that a dear friend and neighbour with a little baby of her own would like to offer a similar post to me. She says that Anne and I will be able to see each other often, since they live so near to each other and both their husbands are doctors in the same hospital. As you will understand, we get very little sleep these nights, for we spend all our free time wondering whether we should stay here in Canada as we had intended, or make the move to Boston and become independent of the authorities who brought us over from Scotland.'

Mirren read the letter through again before putting it back into its envelope. As far as Grace was concerned, the move to Canada had been a good decision. She seemed to have got George Armitage out of her system, and her family had agreed, when Mirren told them of George's death, that Grace must not be told about it.

The Proctors had had a letter from Anne by the same post and when Mirren called the next day she found the entire family in a turmoil about it. Almost before she had time to take her coat off, Anne's letter had been thrust into her hand and she was ordered to read it and give her own views on the matter.

The letter was similar in content to Grace's but with neater writing, for no matter what might be happening around her, Anne always took time to make her handwriting both precise and clear – one of the talents that had stood her in such good stead in the Co-operative.

While Mirren scanned the pages, the arguments flew back and forth over her bent head. For once they were all at home; even Kate and Bill had been summoned from their own marital homes to discuss this latest family crisis. James Proctor was adamant in his belief that his daughters should stay where they were, since they had contracted to work in the Canadian hospital and had had their steamship fares paid in order to do just that. But John and his brother Bill both thought that if the new careers on offer were attractive to their sisters then they should accept.

'The authorities will easily find other Scots lassies eager to take their places,' John argued. 'And it gives them both the chance to see something of America. Working independently will give them new opportunities.'

Catherine was concerned at the prospect of her girls having to face more travelling in another unknown country, 'Just when they had settled down and begun to enjoy their work', while Kate, Maggie and Mary were united in envy at the new opportunities their sisters were being offered.

'Mirren, what do you think?' Catherine wanted to know, and suddenly Mirren was the centre of attention.

She folded Anne's letter and handed it back, desperately wondering what she could say that would satisfy them all without agreeing with one against another. At that moment the grandmother clock in the hall chimed the hour and, even as the final note echoed into silence, inspiration struck.

'It doesn't really matter what any of us think, for both the letters have taken some three weeks to come from Canada. This Mrs Fitz will want a swift decision, and by the time you send your views back to them Anne and Grace will have acted on their own initiative.'

'Sometimes,' Catherine said when the rest of the family had scattered to take up the threads of their own busy lives again, 'it takes an outsider to cut through the tangles and see the sense. Not that you're not one of the family, pet, I just mean that you came in from outside and put a fresh mind to the matter.' She sat back and heaved a sigh, clearly relieved to be free of further decisions. 'Take another cup of tea and tell me what you've been busy with. It's been a while since I last saw you.'

'I'm sorry, Aunt Catherine, but the days go by so fast . . .'

'Tut, Mirren, I was the one who told you to look to your own life after poor Helen died, and you've certainly done that. We'll not lose touch entirely, and that's all that matters.' Then, when Mirren had told all there was to tell, 'No word from your Logan yet? Och, he'll come round one of these days. Family's family, but in the meantime the loss is his.'

When Bert drove the car off the road and down onto the sands at Barassie the great stretch of sandy beach was deserted.

'I thought we'd get the place to ourselves,' he said with satisfaction, 'May's a bit early in the year for folk to come swimming and sunbathing.'

'But it's such a lovely day.' Ella, untying the streamers

of the wide-brimmed hat she had bought specially for the occasion, gazed up at the clear blue sky.

'Ah, but the Scots are creatures of habit.' Martin jumped down from the car and held his arms up to her. 'You'll not get many of them venturing onto a beach before June at the earliest.'

'We could bring our swimsuits next month and enjoy the water properly,' Bert suggested. 'You can both swim, can't you?'

'Of course.' Ella slipped her shoes off and tested the sand with the sole of her stockinged foot, her eyes on the soft little waves rippling invitingly only a short distance away. 'We could have a paddle.'

'Why not?' Bert began to tug his own shoes off.

'I'll soak my stockings,' Mirren objected.

'Take 'em off too.' Martin, dancing about on one foot while he unfastened the laces of the other shoe, nodded up the beach to where the soft white sand above the waterline had been blown by the winds into dunes thick with clumps of tall sea-grass. 'Nobody'll see you up there. Just be careful of the grasses, the blades can be quite sharp.'

'The men are lucky,' Ella said enviously as she hauled her skirt up in the privacy of the dunes so that she could unfasten her suspenders. 'They can just pull their socks off and roll their trouser legs up right out there in public.'

'Why did you tell them we could swim when we can't?'

'They'd think we were stupid if we told the truth. I'm sure that the sort of girls they usually go out with can swim.'

Mirren rolled her stockings up and tucked them into her skirt pocket. 'They're going to get a surprise when they bring us down here in the summer and we drown before their very eyes.'

'We'll learn – we'll start going to Paisley Baths and by the time we come back here we'll be swimming like fish.'

Going barefoot through the dry sand was like walking on cool silk. When they reached the water's edge the men were already wading in the shallows, trousers rolled up to their knees to expose muscular calves. The little waves looked inviting, but as soon as Mirren and Ella ran into them they skipped out again, shrieking.

'It's icy c-cold!' Mirren hopped about on the sand, trying to restore feeling to her numbed toes.

'It's fine once you get into it. Come on, don't be a baby.' Martin bounded from the surf and before Ella could back away he had caught her up in his arms and carried her into the water. She locked her arms about his neck, screaming, as he pretended that her weight was too much for him and he would have to drop her into the waves. When Bert advanced on Mirren she prudently took to her heels.

It was wonderful to be able to run without having to bother about trams and vans and carts, and with no people in the way or corners to dodge round. Her hair came loose as she ran and whipped about her face, while her skirt flared round her bare knees. Underfoot the packed sand was firm and easy to run on, but as she sped up the beach and past the waterline, back into the soft white powdery sand, she began to flounder. A laughing glance over her shoulder showed that Bert was gaining, and she swerved to make a mad dash into the dunes, only to be tackled and pulled to the ground almost at once.

'Gotcha!' Bert said triumphantly as they rolled together down a slope and into a sheltered hollow.

'Bully! Just because you can run faster than I can . . .'

'Of course I can. I'm a man and you're only a weak and feeble little woman.'

'Let me up.'

'There's a penalty for being caught. You'll have to give me a kiss.'

'Must I?'

'There's no appeal, and no bargaining allowed.'

She wound her arms about his neck. 'If you insist, but I won't enjoy it . . .'

'Then I'll have to keep on kissing you until you do.'

His mouth was cool and firm and the tall thick clumps of grass surmounting the dunes created a hidden private world, where the only noise was the whisper of waves coming into the shore, the movement of the grasses in the slight breeze, the harsh cry of a seagull and the occasional sound of laughter from the beach. Mirren, intoxicated by sun and sand and space, felt that time had stopped for them in their secret place, specially made for lovers. Bert's mouth strayed down to caress her throat, then he eased her blouse aside so that his lips could trace the path of her collarbone towards her shoulder. His fingertips brushed against her breast, and she gasped and arched herself against him as his touch sent an unexpected thrill through her entire body. Compared to Bert, Donald had been a circumspect and somewhat dull suitor.

Bert's mouth moved back to claim hers in another long slow kiss, then he raised himself up slightly on his elbows so that he could look down on her. 'You're very lovely, Mirren,' he said huskily, 'My beautiful sand-maiden.' His fingers were cool against her throat as he eased the top button of her blouse free of its buttonhole and stroked the curve of her breast very gently, arousing the same thrill as before, before bending to kiss – no, she realised with surprise – caress her skin lightly with the tip of his tongue. Ripples of pleasure followed his every touch, for all the world as though she were a musical instrument and he the player. One hand stroked her skirt slowly up her leg and, as he shifted slightly, his bare feet entwined with hers. The ripples turned to fire that probed beneath her skin and right into the depths of her.

She shivered, wriggling into the silky sand, greedily savouring the pleasures of the moment. Soon, she knew, this would have to stop. But not yet, not just yet . . .

Then the moment vanished and her eyes flew open. 'Was that Ella calling us?'

'No.'

She put a hand on his shoulder, holding him back when he tried to kiss her again. 'Are you sure?'

'It was only the gulls.' He captured her hand, kissed it, then placed it on the sand, above her head, holding it there.

'We'd best get back to the others.'

'In a moment. There's plenty of time.'

'But if they're looking for us . . .'

'They're not. I told you, it was only a seagull. Lie still, will you?'

She tried to move, then discovered that she was trapped beneath his hard body.

With the sun behind him, his face was in shadow. Mirren began to feel uneasy. He could have been any man, any stranger, holding her down with his superior weight, pinning her hand to the ground by her head. 'Bert, let me up.'

'In a minute, I said . . .' His voice was rasping now, rather than husky, and his breathing was quick and uneven. The hand on her bare leg moved higher, pushing her skirt above her knees, clutching at her thigh.

'Bert . . .' She tried to sit up, but he suddenly shifted so that his full weight was on top of her. He gave a strange groan and fumbled at her legs, trying to force them apart.

'Bert, leave me be, I want to go back to the others!'

Frightened now, she struggled to squirm out from beneath him. This time he deliberately fought against her, the shared caresses of only moments earlier becoming a battle for survival on her part and domination on his.

Dimly Mirren heard someone crashing through the sheltering grasses. A voice, higher and wilder and more harsh than the gulls, screeched, 'Get away from her!' then

Bert gave a sharp, surprised grunt and the weight of him was gone from her. Even as Mirren felt the first shock of cool air on her bare legs, clawed fingers caught at her, dragging her to her feet.

'Look at you!' Ella skirled, shaking her so hard that her teeth felt as though they were loosening in her jaw. 'What d'ye think ye're doin'? Look at the state of ye! Ye're dirty . . . dirty!'

'Ella!'

'Nothin' but a dirty wee slut!' Ella's arm swung up, back, then forward, her open palm hitting Mirren's face with all the force of the upswing. Her head jerked painfully on the stem of her neck and the warm still air echoed with the sound of the slap.

'Steady on!' she heard Bert protesting. Through eyes streaming with tears of shock and pain she saw Ella rounding on him, driving him across the sandy ground as she punched and clawed at him with all the aggression of a terrier dog. He stumbled back under the onslaught, then lost his footing and fell among the sharp-bladed grasses as Martin arrived in the secluded little hollow to grab Ella's arms, pulling her away from his friend when she would have continued the attack.

'What's going on?' he asked, bemused, but with the sense to retain his hold on her upper arms so that she couldn't turn on him.

'Ask him!' Ella glared at Bert, who was clambering to his feet, dabbing at a grass cut on his face. 'Ask that dirty pig what he was doin' tae my friend!'

'I wasn't . . .'

'Liar! I saw ye!' Ella shrieked at him, then to Mirren, 'And I saw you lettin' him touch ye, dirty wee whore!'

'Be quiet!' Martin shook her hard, shouting her down. 'That's enough!'

Suddenly all the fight went out of Ella. Panting and sobbing, she hung from his grasp as he looked at the others over her head. 'What the hell's going on here?'

'Nothing,' Bert mumbled from behind the handkerchief pressed to a scratch on his cheek. 'It was just a few harmless kisses.'

'That's what they all say,' Ella flared up again. '"Just a wee kiss, hen. A wee kiss won't hurt." But it does . . . it does!' She tried to lunge again at Bert, who hurriedly retreated to the dubious protection of the grasses.

'For God's sake keep her away from me!' he squawked while Ella, unable to break free, collapsed once more, wailing, 'Go away! Go away and leave me be!'

'Gladly.' Martin's voice was like ice. He opened his hands and Ella sank to the ground, wrapping her arms about herself. 'Come on, you two.'

'You go. I'm staying with her.'

Martin looked doubtful. 'Will you be all right?'

'Safer with her than . . .' Mirren looked at Bert, who avoided her gaze. She felt dirty, just as Ella had said. Her cheek throbbed from the force of the slap, while the fire that had flared through her entire body under the touch of Bert's lips, hands and tongue had turned to burning shame.

'Come on, Bert, come away!' Martin took his friend's arm and marched him back to the open beach. When they had gone Mirren knelt cautiously by Ella, ready if necessary to retaliate if she was attacked again.

'Ella?'

'Dirty,' Ella keened, huddled into herself.

'Ella, what happened to you?'

'What happened tae me? It's what happened tae you that matters!'

'I'm talking about you. Something happened once, didn't it? Something . . . dirty?' Mirren hazarded cautiously.

Ella suddenly scrambled away from her, grovelling in the sand, snatching up handfuls of the abrasive stuff and scrubbing hard at her face and neck and arms, oblivious to the grains streaming down inside her blouse.

'Stop that, you're hurting yourself!' Mirren tried to restrain her, and Ella struggled to pull free.

'Leave me be! I'm dirty, and it's not me that did the hurtin'. Not me!' Her voice rose. '"No harm in kisses, hen." But there is. It's wicked and then you're wicked, a wicked, dirty girl!'

'Sshhh . . .' Confused, but acting on impulse, Mirren pulled the other girl into her arms and held her tight, ignoring Ella's attempts to fight free. After a moment she stopped struggling and began to weep noisily, like a child. It took some time before the bawling slowed and quietened to sniffles and hiccups, and the Ella that Mirren knew emerged from the stormy, frightened child cowering in the sand to sit up, look around and say fairly calmly, 'We'd best get back.'

'We're not moving from here until you tell me what happened to you.'

'It's none of your business.'

'It is. I'm your friend.'

'That's why I can't tell ye,' Ella muttered, head turned away, lifting handfuls of sand then letting it run back through her fingers. 'Ye'll not want tae know me after.'

'Don't be daft!'

'Ye'll not understand. Nob'dy can, if it's not happened tae them.'

'If what's happened? I'm not moving until you tell me.'

Ella dragged up a deep sigh from the very centre of her being, then straightened and scooped up another handful of powdery sand, this time rubbing it carefully over her face to cleanse the tears. 'All right, but ye'll wish I hadn't.' Her eyes, when she looked at Mirren, were old and sad.

'I'll be the judge of that.'

Ella shrugged and continued to play with the sand as she talked. 'It was when my mam died and it was just me and my da, and he needed a wife more than a daughter,' she said flatly, then stopped as though the story was over.

'So did he get married again?'

'No!' Ella said contemptuously, as though Mirren was too stupid to understand. 'He didn't need tae get married, not while I was there in his house.'

'But . . .' Mirren struggled to make sense of it.

'I said ye'd not understand,' Ella said, and all at once Mirren did.

'You mean . . . ?'

'Aye, that's just what I mean.'

'But you were only wee. How could a wee girl . . .'

The old eyes in Ella's face pitied her confusion. 'Us – we're born female, Mirren. We don't have tae do anythin' but be there and keep quiet about what's goin' on, in case we get put intae the jail for bein' wicked and . . . dirty and . . .' Her voice began to shake on the final words and tears glittered on her lashes.

'Oh, Ella!' Mirren reached out, but the other girl pulled away, shaking her head.

'Leave me!'

'How did you get free of him?'

'My aunts came and said I'd tae go and live with them. I think a neighbour mebbe told them there was somethin' wrong in our house. He didnae want tae let me go. I mind them talkin' tae him – talking at him, more like. I think they threatened him with jail the way he'd threatened me.' A glint of tired amusement flashed across her drawn face. 'When someone says they'll get the police tae ye, ye usually give in.'

'Did you see him again?'

Sand showered from Ella's long dark hair when she shook her head. 'He died that first night after they took me out of the house. He drank a bottle of laudanum, and there's not a day goes by without me hopin' that he's sufferin' in thē bad fires.'

'But you were all right after that.'

'Of course I was.' The stranger's eyes gave way to Ella's. She even managed to summon up a jaunty smile. 'My aunts cured me with religion and guilt. Lots of guilt. They made me go tae the church tae save my soul, but while they prayed for me tae be cleansed and cured, I just kept askin' God tae send my father's soul tae hell. That's why I can't let them know that I go tae the dancin' . . . They think that workin' in the fried-fish shop every night keeps me from gettin' intae mischief.' She dusted sand from her fingers. 'Did I not say ye'd be sorry ye'd asked?'

'I'm not sorry at all.' Mirren forced back the wave of nausea that swept over her, knowing that Ella would misconstrue it as disgust at her, instead of at what had been done to her. 'Friends should be able to share everything.'

Ella hiccuped, sniffed, scrubbed her nose with the back of a hand, then surveyed her and remarked, 'You look like a tink.'

Better to be called a tink than a whore, Mirren thought with relief. Aloud she said, 'I'm not the only one.'

It took a few minutes to put their stockings back on and shake the worst of the sand from their clothes. Fortunately Ella had a comb in her pocket.

'D'you think they'll still be waiting for us?' Mirren asked as she tried to comb the tangles from her hair.

'I'd not blame them if they were halfway back tae Glasgow. If they are, there's a railway station in Troon.' Ella pulled her blouse free of her skirt and sand cascaded down about her feet. 'It's only about a mile away along the sands,' she said briskly as she shook her blouse then tucked it back in. 'I've got some money in my bag.'

'I just hope they thought to leave our bags and shoes behind,' Mirren fretted, but to her surprise they saw when they left the dunes that the car was still there, with two silent figures waiting in the front seats.

21

Not a word passed between any of them as Bert drove the car back to Paisley at top speed. When they reached the corner of Broomlands and Maxwellton Street he stayed where he was, brooding over the steering wheel, while Martin assisted both girls down to the pavement, then jumped back in beside Bert after a hurried 'Cheerio.'

'And that's the last we'll see of them,' Ella said as they watched the car drive off. 'Can I come home with you and get tidied up? I don't want the aunts tae see me like this.'

Mirren had hoped that Robbie would be out, but he was at home when they got there. So was Joe Hepburn, who scrambled to his feet as the door opened.

'I just brought Ella back . . .' Mirren said feebly to the two astonished faces.

'For a cup of tea.' Ella had recovered her ability to think quickly. 'I'm parched, I think it must be somethin' tae do with lookin' at all that sea.'

'Mirren,' Robbie's voice was cautious. 'What's happened to yer face?'

She put a hand to her cheek, still throbbing slightly. 'Nothing.'

He started to argue then changed his mind. Joe picked up his hat. 'I was j-just g-going.'

'I'll come with ye. I could do with the walk.' Robbie followed him. For some reason the sound of the men

crunching over spilled sand as they went through the tiny
lobby struck both Ella and Mirren as funny. As the outer
door closed they dissolved into giggles, clutching at each
other, releasing the afternoon's tension in peal after peal
of laughter. By the time they had sobered Mirren's ribs
were aching and her face was wet with tears, but at the
same time she felt as though she had been relieved of a
great load.

'There's nothin' like a laugh tae cheer ye up.' Ella
mopped her eyes then looked at her fingers, grimacing.
'I've even got sand in my tears.' Then, touching Mirren's
face gently, 'I must've given you a right dunt, pet. Yer
poor face is bruised. Bathe it with vinegar right away,
then we'll have tae take all our clothes off if we want
tae get rid of this sand properly. Where's the old sheet
ye use when ye come home from the mill?'

While Mirren bathed her face, Ella snibbed the door in
case Robbie returned before they had cleaned themselves.
That done, she filled the kettle and set it to boil while she
spread the sheet out before the kitchen fire. Then they both
stripped, shaking out their clothes and rubbing themselves
down with clean rags before washing.

It was the first time Mirren had ever seen another
human being naked, or allowed anyone else to see her in
the nude; at first she was deeply embarrassed, especially
when they happened to brush against each other, but Ella
was completely at ease, laughing when Mirren almost fell
off the sheet trying to avoid contact.

'Ye're awful shy all of a sudden . . .'

'I thought you'd hate to be too near anyone after . . .'
Mirren hesitated, then said daringly, 'after what you
told me.'

'You're a lassie, so it's different. And some men are
different too. They're not all like my da was. And Bert.'
She stepped off the sheet to pour hot water from the kettle
into a basin, moving with a natural grace. 'I was right,
wasn't I? He wasn't just kissin' ye.'

'He was at first.' Mirren's insides curled up at the memory. 'Then he changed.'

Ella added cold water from the tap to the basin, her back to Mirren. 'Did ye want him tae change?' she asked without looking round.

'Of course not!'

'Then it was as well that I stopped him when I did. Ye have tae learn which ones ye can trust, Mirren.' She set the basin on the draining board. 'Come on, we'd best wash together tae save time. Yer brother might come back at any minute. I wish I was skinny like you, instead of fat,' she said casually as they jostled each other at the basin.

Mirren risked a sideways glance. Ella was enviably rounded, her waist generous but neat above the swell of her hips. Even her belly, tensing as she lifted her arms to wash her neck, had a gentle feminine roundness to it, whereas Mirren's was almost as flat as her chest. 'You're not fat.'

'I am. In another few years when they . . .' Ella touched her full firm breasts, 'start tae sag and my hips get fuller I'll look just like Libby.'

'There's nothing wrong with Libby.'

'She's had weans and grandweans – she's got an excuse for lookin' sonsy. Me,' Ella shrugged and her breasts bounced, 'I'm just fat.' She shook water from her hands and stepped away to dry herself and dress again.

Mirren had only intended to swill the last of the sand swiftly from her skin, but once she started to wash she found herself rubbing hard, going over and over the places Bert had touched, trying to clean away the memory of his fingers and his lips. Now she understood the meaning of Ella's keening cry of 'Dirty!' She was still washing when Ella finished dressing herself.

'Come on, ye're surely clean enough now. Here,' Ella thrust the towel into her hands, 'ye'd better dry yerself before ye rub yer skin off altogether. How're we goin' tae tell Ruby that we're not goin' out with our fancy draughtsmen any more? She'll never let us hear the end of it. We'll have tae pretend that we just got tired of them.'

'Will she believe that?'

'Not for a minute – she's not daft. But if we stick tae the same story there's little she can do about it,' Ella said. Then, stooping to gather up the sheet, 'Would ye look at that? It's a wonder there's any sand left on the beach.'

'We must have left some in their car as well.'

'I hope it's all over the duster coats. That'd give Bert some explaining tae do tae his sisters.' Ella deftly folded the sheet corner to corner, careful not to spill its contents. 'I'll take this down tae the back court while you make a cup of tea.'

'Ella . . .'

The other girl paused on her way out the door. 'If ye're goin' tae say anythin' about what I told ye back on the beach, I don't want tae hear it, ever,' she said flatly, then with a return to her old self she added with a grin, 'There's one good thing about today's carry-on – we won't have tae learn tae swim after all.'

'What was going on with you and Ella?' Robbie wanted to know when he came home later.

'Nothing.'

'It didn't seem like nothing. The two of ye looked as if ye'd been dragged through a hedge backwards, and her eyes were red. And your face . . . Did someone hit ye?' His voice rose. 'Was it one of these two lads with the car?'

'They didn't do anything. I hurt my face by accident.'

'Next time ye go out with them,' Robbie said belligerently, 'I want tae have a word with them first.'

'We'll not be seeing them again. There was a bit of a falling-out.'

'Oh.' He peered at the hearth. 'There's a sprinkling of sand on the tiles.'

'I'll sweep it up later. We were sitting on the sand down at Barassie,' Mirren added defensively as he gave her a long, thoughtful look. 'It was very nice but the sea air's made me tired.' She gave an elaborate yawn. 'I think I'll just get to my bed.'

When the women in the twisting department found out that there were going to be no more jaunts for Mirren and Ella in Bert's fine motor car, the two of them had to put up with some teasing and jeering. As was to be expected, Ruby, who had been beside herself with envy, led the chorus.

It was a few weeks before the two of them ventured back to Denniston Palais. 'Even if Bert and Martin are there, we don't need to speak to them,' Mirren said nervously as they hurried towards the hall, their dance shoes in their bags.

'I doubt if they'd want tae speak tae us. And if they did I'd have somethin' tae say tae that Bert McNeil!'

'Don't start anything,' Mirren begged. 'The last thing we want is to be thrown out of a dance hall!' But to her relief there was no sign of their former suitors.

'This is going to be a perfect day!' Mirren, dressed in her best and marching along Broomlands Street arm-in-arm with Ruby and Ella, beamed at the folk that gathered on the pavements to watch the Ferguslie Mill-workers walk to Gilmour Street Railway Station on Sma' Shot Day. The previous July she had been standing with Annie Proctor at the door of the Co-operative shop, watching the procession and pretending that she didn't envy them one bit. This year she was part of the great crowd, on her way to enjoy a day out. It was one of the grandest moments of her life.

'I hope I don't make an exhibition of myself, bein' sick all over the train carriage,' Ella said limply. 'It must have been the . . .' She paused, unable to mention food in any context, then finished with, 'what I had for my tea last night.'

'You'll be all right, Ella,' Ruby said firmly across Mirren. 'Just keep yer mind on the grand time we'll have. And if ye do feel like vomitin', don't do it on my new skirt.'

As they gained the High Street Mirren suddenly noticed Logan and Belle on the pavement, watching the excited, chattering, colourful procession. Her first reaction when she caught her brother's eye was to look away quickly, then she changed her mind and smiled at him. Life was too short for bearing grudges. To her delight he inclined his head slightly. He didn't smile, but even so it was a start in the rebuilding of their relationship.

She squeezed Ella's arm against her side and beamed at Ruby. 'Nob'dy's going to vomit. We'll find a window seat for Ella and the breeze'll do her the world of good. And we're all going to enjoy every minute of this outing.'

County Square boiled and seethed with people as the employees from both Coats' and the Anchor Mills met and mingled, lining up to file into the railway station. It looked as though the entire town was being evacuated. Inside the station train after train, chartered by the mill-owners, arrived, filled up from the queues stretched from the square to each platform and drew out.

When the turn of the adult Ferguslie workers came, Ruby and Mirren managed to find a window seat for Ella. Ignoring protests from their fellow travellers they opened the window and, although her hair was somewhat wind-blown and there was a sooty smut on one cheek from the smoke blowing back from the engine, she had quite recovered by the time they arrived in Callander, a pretty little Perthshire town known as the gateway to the Scottish Highlands. As they walked in a chattering, giggling throng to the large field set aside for their use, Mirren's head swivelled from side to side in an attempt to take in everything – the clean little market town, which relied on agriculture and small woollen mills for its income, the shops and the pretty houses with their flower-packed gardens, the great hills that enclosed and sheltered Callander, giving it the appearance of a pet kitten nestling in the protective palm of its loving owner.

'Imagine being able to live in a place like this!'

'It's all right tae visit,' Ruby said doubtfully. 'But I'd not want tae live here. Ye'd be too far away from the Picture Palaces and the dance halls.'

Ella agreed, but to Mirren, Callander represented heaven on earth and she felt that she could settle very happily into a pretty, tranquil place such as this.

The rest of the day rushed by. Sports had been organised for those looking for an active day out, and while the older folk were happy to wander back into the town to buy mementoes of their visit, or sit in the shade and talk, Mirren and Ruby and Ella, now back to her old self, ran races, jumped hurdles, balanced eggs on spoons, and hopped along at top speed with their feet trapped in sacks, helpless with laughter. When Ella and Ruby paired off with each other for the three-legged race, Gregor Lewis appeared at Mirren's side, wrenching his tie off and kneeling to bind her right ankle to his left.

'You're too quick for me,' she protested as they started their ungainly stumble towards the rope that marked the winning post. 'I'll fall!'

'No ye won't.' He wrapped one arm about her, hugging her so close that she could feel the heat of his body through the material of his shirt and smell his mingled scent of sweat and hair cream. 'Just hold on tae me and we'll win.'

Win they did, with Gregor half-carrying Mirren, who had started to laugh so hard at the absurdity of the race that she could scarcely see the rope.

He stayed by her side while she sampled football and cricket, skittles and darts, all sports she had never tried before. When they were summoned to the huge tent that had been set up at one end of the field to house trestle tables filled to overflowing with trays of sandwiches, sausage rolls, pies, scones, pancakes, crumpets and cakes, he carried her plate.

'You've done well for yerself,' Ella said as he went off to fetch more lemonade.

'Are ye goin' tae start walkin' out with him?' Ruby asked through a mouthful of sausage roll. Her dark eyes glittered enviously at Mirren, who realised that Ella was right when she said that Ruby's real eye-colour was green, for jealousy.

'No, I'm not.'

'Ye could dae a lot worse than the likes of Gregor Lewis.'

'I'm not interested in anyone. Gregor's just a nice lad enjoying his day out like the rest of us. And it's not just me he's fetching for,' Mirren pointed out as Gregor came scudding back bearing a large jug of lemonade and several tin mugs. She had to admit, though, in her new mood of relaxed contentment, that he was one of the best-looking men in the field, and there was something flattering about his attentions.

He was the best dancer too. When everyone had eaten their fill and the tables and the dishes had been cleared away, boarding was put down to form a makeshift floor, and several men who had brought musical instruments with them – an accordion, a fiddle, a banjo and a few mouth organs – took their places. Moving across the floor with Gregor, feeling as light as a puff of thistledown in his arms, she felt that she could ask no more from life. She and Gregor danced every dance, and when the mill-workers wandered back along the road to the little station where the chartered trains waited to take them home, it seemed natural for them to sit shoulder-to-shoulder on the return journey. Just as it seemed natural, when he asked, to agree that he could walk her home.

They meandered through the town arm-in-arm, with

Gregor regulating his long strides to suit her shorter steps, pausing now and again to look into shop windows, reluctant to let the day end. But as they approached the corner of Broomlands and Maxwellton Street, Mirren began to regret her decision to allow Gregor to walk her home. He would expect a goodnight kiss, and he had every right to it, for he had been an attentive escort for most of the day. But would he want more than that? He was a decent enough lad, but Mirren knew only too well that if he asked her to walk out with him and she agreed out of politeness, she would be setting her foot on the road that led to commitment. Men like Gregor grew up expecting to follow in their father's footsteps, which meant marrying and raising a family in one of Paisley's tenements and seeking nothing further from life.

One goodnight kiss, she told herself firmly as they turned the corner and started down the slope of Maxwellton Street, and she would make it clear that it was nothing more than a parting caress between friends. Then she stopped so suddenly that her hand was jerked from the angle of Gregor's arm.

'Did ye catch yer foot on the pavin' stones?' Then, following her gaze, 'Does that car down the street not belong tae one of the men you and Ella were seein'?' he asked with sudden jealous heat.

'No, of course it doesn't. Thank you for walking me back.' She caught hold of his elbows, bounced up on tiptoe and planted a swift kiss on his surprised mouth. 'Goodnight,' she gabbled, and began to hurry towards her close, desperate to reach it before Bert saw her.

Her foot was on the step leading to safety when he emerged from a doorway further down.

'Mirren?' His long legs covered the ground swiftly and he was by her side before she could duck into the close and gain the stairs. 'I've been waiting for you for the past hour. Listen . . .' He took her arm and began to lead her down towards the car. 'I came to apologise. I behaved like a bounder.'

'Bert . . .' She tried to draw away but he was so intent on getting his apology out that he just tightened his grip.

'I don't know why I did . . . what I did. You've no idea how much I've missed you. If you'll just forgive me I swear that I'll never . . .'

'Here, you, what d'ye think ye're doin'?' Gregor interrupted, catching hold of Mirren's free arm.

Bert whirled and stared at him, then said icily, 'Speaking to a friend, not that it's any business of yours, whoever you are.'

'I'm the one that's walkin' her home, that's whoever I am. So ye can just take yer hands off of her. Come on, Mirren, I'll see ye safely intae the house.' Gregor began to lead her back to her own close, but Bert held on so that she was being jostled between them both.

'If you'd prefer it, Mirren, I'm willing to go into your home and meet your family and apologise to them as well.'

'I said, I'm takin' her home,' Gregor interrupted grimly. 'Anyway, she doesnae live up that close, she lives up this one.'

'This one?' Surprise caused Bert to release her and Gregor, seizing the victory, hustled Mirren into the close, muttering, 'I thought ye werenae seein' him any more.'

'I'm not.'

'Then what's he doin' here?'

'I don't know! Gregor, why don't you just go home?'

'And leave you alone with him? I'll see ye intae the house.'

'Mirren?' Bert followed them. 'Why did you tell me that you lived somewhere else?'

'Why don't you get intae that fancy car of yours and go back tae where ye belong and stop botherin' us?' Gregor invited.

Bert pushed past him to confront Mirren. 'I told you, I want to apologise.'

'Apologise for what?' Gregor wanted to know belligerently. He tapped Bert on the shoulder. 'What did ye do tae her that needs apologisin' for?'

'Go home, the two of you, and leave me in peace!' Mirren put one foot on the stairs, worried now that the ground-floor tenants would hear the argument and open their doors to investigate.

'Ye heard what she said. We've had a very nice day at the mill outin', me and Mirren, and we're both tired. So why don't ye just go home and let us dae the same?'

'Mill outing?' Bert asked, puzzled. 'What were you doing on a mill outing?'

'She's entitled tae go, as one of the mill-girls.'

'A mill-girl? But I thought . . . Mirren, what's going on?' Bert caught her arm. 'You don't live where you said you did, you don't work in a lawyer's office . . .'

'You take yer hands off of her!' Gregor tried to pull the other man away, then reeled back as Bert swung round on him, lashing out with his fist. The blow landed on Gregor's jaw; taken by surprise he staggered away, his shoulder rebounding off the concrete wall, then came straight back at Bert. In seconds they were locked together, staggering and swaying, each trying to break free in order to hit the other, almost falling against a house door but mercifully avoiding it just in time to reel along the short length of the back close, hissing and grunting through gritted teeth as they scuffled, careering off the walls on each side. Mirren watched helplessly, both hands fisted at her mouth.

Finally Bert managed to break free and swing a strong punch at Gregor, who gave a yelp of pain and retaliated with a furious flurry of blows that dropped Bert to the ground like a sack of potatoes.

'Oh my God, you've killed him!'

'It'd take more than that wee slap tae kill anyone.' Gregor used his sleeve to wipe blood from his chin. 'And even if I have, he deserved it. The bastard near punched my eye out!'

As Mirren dropped to her knees Bert stirred and raised himself on one elbow, looking up at her groggily. He too was bleeding, from the nose. 'Leave me alone!' He pushed her hands away when she tried to help him and had got to his knees, dripping blood on the flagstones, when booted feet came down the pavement and into the close. The three of them froze instinctively, Gregor on his feet, Bert and Mirren kneeling. Fortunately they had moved into the back close during the struggle and were out of sight of anyone coming in from the street. But if the newcomer was to come to the nearby door, or to go through to the back court for some reason, they would be discovered. The thought was almost more than Mirren could bear. Why, she asked herself frantically, why hadn't she just hurried home from the station? Then she might well have been safely indoors when Bert arrived, never to be discovered.

A wheezy, crackling cough from the depths of damaged lungs echoed through from the front section of the close, then the darkness about them suddenly lifted as the gas mantle near the stairs was lit. As the lamplighter moved on to the next close Mirren scrambled to her feet. 'Are you all right, Bert?'

He got up, leaning against the wall for support and mopping at his face with a handkerchief. When he took it from his face he stared, aghast, at the material in the faint glow from the gas-lamp. 'I'm bleeding!'

'So am I . . . and I'm half-blind and all,' Gregor told him sourly, his hand still clapped over his left eye.

'Come upstairs and I'll put a cold cloth to the back of your neck.'

'Upstairs? With you and him?' Bert gave a short snuffly laugh. 'I value my life higher than that. I'm getting out of this godforsaken town right now and you needn't think I'll be back!' Over the handkerchief clasped to his nose his eyes glittered malevolently at Mirren. 'I must have been mad, driving all this way to apologise to a common mill-worker who lives in a . . .' he glared round the small shabby close, 'a hovel like this!'

Gregor rumbled angrily and took a step forward, fists bunching. Mirren moved to hold him back as Bert stormed out of the close. The car's engine noisily chugged into life, the hooter, so often sounded in Mirren's presence as a triumphant flourish, gave a derisive sneer, and Bert drove out of her life for ever.

'Good riddance tae bad rubbish,' Gregor snarled, 'How ye ever wanted tae have anythin' tae dae with . . . Where are ye goin'?'

'Home,' she told him crisply from halfway up the stairs. 'And you should be, too.'

'Am I not even tae get a wee cup of tea first?'

'After what you've done?'

'I was only lookin' after ye.'

She marched back down the stairs. 'I don't need looking after, Gregor, and I don't like to have men fighting over me.'

'But . . .'

One of the two doors at the foot of the stairs opened and a bald head appeared. 'Will ye for God's sake stop yer natterin' and get out of here! How's a body tae get any sleep?'

'I'm sorry, Mr McCrae.'

'Oh, it's you. I don't know,' the old man said peevishly. 'First it's weans fightin' right outside my own door then it's youse two!'

'We were just sayin' goodnight,' Gregor mumbled.

'Well say it an' get off home!'

'You're quite right, Mr McCrae. Goodnight, Gregor,' Mirren said, and escaped.

22

'I don't know what Gregor Lewis tried tae do tae ye on Saturday night,' Ruby said slyly on Monday morning. 'But he's got a grand black eye.'

'He never has!' Ella said.

'I'm tellin' ye. When I asked what he'd been up tae he gave me a right squint . . . not that it's easy tae squint with a black eye.' Ruby howled with laughter at her own wit.

'Ye hit him, Mirren?' Ella's own eyes were huge with curiosity. 'What was he tryin' tae do?'

'He wasn't trying to do anything and I didn't hit him. He just walked me home then went off to his own bed,' Mirren protested. 'Mebbe he walked into a lamp-post on his way home.'

Gregor avoided her all morning, but she managed to catch him on his own on her way to the privy. As Ruby had said, his eye and the area all around it were badly bruised.

'Oh, Gregor, I'm sorry!'

'It wasnae all your fault, I suppose,' he said gruffly. 'Though I still don't know what was goin' on.'

'What did you tell folk about . . .' She indicated the eye.

'That I fell over a broken pavin'-stone and hit my face off a wall. I've been takin' a terrible ribbin' about it.'

'You should never have tried to help me.'

'I wasnae goin' tae let that daft fool drag ye intae his car. God knows what might have happened tae ye then. I don't really mind this keeker,' Gregor said manfully. 'Not if it helped ye tae get rid of him. Anyway,' a sly grin crept over his face, 'I doubt if he's lookin' too smart himself this mornin', with his nose all over his face.' He sniggered, then said, 'I was wonderin', Mirren – we never got tae say goodnight properly because of him, so I was wonderin' if we could . . .'

'No, Gregor,' she told him firmly. 'You're a nice man, but I think you and me'd be best just to leave things as they are. I've got you into enough trouble as it is.'

Ella heard the whole story during the midday break when the two of them were on their own and apart from the others. 'Bert must've really liked ye, if he came here specially tae apologise.'

'Mebbe so, but I couldn't bear to be with him again.' Mirren shivered, remembering how swiftly he had changed from a friend into a frightening stranger, and the weight and strength of him pinning her down when she tried to push him away. Sometimes in the dead of night, jumping from sleep to wakefulness after a nightmare about the dunes, she wondered what would have happened if Ella hadn't stopped him.

'And it was him that blacked Gregor's eye?'

'Just before Gregor burst his nose for him.'

'And I missed it all,' Ella mourned.

'I wish I had.'

'At least Gregor stood up for ye.'

'I didn't want him to! You should have seen them, Ella, they were like a pair of dogs fighting over a bone. I'm done with Gregor, apart from dancing with him sometimes . . . if he ever asks me again. I don't want him to think that he won me in some daft fight.'

'Did Bert mention Martin at all?'

'He didn't have time to chat, and anyway we'll not

see either of them again now that Bert knows we're
mill-girls.' She shuddered at the memory. 'He looked
at me as if I was dirt!'

'Cheeky bugger!' Ella was outraged.

'I wish you'd never said that we worked in a lawyer's
office, Ella. I hated having to pretend, and fibs are always
found out.'

'If they'd known the truth we'd never have got even
one ride in their nice car. Ye should have told him that
us women in the mills earn more money than office
workers anyway. A lassie I went tae school with works in
Gardner's, the lawyers in County Place, and she doesnae
make as much as me. And,' Ella ended triumphantly, 'ye
should've told him about the pension too. That would've
put his toffee nose out of joint.'

'I could scarcely stand in the back close and tell him
all that while Gregor was breaking his nose for him, could
I?' Mirren snapped, and flounced back to join the others
as the great bell rang from its tower to signal the return
to work.

After work on Friday she took the gifts she had bought
in Callander – a book for Thomas, a knitted toy for the
unborn baby, a brooch for Agnes and tobacco for Bob
– to Lady Lane, intending to go straight from there to
her evening stint at the shop. She looked forward to
spending an hour with the family, for Bob and Agnes
were always welcoming and Thomas would be sure to
have some adventure, real or imagined, to relate.

Bob opened the door, his normally cheerful face creased
with worry. 'I'm awful glad ye came, Mirren. Agnes is
poorly and I don't know what tae do for the best.'

In the kitchen Agnes was crouched over her swollen
belly, breathing quickly and noisily, while Thomas played
happily at her feet with a brightly painted train Bob had
made from thread bobbins. Her face, when she lifted it
at Mirren's entrance, was deeply flushed.

'Mirren, it's . . . yerself.' She summoned up a sickly smile. 'Sit down and . . . Bob'll put on the . . . kettle.'

'He will indeed, but I'm not sitting down.' Mirren dropped her bag and the parcels she had brought onto the table and rounded on Bob. 'For goodness sake, man, her bairn's coming.'

'Eh?' His jaw dropped. 'But it's not due for another two weeks.'

'Mebbe it doesn't know that. Did you not tell him, Agnes?'

'I didnae want tae say till nearer the time for my mother tae get home from her work,' Agnes gasped apologetically. 'Poor Bob's not good with illness.'

'Poor Bob' had indeed gone grey. 'I wouldnae know what labour looks like.' He wet his lips nervously, peering at his wife. 'I've never fathered a bairn before.'

'Neither have I, or birthed one either, but I've a good idea of what we're looking at here. Get that kettle on while I run to fetch a midwife!'

'Never mind a midwife, just get my mother,' Agnes begged. 'She'll surely be home by the time ye get there.'

'I'll go.' Bob snatched up his jacket. 'You stay with her, Mirren.'

'It's your baby, not mine. You put it in there,' Mirren was heedless, in her panic, of what she was saying. 'It's your duty to see that it gets back out safely, not mine.'

'Mirren!' Even in her distress Agnes found time to be shocked. 'There's a bairn wi' big ears in this house! Ye'll have tae take him with ye, Bob. My mother's neighbour'll . . . look after him, she's a kindly soul. Put the kettle on before ye go. And will ye rub my back, Mirren, for it's awful sore.'

As Bob snatched up the kettle and hurried to the sink Mirren massaged her sister-in-law's spine. 'Should you not be lying down?'

'I will in a . . . minute, but get wee Thomas out of here first, for I don't want him frighted.'

As soon as the kettle was on the stove Bob gathered up the little boy, who was quite happy where he was and only went with his step-father on the false promise of a visit to the park, and hurried him out of the flat.

'Mebbe you should just get whoever you can instead of going all the way to Gauze Street,' Mirren called after him as a whimper escaped Agnes's bloodless lips. 'You should have told Bob what ailed you!' she scolded as she helped the other girl to her feet. 'He's the father – surely he should know when his own child's arriving.'

'I didnae like tae say, with him never havin' . . .' Agnes gasped and clutched at Mirren, then faltered on after a moment, 'never havin' seen a woman in labour before. I kept hopin' my mother might look in after work, the way she sometimes does. Anyway, I wasnae sure myself until just before you came, for the pain's . . . all in my back and that's not the way it was with Thomas. And my water's not broke yet. That's supposed to be the first . . . Oh!' She looked in dismay at the pool that had suddenly appeared on the floor where Thomas had been playing only minutes earlier. 'Oh, my good rug!'

'Never mind your rug, let's get you undressed and onto the bed.'

By the time Agnes was in a night-dress and on the bed, her back pain had turned into unmistakable contractions, arriving regularly and frequently. Mirren, who had never witnessed childbirth before, longed for Mrs McNair to arrive and take over before things went much further. While waiting for the woman she turned down the gas beneath the kettle, which was filling the room with steam, then began to mop up the mess on the floor. Before she was half-done Agnes let out a hoarse scream.

'What's wrong?'

'It's comin', that's what's wrong,' her sister-in-law said through gritted teeth. 'And it's comin' fast. Look in that top drawer of the cupboard. There's some . . . oh! . . . some strips of cloth. Bring them . . .' She broke off as the contraction deepened, gripping Mirren's forearms and holding on tight, digging her fingers deep into the flesh. By the time she finally relaxed they were both breathless, Agnes with exhaustion and Mirren with the strain of holding back her own yelps of pain.

She used the lull to fetch the bundle of clean rags Agnes had carefully stored in the cupboard in readiness. Following the older woman's panted instructions she tied the two longest to the head of the bed, knotted the free ends and placed them into Agnes's hands, so that she could pull on them when the next contraction came, which it did almost as soon as the rags were in position. While Agnes dragged on them and roared out her suffering at the top of her voice, Mirren soaked another piece of cloth under the tap and hurried back to mop her sister-in-law's sweating crimson face. Just then, to her great relief, she heard the door open.

'It's all right, Agnes, your mother's here.'

'Thank God . . .' Agnes panted, exhausted. But it was Bob, on his own.

'She's not home yet,' he gabbled. 'The wee chap's sittin' on the stairs outside, I didnae know what else tae do with him.' Then as his wife let out another scream he started past Mirren, his face ashen. 'Agnes . . .'

'Go away!' Half-raised on her pillows, her face swollen with blood and running with sweat, her hair loose and her eyes wild, she looked like a harridan. 'Get out of here!' she shouted at him, and he fled.

'And find someone – anyone!' Mirren ordered in a panic as he disappeared through the outer door. Then, to Agnes, 'I don't know what to do!'

'You don't have tae do . . . anythin'. It's me that has to do all the . . . work . . .' The last word rose into a banshee's screaming as Agnes fell back, snatching at her night-dress in her pain and pulling it up to her waist.

'Oh Mammy . . . !' she gasped as the contraction

washed over her then ebbed, leaving her shaking on the mattress. 'Oh dear Jesus, help me!'

'Oh God, oh God . . . !' Mirren chattered in harmony, her eyes fixed on Agnes's flabby blue-veined white legs and a stomach so bloated that she was convinced it must split wide open at any minute. Surely Bob must be able to find someone more capable than herself to help Agnes!

For a few moments they had a respite. Mirren mopped Agnes's face and brushed her hair back while her sister-in-law lay still, eyes closed. 'I wish my mammy was here,' she said, her voice weak and childlike. 'I want my mammy.'

'She's just coming. She'll be here any minute.' Please God, Mirren thought, dabbing Agnes's forehead, then her own as she went to the sink for more cold water.

Behind her she heard a sudden surge of movement from the wall bed. 'It's comin', Mirren, it's . . .' Agnes raised herself up on her elbows, her face almost purple and her lips dragging back from her teeth with the strain of a massive contraction. 'Take . . .' she said, then the words were lost in a long animal-like snarl of effort. It was then that Mirren saw the blood flooding over the sheet and something emerging from between Agnes's spread thighs. She reeled back, while about her the room turned grey and hazy, as though suddenly filling with steam from the kettle that still simmered away on the stove.

'Agnes . . .' she quavered, just as the door opened and an elderly woman came bustling in, rolling her sleeves up.

'It's all right, Mrs McCulloch hen, I'm here. We'll get that bairn o' yours born in nae time at all.' She advanced on the bed with relish, just as grey turned to black and Mirren's knees gave way beneath her.

'Ye're late. Ye should have been here fifteen minutes ago,' Maria snapped when Mirren walked into the shop on shaky legs.

'I'm sorry. When I went to see my sister-in-law she'd gone into labour and I'd to stay and help her.' Mirren still felt queasy and the smell of food frying didn't help. When she went into the small back shop to hang up her coat and put on her apron she took a moment to drink some cold water and take a few deep breaths before plunging back into the warmth and the smell.

'Are you sure you're all right?' Vanni asked. Mindful of Maria's sharp eyes, she smiled and nodded.

'Has Agnes had her baby?' Ella whispered as they worked side by side at the counter.

'A wee boy.'

'And you were there? Ye saw it happenin'?'

'Most of . . .'

'Ye're welcome tae chatter all night if ye want,' Maria said from behind them, 'but I'd ask ye tae do it on the pavement. Ye're here tae work, not gossip.'

The evening seemed to go on for ever and Mirren, already worn out by all that had happened in such a brief space of time, was reminded of the bad old days when she used to come in to work exhausted after staying up with her mother all night, then putting in a full day at the mill.

'I've never seen our Agnes look so bonny or so happy,' she marvelled to Ella as they walked home. It was a miracle the way the woman had put all the horror of childbirth behind her, once she had been washed and changed and given her new son to hold.

'Did she . . .' Ella hesitated, then pushed on, 'did she hurt badly?'

'I think it was more uncomfortable than sore,' Mirren lied, not particularly keen to recall the details.

'I mind when I was wee, the woman that lived through the wall from us had a bairn and she screamed as if her throat was bein' cut.' Ella's eyes were dark with the memory.

'Agnes roared a bit – but I think it was just with the effort of it all.'

'Was there a lot of blood?'

The air about Mirren took on an ominously grey tinge. She swallowed, then said carefully. 'Not much. It all happened so quickly.'

'I thought it took a long time tae have a bairn. One of my aunts told me once that my mother was in labour with me for thirty hours.'

'It must be different for different folk then, for it was very quick with Agnes.' Too quick. Mirren wouldn't have minded thirty hours at all, for then the birth would have been in the capable hands of Agnes's mother, who had finally arrived just before Mirren left, quite put out to discover that she had missed all the excitement.

Ella's eyes were huge in her pale face. 'What was it like when the baby actually came?'

'I don't know,' Mirren confessed. 'I fainted just as one of the neighbours came in to help Agnes, and the next thing I knew was the noise of the wee lad yelling. I felt such a fool, Ella. I was shakier than Agnes was afterwards. Poor Bob had to walk me to the shop, when all he wanted was to be with her and the wee one.'

'It must've been bad if ye fainted.' There was a tremor in Ella's voice.

'It was just the shock of it all and worrying about delivering the bairn on my lone. I might have dropped it – and then there's a cord to cut, isn't there? I wouldn't know how to do that.'

'Ye'd have found out if ye'd just stayed awake. Now we still don't know any more than we learned in the school playground.'

The greyness intensified and Mirren stopped walking, putting a hand on a house wall for support. 'Mebbe I should ask Agnes to put the baby back and then go through it all again for your benefit.' She had meant to speak sharply, but instead it sounded to her own ears as though a thick woollen scarf had been wrapped over her mouth.

'Here, you're lookin' a bit peelly-wally.' Ella peered into her face. 'Put yer head between yer knees.'

'Not out in the street,' Mirren objected thickly.

'Bend down, then, as if ye're lookin' at something on the ground.' A hand caught the back of her neck and forced her head down. Although she felt stupid, she had to admit that it helped to combat the nausea and giddiness. When Ella gave in to her muffled squawks and let her stand upright again, the nausea was gone and the greyness had retreated to the perimeter of her vision, where it hovered.

'How d'ye feel now?'

'A bit better.'

'When did ye eat last?'

Mirren had to think for a minute. 'At the dinner break.'

'That was ten hours ago! No wonder ye're feelin' faint.'

'I'm not hungry.' At that moment she felt as though she never wanted to eat again.

'You are, but ye just don't know it.' Ella opened her parcel and plucked out a piece of fried fish. 'Eat that.'

'I couldn't!'

'Yes, ye could,' Ella insisted, and to her surprise Mirren discovered that she was right. Under her friend's supervision she ate all the fish and even managed a few chips.

'Is that better?'

'A bit. Are you not eating anything?'

'I'd not be able to keep it down.'

Mirren frowned. Recently Ella had taken to handing over her fish supper to Robbie, claiming that the summer heat had ruined her appetite. 'You'll waste away to nothing if you don't start eating again.'

Ella made a strange noise that sounded like a collision between a laugh and a sob. 'No fear of that. I'll just get bigger and bigger even if I never eat another morsel. Mirren, I'm expectin'.'

'Expecting? You can't be!'

'If I'm not, then there's somethin' else wrong with me, for my monthlies haven't come and you know me, I've always been that regular that you could put the kettle on by me.'

'It could be the hot weather. When are they due again?'

'Tomorrow. But Mirren,' Ella's voice was so small that it was almost away to a whisper, 'mind I felt awful sick on Sma' Shot Day? I've been like that every mornin' since.'

'Oh, Ella!'

'I know!' They gazed helplessly at each other.

'You'll have to tell Martin.'

'Why should I tell him?' Ella asked, puzzled.

'He's going to have to take responsibility.'

'No he's not, for it's not his wean.'

'But . . . you wanted to marry him.'

'Only because marryin' him would have made me free of my aunts.'

'If it's not Martin's, then whose is it?'

Despite the warmth of the night Ella wrapped her arms protectively about her body. 'Vanni's.'

'Vanni's?' Again Mirren reeled back against the house wall, but this time, fortunately, the fish that Ella had made her eat was doing its work and the grey dizziness was kept at bay. 'Vanni Perrini?'

'Aye.'

'It can't be him!'

'If it's not, then I don't know whose it can be, for there was never anyone else but Vanni.' A softness came to Ella's voice, and the grip she had on herself seemed to loosen into an embrace. 'Mind me tellin' ye that I knew there were men more lovin' than my father was? It's Vanni I was talkin' about.'

'But he's married!'

'I know that, but ye cannae choose who tae love, Mirren, it just happens.'

'Does he know about . . . ?'

Ella shook her head. 'I needed tae be sure, then when I was, I couldnae give him the added worry, with Maria bein' so difficult these past weeks.'

A terrible thought struck Mirren. 'You don't think it's because she knows about the two of you?'

Ella gave another strangled laugh. 'If she knew, d'ye not think we'd have heard about it by now? I'd be out on my ear and God knows what she would have done tae my poor Vanni.'

'You'll have to tell him.'

'I know,' Ella said bleakly. 'When I can find the right time.'

'What d'you think he'll do about it?'

'He'll be pleased, there's no doubt of that. He loves bairns, and he loves me.'

'Are you sure of that? He's married to someone else.'

'I know, but you've seen for yerself the way Maria treats him. He does love me, Mirren, and he'll want the two of us . . . the three of us tae be together, I know it.'

'Maria won't allow it.'

'She'll have tae,' Ella said, an uncertain tremor in her voice.

23

Unusually for the west of Scotland, used to wet summers, day after day brought a dry heat as rich and ripe and sultry as the heart of the roses blooming alongside pinks, lilies and geraniums in the gardens of those fortunate and wealthy enough to have ground of their own. The cat's cradles of washing lines in every communal back court blossomed with clothes drying almost as soon as they were pegged out on the lines, while the town's parks blossomed with local citizens taking the air. A flotilla of miniature sails decorated the boating pond at Barshaw Park and in the narrow streets, ill-fitting windows that had been stuffed with newspaper and rags to keep out the winter draughts were forced open to ventilate frowsy, overcrowded little rooms. The bowling greens were busy again, and the cycling-club members, bells jangling impatiently at anyone who accidentally got in their way, sped on swift wheels into the countryside to exhaust themselves and overstrain muscles weakened by months of disuse.

Housewives, some perhaps forced during the winter to burn the linoleum covering their floors in order to keep their families warm, dragged kitchen chairs or wooden crates to the close-mouths, where they sat fanning flushed faces with newspapers, as many buttons unfastened as common decency would allow, skirts eased back above their knees and legs splayed. Small children playing in the gutters were clad only in short vests, and dogs panted in whatever scraps of shade they could find, and became irritable and snappy. Cats scratched and small girls playing hopscotch burned the soles of their bare feet as they bounced nimbly over the sun-heated, chalked stone pavement flags. Whenever the water carts appeared, half-naked children swarmed from buildings and back courts to run alongside, desperate for the touch of cool water spraying their skin.

The sprawling mill buildings, snugly warm in the winter, were just as warm in the summer although, in the twisting department, working with bare feet brought some relief. The ice-cream vendors who brought their barrows to the mill gates at the midday break did a roaring trade. Even when the sun went down there was little ease, for the air remained still and sultry, and the cobbles and flagstones that had absorbed the sun's heat all day threw it back into the night air, to filter in through the open tenement windows and make sleep almost impossible.

The fried-fish shop reminded Mirren of stories she had heard about hell, where the sinners laboured in the heat from the flames. 'You'd think that in this weather folk wouldn't want hot food,' she muttered to Ella out of the side of her mouth as they coped with a queue of folk fresh from the cinemas and eager for nourishment. Ella simply shrugged and rubbed an arm over her damp pale face and kept on working.

Vanni had the worst job of them all, toiling over the vats of bubbling fat, constantly mopping his face and throat with the towel kept close to hand and emptying jug after jug of tap water. Maria, who had reacted to the heat in the same way as the town's dogs – by becoming snappier than ever – had decreed that he was not to be allowed to drink lemonade as he was swallowing all their profits. The chief target for her acidic tongue-lashings, Vanni had lost his ready smile, and between the heat and his wife's nagging, his lovely dark eyes, normally sparkling with life and humour, were like dusty glass beneath half-lowered lids.

Mirren, heart-sorry for the man, could well understand why Ella was reluctant to add to his problems.

Now that she knew of the secret relationship between them, she saw how hard he and Ella worked at ignoring each other. The easy banter there had once been between them had vanished and, if their hands happened to brush together when they both stood at the vats, they immediately pulled away from each other. At the end of the evening, going through his usual ritual of handing both assistants a bundle of fish and chips, Vanni gazed past Ella's shoulder instead of meeting her eyes, and she did the same with him. Their precautions were so elaborate that Mirren began to fear that Maria would notice and suspect.

'It'll be a relief when this heat breaks,' Ella said limply when they left the shop. 'My corset's so tight on me now that I feel as if I'm being cut in half.'

'You surely shouldn't be wearing tight clothing. It'll damage the baby.'

'Not as much as Maria and my aunts'd damage me if they knew the truth. I can manage for a wee while longer,' Ella insisted. 'It'll all work out, you'll see.'

Even so, Mirren worried about her all the time – in the mill, in the shop and at home, tossing and turning in the wall bed, trying to recall the persistence of a cold draught coming through the ill-fitting window or the sound of rain on the glass panes.

Grace Proctor's next letter bore American stamps and was postmarked Boston. After much discussion, Grace wrote, she and Anne had accepted the positions of nursery maids to the two doctors' families, and in doing so they found themselves plunged into 'yet another great adventure. Anne is writing to Mother and Father, but of course she won't tell them all that happened, since Mother would only worry and Father might think that we are not capable of looking after ourselves, which is quite wrong.'

Mrs Fitz had sent their train tickets and all the papers necessary for their journey, explaining that they would be met at Boston's North Station on arrival. 'So it was a matter of packing our trunk and setting off on our next journey,' wrote Grace. 'It passed without any problems, even when we crossed into America at Vermont and had our papers checked by the immigration officials at Newport. Everything was correct and we were allowed to continue on our way to the North Station. Our train was late in arriving there and there was no sign of the chauffeur Mrs Fitz had promised would meet us. After we had been waiting for a good half-hour with our baggage around us, a big burly man approached and asked in a strong Irish accent if we were the Proctor sisters. Upon Anne saying that we were, he picked up our luggage and marched off with it, telling us to follow on behind.

'I wasn't at all sure of him, but when I asked Anne in a whisper if she thought he had been sent by Mrs Fitz she was very calm and said that he must have been, for how else would he have known our names. "In any case," she said, "he has our luggage away with him, and we must follow, for I'm not letting it out of my sight." He hurried us into a large limousine with glass between the driver and the passenger area and off we went, driving all round the streets of Boston, with me getting more and more nervous by the minute. So was Anne, I could tell, though she tried hard not to show it.

'After about twenty minutes of this, Mirren, I had worked myself into such a certainty that we had been kidnapped and would never see Mrs Fitz, or anyone else, ever again that when the car stopped in traffic I had the door open in a trice. I grabbed Anne's hand and, before she could say a word, we were both out of the car and running for our lives. Fortunately we had stopped beside a large park, and off we flew across the grass, away from the street. When I looked back to see if the Irishman was chasing us I could see him staring at us from the car, his mouth and his eyes wide open.'

It was almost as good as reading one of Mr Dickens's books. Mirren, heedless of the need to get to work, turned the pages, frantic to find out what had happened to her friends.

'When we finally stopped running I was in tears with worry. There we were, in a strange city in a strange country where nobody knew us, and all that we possessed in the world had been taken off to goodness knows where by an Irishman. All I could think of was that I bitterly regretted leaving Paisley. I would have given every tooth in my head in return for seeing you and Mother and Father and my brothers and sisters at that moment. Then, by a mercy Anne recollected that she had Mrs Fitz's letter in her pocket, with the address on it. So she hailed a taxi-cab, for all the world as though she was used to doing such things every day of her life, and ordered the man to drive us to the house, where we found everyone in quite a state of worry as to what had become of us.

'Fortunately Mrs Fitz was very understanding, though as Anne said to me later, quite sharply, she could well have been wondering just what sort of ninnies she and her friend had hired to care for their innocent little children. She even brought in the chauffeur to tell us how sorry he was for having frightened us. A very nice man, he is; his name is Tommie. Mrs Sheridan, my new employer, is just as friendly as Mrs Fitz, with a beautiful house and two sweet little children. I know that I will be very happy here, which is just as well, for here, Anne says, we stay! I have enclosed a respectable version of our travels for you to show to Mother.'

Anne's letter to her parents gave the impression that the journey to America had been an easy business with no problems whatsoever. 'They seem to be very well suited,' Catherine Proctor admitted when she had read Grace's 'respectable' letter. 'But I can't keep up with them at all.

Last year at this time they were both right here under this roof with no thought at all of ever leaving Paisley. And now they've been in Canada and moved from there to America!'

'It's as well that Grace did go away from here.'

'Aye, I'll grant ye that. She'd have broken her heart if she'd known of poor George's death. But this travelling around bothers me. When all's said and done, they're still two young women on their own.'

'Not on their own any more. They're both with families now, and being well looked after. I'm sure they're settled now.' What on earth would Aunt Catherine say, Mirren wondered, if she had heard about her daughters escaping from a limousine in the heart of Boston and fleeing hand-in-hand across a city park from a large, puzzled Irishman?

'Aye, well . . . I suppose so,' Catherine said, then her eyes filled with tears, 'but there's times I can't help thinking about the way things might have gone if George hadn't been so badly injured in the war. He and Grace could have been married and settled by now, and I'd have had my two lassies where I could see them whenever I wanted. Mind you, even if she had wed George they might well have gone away together, just as you would have gone with your Donald if Helen hadn't been so poorly. D'you pine for him, Mirren?'

'No. What's bye is bye, and I'm happy enough with what I have now.'

'Have you been at the dancing recently?'

'It's too hot for that just now, and Ella's . . . her stomach's not right with this heat, so we've not bothered over the past week or so. We'll get back to it soon enough. Agnes was fair delighted with the wee cap and booties you knitted for Robert.'

'How are they both?'

'Grand, and Thomas is as proud as punch to be a big brother.'

'Bless him. I enjoyed making the wee clothes for Agnes.' Catherine's eyes misted again. 'She's fortunate to have little ones to care for. They grow up so fast; in no time at all they're off to the school, then next thing you know they've gone even further – too far away altogether.' Then she blinked, and added cheerfully, 'And you just have to be pleased for them, for there's no turning the clock back.'

It was as if her aunt's mention of his name had stirred Donald, far off in America, and brought him back into Mirren's life.

'There's a letter for ye,' Robbie said when she came in from the shops.

'What sort of letter?' She had just heard from Grace, her only correspondent.

'See for yerself.' There was a strange look on his face, half-curious, half-apprehensive. He took the envelope down from the mantelshelf; then, tactfully, he left the room, but Mirren didn't notice him go. As she stared down at the envelope with its American stamps and her own name written across it in the large, clear hand she had once known so well, it was as if time had stopped, or, rather, as if it had taken a great leap backwards, dragging her with it. There was no need to turn the envelope over, but she did so anyway, partly because it put off the moment of opening for a little longer.

It was when she saw the name, 'Mr Donald Nesbitt,' that her heart began to leap about like a mad thing, pounding so hard that she had to sit down.

At last, she opened the envelope, drew out Donald's letter and began to read.

When Robbie returned to the kitchen, driven by hunger, Mirren handed the letter to him without comment. She had already studied the single page so closely that, as his eyes moved from line to line, she knew almost to the word what he was reading.

'My dear Mirren,' it began. 'I am no longer certain that I may still address you in this way, although I would like to think that I can do so for the rest of my life. In the months since I last wrote to you I have reproached myself bitterly over and over again for those cruel words. I can only say that at that time I was seized by such an impatient longing to see you that I felt you must come to me at once. And of course, being the honest and dutiful young woman that I first fell in love with, you could not bring yourself to turn your back on your mother when she was in such frail health.

'Instead of understanding your dilemma and offering you my strongest support, I can only believe that I was taken over by a sort of madness, and fancied that I could find the love that we had – and still have, I dare to hope – with someone else. I was wrong, Mirren. I knew it almost at once, but I have not been able to tell you so before now, because I was so bitterly ashamed of the hurt I must have caused you. I would have come to Scotland to see you in person but the shame would not let me. It is only now that I feel able to ask your forgiveness and much more . . . I want you to come to America, Mirren, and marry me.

'If you will only agree, you can be assured that the brief madness that caused us both so much unhappiness has gone for ever, and I will pledge myself to care for you and make you happy for the rest of your life. As for Robbie, there is work here for a good Scots-trained engineer and he would be more than welcome to live with us until he is ready to branch out on his own. I hope that he agrees to this, for as well as being a companion and help to you on the journey here, he would be in a position to see for himself how I will atone for my previous behaviour.

'With this in mind, I have taken the liberty of booking passage for you both on an October sailing, to give you time to make your preparations.

'I trust that you will use the enclosed tickets and that you can find it in your heart to be generous and understanding, Mirren. I will be in torment until I hear from you. Your most loving and most penitent suitor, Donald.'

'Well now,' Robbie said slowly, handing the letter back. 'I never thought ye'd hear from him again. Did he send the tickets right enough?'

Wordlessly, Mirren handed them over. He studied them with interest. 'Will ye go?'

'I don't know. There are so many things to think about.'

'I suppose so,' Robbie agreed. Then, ever mindful of his stomach, 'What're we eatin'?'

Mirren roused herself. 'Potted hough and boiled potatoes. I cooked them this morning so they just need to be sliced. And I stewed some apples for afterwards.'

'I'll slice the meat and potatoes for you.'

'They're out on the sill and the apples are in the press,' Mirren told him. 'I'll fetch them.' Normally the cold meat and boiled potatoes would also have been in the press – a high, narrow wall cupboard kept scrupulously clean and used for food storage. But in hot weather meat and fish had a better chance of keeping fresh in a small wire cage left out on the window sill.

The two of them ate in silence for some time before Mirren asked, 'Even if I decide against going, will you go?'

He forked the last piece of potato, then used a slice of bread to clean his plate. 'No.'

'But it would be such a chance for you!'

'I like it well enough here.'

'Never knowing if you'll be laid off again?'

'I've got things tae do in Paisley.'

'Political things, with Joe Hepburn?'

His mouth tightened. 'Mebbe,' he said, then urged, 'But

you should go. If anyone deserves happiness and a new life it's you.'

'I don't know,' Mirren said wretchedly, 'So much has happened . . . and I'm not certain that I can trust Donald now.'

'He'll not let ye down again. He's learned from his mistake.'

'Mebbe. I'm going to write and tell him that I need time to think about it.'

'Of course ye should go,' Ella said. 'What is there here tae keep ye?'

'If Robbie'd agree to go with me I might consider it, but I don't want to leave him behind.'

'He's not a bairn, Mirren, he's a young man – and a good-looking one at that. He's sure tae find himself a wifc soon, and then where'll you be?'

'I just wish he'd stop getting himself involved in these daft ploys of Joe Hepburn's. Going to America would take him away from the meetings and the trouble they can bring.'

'Ye cannae agree tae marry Donald Nesbitt just tae keep yer brother out of trouble. Whether Robbie goes or stays, ye've got yer own decision tae make. The hoist's fillin' up.' Ella, who had been heading for the big lift, changed direction. 'We'll take the stairs tae work, for I need tae talk some sense intae ye and ye'll not want the rest of them tae know what's happened.'

'And then there's you . . .'

'For any favour, Mirren Jarvis, will ye stop tryin' tae be responsible for the whole world?' Ella said, exasperated. 'I'll be away myself soon, with Vanni. So there'll be no sense in stayin' here for my sake. My . . .' She stopped on the landing, fanning herself with one hand. 'It's that close in here ye cannae draw a decent lungful of air. I'll be glad tae see a break in this weather!'

*   *   *

Mirren and Joe Hepburn stood as godparents to young
Robert McCulloch when he was christened at the beginning of August. Logan and Belle had been invited to the
christening, but to Mirren's disappointment they had sent
a brief note regretting that they were too caught up with
business matters to attend.

Logan had called on his brother and sister one evening
shortly after Sma' Shot Day – a brief, uncomfortably
formal visit during which they discussed the weather,
enquired after each other's health and spoke of the mill,
the shipyard where Robbie now worked and Logan's
father-in-law's shop. The more important unspoken words
had hung in the air around them like clusters of grapes, full
and ready to burst, yet ignored throughout. But at least he
had called, and that, Mirren felt, marked a step forward.

Agnes accepted their absence from the christening celebrations without umbrage. 'I never thought they'd come,
but me and Bob wanted tae let them know that they'd be
welcome,' she said as the christening party walked to the
church, with Agnes, Mirren and Mrs McNair leading the
way while the menfolk followed; Thomas, in his sailor
suit and with his hair brushed flat against his skull, trotting
morosely between his step-father and Joe Hepburn. Wee
Robert slept contentedly in his mother's arms, and Agnes
was careful to keep close to the house walls in an attempt
to prevent the bright sunlight from falling on his face and
disturbing him. Resplendent in his christening gown and
shawl and little lace cap, he caught the eyes of passers-by
and the group had to stop several times to allow people
to admire him.

'I thought Logan at least might have made the effort.'
Mirren picked up the conversation as they left another
admirer and continued on their way.

'So did I,' Mrs McNair chimed in, then, as the baby
stirred and murmured, 'Here . . . I'll take him and let you
rest yer arms.'

'He's fine where he is for the moment.' Agnes made

little kissing noises at her younger son and bounced him gently. 'I hope he's going tae behave himself.'

'So dae I,' the fond grandmother said grimly. 'Ye'd not believe the noise he can make, Mirren. If he starts his cryin', the stones in the church walls'll be dingin' with the noise.'

'It shows he's healthy, Mam. It's got nothin' tae do with effort,' Agnes went on as Robert settled again. 'It's poor Belle not bein' able tae have bairns of her own that's the trouble.'

'Can she not? I thought they didn't want children.'

'No, no. It's a tragedy, so it is. When they were goin' off tae the war Logan told Crawford that he and Belle wished they'd a bairn, 'cause then she'd have someone of her own tae care for if he didnae come back. That father of hers is a right cold fish. When Crawford told me, I felt bad about us havin' Thomas. Even when it was my poor Crawford that was killed, and not Logan, there were times when I felt that Belle grudged me my bairn.'

'That's terrible, and you a young widow!'

'Och, there was never any real harm meant. It can be a terrible pain,' Agnes said, 'wantin' somethin' bad and not bein' able tae get it.'

Fortunately for the church building and all those within it, Robert slept through the brief ceremony, not even wakening himself when he gave a loud sneeze as the holy water landed on his smooth, untroubled forehead. Once the ceremony ended the guests walked back to Bob's flat for sandwiches and cake. Thomas, flushed and irritable with the heat, demanded to be taken instead to the ice-cream parlour they had visited after his mother's marriage to Bob.

'Robert's too young for that, and it's his christenin' we're celebratin',' Agnes told him. 'Be a good laddie now, and mebbe we'll get you a cone later.'

Thomas's bottom lip thrust itself forward and he moped about the crowded kitchen, finally ending up by the cot, where he stood staring at his small half-brother until the baby, uneasily aware even in his sleep of the belligerent glare only inches away, woke and began to yell for attention. Joe saved the situation by suggesting that he and Robbie should take the little boy to Nardini's for ice-cream and then into the Fountain Gardens.

'I don't know,' Agnes fretted. 'Thomas'll have tae learn that he cannae always get his own way.'

'I think we could let him have his ice-cream this once, since it's a special day and he was such a good laddie.' Bob took the screaming baby from his wife.

'You spoil that boy.'

'I'm in the mood tae spoil the whole world today,' he confessed, tucking his tiny namesake on his shoulder and patting his back soothingly. 'For ye've brought me a whole family just when I thought there was nothin' left for me in the world.'

24

Thomas insisted on Mirren's company as well and she was glad to go for, as Mrs McNair had said, little Robert had a very good pair of lungs. The ice-cream, topped with raspberry sauce, was deliciously cold on such a hot day, and the trees in the elegant Fountain Gardens offered welcome shade. In hot weather the gardens, created with money donated by the Coats family, lived up to their intended use as the 'lungs of the town'. Robbie produced a ball from his pocket and he and Thomas began kicking it to and fro along one of the paths, while Mirren and Joe followed at a more sedate pace.

'I was surprised to see you standing godfather to wee Robert,' Mirren said. 'I thought that a man with your beliefs wouldn't believe in religion.'

'It's strange how folk that know nothin' of socialism jump tae conclusions about it. There's few men as dedicated tae the betterment of the workin' class as Willie Gallacher.' Joe's voice, which had not shown any trace of a stammer that day, warmed at the very mention of the great son of Paisley who, with his fiery speeches and his tireless crusading on behalf of his own kind, was rarely out of the public eye. 'And he was born intae the Roman Catholic faith. Why should religion and politics not sit comfortably together? Didn't Christ himsel' believe passionately in justice and equality?'

She was half-intrigued by his views and at the same

time half-shocked. 'There's some that would see you thrown in the jail for saying such a thing.'

'That's probably the way they'd treat the man himsel' if he was tae come back and preach his beliefs today. It's one thing readin' about him in a wee book with gold edging tae the pages,' he said tersely, 'but let ordinary flesh and blood folk try tae say the same things he did and the factory owners, landowners and politicians want tae see them persecuted the way John McLean was. They flutter and panic like hens in a coop when the fox visits.'

'So you take your religion from the likes of Willie Gallacher?' Mirren prompted. When it came down to it, she would rather discuss religion than politics.

'Not a bit of it. I was a church-goer all my life, intae adulthood. My father was religious and I still mind bein' carried tae the church in his arms before I could walk. I even sang in the choir and taught a Sunday School class.' He laughed at the astonishment in the face lifted to his. 'Oh, you'd have thought me a grand fellow in those days, Mirren Jarvis.'

She refused to be drawn. 'So you admire Willie Gallacher.'

'Of course. Who wouldn't?'

John Proctor for one, Mirren thought, with his love of the Liberal movement. 'But Gallacher doesn't believe in going to war and neither did John McLean. Yet you enlisted in the Army.'

'Ye're very learned about socialism all of a sudden.'

'Don't go thinking I'm one of your converts. I'm just saying what I've heard from Robbie.'

'Since ye ask, I'd not really started tae follow their teachings when I enlisted in the Army. I joined because it seemed tae me that I'd no option but tae fight. War's a filthy business with no glory in it at all. It causes more sufferin' among ordinary folk than any other class, so the sooner it can be ended, the fewer the number of decent men on both sides that have tae die. But it was the war that changed me from a Sunday School teacher tae a socialist.' A grim note came into his voice. 'It changed more folk than me. I saw atheists converted overnight, while others like mysel' came tae realise that if we want change in this country we need tae work tae get it. That's another difference between me and McLean and Gallacher – they've no time for the Parliament because they see it as a gatherin' of titles and landowners and factory owners, while I believe that we have tae make use of it tae bring about the changes we want. And tae do that we need tae get more workin'-class folk intae the place. It'll happen sooner or later.'

'Would you stand for Parliament yourself?'

'Mebbe. One day. That's why I went tae McLean's classes on literature and economics. And I've listened tae Gallacher a lot too, and read everythin' that I could get my hands on. If ye want tae change things,' Joe said earnestly, 'ye first have tae understand what ye're up against.'

Robbie arrived with Thomas riding up on his shoulders. 'It's time we got this laddie home before it's him havin' tae carry me.'

'Would ye care tae go for a walk up the braes next Sunday afternoon, Mirren?' Joe asked diffidently as she reached up to mop the last vestiges of ice-cream from the little boy's face. 'It seems a shame not tae make the most of this grand weather.'

'Can I come too?' Thomas wanted to know.

'We'll be doin' a lot of walkin'. Yer legs arenae long enough,' Joe told him, and Thomas stuck his feet out on either side of Robbie's head, stretching his legs as far as he could.

'They are! They go all the way down to the ground when I'm standing.'

'Another day, mebbe.'

'I'll take ye tae the river on Sunday,' Robbie offered. 'We might see some boats and catch a fish. It'll be more fun than their walk.'

'Mirren's not agreed yet,' Joe pointed out. 'She might prefer tae go tae the river with you.'

'I'd enjoy a trip to the braes,' Mirren said. Despite herself, she was interested in Joe Hepburn. There were so many facets to his character, and she had never before met anyone with the ability to surprise her over and over again. In any case, she wanted to talk to him about Robbie's stubborn refusal to consider going to America.

The countryside was no cooler than the town, but there was a sense of space and the air was fresher. Freedom from the pavements and the tenement buildings that cut the town sky into parsimonious slices seemed to loosen Joe Hepburn's tongue. As he and Mirren strolled up the narrow road leading to the Bonnie Wee Well he tickled the lush roadside grasses with a stick and talked about his sister Molly, Bob McCulloch's first wife, who had died of tuberculosis.

'Did they not send her to the Peasweep Sanatorium?' Mirren asked. Tuberculosis was common among the mill-workers and Molly, employed in the bleaching department at Anchor Mills, would have been eligible for admission to the large sanatorium that the Coats family had built on top of the braes for afflicted employees.

'Aye, but that couldnae save her. Poor Bob . . . after all he'd been through, tae come back safe and well tae an empty house.'

A group of cyclists came free-wheeling down the brae towards them; as Mirren and Joe stepped against the hedgerow to let them pass they were bathed in heady perfume from clusters of creamy, purple-tipped honeysuckle.

'You came home to an empty house too.' Robbie had told her that Joe's two older sisters had married and left Paisley by then, and his widowed mother had died early in the war.

'It was different for me, because I don't mind bein' on

my lone and I've got my political interests tae keep me occupied,' he said, then launched into the usual subject.

Mirren allowed his voice to become a background drone while she enjoyed her surroundings. Delicate, shell-pink wild roses hovered shyly beside the honeysuckle as though hesitant to intrude on such lush beauty, and she stopped briefly to inhale their perfume, recalling the days when she and Grace, as children, visited the braes every autumn to gather rosehips and make necklaces and bracelets from them with the aid of large darning needles and bits of wool. It was a dangerous procedure, resulting in many a pierced finger if the needles slipped – as they often did – while being forced through the hard red fruits, or emerged faster than expected at the other side to draw blood as red and shiny as the rosehips themselves. But the toil was worth it, for there was no greater delight than the finished jewellery, glowing as red as any precious ruby.

By the time they reached the Bonnie Wee Well she and Joe were more than ready to cup their hands and drink some of the clear, cold spring water bubbling into its bowl before leaving the road to walk across springy grass, skirting whin bushes and clumps of purple heather.

When they reached a shallow grassy bowl at the edge of a bluff overlooking the town, Joe, who had been carrying his jacket over his shoulder, spread it on the grass for Mirren to sit on. She took off her own jacket, relishing the sun on her arms, glad that she had chosen to wear her green-and-white striped blouse with the short sleeves. For a while they amused themselves by looking down on the town, identifying landmarks such as the Abbey roof, the elegant pale green dome of the John Neilson School, the Town Hall and the great sprawling mills at either end of Paisley. Joe took his tie off and rolled his shirt sleeves up, while Mirren leaned back on her elbows and let the sun caress her face and throat. Butterflies danced around the wildflowers that dotted the grass, and birds swooped overhead and chirped in the bushes and trees nearby. Mirren wondered idly if America had anything as beautiful and tranquil as this place to offer her. The thought of the decision she still had to make reminded her of her main reason for walking with Joe.

'Robbie'll have told you that I might be going to America?' she put in as soon as he gave her the chance.

'He said somethin' about it. Have ye made up yer mind, then?'

'I've told Donald that I need time to think about it. After all,' Mirren heard the sharp edge coming into her own voice, 'he took long enough to reconsider the matter, and now it's my turn. I'd be more willing to go if Robbie would come with me. He says he's not sure it'd be right for him, but I think it is.' She paused, then said carefully, 'He listens to you. You could persuade him.'

'Me?' He had been lying back on the grass; now he sat up, elbows on knees, his long bony hands loosely linked. There was amusement in his voice when he said, 'But is it not me ye want tae protect him from?'

'Not you – the things you stand for.' She turned to face him. 'I don't like seeing him come home some nights with bruises on his face and cuts on his fists. I don't want him to end up like John McLean, dead before his time because of harsh imprisonment. Can you not understand that?'

'Aye, I can . . . but I'd never try tae influence him, not even for you. He's his own master.'

'You think I'd be happy all that distance away, worrying about him?'

'I'm not even sure ye'd be all that happy anyway, from what Robbie says.'

'What d'you mean by that?'

He plucked a blade of grass and considered it closely. 'A man who jilts a lassie once could do it again.'

'You don't know anything about Donald, or his situation.'

'I know that if I cared enough for a woman, I'd not change my mind then change it back again.'

'It's well seen that you've never been . . . had . . .' Mirren floundered in a quagmire of her own making.

'Ye're right, I never have . . . been . . .' His voice was solemn, though she knew without looking at him that he was grinning. 'My mind's always been concentrated on other things.'

'Like being a Member of Parliament?'

'Aye, that as well.' Joe lay back on the grass, his arms folded above his head. 'You know, Mirren, you've got a good brain; mebbe ye shouldnae waste it on domestic concerns. Ye could do a lot for other folk – yer fellow workers, for instance.'

'Me?'

'I've already said that there's one thing that damned war taught us – the power we have over the employers. Even women have started tae take matters into their own hands now and demand better treatment. You could teach them how to go about it.'

She turned over so that she was still propped on her elbows, but looking down at him. 'What d'you mean, even women?'

'I mean there's no need for ye tae be subservient or helpless any more. There's more of us than there is of them, and without us they'd be nothin'.'

'You're saying that I'm subservient and exploited?'

'Of course – all workers are.'

'You might be, Joe Hepburn, but I'm not.'

'Are you tellin' me that you slave in those mills for the pleasure of it?'

'Of course not. I'm not stupid. It's hard work and the hours are long and most days I hate every minute of it. But slaves don't have a choice, and I'm nobody's slave, for I could leave whenever I want and get work in a shop or mebbe even an office, or take in washing or scrub stairs or . . . or sell my body, come to that,' she said, too angry to choose her words carefully. 'I stay in the mill because I choose to. Because I'd not get as good pay in any of these other jobs and I'd probably not be so well treated either.'

'Well treated?' he asked scathingly, getting up on one elbow and confronting her, almost nose to nose.

'I know there are bad supervisors and foremen. You get bullies in every factory and mill. I've heard about . . . I've heard stories.' She would never forget Agnes telling her about an older woman in the gassing flat at the Anchor Mills who had for some reason been the butt of the male overseer. He took delight in ignoring her every time she flapped her apron, a sign that the worker wanted permission to visit the privy. Time and again the poor woman had been forced to work on, discomfort turning to pain. Finally, she had had to give up the job because of the permanent damage visited on her by the callous supervisor. 'But at the same time we're respected, me and the others. We're valued – the management knows fine that we could find work elsewhere if we wanted it. Why else d'you think they pay us well and set up all these clubs and classes for us? To keep their workers happy, that's why, and if you're saying that me and the ten thousand other men and women that work in the Paisley mills are so daft that they put up with bad treatment and say not a word in protest, your brains must be addled!'

He tried to speak, but she swept on, determined to finish. 'Look at what the Coats have done for this town – where d'you find all these books you talk about reading? In the library, that's where. And who built it, and the museum, and the observatory? The Coats!'

'I'll grant ye that. But while I'm reading books in Paisley's fine library, folk are livin' in such crowded conditions in some of the houses down there,' he indicated the town spread beneath them, 'that they're almost standin' on each other's toes. The rich manufacturers would've been better building more houses.'

'And I suppose they started the Great War and caused the influenza epidemic too.' She was furious with him for turning a pleasant afternoon walk into an argument. 'Just you save your compassion for those that are truly exploited and leave the mill-girls be!'

'By God, ye're everythin' that Robbie told me ye were. Ye're a right wee fighter,' Joe said admiringly.

'I've had to be.'

'I know. Tae tell the truth, I've wanted tae meet with ye from the first time Robbie talked about ye.'

'I find that hard to believe, considering what happened the first time we did meet.'

'Oh God, don't remind me,' he groaned. 'I could've hit my head off that church wall when I saw ye comin' along the road with Agnes and realised who ye were. Tae think I treated ye so badly, after all I'd heard about the way ye were carin' for yer mother and workin' all hours so's Robbie could serve his apprenticeship.'

'Robbie exaggerates sometimes,' Mirren said, embarrassed.

'He didnae exaggerate, not a bit of it. He thinks the world of ye, and I can understand why, now I've got tae know ye.' He raised himself on one elbow so that he could look into her face. 'That's why I asked ye tae come walkin' with me today, so's we could talk with nob'dy else about. I've never met anyone like you, Mirren.'

It was all too much. She already had more than enough on her mind, what with Ella's situation, and Donald still awaiting a decision from her. 'Listen, Joe . . .'

'We could fairly do with ye in the Independent Labour Party.'

'What?'

'There's women joinin' as well as men. Ye've got a good brain and a lot of courage. Ye'd be an asset tae any organisation.'

Mirren didn't know whether to laugh or cry. 'Well, you can just do without me in the ILP, because one member of the family coming home from meetings with a bruised face and sore knuckles is enough,' she said, pulling a blameless daisy from the grass and shredding it between her nails.

On the following day Ella fainted in the twisting department, folding neatly at the knees and sinking to the floor before one of her machines quietly and without fuss. Fortunately the machine was off at the time and being tended by Gregor Lewis, who was so taken aback by the suddenness of the collapse that he stood staring down at her in dumb disbelief, until the woman on the neighbouring machine shouted at him to give up standing there like a big dowfie and run for Mrs Drysdale.

By the time the Mistress pushed her way through the crowd gathered about Ella the girl had come round and was insisting that she had just slipped on the greasy floor and was well able to get back to her work.

'Not on one of my machines,' Mrs Drysdale told her. 'Not until the nurse has had a look at ye.'

What little colour there was in Ella's face drained away. 'I don't need the nurse! It's the heat that did it, that's all.'

'I'll be the judge of that. Sylvia,' the Mistress nodded to the six-sider whose job it was to take over from any operators who had to leave their machines for any reason, 'You see tae Ella's frames. And you can just get back tae yer work,' she told Mirren, who had stepped forward to stand protectively by Ella's side. 'That goes for the rest of ye as well.'

'But . . .'

'I'm quite able tae see tae the lassie on my own, Mirren Jarvis, and I'm not minded tae have any more twiners idle. Come along,' the woman ordered Ella, who cast an imploring glance at Mirren as she was led away.

'That's her turned off for sure,' Ruby said sombrely. There was no place in the mills for workers who collapsed while tending machinery, for the job was dangerous enough without permitting further risk.

'She'd not have been stayin' on for much longer anyway, in her condition,' Sylvia put in, and Ruby's eyes widened.

'Ye mean . . .' she said, then when Sylvia nodded significantly her voice rose a full octave. 'Ella Caldwell?'

'I knew ages ago,' Sylvia told her smugly, and some of the others nodded in agreement. 'Ye can always tell,' one of them said sagely, 'if ye've had weans of yer own.'

'But . . .' Ruby rounded on Mirren. 'Did you know about this? Who is it – one of these fancy Glasgow men ye both went out with?'

'Whether it is or whether it isn't is no business of ours,' Libby McDaid came to Mirren's rescue. 'And ye'd be wise tae keep yer tongue still, Ruby, till yer sure of yer facts. Mind, it could just as easy happen tae you.'

Ruby drew herself up self-righteously. 'I hope I'd know better.'

'That's right, hen, you keep yer hand on yer ha'penny,' Libby advised. 'And yer legs crossed . . . and yer desk work done if ye want tac keep yer own job. And that goes for the lot of yez,' she added, glaring at Sylvia. 'We shouldnae judge folk until we know the truth.'

Sylvia glared back, then flounced to Ella's machines while Mirren returned to her own work, wondering all the while what was happening to Ella.

'Sit down, lassie, and tell me what's amiss.' Mrs Drysdale gestured to the worn leather couch that took up most of the space in her small office.

'It's just the heat. I'm fine!'

'Indeed ye are, if "fine" means lookin' like a tray of tripe in a butcher's window.' The woman eyed Ella long and hard then asked, 'When's it due?'

'When's what due?'

'Don't play about with me, lass, I'm not daft and neither are you. When's the bairn due, I'm askin'?'

Ella bit her lip and fiddled with her apron, then admitted in a near-whisper, 'Early on in the New Year.'

'And will ye be safely wed before then . . . or is he wed already?'

'He . . .' Ella began, then burst into a flood of tears.

Mrs Drysdale silently handed her a towel then waited at her small, cluttered desk. It wasn't the first time she had had such a situation to deal with, and it would not be the last. In each department the overseers were answerable to the foreman, who was answerable to the sub-manager who, in turn, was answerable to the manager. Whenever possible, problems were dealt with at floor level and those higher up the ladder than overseers were only called in when absolutely necessary. In this case the Mistress was quite certain that it was not a matter for her superiors.

'I'm sorry,' Ella gulped when she finally emerged swollen-eyed from the damp towel.

'Well, at least that's one burden ye've got rid of. As tae the other . . .' The older woman sighed and took a bottle and a glass from a drawer. Pouring half an inch of amber liquid into the glass she held it out. 'Here.'

Ella reared away, eyes wide. 'What is it?'

'God, lassie, I'm an overseer, no' an old backstreet woman wi' a knittin' needle! Sinnin's bad enough but I'd never be a party tae murder! This is medicinal brandy and before ye get any ideas in yer head, I touch none of it myself for I'm teetotal. Drink all of it, mind. It's only a drop I've given ye, and it'll not do you or yer bairn any harm provided ye don't make a habit of it.' She well knew that most of the women working in the department thought her harsh and domineering, but a Mistress who wanted to be liked rather than feared usually ended up with a badly run department. Now, as Mrs Drysdale watched Ella empty the glass, sip by reluctant sip, she felt sorry for the girl. Ella Caldwell was a hard worker and a decent enough lassie; it was too bad that she had been foolish enough to get herself into trouble with a married man.

Mebbe something could be salvaged, if the matter was dealt with carefully. 'Now,' she said briskly when Ella handed the empty glass back, 'you and me'll take a walk over tae the first-aid room. After they've had a look at ye, ye'd best go home.'

The brandy burned into Ella's stomach, adding strength to her limbs and bringing a flush of colour to her cheeks, but at the Mistress's words she felt all the good of the drink ebbing away. 'I can't go home at this time of day . . . My aunts'll want tae know why I'm not at work and, if they find out the truth, they'll put me out the house!'

'Ye cannae be sure of that, lass. And ye'll have need of them, since it seems tae me that the father's already spoken for.'

'I am sure. You don't know them!'

'They'll have tae be told eventually.'

'I know, but . . . things'll have been decided by then,' Ella said desperately. 'He'll stand by me, I know he will!'

The Mistress gave her a long, thoughtful look, then said, 'Ye can tell yer aunties what I'll tell the women out there – that yer stomach's bad and ye'll be back at work in the mornin'. And see and be here early, tae make up for the time ye've lost today.'

'Ye're not turnin' me off?'

'Ye're a good worker and ye've never caused trouble before. We might be able tae help ye, but ye're goin' tae have tae be sensible and look after yerself and the bairn. No more faintin' at yer work.'

'No, Mrs Drysdale. Thank you, Mrs Drysdale.'

The woman nodded and levered herself to her feet. 'Come on then, let's get it over with. Once the nurse has had a look at ye and ye've had a rest, we'll talk about what's tae happen next.'

When the Mistress announced curtly that Ella had been sent home suffering from colic and would be back at her

frames in the morning, the women accepted the explanation without question, though in the privacy of the toilets
later there was a buzz of speculation.

Ruby, with sly sidelong glances at Mirren, declared that
Ella had been 'up tae no good' with that posh boyfriend
with the car, adding smugly, 'That's why things have gone
wrong between them. She told him she's in the family way
and he's taken tae his heels.'

'That's not true, and you're a jealous cat, Ruby!'
Mirren blazed at her. 'Ella's got the colic!'

'Are ye sure? I've never seen her faint before.'

'Even if the lassie is carryin' – and I'm not sayin'
she is, mind – it won't be the first time in these mills,
nor the last.' Libby McDaid lit up a forbidden cigarette.
'Any place with five thousand women working in it's
bound tae see its fair share of lassies gettin' caught.'
She puffed contentedly, perched on the edge of the big
wooden toilet seat. 'It's different in engineerin' works
and the like, where there's only men. Mind you, every
unborn wean's got a father as well as a mother, but since
the men don't have tae dae the carryin', nob'dy knows
what they've been up tae.'

'But Ella Caldwell, of all folk,' Ruby persisted, her
eyes gleaming. 'Her that'd never even let a lad see her
home after the dancin'!'

'It might just be the curse comin' hard on her this
month. And if it is anythin' else, Mrs Drysdale and
the nurses'll know how tae help her through what's
to come. That's one thing ye can say about the mills
in this town, they look after their own,' Libby said,
then as the girl posted outside the door broke into a
warning fit of coughing the cigarette was stubbed out
and secreted, the cistern flushed and Libby was on her
way into the corridor, innocent of expression and sucking
a peppermint sweetie.

25

Ella didn't put in an appearance at the shop that night and there was no message from her or her aunts. Mirren's explanation about the colic did nothing to improve Maria's temper, which seemed to permeate the entire shop, even affecting the customers. Those who came through the door in high spirits after an enjoyable night out were instantly silenced by the atmosphere and slunk out as soon as they had received their orders and paid for them. One brave soul who dared to say, when Mirren asked if he wanted vinegar on his fish supper, that there was enough around the place without adding more from a bottle, was subjected to one of Maria's tongue-lashings and left vowing never to set foot in the shop again.

The next morning Ella was back in the twisting department, pale-faced, unusually subdued and refusing to rise to Ruby's continuous baiting. Mirren had to wait until the midday break to find out that, under Mrs Drysdale's supervision, Ella had been examined in the mill's first-aid room, which was run by a doctor and a nursing sister with the assistance of two nursing aides drawn from a rota of trained volunteer mill-workers. After that Ella, the nursing sister and the Mistress had had a long consultation.

'I never knew Mrs Drysdale could be so kind, Mirren. I didn't tell her about Vanni and she never asked for his name. She said that her job was tae deal with what had happened, not tae preach about what's done and can't be undone. And she says she'll not dismiss me as long as I go on doin' my work properly. Then the nurse told me about eatin' well and how I should look after myself, then they sent me home.'

'Some of the women are saying that you're expecting.'

Ella bit her lip. 'Ye cannae keep anythin' from them. I'll be glad tae get away from their tattlin', just me and Vanni, together. I cannae wait!'

'Neither can the bairn. When are you telling him?'

'Next Saturday afternoon. Maria visits her family on a Saturday.' Ella's eyes misted over with memories and a smile curved her mouth. 'That's how we first met by accident. I'd gone tae Barshaw Park one Saturday afternoon tae get away from my aunties and he was there on his lone, watchin' folk sailin' their boats on the pond and we just got talkin' . . .'

'Ella!'

'I know, I know. I'll definitely tell him next Saturday afternoon,' Ella promised, crossing her heart. 'And he'll make everythin' work out right for us.'

Mirren, who had learned the hard way not to expect too much out of life, could only hope that the other girl's confidence was not misplaced.

'If this heat goes on we'll have tae think of layin' folk off,' Maria told Vanni on Friday night, her voice deliberately pitched so that Mirren and Ella could hear her. 'We're not gettin' as many customers as usual and I'm not payin' staff good money just tae stand around doin' nothin'.'

'The weather will break soon,' he tried to placate her. 'We'll be as busy as ever next week, you'll see.'

'We'd better be,' his wife said sourly. 'Because if we're not, there's goin' tae be changes here.'

'Mebbe changes she doesnae expect,' Ella muttered to Mirren from the corner of her mouth as the two of them industriously cleaned the counter. Spots of excited colour glowed in her cheeks tonight and her eyes were bright with happy anticipation of the following afternoon, when she would meet Vanni and tell him her news.

The evening dragged by so slowly that it seemed as if time had stopped completely; when the door opened they all looked up, relieved to have some diversion. Ruby trailed in, her heavily made-up face set in discontented lines and little tendrils of red hair sticking to her perspiring brow.

'You look as if ye'd lost a sixpence and found a ha'penny,' Ella greeted her.

'Mind yer own business.' Ruby surveyed the empty shop. 'God, I've seen graveyards wi' more life in them than this place.'

'If we want your opinion we'll ask for it,' Maria snapped. 'Either buy or get out.'

Vanni shot a reproving glance at her over his shoulder while Ruby raised pencilled eyebrows and drawled to Mirren, 'Now that I'm through the door ye might as well give me two pennyworth o' chips and a bottle o' juice.'

'Don't do us any favours, will ye?' Maria sneered.

'Maria . . .'

'You be quiet, Vanni. I'm not puttin' up with impertinence from the likes of her.'

'I'm a customer, in here tae pay good money,' Ruby squawked. 'I can say what I like.'

'Not in my shop. Not for two penn'orth of chips.'

Ruby satisfied herself with a contemptuous snort, while Mirren scooped the chips hurriedly onto a square of greased paper, shook the salt cellar and the vinegar bottle over them, then wrapped them up in newspaper. The heat was causing tempers to rise and she had had to listen to the same petty sniping among the women at work over the past few days. She prayed that Ruby would take her chips and go, but that night Ella, perky now that she knew she would be alone with Vanni in less than twenty-four hours, was just as bad as the other two women.

'What's happened tae the dancin' tonight?' she asked as she took Ruby's money. 'Don't tell me Gregor's stood ye up already?'

Ruby's face, already flushed from the still heat outside, took on a deeper hue. During the past week she had been eager to make it clear to everyone at work, especially when Mirren was within earshot, that she and Gregor Lewis were walking out together.

'Nob'dy stands me up!' she said belligerently. 'If ye must know, Gregor's gran's poorly and he's gone with his ma tae visit her.'

'So he's told ye,' Ella needled.

'That's rich, comin' from you! Did she tell ye that tale about havin' the colic earlier in the week?' Ruby asked Maria. 'Fainted over her machine, she did – if she wasnae one of the Mistress's pets, she'd've been out on her ear.'

Vanni's back stiffened, while Ella said sharply, 'Get out of here, Ruby.'

'Oh, I'm goin', before the smell of the grease in here makes me sick. Mebbe that's what was wrong with ye?' Ruby tucked the bottle under her arm and sauntered towards the door, turning at the last minute to deliver her final broadside. 'Since Gregor's so busy tonight, mebbe I'll just go home and knit a nice wee shawl for yer colic . . . eh, Ella? It should be ready tae wear it in about five months' time.'

Maria scarcely waited until the door closed before confronting Ella. 'Is it true what she's sayin'? Are you expectin'?' Behind her, Vanni had whirled round, eyes huge in a handsome face that had gone grey with shock, not even noticing that he still held the scoop used to lift the chips from the boiling fat, and that it was dripping grease over Maria's clean floor.

'Of course not!'

'Ye're lyin',' Maria said flatly. 'I can see it in yer eyes. I should've known.' Before Ella could resist, the

older woman had grabbed her and ripped her apron off.
'Look!' One bony finger stabbed into Ella's stomach. 'I
thought ye'd put on weight . . . and I was right, ye dirty
wee whore!'

'Maria, stop it!'

'You get back tae yer fish-fryin' and leave her tae me!
Look at this!' Maria caught hold of Ella's left wrist and
shook the ringless hand under Vanni's nose. 'A lassie that
falls pregnant when she's no' wearin' a ring's nothin' but
a harlot, and I'll not have folk like that workin' in my
shop.' She released Ella's wrist, giving the girl a push
towards the back shop. 'I've been wantin' tae get shot
of you for a good while, ye cheeky wee midden. Go
on, out ye go. Let the man that put ye in the family
way support ye, for ye're no' takin' any more of my
hard-earned money!'

'Maria, that's enough!' Vanni stepped in front of his
wife. 'Ye've got no right tae say such things tae Ella.'

'I have if they're true, and they are. Ask her yersel'
if I'm no' right in what I say,' Maria ordered. 'Go on,
ask her!'

Vanni turned his back on his wife and looked down at
Ella. 'Are ye . . . ?'

Mirren caught her breath at the expression that swept
across his face when Ella nodded. It could only be
described as radiant. She knew now that Ella had not
been fantasising when she said that Vanni loved her, and
would want their child.

'Oh, Ella . . .' Oblivious now to his surroundings, he
would have taken her hands, but Ella stepped round the
shelter of his body to confront his wife.

'There's nothin' wrong wi' lovin' a good man and bein'
proud tae carry his bairn,' she told the woman, putting her
hands protectively over her belly. 'At least the world'll
know that I'm a real woman, and not a dried-up stick
of bitterness that can't keep the edge of her tongue off
everyone in sight.'

Maria gave a witchlike screech and lashed out, just as Ella herself had once struck at Mirren in the sand dunes at Barassie. Unprepared for the vicious blow, the girl staggered to one side and would have fallen heavily against the counter if Vanni hadn't caught her.

'Leave her alone!' Instead of releasing her at once, as he should have, he kept his arm about her. 'Are you all right?' He put a hand to her reddening cheek, touching it so carefully, so gently, that Mirren, unnoticed in a corner, caught her breath. The caress – for it was undeniably a caress – was a declaration that Maria could scarcely miss. Nor could she miss the adoration on her husband's face as he looked down at the girl within his embrace.

'Oh God,' she said low-voiced. 'Oh, dear God! You?'

'Aye, me.'

Maria looked as though she was going to be sick.

'You and that . . . that slut?'

'Keep your tongue off her, Maria.' Vanni's eyes were blazing but his voice was quiet. 'Send the lassies home and we'll close the shop and talk about what's tae be done.'

'Get away from my man!' Maria screamed at Ella, her voice so shrill that it hurt Mirren's eardrums. Then, to Vanni, 'Take yer hands off her!' She launched herself at the two of them; at first it looked as though her clawed hands were reaching for Vanni's face, then she swerved suddenly, a bony elbow catching her husband in the ribs and throwing him off balance. As he reeled away, releasing Ella, Maria reached for the girl, snatching and scratching at her face. 'Bitch!' she screamed as she drove her prey back along the counter. 'Whore! Jezebel!'

It all happened in a matter of seconds, yet to Mirren it was as though everything suddenly slowed down. As Ella retreated, one hand going up to protect her eyes from the older woman's reaching fingernails, Vanni, quickly recovering his balance, tried to grab Maria's shoulders. She swung round on him, the talons changing to small knobbly fists that rained punches on him, while all the time curses and obscenities poured from her gaping mouth.

Unable to catch hold of her wrists, he was forced to swing away so that the blows landed on his broad back and shoulders. As he did so one foot skidded on the solidifying fat that had dripped from the scoop and went from under him. He tried to catch his balance, but failed and fell heavily against one of the vats. Its rim caught him across the midriff and the momentum of his fall sent him toppling head-first into the seething, boiling fat below.

When the ambulance van had gone careering off to the Royal Alexandra Infirmary and the gaping crowds had dispersed, Mirren lifted Ella from the corner where she had collapsed, and half-carried, half-dragged her to Maxwellton Street, arriving at the close-mouth just as Robbie and Joe came along the street from the opposite direction.

Robbie took one look at Ella's bleeding, dazed face and scooped her up into his arms. 'Go ahead and open the door, Mirren.'

In the flat he fetched everything that was needed, then without wasting time on questions he retreated to the front room with Joe, leaving Mirren to tend to the wounds that Maria's nails had inflicted on Ella's face. The other girl submitted to the treatment without a word, not even flinching when iodine was dabbed onto the long scratches. She was like a life-sized doll, mute and dazed, not responding to anything that was said to her. When Mirren had done all she could, she undressed Ella then helped her into the kitchen bed, where she turned her face to the wall and plunged into restless unconsciousness.

'You're shakin',' Robbie said when Mirren went into the front room. He drew her to a chair and sat her down, crouching in front of her. 'What's happened?'

'D'ye have any brandy, or whisky in the house?' Joe wanted to know.

'I don't want anything. It's . . . Vanni got hurt tonight, hurt awful bad.' At the memory of it her voice began to break up. Robbie would have stopped her there and then but Joe interceded, pushing Robbie out of the way and kneeling before Mirren to take her hands in his.

'Get it all out now,' he said, his voice low and intense. 'Just look at me and tell me every bit of it and clear it out of your head, else it'll fester in there.'

She did as she was told, finding strength from the unwavering gaze of his blue eyes, darker than her own, and the warmth of his grip. She told them the whole story, for the time for secrets was over, and she kept no detail back, even re-living the way Vanni had managed to pull himself out of the vat almost at once and had dropped to the floor where he writhed, his hands locked over his eyes, his entire body twisting, and curling, then straightening and arching, heels drumming against the floor, only to curl up again into a ball of pure undiluted agony.

She told how Maria, screaming, had wrestled her husband across the floor, trying without success to drag him to the cold-water tap in the back room. And how Ella, after one look at her lover's blistering, bursting features, doubled over on herself in a violent paroxysm of vomiting. Meanwhile Mirren, not knowing what else to do, had embarked on the long journey round the counter and across to the door. It had been a hazardous trip, for it meant having to pass Vanni's writhing figure and flailing legs without falling over him or, worse still, falling on top of him. She had finally managed to reach the door, throw it open and run out onto the pavement, screaming to gaping passers-by to fetch the ambulance.

Some of them had come into the shop and helped to drag Vanni, fighting every inch of the way, into the back shop, where water could be trickled onto his ruined face in a futile attempt to ease his pain. More had gathered outside to stare through the windows and by the time the ambulance van arrived there was a good crowd watching as Vanni, still screaming and struggling against his pain, so that he had to be held down on the stretcher by volunteers, was carried out of the shop. Maria, of course, went with him; once they had gone the crowd melted away, leaving Mirren to lead her friend, shaking and weeping, out of the place.

'Sh . . . she'd not go home, and it's just as well for she was in such a s-state that those poor old ladies would have been alarmed. Sh-she wanted to go to the infirmary to see Vanni, but I couldn't let her do that, not with M-Maria there.' Shock was tying Mirren's tongue up in knots and now she understood why Joe had come out of the war with a stammer. 'I managed to persuade her that visitors wouldn't be allowed at this time of n-night and . . . and . . .'

'And now we're here tae help ye.' Joe gave a brief nod, part approval for finding the courage to tell her story, part reassurance, and got to his feet. 'First of all, Ella's aunts'll have tae know that she's safe and that she's goin' tae spend the night here.'

'I'll go,' Robbie said at once.

'They're maiden ladies . . . It'll probably be bad enough for them to see a stranger at their door at this time of night, without it being a man into the bargain. I'll do it,' Mirren insisted.

'You're not fit!'

'I'm more fit than poor Vanni.' An involuntary shudder shook Mirren.

'I'll go too,' Joe said. 'Ye should have someone with ye.'

'Could you keep watch over Ella, Robbie? I'm worried she might try to go to the infirmary.'

'I'll see tae her,' he said gruffly. 'And Joe, you mind and look after my sister.'

*   *   *

When the other two had gone Robbie went into the kitchen, where Ella twitched and thrashed and muttered feverishly in a sleep that was not really a sleep. As he stood looking down on her, she cried out and her eyes flew open. She stared wildly round then began to struggle upright, and he dropped to the edge of the bed, speaking to her quietly, easing her back down with a hand on her shoulder. She calmed and fell back to the pillow, her eyes closing, and in a moment she was asleep again.

Warm though the night was, her shoulder had felt cold beneath the night-gown Mirren had put on her. Robbie drew the blanket up over her, then pulled an upright chair from the table to the bed so that he could keep an eye on her. Although he liked Ella well enough he had always been wary of her, finding her quick tongue and her confidence daunting at times. Strangely, the revelation about her secret love for another woman's husband and her pregnancy, instead of shocking him, made her more human in his eyes.

She moaned and her eyelashes fluttered then stilled again. Robbie lifted a strand of dark hair back from the curve of her cheek and resumed his vigil, marvelling over her vulnerability, remembering how she had felt in his arms when he carried her upstairs.

'D'you think Vanni'll be all right?' Mirren asked Joe fearfully as they walked to Well Street.

'It depends on how badly he's been burned.'

'I'll never forget the way he screamed and the way he threw himself about the floor, being burned alive . . .'

'Ye've already spoken it out and now ye must learn not tae dwell on it. Memories like that need time tae fade, though they'll never go right away.'

'This is what you've talked about, isn't it? This is the sort of thing you and George Armitage and all the other men saw during the war. That's why you made me tell it all to you and Robbie.'

'Aye,' Joe said. 'But you should never have had tae see it, not here in yer own town.'

By agreement he waited at the close-mouth while Mirren went upstairs alone to face Ella's aunts. Her timid tap on the door was greeted at first with total silence, then just as she was considering lifting the shining brass knocker to administer another tap on the equally shining plate, there was a slight scuffling noise on the other side of the door and a high-pitched voice asked, 'Who is it?'

Mirren put her mouth close to the door, unwilling to divulge her business to any neighbours who might be listening behind their own doors. 'Mirren Jarvis, Miss Peacock. I'm Ella's friend.'

She could hear a whispered consultation, then the same voice said, 'Ella's not at home, she's at work.'

'I know she's not at home, she's at my house. She's not well. Can I come in for a minute?'

'It's very late!'

'I know it is, but I need to explain about Ella,' Mirren said frantically. There was silence, though she thought that she could hear whispering from inside the flat. Then to her relief the door opened, though just wide enough to reveal a pointed nose surmounted by a sharp eye and a fringe of grey hair.

The eye surveyed her, then 'You'd best come in and stop spreading our niece's business all over the building,' the voice reproved, and the door opened to reveal a dark narrow hall. Stepping over the threshold, Mirren was suddenly surrounded by the mingled scent of lavender, moth balls and pot pourri. Whenever they went dancing together Ella always used perfume lavishly because, she said, she had to get the smell of her aunts' flat out of her nostrils. Now Mirren understood why. As the door was closed behind her she saw that two other old ladies were huddled at the end of the long narrow lobby, eyeing her cautiously.

'In there,' the spokeswoman said from the door, and

the two backed before Mirren to allow her entry into a parlour where the predominant smell was that of furniture polish and the air felt chilly, even on that hot stuffy night. The few pieces of furniture were large and dark and the chairs looked as though nobody ever sat on them.

The three facing her were clearly sisters, all plump but thin-faced, and with grey hair which, at that time of night, hung in long pleats over their shoulders. They were all wearing outdoor coats over white night-gowns – it was obvious that she had brought them from their beds.

'Now then, what did you say your name is?' the woman who had opened the door asked. Like Ella herself, all the women were slightly smaller than Mirren; their spokes-woman was the smallest, yet she exuded a strength and power none of the others showed. This, no doubt was Aunt Lillian, the matriarch of the family.

'Mirren Jarvis, Miss Peacock. I work with Ella at the mill and at the fried-fish shop. Vanni . . . Mr Perrini, the owner, was badly hurt in an accident tonight and Ella's ill with the shock of it.'

'If our niece is unwell she should be here, at her home.'

'She's very upset. I thought it best to take her home with me, just for the one night.'

'We do not approve. Eleanor knows very well that our door is bolted at eleven o'clock every night. It is now,' Lillian Peacock turned to consult the clock that stood in solitary possession of the mantelshelf, 'half past ten. There is still time for her to come home before eleven.'

Mirren swallowed back her surprise at hearing Ella's real name. 'She's asleep now. It would be best to leave her for the night. She'll be home tomorrow.'

'She'll be through that front door by eleven o'clock tonight, young woman, if she wants to continue to regard this as her home.'

'Accident?' one of the other women said. 'What sort

of accident? Was our niece involved in it? We'll not have her bringing scandal down on our good name.'

Mirren wished that she had asked Joe to come to the flat with her. 'Va . . . Mr Perrini slipped and fell into one of the vats.'

'Oh!' the third woman clapped a hand to her mouth, her brown eyes, greatly magnified by thick spectacles, blinking in owlish concern. 'The poor man. Was he . . . is he . . . ?'

This must be Ella's favourite aunt, Bea. 'He was taken to the infirmary, but we haven't heard how he is.' The room began to dip and sway gently and the grey curtain she recalled only too well from the day Agnes had given birth to wee Robert drifted over Mirren's eyes. She wondered which would be the worse crime – sinking down onto one of the forbidding chairs or sprawling over the carpet at the sisters' feet in a dead faint.

'I trust that Eleanor was not involved in any way?'

'No, of course not, but she . . . we were both very upset.'

'I did say, Lillian, that it was not a good idea to allow her to work in that place, and now I've been proved right.' There was almost a note of glee in the speaker's voice and a glitter in the depths of her otherwise expressionless eyes. Digging into her memory, Mirren established her as Margaret, the middle sister.

Lillian glared at her, then said frostily to Mirren, 'Eleanor agreed to abide by our rules when we first took her in and she is aware of the consequences of breaking them. Please leave now and remind her that we are not some charity at the beck and call of young women who ought to know better.'

'Lillian,' Bea said anxiously, while Mirren, so astonished that the grey curtain cleared from her eyes for a moment, asked, 'D'you mean that you'd put her out of the house just for staying with me for one night?'

'Every well-ordered household has its regulations. There

is still time for her to walk here if she puts her mind to it.' The woman's gaze was as chilly as the room. 'That is, if you go and fetch her instead of standing around here wasting time.'

'But she can't walk as far as this tonight, not in her condition!' As three heads jerked upright and three pairs of eyes fastened onto her face, Mirren could have bitten her tongue out.

'Condition? Are you telling us that our niece is . . .'

'I'm just saying that she was very sick tonight – and who could blame her, with what happened?'

Aunt Bea gave a little whimper, then said shakily, 'Oh, Lillian! She's been sick such a lot recently. Surely . . . ?'

'Why was I not told?'

'I thought it was just the heat. I've felt quite queasy myself more than once recently.'

'I knew it,' Margaret's dry voice rustled triumphantly. 'Did I not say all along that there was probably badness in that child? That the fault may not have been her father's entirely?'

'That's a wicked thing to say!' Mirren burst out. 'Ella's a good, decent girl!'

'So she told you?' Lillian's eyes flashed. 'She's boasted to you about her shameful past?'

'She's done no such thing!'

'This conversation is at an end.' Lillian Peacock swept to the door and threw it open. 'You may inform Eleanor that as from this moment she is no blood-kin of ours.'

'But what's to happen to her?' Bea squeaked.

'That is between herself and the devil, as far as we are concerned.' The woman threw the words over her shoulder as she marched along the lobby. 'Her belongings will be packed and handed in to the grocer's shop on the ground floor.' She wrenched open the door and stepped back to allow Mirren to exit. 'She may collect them from there when she has a mind to. Goodnight to you.'

Back on the landing, Mirren turned. 'You're a cruel,

bad-minded old woman,' she said, 'and Ella's better off without you.' The door banged shut and she caught the beginnings of what sounded like a bout of hysteria as she started down the stairs. Probably it was Aunt Bea; she couldn't see either of the other two succumbing to any form of emotion whatsoever.

It was such a relief to see Joe Hepburn pacing the close and looking so normal and human that she would have flown down the final steps and right into his arms if she had had the energy.

His penetrating gaze searched her face. 'Was it awful bad?'

'They were . . .' She stopped suddenly and pushed him rudely aside in her rush to get through the back close and into the yard. Hours, or perhaps seconds, later she spat the last of the sour taste from her mouth and straightened, glad of Joe's supporting arm. He had been there all along, she realised, holding her head, rubbing her back, but otherwise leaving her unhindered to empty herself of the physical manifestation of the night's horror. Now he offered her a handkerchief.

'It's clean.'

'I suppose this is something else you were used to seeing in the war,' she said shakily.

'All the time, and I did my fair share of it too. D'ye feel ready tae walk back tae Broomlands Street?'

She nodded. 'I'd crawl over broken glass to get out of this place. Have you ever heard of witches' covens, Joe?'

'Aye, I have.'

'I've just been in one,' Mirren said. 'And now I want to go home!'

26

'She'll stay here, of course,' Robbie said. They had returned to Maxwellton Street to find him sitting by the wall bed, his eyes fixed on Ella's sleeping face. Now the three of them were in the front room in low-voiced consultation.

'You'd not mind?'

'Why should I? From what ye say she's far better here with us than with those old aunts of hers.'

'Not tae mention it bein' better for her bairn,' Joe nodded, and Mirren shivered at the thought of an innocent baby in the hands of the women she had recently faced.

'I never suspected how bad they were. She never said a word against them, just made a joke of her life with them.' Now Mirren understood why Ella had been so eager to inveigle Martin into marriage. 'How could she have kept so cheery all the years when she was going home every night to that place?'

'She must have a lot more courage than any of us realised,' Robbie said soberly.

'She'll need all of it and more tae get her through what's ahead of her, poor lass.' Joe stretched and yawned deeply. 'I'd best get home and let ye go tae yer beds.'

'You could stay here,' Mirren suggested tentatively, but he shook his head.

'I'll call at the infirmary in the mornin' and try tae get word of how the man is. Then I'll come and let ye know.'

*　　*　　*

During the night the long-awaited thunderstorm arrived, the first indication a vivid, searing flash of lightning that lit the kitchen so strongly for a few seconds that Mirren, lying sleepless in the wall bed, could see the cracks in the ceiling and the patch of damp high in one corner. Within seconds she was plunged again into darkness and there was a rumbling crash right above the town and then, at last, the heavy drumming that meant rain.

Mirren, usually nervous in thunderstorms, was indifferent for once to the lightning's vicious brilliance and the thunder's angry threats, for they were as nothing compared to the storms she had been through in the past few hours. She lay wide-eyed while Ella tossed and moaned and muttered by her side, watching the kitchen appear and disappear at the whim of the lightning, listening to the lion's roar of the thunder and the hiss of rain, but hearing only Vanni Perrini's terrible choked screaming and seeing with each lightning flash the horror of the skin, shiny with burning fat, flaking from his face. Joe was right, she must try to cleanse her mind of the memories, or else they might drive her mad.

He arrived late on Sunday morning, rain soaking through the material of his old, thin coat and glittering in his dark hair, to report that Vanni was 'doing as well as could be expected', and that there were to be no visitors apart from family.

'So there's no sense in goin' tae the infirmary, for they'll not let ye see him,' he explained to Ella, who had slept late and refused food or drink.

'Of course I'm going.' Her eyes were huge in an ashen face and her long hair was lifeless. She looked like her own ghost.

'Ye're not well enough,' Robbie said gently, 'and they'll not let ye in tae see him anyway.'

'But he'll be lookin' for me, mebbe askin' for me.'

Ready tears filled Ella's eyes and flowed down her
cheeks. 'It was a terrible way he found out about our
bairn,' she sobbed. 'And we never had a minute tae talk
about it together.' She was inconsolable and, at her wit's
end, Mirren finally sent Robbie down the road to fetch
Catherine Proctor, who walked back with him.

'We've got our work to go to in the morning, and there's
Ella's clothes to be fetched from the grocer's shop, and
she's determined to go and see Vanni even though she's
not fit for it . . .' Mirren poured out her worries, with
Catherine nodding her understanding of each point.

'Even if they did let her in, the lassie isn't fit to visit.
You just need to look at her to see that she's not herself.'

'Shell shock,' said Joe Hepburn, and she looked up at
him, startled.

'I've never seen it myself, but from what I've read of it
I suppose you're quite right. Why don't you let me take
her in for a few days, Mirren, just until she feels a bit
better?'

'I couldn't ask . . . !'

'You didn't ask, dear, I offered. It would be the best
thing all round, for I'm at home during the day and I can
keep a watch over her. She can sleep in the wee room Mary
had before she moved into Grace and Anne's bedroom.
You'll be just up the road and mebbe having the rest of
the family round the place will help her.' Catherine got
to her feet. 'Someone will have to fetch her belongings
tomorrow, but in the meantime I'm sure my lassies can
provide her with whatever she needs.'

Once it arrived the rain, in true Scottish fashion, declined
to leave. It drizzled down throughout Sunday and when
Mirren went to work on Monday morning it was still falling
from a heavy grey sky. Not that anyone minded as yet, for
the air smelled fresher and felt cooler, and children on their
way to school splashed joyfully through the puddles, heedless of the coming misery of having to sit in the classroom

with wet, chilled feet. In another twenty-four hours, if the weather didn't brighten, folk would begin to complain and wonder if summer was ever coming back.

'Is it true what they're sayin'?' Ruby asked as soon as Mirren stepped off the hoist and into the twisting department. 'Was there an accident in the fried-fish shop on Saturday night?'

The sight of the girl who had heedlessly triggered off events with her barbed tongue infuriated Mirren. 'Yes there was, and a decent kindly man was hurt bad. And I wish your two penn'orth of chips had choked you,' she said. Then, spinning away from the other girl's astonished face, she went in search of the Mistress, who heard her out without interruption before saying heavily, 'I'd a feelin' in my bones that it wouldnae turn out the way Ella planned. Sin's sin, no matter how many good intentions are behind it.'

'He would have seen her right, I know it, if . . .'

'So she'll not be back for a while, then?'

'Not till she gets over the shock of what happened.'

'And I'll be expected tae keep her place open, will I?'

'I know it's a lot to ask, but it would be a help, Mrs Drysdale.'

The woman sighed heavily. 'And in the meantime here's me with one six-sider short and expected tae turn out the same amount of work. Give me your auntie's address, and I'll go and see her and Ella after work.'

Mirren had no sooner brushed all the oose from her clothing and combed it from her hair than the door knocker rattled.

'Good afternoon, miss.' The small, dapper man standing on the doormat raised his bowler hat and gave her a little bow. 'I must apologise for disturbing you, but I'm looking for Miss Ella Caldwell?' His voice, Scottish and yet not Scottish, lifted enquiringly at the end of the sentence.

'She's not here.'

'Perhaps she will be back soon?'

Mirren studied him, faintly uneasy without knowing why. He must have been handsome once, when his flat dark eyes probably sparkled with youth, the ivory teeth now bared in a shallow smile were strong and white and the balding head was covered in thick black hair. But perhaps, even then, there had been a sinister air about him.

'Ella doesn't live here.' Her fingers gripped the edge of the door, ready to close it if he made to enter.

'No?' His eyebrows, thick and bushy, lifted. 'I was told that I would find her at this address,' he said. 'You are the young lady who worked beside her in my nephew Giovanni's shop?'

'Vanni? How is he?'

The old man pursed his lips slightly, then shrugged. 'Quite well. Uncomfortable, but who would not be uncomfortable if they had suffered as he has?'

'Can he have visitors?'

'No visitors,' he said flatly. 'Only family. You will appreciate that he needs to rest quietly. His poor wife is quite distraught with grief and worry. It has been decided that as soon as Giovanni is recovered enough to leave the infirmary, he and Maria will go away on a holiday to visit family elsewhere. They will not return to Paisley. I'm sure you will understand that this town holds too many memories for them now. Bad memories,' he emphasised, his dark eyes holding hers. 'I was asked to explain to Miss Caldwell – and to yourself, of course – that unfortunately your services in the shop will no longer be required. I am so sorry. Perhaps you will tell your friend, wherever she may be?'

'I will.' Mirren began to close the door, but he put out a wrinkled brown hand to stop her.

'Please, miss, make it quite clear to your friend that it would not be wise for her or for you to think of attempting to see my nephew. It would only cause great upset, and a lot of trouble too.' His teeth, the colour of the keys of the old piano in William Primrose's dancing studio, were bared in another shallow smile. 'You may rest assured that we, the Perrini family, will look after both of them.'

He gave her another little bow and turned away, replacing his hat as he did so. Mirren immediately shut the door and stood in the little lobby, too shaken to take the few steps back into the kitchen. When the snib rattled, she jumped and leaned her weight on the door to hold it shut.

'Mirren?' The snib banged up and down. 'I can't get the door open. Are ye there?'

'Robbie?'

'Of course it's me, and Joe too. What's amiss?' he wanted to know as she opened the door to admit the two of them, each carrying a brown-paper parcel. She had forgotten that they had offered to collect Ella's belongings from the grocer's shop after work.

'Come in, quick!' When they were inside she closed the door and put the snib down to lock it before following them into the kitchen, where they had laid the two pathetically small bundles that held all Ella's possessions on the table. 'Did you meet anyone on the stairs?'

'Only a wee, well-dressed chap. We passed him in the close. What about it?' Robbie wanted to know. When she told them about her visitor he and Joe looked at each other, then Joe said, 'I've heard that Italian families are very close. They look after their own.'

'Ella once said that it was Vanni's relatives that got them the shop.'

'I think the two of ye'd be as well tae heed the wee man and let matters be,' Joe advised.

'She'll want to go to the infirmary as soon as she's able.'

'Then we'll have tae find ways of stoppin' her. I'll say that I've been back tae ask for him, and only family are allowed tae visit.'

'They couldn't do anything to Ella even if she did manage to get to Vanni. Could they?'

Again, the men looked at each other before Joe said grimly, 'Best that she doesnae take that chance. And mebbe best that she stays on with yer aunt, if that's all right, instead of comin' back here.'

'And what about Vanni?'

'I doubt if ye'll see him or his wife again. And mebbe,' said Robbie, 'that's as well. Mirren, I wish ye'd go tae Donald. You'd be best out of this place.'

'How can I go away until I know what's to happen to Ella?'

'Yer sister can make up her own mind in her own time,' Joe said unexpectedly. 'She has as much right tae do that as you have.'

By the time Ella was strong enough to walk across town to the infirmary Vanni had gone, and she had no way of finding out where. She returned to the twisting department where the other women had been well warned by the Mistress concerning their behaviour towards her. Even without the warning none of them, Ruby included, would have said a word to their errant workmate, who had changed overnight from a cheerful young girl into a pale, withdrawn woman. Her thin, wan face and shadowed eyes, together with her swelling belly, gave the impression that the child was thriving at the expense of its mother.

'Surely she shouldnae be workin' in her condition,' Robbie said anxiously to Mirren. 'She doesnae look as if she'd the strength tae walk from one end of the town tae the other, let alone birth a child.'

'She needs to work. Women like us don't stop doing things just because they're expecting bairns, and she needs to keep busy, let alone having to earn her keep for as long as she can.'

He began to worry at his hair, twisting a forelock around his finger just as he had done when studying for his apprenticeship. 'But our Agnes had red cheeks and bright eyes all the while she was carryin' wee Robert. Ella looks like a ghost.'

'Agnes had her man by her side. Poor Ella doesn't even know where Vanni is, and she never will.'

The fried-fish shop remained closed for some time before re-opening under new management. And for the rest of her life Mirren was haunted by the thought of good-looking, gentle, caring Vanni Perrini, horrifically scarred, possibly blinded, living out the rest of his life in some unknown place, at the mercy of Maria and perhaps wondering – and never knowing – what had happened to Ella and their child.

Catherine Proctor proved, once again, to be a godsend. She persuaded Ella to remain in her home, using the excuse that Ella would help to fill the gap left by Grace and Anne, while Mrs Drysdale saw to it that when the girl had to leave work to give birth, her keep would be paid from a special mill fund set up for such emergencies.

Like Joe Hepburn, Ella took to spending most of her spare time in the Maxwellton Street flat, where, although there were no longer fried-fish suppers to be divided amongst the four of them, the talk was as lively as ever, with Mirren, Joe and Robbie locked in heated discussion almost always set off by some political comment. The debates became passionate, with each of them raising his or her voice in order to be heard above the others.

At first Ella simply listened, but gradually she began to put in a word here or there, until finally she was playing her full part and going back to the Proctors' house most nights with her face flushed and her eyes bright.

'It's a shame we've tae get her angry tae see colour in her face,' Robbie said one night on his return from walking her down the road.

'It's nice to have someone taking my side for once, when you and your precious friend start airing your views,' Mirren responded tartly.

He sat down to pull his boots off. 'Growin' up in that house with those old aunties of hers . . . She must have had a lot of courage tae stay so bright and cheerful all the time.'

'Ella's always had courage – and she'll need all of it. Mrs Drysdale's been talking to her about giving the bairn away when it comes, but Ella's determined to keep it.'

'How could she, on her lone?'

'That's what Mrs Drysdale says, and Aunt Catherine too, but as far as Ella's concerned, the child's all she'll have left of Vanni and she's determined not to let it go. It'll come hard on her when she has to face the truth.'

Robbie took the second boot off and stood it neatly beside its partner in the hearth. 'There's times,' he said soberly, 'that I'm glad I'm just a man.'

Grieving though Ella was, the natural resilience that had already brought her through her father's abuse, then through years of living with her repressive aunts, slowly began to surface as the weeks passed. The colour returned to her face, though anyone catching her during a quiet moment could not miss the deep sorrow in her eyes and the way her mouth, in repose, now curved down at the corners.

'I'll hand a jar in to Mrs White across the landing tomorrow and you can take two back to Aunt Catherine tonight.' Mirren studied the eight jars set on the draining board to cool. 'We'll give one to Joe and one to Agnes and Bob, and that leaves three.'

'Best make it two jars for Joe,' Ella advised, running the back of one hand over her hot forehead. 'I've noticed he's got a sweet tooth.'

They had spent Saturday afternoon on the braes with Robbie and Joe, who had taken them to a spot Joe knew where raspberry plants that had once been cultivated still flourished in an overgrown garden close by the tumbled ruins of a farmer's cottage. They had brought back a good supply of the soft red berries with their delicate, almost perfumed flavour, and now the flat was filled with the rich aroma of boiling fruit.

'You're right. Two jars for Joe, then.' Mirren ran the back of one finger round the warm curve of a jar. 'They look like rubies, don't they? There's nothing like the sight of fresh-made jam.' She glanced at the clock. 'They're late back from their meeting tonight. You sit down and I'll mebbe get this place tidy before they arrive.'

'Indeed I'll not sit down! I'm not an invalid. Come on, two of us'll get things done twice as fast.' The afternoon out in the countryside had done Ella the world of good and now, tired and hot though she was after the jam-making, she set to with a will. Between them they had put the kitchen to rights by the time the outer door opened.

'Here they are, and I've no doubt they'll empty one of the jars tonight before it even has a chance to go cold. Put the kettle on, Ella, while I slice the bread. They'll be starving.'

But only Robbie came into the kitchen, his jacket torn and his face swollen and bloody.

Ella's horrified 'What's happened tae ye?' clashed with Mirren's 'Where's Joe?' She had no need to ask what had happened, for she well knew; but usually when tempers ran high at a meeting she was presented with two sets of cuts and bruises to tend to.

'He's in the jail,' Robbie said thickly through a swollen mouth. 'I'm lucky not tae be there myself.'

'You ran off and left him?'

'Of course not! What d'ye take me for? Joe was on the platform, speakin', when the police arrived. If they'd been ten minutes earlier it's me they'd have arrested, not him.'

'So it was an illegal meeting.'

'In this country most of the workin' folk's meetings are illegal. You should know that by now.'

'Oh, I do. So what cause were the two of you supporting this time?'

'It was tae do with a grievance the shipyard workers
have in Greenock. A justified grievance,' Robbie added
firmly, dabbing at his bloody, swollen nose with a gory
handkerchief.

'For any favour, are ye goin' tae let the man bleed tae
death while ye plague him with yer questions?' Ella asked
frantically, taking his arm and leading him to the sink.
'Stand there while I bring a chair over.'

Mirren had already assured herself with a glance that the
nosebleed that had caused most of the mess was over. 'If
there was any danger of him bleeding to death it would've
happened last time or the time before, or the time before
that. Lift the vinegar down from the shelf, will you? And
you'll find some clean rags in that drawer – put some hot
water from the kettle into the basin and add a good helping
of vinegar before you wring the cloths out in it. Use one
to clean his face and the other on the cuts. I'll fetch the
iodine.'

'It's not that bad,' Robbie said swiftly, screwing up his
face in anticipation of the iodine's sting, then wincing
as the movement caused additional pain. 'I don't need
iodine.'

'You're getting it anyway,' Mirren told him mercilessly.
Together she and Ella tended him, Mirren with the brisk
efficiency of a hospital nurse and Ella, new to the business,
with gentle care.

'What's goin' tae happen tae Joe?' she asked when the
blood and grime had been washed away and Robbie was
looking more like himself. 'Did ye see him after he was
put intae the jail?'

'I could scarce go in and demand tae talk tae him
when I looked like . . . ow!' Robbie winced and looked
reproachfully at Mirren, who was putting the iodine on
with a lavish hand. 'I don't need the whole bottle! I hung
about outside for a wee while and a policeman friendlier
than most told me Joe'd be kept in and sent before the
magistrate on Monday mornin'.'

'He's supposed to be at his work on Monday morning.'

'I'll tell the gaffer he's got a bad stomach.'

'And what if he's sent tae prison?' Ella asked.

'That won't happen . . . will it, Robbie?'

'Not for a wee stramash like tonight's,' he assured them both. 'He'll mebbe have tae pay a fine but he'll be out in time tae get back tae the shipyard by midday. Can I get up now? Are ye finished?'

'We're finished, but your face looks like a patchwork quilt. It'll still be a mess when you go into work on Monday,' Mirren fretted.

'I'm employed for my expertise as an engineer, no' for my looks.' His eyes brightened as he spotted the jars. 'Any chance of some bread and jam? I'm that hungry my stomach thinks my throat's been cut. And I'd fair enjoy a cup of tea.' He looked hopefully at Ella, who succumbed at once.

'I'll make it for you . . . and see tae the bread and jam too.'

'If it was Joe the police wanted, what happened to you?' Mirren wanted to know.

'Aye, well, tempers were gettin' a bit heated durin' the meetin' anyway. The bosses must've heard about it and sent some men of their own in. They do that sometimes, tae try tae set us against each other. So even before the police arrived there were fights breakin' out all over the place. I just got caught up in one of them. Poor Joe was on the platform tryin' tae calm folk down.' He snuffled at the air then mourned, 'I cannae smell a thing tonight – and I love the smell of the jam-makin' too!'

'It serves you right,' Mirren snapped.

Battered though he was, Robbie insisted on walking to the Proctors' building with Ella, as he always did. When he came back, he said, 'I'd best go tae see Joe tomorrow.'

'Looking like that? They'll keep you in!'

'They'll not. I just want tae make sure he's all right.'

'Did he get hurt as well?'

'A bit, but nothin' too bad. He's used tae it.'

'D'you want me to go with you tomorrow?'

'Best not,' he advised, and she didn't argue, for she had no real wish to see Joe locked up in prison. The very thought made her shiver and she found it hard to sleep that night for worrying. Maddening though he was, Joe Hepburn had become part of her family.

She got up early on Sunday morning and did a baking. When Robbie, his face still badly bruised and his nose swollen, was ready to leave for Greenock, she put a small bag into his coat pocket. 'A few scones with some raspberry jam on them. Mind and keep your cap pulled down over your face when you go into the jail, for you're still marked. You look like a man on the run. And tell Joe not to argue back in the court tomorrow. That's not the place for him to start his lecturing.'

He returned home to report that Joe was managing fine, and grateful for the scones.

'You're not going to Greenock for his court appearance, are you?' Mirren asked anxiously.

'I can't, for I'll have tae go tae work tae try and persuade the gaffer that Joe'll be in after dinnertime. And I hope tae God that he is. Someone's goin' tae get word tae me about what happens. We've arranged for the fine tae be paid, whatever it may be, so that Joe can get back tae Paisley as quickly as possible.'

27

On Monday Robbie came home from work in a state of shock and announced that Joe Hepburn had been sent to prison for seven days for the part he had played in the Greenock meeting.

'But you said he'd never be sent to the jail!' Mirren was as stunned as her brother.

'I was certain of it, and so were the others I spoke tae. But we're not the ones in control, are we?' he said bitterly. 'It means he's lost his place in the shipyard, for the gaffer'd never believe that a pain in the gut could last for a whole week. Anyway, he'll hear about it one way or another.' He pushed his dinner away, half-eaten. 'I've lost my appetite entirely. I'll have tae fetch some things from his house and take them down tae him tonight.'

'Be sure to take him some books and mebbe paper to write on. He'll not be able to manage without them.'

'What books should I take?' he asked, at a loss.

'I'll go with you to his house and find something suitable.'

Joe lived in a single room in Orchard Street, which bore no resemblance whatsoever to its pretty name but had been built on ground where, some 600 or 700 years before, the monks of Paisley's great Abbey had grown fruit. Robbie unlocked the door and Mirren followed him in, feeling as she did so that they were invading Joe's privacy. She stood for a moment, staring, then said, shocked, 'This is no place for the man to live!'

'What's wrong with it?'

'It's . . . it's so . . .' she fumbled for the right word but could only come up with, 'so bare.'

'It suits Joe's needs well enough,' Robbie said, clearly surprised by her comment. 'He's not here much anyway.' He got down on his knees and peered beneath the narrow cot, then pulled out a small suitcase.

Apart from linoleum, clean but so faded that the pattern could no longer be seen, the only covering on the floor was a small, thin cloth rug before the fireplace. Posters – all announcing political meetings – and newspaper photographs had been pinned on the walls and the few furnishings consisted of a sink below the window, a small gas cooker, a table almost buried beneath its burden of books and papers, with an ordinary wooden kitchen chair at each side, one shabby fireside chair, a small set of drawers and the cot. The way in which its bedding was neatly folded and stacked at the foot of the mattress reminded Mirren of Donald explaining to her how he was taught to set out his Army cot each morning for inspection.

'Most houses have something lying around – a newspaper, mebbe, or slippers in the hearth. There's nothing here.'

'That's tae do with his upbringin'.' Robbie was rummaging in the little chest of drawers. 'Joe told me once that because he was raised in a wee house that had tae hold the family, as well as his old grandpa, his mother was very strict about possessions. Everythin' that wasnae needed was put out. Even the books he got for Sunday School prizes were thrown away as soon as he'd read them.'

'That's terrible!' Mirren started to search through the neat piles on the table for suitable books to send to Joe.

'I'd not care for it myself,' Robbie admitted. 'It meant that he'd tae learn tae do with very little. He said his upbringin' was helpful when it came tae bein' in the

Army, because the soldiers had tae do with very few possessions.'

All the books were political, and she felt that it would not be wise to send them, given the charges of sedition that had been made against Joe. 'But where are the books he loaned me?'

'They're kept here . . .' Robbie swept aside the curtains over the recess that would normally have held a bed. Hooks in a small section of wall served as a wardrobe, holding the familiar dark, pin-striped, old-fashioned suit and two clean shirts, but the rest of the space behind the curtain was filled with books. Here there was no attempt to keep things uniformly tidy. Fat and thin volumes, large and small, crowded together on tier upon tier of rough shelving that covered the recess walls from floor to ceiling. More books spilled from orange boxes and cardboard cartons on the floor. Compared to the rest of the room, the wall recess was a treasure trove.

'He's read every one of them too,' Robbie boasted, pleased by his sister's awed reaction. 'He buys them from second-hand shops and pawnshops and he'll never throw one of them out, no matter how ragged it gets with bein' read over and over again. Pick somethin' suitable for him while I see tae some clothin'.'

While he carefully packed the cardboard case, Mirren studied Joe Hepburn's library. There were all sorts of books: poetry and prose, novels and essays, political writings and volumes on geography, geology, flora and fauna. The names danced at her, some familiar, others not – Charles Kingsley, William Thackeray, Daniel Defoe, Jane Austen, Anthony Trollope, H.G. Wells, Shakespeare, Byron, Robert Browning, Tennyson living cheek-by-jowl in no specific order, with only one thing in common. They were all old and shabby.

She was so busy looking that she forgot what she was supposed to be doing until Robbie asked, 'Did ye find anythin'?'

'This, mebbe . . . and this.' Mirren picked out a Charles Dickens novel at random, then took down a volume of poetry as well. From the table which, although crowded, held everything in neat piles and stacks, she took an exercise book and two pencils.

When Robbie tried to close the case he discovered that the catches were broken. After a brief hunt Mirren found some string neatly rolled up in bundles in the chest of drawers, and he tied the case shut. 'I'll catch a train, it'll be quicker than the bus.'

Before following him out she took quick stock of the place again, and realised what had been bothering her since she first walked into it. The small room spoke clearly to her of the man who lived in it: his background, his character, his beliefs and, when the curtain was lifted, his hopes and his longings and his soul. And having seen it, been part of it for a few brief moments, she had the uneasy feeling that she herself would never be the same again.

Robbie was pale and withdrawn when he came home that night, saying only that Joe was fine, and grateful for the books, the writing material and the scones.

'But he doesnae want ye tae visit him. I can see why,' he added with a shiver. 'Those big doors and the sound of keys in the locks, and the look in some of the other men's eyes . . . Ye'd not want tae go there if ye didnae have tae.'

'Mebbe you'd best leave it be, yourself,' Mirren suggested. His eyes were haunted, his normally open young face closed in a way she had not seen since he had been turned off after completing his apprenticeship. 'He's only in for a week.'

'The least I can do is tae visit the man,' Robbie snapped at her, but after his second visit he looked even more haggard.

'He's off his food, and that's not like Robbie at all,' Mirren said to Ella on the Wednesday evening. 'And last night I heard him walking up and down his wee room when he should have been asleep. But if I say anything he just bites the nose off me.'

'Best leave him alone. Joe'll be out soon enough and then Robbie'll get back tae his old self. If ye ask me,' Ella began, then changed tack swiftly as the outer door opened, 'that Ruby Liddell's got above herself since she started walking out with Gregor Lewis. There'll be a bottlin' before . . . It's yourself, Robbie. How's Joe?'

'Bearin' up.'

'I'll make some fresh tea.' Mirren picked up the pot then put it down again as Robbie said, 'I'm not bothered.'

The two girls exchanged glances, then Ella reached into the bed recess and picked up her coat, 'I'd best be going.'

'I'll walk down with ye.' Robbie, hanging his cap on the peg behind the kitchen door, lifted it down again.

'Are you certain? You're just in, and I can manage that wee bit of street on my lone.'

'I always walk ye back tae George Street,' he said, jamming the cap over his head. As he led the way out Ella raised her eyebrows at Mirren behind his back. Mirren shook her head helplessly, at her wits' end.

On the way down the stairs Ella kept Robbie's moody silence at bay with a stream of meaningless chatter, which was suddenly interrupted when he muttered something and went bounding down the last few steps ahead of her.

'Robbie . . . ?' But he had gone, rushing out through the close into the big back court. Reaching the final step, she followed him into the September darkness.

'Robbie?' When there was no reply she moved forward slowly, testing the ground with a cautious foot before each step. Although the court was better cared for than some, there was no knowing what might have been left out – a child's toy, or perhaps a basket of clothes-pegs forgotten by some woman already burdened with a big washing from the line. Off to one side she heard the flap and whisper of clothes left out in the night winds because of pressure of time, or perhaps to give them a good freshening. As her eyes grew accustomed to the darkness she could see the flickering restlessness of bedsheets pulling against the pegs that anchored them.

'Robbie?' There was still no reply and she was debating whether or not to turn back into the close when he said from quite nearby, 'I'm here.'

'Where?'

'Here.' There was a movement to her right, then all at once she saw his face, a white glimmer against the darkness of the tenement wall.

'Are you all right?'

'I'm . . . I just thought for a minute that I was goin' tae be sick. I had tae get outside.'

'How d'you feel now?'

'A bit better.' His voice sounded shaky and Ella fumbled in her bag.

'Wait a minute.' Her questing fingers found the small bottle and she drew it out, unscrewed the lid, and held it to his nose. 'Take a sniff of that.'

He did so and immediately shied away so sharply that she heard the back of his head rebound against the wall. 'God . . . !' He grabbed at her hand and pushed both it and the bottle away, coughing. 'What's that?'

'Sal volatile.'

'It's vicious! It near killed me!' He rubbed his head.

'I'm sorry about the bump. I meant it tae clear your head, not hurt it. I carry it around with me because since I . . . since the bairn started I sometimes feel a bit faint. It helps me every time. D'ye want tae try it again, more carefully this time?' she suggested.

'No no, I'm fine.'

'You're not fine at all, Robbie Jarvis. When ye came home tonight ye looked for all the world as if it was you in prison and not J . . . What is it?' she asked sharply as he gave a muffled groan and turned in against the wall, forehead against the cold stone. 'Ye might as well tell me, for ye're worryin' the life out of poor Mirren, and now ye're worryin' me.'

'I'm a coward, Ella.'

'Ye are not! Who said such a thing?'

'I'm sayin' it, and I'm sayin' the truth.' He took a long ragged breath. 'It's as well I wasnae old enough tae fight in the war for I'd never have been any good at it. I'd've turned and run for home and been shot for a deserter if I'd . . .'

His voice broke and when she touched his back she could feel the tremor shuddering all through his body. 'Robbie?'

'I couldnae do it, Ella,' he said. 'I couldnae do a spell in the jail like Joe. Just walkin' intae the place tae see him has me near vomitin' with fear, even knowin' that in an hour I'll be able tae walk out again and come home. Joe can take it, but I cannae. And it'll come tae that, as sure as anythin', if I go on with the meetin's.' In one convulsive movement he turned and pulled her into his arms, clinging to her as though she was his anchor. 'I believe in it all, but not enough. It's one thing clappin' and cheerin' and talkin' about it, but I could never go tae prison for it. That's what did for John McLean and . . . Oh, Ella, I'm that ashamed!'

'Shush now, there's nothin' wrong with bein' frightened.' She held him close, talking, trying to still the tremors that shook him from head to toe. 'Listen tae me, Robbie. Cowards are folk that arenae even true to themselves. There's nothin' wrong with bein' the person ye are. Look at me. Folk think I've made a mistake – the kindly ones, that is, the others just think I'm sinful – but tae my mind the only thing I did wrong was tae love a man that belonged tae someone else. I'll never regret Vanni . . .' She had reached the stage where she could use his name without crying but, even so, the taste of those two short syllables in her mouth still caused a jolt of pain near her heart.

'Because he made me happy and he's given me a bairn tae love. D'ye know what Mrs Drysdale said tae me last week?'

'What?' At least he was listening to her.

'She said that if I kept the bairn, folk would always see the poor wee innocent soul as livin' proof of my sinnin'.'

'What?' Robbie straightened, holding her back from him so that he could see her face in the dim light from the surrounding windows. 'The old bitch!'

'She's been very good tae me, and she was only tryin' tae explain how hard it would be for me if I keep him. But it'd be a lot harder tae let him go. I've not got the courage tae do that. I've just got tae hope that mebbe one day he'll understand, even if nob'dy else does. And mebbe,' she said, low-voiced, 'he'll agree with Mrs Drysdale and tell me that I ruined his life, bringin' him intae the world a bastard. But I've made up my mind, Robbie, and so should you. Surely Joe wouldnae think any the less of you for not wantin' tae go tae prison for your beliefs. Specially if you'd the courage tae tell him face tae face. Man tae man.'

She was close enough to feel his body slump as he recalled his own problem. 'Ye don't understand . . .'

'If you could do anythin' ye wanted in the whole world, no matter what, what would ye do?'

'I'd go tae America with Mirren. I've said I don't want tae go, but I do.'

'Then go. Joe'll understand.'

'Joe's not the only reason why I said no,' he said abruptly. 'There's you.'

'Me?'

'I thought mebbe one day, if I'd the patience tae wait until . . .' He gulped down air, then said in a rush, 'Come tae America, Ella, with us . . . with me.'

'But . . .'

'I know I'm younger than you, but only a year or two, not enough tae make a differ—'

She put her hand up to cover his mouth.

'Robbie, it's got nothin' tae do with age. It wouldnae be right for me tae let ye take on responsibility for another man's bairn.'

He caught her wrist and pressed her fingers closer so that he could kiss them, then held them against his cheek. 'It's your bairn, and that's all that matters tae me. I swear I'd never be jealous of Vanni, or what he meant tae ye. Ye don't even have tae love me, not till ye're ready. I've enough love for the both of us, and it's been growin' since that night Mirren brought ye home and I sat beside the bed and watched ye cryin' in yer sleep. It near broke my heart, not bein' able tae help ye. But now I can. I'm talkin' about a new life for us both, far away where nob'dy knows us and we can both start again.' He gulped again, then gave a husky laugh. 'And if ye're angry with me for talkin' tae ye like this, it's yer own fault, for you're the one that's tellin' me tae be honest and face the consequences.'

'But I didnae think tae hear that sort of truth,' Ella said feebly.

'Now that ye have, d'ye have an answer for me? I don't mind what it is . . . well, I do, but I'll accept your decision. I just have tae know, Ella, for I cannae bear the wantin' and the wonderin' any longer.'

She could have done with the sal-volatile bottle, but she had no idea what had become of it. 'What would Mirren say?'

'Ach, tae hell with Mirren and all the rest of them,' Robbie said, taking her into his arms. His mouth was warm against hers, his arms strong. The need that had ached like a rotting tooth deep inside Ella for weeks stirred and responded. Although common-sense tried to advise otherwise, her arms drew him close, and her mouth returned the kiss. Vanni Perrini had awakened something in her that would not now be denied, and although the man who held her was not Vanni, and never could be, he too was gentle and loving, able and willing to give as well as take.

They clung together in the darkness of the back court where once the Bargarran witches had died in front of a baying crowd, while a few yards away someone's abandoned washing flapped and fussed on the clothes-line.

— • —

'It must have come as a shock tae you,' Joe said.

'It was, but once I got used to the idea I realised that it was the best thing that could happen to Ella, and I've never seen Robbie so happy.'

'When he came tae the jail tae tell me, he seemed tae be a good few years older and six feet taller. I'd say he's ready for the responsibility he's takin' on.'

Mirren had been in the middle of the ironing when Joe arrived, and at his insistence she had continued with it. In any case, it gave her something to do with her hands, and the chance to sneak the occasional glance at him under the pretext of reaching for another garment or hanging something on the clothes-horse to air. He looked well enough despite his week-long incarceration, although patches here and there on his face had a yellow tinge – the final remnants of the bruises he must have received at the meeting when he was arrested.

'He was worried about how you'd take it,' Mirren told him.

'Me?'

'He thought he might be letting you down, going off to America.'

'That's daft. We've all got our own roads tae walk. We'll all miss him, though, for he's got a good head on his shoulders and a clever way with words. I hope he'll keep on with his writin' in America. Talkin' about writin',

I believe I've you tae thank for the paper, pencils and books Robbie brought tae me. He said you'd picked them out.'

'Were they all right?'

'Aye, but what made ye send *Great Expectations*?'

'It was just the first one that came to hand. Why? D'you not like that one? I thought you enjoyed Charles Dickens.'

'Oh I do, but I just wondered, with it havin' a right desperate convict in it that managed tae escape from the jail. You werenae sendin' me some sort of message, were ye?'

'Oh!' Her hand flew to her mouth. 'I'd no notion – I just took the book from the shelf . . .' she said in confusion, then on seeing the glint in his eyes, 'You must think I'm daft!'

'No, but I got a good laugh out of it, and it's nice tae have somethin' tae laugh at in a place like Gateside.'

'Was it bad?'

'Och, I managed fine. I'd not want tae be in a place like that for much longer than a week, though – or tae be sent tae the prison hulks like that poor man in Dickens's book.'

His blue eyes seemed to Mirren, in her newly heightened awareness of him, to be more blue, more direct than before, his long hands more eloquent in their movements. His presence filled the kitchen now, or perhaps that was just her imagination.

She gave herself a shake and took one of Robbie's shirts from the pile on the table.

'So, when d'ye go then?'

'Robbie and Ella are off in two weeks' time, just. It doesn't give them a lot of time, but they're using the steamship tickets Donald sent, and with Ella's condition, the sooner she gets to America the better. Once they'd made their minds up, they didn't want to wait until after the bairn was born, for that's another four months away yet. That's where they are today – in Glasgow seeing to the paperwork. They'll get married in America.'

'And when do you go?'

One particular crease in the shirt was being very obstinate. She ran the iron over it again, pressing down hard. 'I'm not going at all.'

'You're staying in Paisley?'

'I don't want to marry Donald now.' The crease was still there. She leaned even harder on the iron. 'There's no point in going halfway round the world to spend the rest of my life with a man I don't love any more.'

He got up from the chair with that swift unfolding motion that belonged only to him, and came to touch the iron, a quick, tentative tap at first, then a firm clasp round the base.

'This is cold.'

'Is it?'

'Aye. Ye'll never iron things smooth with it like that.' His hand brushed against hers as he took the iron away and she drew her breath in sharply. When he had placed it back on the gas ring to heat he asked, 'What made ye decide against marryin' Donald Nesbitt?'

One day she might be in a position to tell him that the decision had been made for her when she stood in the cold little room that housed all his worldly possessions and suddenly felt such a strong sense of him, to her very core, that she hadn't been the same since. But that day lay in the future, and instead she said primly, 'I just realised that there were things I wanted to see to in the town. Unfinished work.'

'Are you considering my suggestion about takin' an interest in politics?'

'Indeed I am not.'

'It's such a waste,' he mourned. 'Ye'd be a grand speaker, Mirren.'

'Each to his own, Joe. I'd like more time to read, though. You've got a lot of books – you might want to store them here once Robbie's gone.'

'Why would I do that?' he asked, and she sighed inwardly.

'I'm only making the offer because there'll be more room here and it'd be more convenient for me to read them.' And she would iron his shirts and see that he was properly fed, and mop the blood from his face and his knuckles after the more vigorous meetings, and put vinegar on his bruises. She might even, God help her, wait for him to come out through the prison gates if she had to.

'Is the iron ready yet?' she asked in an attempt to distract her thoughts before they appeared on her features or, even worse, jumped of their own accord to her lips. No sense in frightening the man away before her campaign had even begun.

Thoughtlessly, he lifted it off the gas ring without using the padded cloth holder that lay near to hand, and yelped as his fingers came into contact with the hot metal handle. 'Damn!'

Mirren flew to the small cupboard by the window. 'Run cold water over it. There's bicarbonate of soda in here somewhere.'

'I'm fine. Mirren,' he spoke indistinctly round the injured fingers, which he had jammed into his mouth. 'I think you should reconsider going to America.'

'D'you want rid of me that badly?' she asked tartly, and was gratified to see a tide of red sweep over his face. He lowered his hand. 'N-no of course not. I was j-just thinkin' of what's b-best for y-you.'

His stammer, that barometer that measured his inner conflict, was like music to her ears. She had located the bicarbonate; now she beckoned him over to the sink.

'I tell you what, Mr Hepburn,' she said sweetly, 'I'll go off to America when you've taken your seat in the Houses of Parliament.'

Almost a year had passed since the last time Mirren had been at Greenock harbour, but the air was still heavy with sadness, flavoured slightly by the excitement of those facing a new life on distant shores. This time, for her, there was optimism too. If Robbie and Ella did as well as Grace and Anne Proctor, both now settled and happy in Boston, they would be fine.

Robbie had argued long and hard before accepting his sister's decision to stay behind when he and Ella left for America. Now, as a queue began to form for the tender, he swept Mirren off her feet in a hug that almost cut her in two. 'Take care, and promise that you'll come tae us if ever . . .'

'I promise, but I'll be fine,' she said through a throat aching with unshed tears. 'Ella . . .'

'We'll go tae the dancin' again some day, you and me.' Ella's hug was almost as fierce as Robbie's. 'Somehow or other.'

'Of course we will.'

'Ye'll keep an eye on her?' Mirren heard Robbie mutter to Joe. And she heard the other man's, 'Ye've my word on it.'

Time was running out. 'Come on.' Robbie put an arm about Ella's shoulders and led her away. Once in the queue, he looked over at his sister and nodded. She nodded back, with no need for words.

The night before she had put an envelope into his hand. 'That's for you and Ella, to see you started in America.'

When he opened it his eyes widened. 'Where did ye get this?'

'Half of mother's money, and I pawned the engagement ring Donald gave me. I thought it might as well be put to a good use.'

Robbie's eyes widened. 'You went intae a pawnshop?'

'Aye.' She gave a nervous giggle. Pawnshops were a way of life to most Paisley folk; it was the done thing for their best china and their Sunday clothes to spend more time in the pawnshop than in the house, redeemed when needed, then pledged again the next day. But Helen Jarvis, who as a young woman had seen the despair of a close friend who was forced to pledge everything and had the been unable to redeem it, had brought to her marriage a deep-seated fear of relying on the pawnshop. As a result, Mirren had never been inside one of those shops in her life. 'It was a strange feeling, but I managed it,' she said proudly to Robbie. 'Though I'd hope never to do it again.'

'I'm not sure I like the idea of usin' the man's boat tickets and now the money from the ring he gave ye . . .'

'Robbie, you saw the letter I sent to him, explaining about the tickets. He's a decent man, Donald, he'll see you right, and you can repay the money for the tickets when you've found work. Until then, you need a wee bit extra. And the ring was given to me. It's mine to use as I think fit. I'll never wear it again and I can think of no better use for it.'

'One day you might need this money for yourself.'

'If I do I'll write and ask you for it, for you'll be a wealthy man by then. Anyway, you're forgetting that I'm a mill-worker,' Mirren said jauntily. 'I've got the pension!'

'We'd best catch that train,' Joe said when the tender was well on its way to the liner waiting at the Tail of the Bank. 'I've got tae get back tae . . .'

'A meeting.' Mirren lowered her arm, which ached from vigorous waving. 'Come on then.'

They turned towards the station, walking almost shoulder-to-shoulder in a companionable procession of two. The train was busy, but they managed to find seats opposite each other. As they drew out of Greenock, Mirren caught Joe's eye. His smile, meant to be reassuring, made her toes curl most pleasantly inside her good shoes.

They were walking out now – in a manner of speaking. Two days ago they had gone, just the two of them, up the braes to collect brambles. Tonight, while he was at his meeting, she would make bramble jelly, and later, when he called in to make sure that she was all right on her first evening without Robbie, they would drink tea together and at bread thickly spread with the still-warm jelly.

He had kissed her, up the braes where nobody could see them. At the recollection her toes curled again, so much this time that she shuffled her feet uncomfortably, convinced that each shoe must have a telltale row of bumps along the front.

She glanced across at Joe again, but he was staring out of the window. He had found another job, this time as a welder in a Clydeside shipyard. He was good at his trade, Robbie had told her. It was a pity, she thought now, that he couldn't just be like most other men, content to concentrate on his own work instead of fretting about others. But then again, if he were like that, he would not be Joe.

She could tell by the far-away look in the blue eyes beneath half-lowered lids that he saw nothing of the countryside flashing past the train. His mind would be on the coming meeting. She studied him openly, knowing that in that state of mind he would never notice her boldness. His long face was perhaps a touch too thin, but the thinness showed up the bone structure beneath the skin. He was too sombre to be good-looking, but it seemed to Mirren's eyes that his was the type of face that would improve with time. In middle- and old-age, when other men were past their best, Joe Hepburn would be in his handsome prime. He'd be distinguished-looking. Come to think of it, he had a right politician's face . . .

She hummed a tune beneath her breath and sat back to enjoy the return journey to Paisley.

Bibliography

Modern Ballroom Dancing, by Victor Sylvester. First published 1977 by Barrie & Jenkins Ltd. Reprinted by Stanley Paul & Co. Ltd, 1982.

Oh, How We Danced! – The History of Ballroom Dancing in Scotland, by Elizabeth Casciani. Published by Mercat Press, 1994.

Six Cord Thread – The story of Coats' and Clarks' Paisley Threadmills, compiled and published by Phil Anderson, Iain Cameron, David Campbell, Ian Campbell, Irene Conroy, Frank Dever, Andrew Findlay, Fred Lawrence, John Leishman, Colin Livingstone, Doreen McCall, Colin McMillan, Ann McPherson, Stewart Menzies and Robert Todd. 1994.

A Social Geography of Paisley by Mary McCarthy. Published by Paisley Public Library, 1969.

Thread Lines – Extracts and notes from Paisley and Glasgow newspapers regarding the Paisley Threadmills 1812–1993. Researched, compiled and published by David Campbell, John Leishman, Doreen McCall, Bobby Todd, Frank Dever, Stuart Menzies and Andrew Findlay, 1994.